BEN H. WINTERS
UNDERGROUND
AIRLINES

arrow books

1 3 5 7 9 10 8 6 4 2

Arrow Books
20 Vauxhall Bridge Road
London SW1V 2SA

Arrow Books is part of the Penguin Random House group of companies
whose addresses can be found at global.penguinrandomhouse.com.

Copyright © Ben H. Winters 2016

Ben H. Winters has asserted his right to be identified as the author of this
Work in accordance with the Copyright, Designs and Patents Act 1988.

First published in Great Britain by Century in 2016
First published in paperback by Arrow Books in 2017

www.penguin.co.uk

A CIP catalogue record for this book is available from the British Library.

ISBN 9781784751753

Map by Darren Bennett / DKB Creative (www.dkbcreative.com)

Printed and bound in Great Britain by Clays Ltd, St Ives Plc

Penguin Random House is committed to a
sustainable future for our business, our readers
and our planet. This book is made from Forest
Stewardship Council® certified paper.

For my kids, and their friends

CAN
NORTH DAKOTA
The Great Lakes
MINNESOTA
WISCONSIN
SOUTH DAKOTA
MICHIGAN
IOWA
NEBRASKA
UNITED STATES
ILLINOIS
INDIANA
OHIO
OF AMERICA
KANSAS
MISSOURI
KENTUCKY
TENNESSEE
OKLAHOMA
ARKANSAS
ALABAMA
MISSISSIPPI
LOUISIANA
REPUBLIC OF
TEXAS (DISPUTED)
SPECIAL ECONOMIC ZONE (US)
Gulf of
Mexico

D A

'LITTLE
AMERICA'

MAINE

VERMONT

NEW HAMPSHIRE

MASSACHUSETTS

NEW YORK

RHODE ISLAND

CONNECTICUT

PENNSYLVANIA

NEW JERSEY

DELAWARE

MARYLAND

VIRGINIA

CAROLINA

ATLANTIC
OCEAN

FLORIDA

SLAVE STATES

FREE STATES

No future amendment of the Constitution shall affect the five preceding articles . . . and no amendment shall be made to the Constitution which shall authorize or give to Congress any power to abolish or interfere with slavery in any of the States by whose laws it is, or may be, allowed or permitted.

—From the Eighteenth Amendment to the United States Constitution. It is the last of six amendments that, together with four congressional resolutions, make up the so-called Crittenden Compromise, proposed by Senator John J. Crittenden of Kentucky on December 18, 1860, and ratified by Congress on May 9, 1861

Part One

NORTH

It is a strange kind of fire, the fire of self-righteousness, which gives us such pleasure by its warmth but does so little to banish the darkness.

—*Augustin Craig White, from* The Dark Tower, *a pamphlet of the American Abolitionist Society, 1911*

1.

"So," said the young priest. "I think that I'm the man you're looking for."

"Oh, I hope so," I said to him. "Oh, Lord, I do hope you are."

I knitted my fingers together and leaned forward across the table. I was aware of how I looked: I looked pathetic. Eager, nervous, confessional. I could feel my thin, cheap spectacles slipping down my nose. I could feel my needfulness dripping from my brow. I took a breath, but before I could speak, the waitress came over to pour our coffee and hand out the menus, and Father Barton and I went silent, smiled stiff and polite at the girl and at each other.

Then, when she was gone, Father Barton talked before I could.

"Well, I must say, Mr. Dirkson—"

"Go on and call me Jim, Father. Jim's just fine."

"I must say, you gave LuEllen quite a start."

I looked down, embarrassed. LuEllen was the receptionist, church secretary, what have you. White-haired, apple-cheeked lady, sitting behind her desk at that big church up there on Meridian Street, Saint Catherine's, and I suppose I behaved like a wild thing in her tidy little office that afternoon, gnashing my teeth and carrying on. Throwing myself on her mercy. Pleading for an appointment with the father. It worked, though. Here we were, breaking bread together, the gentle young priest and I. If there's one thing they understand, these church folks, it's wailing and lamentation.

But I bowed my head and apologized to Father Barton for the scene I'd caused. I told him to please carry my apologies to Ms. LuEllen. And then I brought my voice way down to a whisper.

5

"Listen, I'm just gonna be honest with you and say it, sir. I'm a desperate man. I got nowhere else to turn."

"Yes, I see. I do see. I only wish..." The priest looked at me solemnly. "I only wish there was something I could do."

"What?"

He was shaking his head, and I felt my face get shocked. I felt my eyes get wide. I felt my skin getting hot and tight on my cheeks. "Wait, wait. Hold on, now, Father. I ain't even——"

Father Barton raised one hand gently, palm out, and I hushed up. The waitress had come back to take our orders. I can remember that moment perfectly, can picture the restaurant, dusk-lit through its big windows. The Fountain Diner was the place, a nice family-style place, in what they call the Near Northside, in Indianapolis, Indiana. On that same Meridian Street as the church, about fifty blocks farther downtown. Handsome, boyish Barton there across from me, no more than thirty years old, a tousle of blond hair, blue Irish eyes, pale skin glowing like it had been scrubbed. Our table was right in the center of the restaurant, and there was a big ceiling fan high above us, its blades turning lazily around and around. The bright, sizzling smell of something frying, the low ting-ting of forks and knives. There were three old ladies at the booth behind us with thin beauty-shop hair and red lipstick, their walkers parked in a neat row like waiting carriages. There was a pair of policemen, one black and one white, in a corner booth. The black cop was leaning halfway across the table to look at something on the white one's phone, the two of them chortling over some policeman joke.

Somehow I got through ordering my food, and when the waitress went away the priest launched into a speech as carefully crafted as any homily. "I fear that you have gotten the wrong impression, which of course is in no way your fault." He was speaking very softly. We were both of us aware of those cops. "I know what people say, but it's not true. I've never been involved in...in...in those sorts of activities. I'm sorry, my friend." He placed his hand gently over mine. "I am terribly sorry."

6

And he *sounded* sorry. Oh, he did. His calm Catholic voice glowed with gentle apology. He squeezed my hands as a real father would, never mind that I was a decade or more his senior. "I know this is not what you wanted to hear."

"But—wait, now, Father, hold on a moment. You're here. You came."

"Out of compassion," he said. "Compassion compelled me."

"Oh, Lord." I leaned away from him, feeling like a damn fool, and dropped my face into my hands. My heart was trembling. "Lord almighty."

"You have my sympathy, and you have my prayers." When I looked up his eyes were straight on me and steady, crystal blue and radiating kindness. "But I must be truthful and say there is nothing else that I can offer you."

He watched me, unblinking, waiting for me to nod and say, "I understand." Waiting for me to give up. But I couldn't give up. How could I?

"Listen. Just—I am a free man, as you see, sir, legally so," I said, then charging on before he could interrupt. "Manumitted years ago, thanks to the good Lord in heaven and my master's merciful last will and testament. I have my papers; my papers are in order. I got my high school equivalency, and I'm working, sir, a good job, and I'm in no kind of trouble. It's my wife, sir, my *wife*. I have searched for years to find her, and I've found her. I tracked her down, sir!"

"I understand," said Father Barton, grimacing, shaking his head. "But . . . Jim—"

"She is called Gentle, sir. Her name's Gentle. She is thirty-three years old, thirty-three or thirty-four. I—" I stopped, blinking away tears, gathering my dignity. "I'm afraid I have no photograph."

"Please. Jim. *Please.*"

He spread his hands. My mouth was dry. I licked my lips. The fan turned overhead, disinterested. One of the cops, the white one, thick-necked and pink-skinned, reared back and slapped the table, cracking up at something his black partner had said.

I held myself steady and let my eyes bore into the priest's. Let him see me clear, hear me properly.

"Gentle is at a strip mine in western Carolina, sir. The conditions are of the utmost privation. Her owner employs overseers, sir, of the cruelest stripe, from one of these services—you know, private contractors. And, now, this mine—I've been looking, Father, and this mine has been sanctioned half a dozen times by the BLP. They've been fined, you know, paid millions in these fines, for treatment violations, but you... you know how it is with these fines, it's a drop in the—you know, it's a drop in the bucket." Barton was shaking his head, gritting his teeth emphatically, but I wouldn't stop—I couldn't stop—my words had become a hot rush by then, fervent and angry. "Now, this mine, this is a *bauxite* mine, and a female PB, one of her age and... and her weight, you see? According to the law, you see—"

"Please, Jim."

Father Barton tapped his fingertips twice on the table, a small but firm gesture, like he was calling me to order or calling me to heel. The compassionate glow in his voice was beginning to dim. "You need to listen to me, now. We don't *do* it. I know what is said of me and of my church. I do. And I believe in the Cause, and the church believes in the Cause, as a matter of policy and faith. I have spoken on it and will continue to speak on it, but speaking is all that I do." He shook his young head again, looked quickly at me and then away, away from my frustration and grief. "I feel deeply for your situation, and my prayers are with you and your wife. But I cannot be her savior."

I was silent then. I had more words, but I swallowed them. This was a bitter result.

I got through our brief supper as best I could, keeping my eyes on my plate, on my fish sandwich and coleslaw and iced tea. God only knows what I'd been expecting. Surely I had not imagined that this man, this *child,* would be so moved by the plight of my suffering Gentle that he would leap to his feet and charge southward with pistols bared; that he would muster up a posse to kick in the doors of a Carolina bauxite mine; that he would take out his cell phone and summon up the army of abolition.

For one thing, there is no such army. Everybody knows that. Everybody with sense, anyway. No such thing as the Underground Airlines, not really, not in any grand, organized sense. No command center in the deserts of New Mexico, like there was in that movie they did a few years ago; no paramilitary force with helicopters and flash bombs, waiting on the orders of a mighty antislavery general to rush into motion.

There *are* rescues, though. There *are* saviors. It's piecemeal; it's small-group action, teams of northerners, daring or crazy, making pinprick raids into the Hard Four, grabbing people up and hustling them to freedom. There are ad hoc efforts, small organizations, cells, each running its own route of the Airlines. You just gotta know the right people. And this man, this Father Barton here, he was supposed to be the right people. The man to get with. Everything I had heard, all the information I had collected, it all said that here in Indianapolis, in central Indiana, Father Barton up at Saint Cat's—this was supposed to be the man.

And now here I was, helpless, watching him eat a hamburger with a paper napkin tucked into his clerical collar, fussily dabbing ketchup from the corners of his mouth. Listening to him assuring me in his soft voice—"to allay any concerns"—that everything on the menu had been certified by the North American Human Rights Association, a Montreal-based outfit that inspects supply lines. I nodded blankly. I murmured "Oh" into my coffee. "Oh, good." Like it mattered. Indiana was, like most states, a Clean Hands state, having a law on the books barring places of public accommodation from serving anything out of the Four. All the rest of it, all the Canadian supply-chain auditors, all the independent inspectorates and "cruelty-free" certification programs—well, that's all marketing. Fancy-sounding words to gin up donations for the antislavery nonprofits. But Father Barton, he pointed his skinny finger at the

9

little gold seal on my menu like it was some kind of consolation prize. *I can't get your beloved out of shackles, you poor bastard, but I can assure you that your tomatoes weren't harvested by a shackled line.*

When dinner was done, Barton took out his wallet, and I put out my hand and laid it over his.

"Hold on, now." A little tremor rolled through my voice. "I'm gonna get this."

"Oh, no." Father Barton shook his head and didn't pull away his hand, and we held that pose like an artwork: white hand on a brown wallet, black hand on the white hand. "I can't let you do that."

"Come on, now." I peered at him through my spectacles. "I wanna thank you for taking the time, that's all. It was good of you to take the time."

The priest exhaled, nodded slightly, slowly removing his hand from our little pileup. Here's what he was thinking right then: he was thinking, *Go on and let the man pick up the check—it's a gift to him, to let him feel he's done something.* I do not want to sound crazy or something, but I do believe that I have this strange power in certain situations. To read minds, I mean. Not to read *thoughts,* not exactly, but to read *feelings.* To read *people.* To know how people *feel.*

I dug a few crumpled bills from my coat pocket and smoothed them out on top of the check. Then I pushed a piece of paper across the table, a smudged scrap of napkin. "Here, though. That's my cell phone number right there. Just in case you change your mind."

Father Barton stared at the napkin.

"Please, Father," I said. "Would you please just take it?"

He took it, and he rose and adjusted his collar, and for a split second, I *hated* this man, this confident boy. *And I believe in the Cause . . . as a matter of policy and faith . . .* Go to hell, son, I was thinking, just for a moment, just a bare half of a moment. With your pity for me and your stiff collar and your alabaster cheeks. *You go to hell.* I didn't say it, though. Nothing of the sort. I did not raise my voice or bang a closed fist on the table. Anger wouldn't help.

All it would do, maybe, is draw the attention of those two cops, the white one with the thick neck and his laughing black partner, maybe cause them to amble over here in that slow cop way and ask Father Barton if everything was okay. Ask me if I wouldn't mind providing my paperwork for them to have a peek at, if it wasn't too much trouble.

I excused myself to use the bathroom and hurried away, just barely keeping it together.

Once, I saw a businessman on TV, the owner of a midwestern football franchise, and this very wealthy man was proclaiming his personal abolitionist sentiment while defending his use of the infamous "temporary suspension of status" rule to add PB muscle to his defensive line. "Do I like the system?" the man had said, shaking his head, in his thousand-dollar suit, his hundred-dollar haircut. "Well, of course I don't. But I'll tell you what: this is an opportunity for these boys. And I love 'em. It's a bad system, but I love my boys."

I hated that man so much, watching him talk, and I hated Father Barton the same way there in the diner. Slavery was a game to this child, as it was for that slick team owner, as it is for all the football fans who tsk-tsk about the black-hand teams but watch every Sunday in the privacy of their living rooms. Declaring hatred for slavery was easy for a man like Father Barton; not only easy but useful, gratifying—*satisfying*. And of course its cold and terrible grip could never fall on him directly.

My anger swelled, then it drained, as anger does. By the time he hugged me consolingly at the door of the diner, by the time the priest was on his way to his car, by the time he stopped to cast a troubled glance back toward me—as I had predicted he would, as I had known he would—that glance found me standing perfectly still in the doorway, a humble man, broken by pain. I had taken off my glasses, and there were tears slipping slowly, one at a time, down my weathered cheeks. The waitress poked her head out, reminded me that she had the rest of my supper for me all boxed up, and I could barely hear her, so busy was I composing this face of grief.

2.

I've been free since I was fourteen years old, and on this particular evening, as my dashboard GPS navigated me through the unfamiliar streets of Indianapolis, I was approaching my fortieth birthday.

The great bulk of my life, then, had passed outside the Hard Four, in the free part of the land of the free. But even after all these years, I still found myself astonished daily by the small miracles of liberty. Just walking out of a restaurant with a clear head and a full stomach, holding a Styrofoam box with leftover food inside it. Just lingering in the parking lot a minute before getting in the car, smelling the wet asphalt, feeling a light drizzle as it condensed on my forehead. Just knowing I could take a walk around the block if I wanted to, go to a park and sit on a bench and read a newspaper. Just getting in that car and feeling the vinyl give under my ass, feeling the cough and purr of the engine. All these things were small astonishments. Miracles of freedom.

I was in a modest Nissan Altima with a serviceable 175-horsepower engine and a dull tan interior, but I enjoyed driving it a whole lot. For most of my driving years you couldn't get a Japanese car because the Japanese were signatories to the European Consensus, blocked from most trade with the United States. Luckily for me, a new prime minister had been elected in 2012 and switched them over to a policy of "stakeholder influence," a phrase borrowed from the Israelis. Hate the sin, love the sinner. Open borders mean open dialogue, that whole line.

I don't give much of a shit about international diplomacy, but I fucking loved that Altima. It started up with no trouble, the heater worked and the wipers worked, and the brakes and the windows and the tape deck worked, too.

I drove north on Meridian Street carefully, away from the Fountain Diner, away from Father Barton and his empty apologies. The world I heard described on the radio was the same as the one I could see through the streaky window of the car: gray and ugly, redolent of violence and the fear of violence. This was the week of the Batlisch hearings: fulminating in the Senate, furor in the streets. This woman's nomination had "ignited a firestorm," as the radio liked to hype it. Protests and counterprotests in Washington, DC, in the nominee's hometown of Philadelphia, and in plenty of other places besides. Violence—violence and fear.

There was some little local controversy, too, about a fund-raising effort called Suzie's Closet: folks getting together in church basements to make care packages for the plantations—blankets and candy bars and all that kind of thing. First they interviewed a local advocate for the homeless, asking why our attention should be down there "when there's so much suffering right here at home!" Then came a spokesman for the Black Panthers, denouncing the campaign as "mere ameliorationism," calling Suzie naive. Which struck me as a little harsh, the girl being nine years old and all.

It was the usual stuff—all the new stories are just the old stories over again.

I turned off the radio and fished a Michael Jackson cassette out of the glove box. The tape hissed when I pushed it in. It was a mix tape that I had made myself, many, many years before. Soon, they were saying, new cars wouldn't have tape decks anymore, since the American market was finally catching up with CDs. Not yet, though.

I turned up the volume. MJ sang "Human Nature," from *Thriller,* and I sang along.

I was stopped at a checkpoint on my way back to my hotel, which I'd been expecting. Tensions were high because of the Batlisch business and because of a couple nasty incidents up along the 49th parallel. Indianapolis, like a lot of cities, had declared a "heightened security environment," so cops were free to pull over black drivers when they felt like it—not that they ever needed a reason in particular. It was at 79th Street and Ditch Road that I heard the bloop-bloop of the sirens, and I got out slowly, giving no trouble, showing my hands, standing where they told me to stand, staring blankly into the doorway of a grocery store while I got frisked by a beefy patrolman with bad breath and razor burn.

He looked closely at my papers. My papers held up just fine. The sun was almost done sinking. A yellow smear against a dishwater horizon.

3.

At the tail end of our dinner together, while we were tussling over the bill, I lifted Father Barton's wallet. This small and seamless maneuver caused me no difficulty or concern: I had performed the same quick action dozens of times in the past. There he was, poor man, embarrassed by my grief, flustered by my adamance, anxious to escape an emotionally charged moment. It would be a lot to ask, in such complicated circumstances, to keep track of something so prosaic, so secular, as a wallet. In the bathroom I photographed its contents, utilizing a tiny device that attaches to my cell phone, then I slipped the wallet back into his pocket when I embraced him good-bye.

And now, back in the Capital City Crossroads Hotel on 86th Street, with the door locked, with the shades pulled, I opened my laptop and began entering data into the remarkable mapping program I had on there. I entered the home address from Father Barton's driver's license. I entered the addresses of three restaurants and five gas stations he had recently patronized and from which he had helpfully held on to the credit-card receipts. I entered the address of his gym, his local branch library, and the Sport Clips where he got his hair cut. I entered, too, the Meridian Street address of the restaurant where we had just eaten at his suggestion and that of the parish church of Saint Catherine's, where I had accosted poor old LuEllen a few hours earlier.

I had never been to Indianapolis before, but I had been to lots of other cities, and every city is the same. Neighborhoods and waterways, big roads and side roads. A circle of downtown in the middle, a circle of highway around the perimeter, like a dog fence. Rich neighborhoods and poor neighborhoods. Black areas, white areas, mixed. CVS and Starbucks, Walmart and Townes Stores. The world is the same everywhere you go.

In the North, I should say. The world is about the same in every northern city. I'm a lot less familiar with the South these days.

What the mapping software did was turn each of the addresses into a blinking red dot. When I was done with the data entry and could take a look at the map, one of the dots sang out to me right away. It called my name. Most of the other dots were clustered together, centered around the priest's church up there on Meridian and just north of it, along the crowded shopping corridor of 86th Street, a mile or two west of where I was sitting. But this one dot was way, way down, in a different part of town. It sat at the intersection of 38th and Graceland, in a neighborhood the map called Mapleton–Fall Creek.

"All right," I said out loud. "Well, all right." I laid a fingertip on that dot, as if to feel it, to measure its strength.

My name is not Jim Dirkson.

Neither is my name Dudley Vincent, the identity under which I'd been staying at the Hilton Garden Inn near the Cleveland, Ohio, airport until last night, when Mr. Bridge called me and woke me and told me to start packing. Mr. Vincent's driver's license and American Express card had since been cut to pieces, and those pieces were now buried in a construction-site Dumpster behind a Cleveland shopping mall.

I had a lot of names. Or, more precisely, it was my practice at the beginning of a new job to think of myself as having no name at all. As being not really a person at all. A man was missing, that's all — missing and hiding, and I was not a person but a manifestation of will. I was a mechanism — a device. That's all I was.

I looked at the dot on 38th Street. The dot blinked, and I blinked back at the dot. That address had come from a cash machine receipt dated three days ago — Sunday, at 4:32 p.m. Two hundred dollars from a Regions bank ATM. I tapped a few more keys, and the laptop whirred to life, accenting my map with the requested demographic information, shading every square block of the city according to its African American population.

When this was done I sat back and laid my hands flat on the desk, on either side of the computer keyboard. The main cluster of dots, representing Father Barton's usual stomping ground—those dots were in pale areas: blocks with an African American population of 10 percent or less, 5 percent or less. That one dot, though, the one blinking lonesome dot down in Mapleton–Fall Creek: that one was singing a different song. It wasn't in the darkest part of the map— that was a six-square-block area just northwest of downtown. That would be Freedman Town, I figured. But the area where Father Barton had taken out two hundred bucks on Sunday afternoon— there was some pigmentation down there, no question about it.

I whistled very softly, still sitting motionless, hands still flat on the table.

"All right," I whispered. "All right, all right, all right."

4.

At 9:49 p.m. I stood from the wobbly wooden desk and stretched, raising my hands until they grazed the low ceiling of the hotel room. I felt around in the coat I had taken off and found a pack of Babas, tapped it on the edge of the desk, peeled off the foil, and took out a single cigarette.

At exactly 9:50 my cell phone rang. It always rang at 9:50 exactly.

"Hello."

"Good evening, Victor," said the voice on the other end, low and even. "How is your progress?"

That's what Mr. Bridge always said—every time—when a case was on, when a file was active. He always called at 9:50, and his voice always sounded the same.

"She's doin' great, thanks," I said. "How's *your* mother?"

Mr. Bridge didn't laugh. He never laughed. He repeated himself. "How is your progress?"

"So far so good." I slipped out onto the little balcony. The room was on the second floor, and I could smell the bitter fumes of the parking lot. "To be honest with you, it would be a lot better if I had the full file."

"You will."

"So you've said." I lit the Baba and took a drag.

"Janice will post the full file by tomorrow noon at the absolute latest. It will be available for download from the second server."

"Yes, Massa. Sho' nuff."

Cold silence. No chance of getting a laugh out of Mr. Bridge on *that* one. I trusted his assurances about the file. My handler at the US Marshals Service was a serious man, and he rarely made promises on which he did not deliver. And even with the full file being unaccountably late, I already knew the most important details. A Person Bound to Labor had escaped. His service name was Jackdaw. His PIN was 78312-99. The company to whom he owed service was a textile plantation called Garments of the Greater South, of Pine Woods, Alabama, a Tuscaloosa suburb.

A man had run. It was my job to find him.

"Victor? How is your progress?"

I took a quick drag off the Baba. "Well, the good father and I broke bread. My name is Dirkson. My wife is Gentle, and she is bound to subterranean service in Carolina."

More silence on the other end. Mr. Bridge, not interested in the nitty-gritty. Mr. Bridge, waiting for information. He and I had never met face-to-face, but we'd been talking on the phone now going on six years, and I had a clear picture in my mind of the man behind his desk in Gaithersburg. Upright behind his computer keyboard, with a round pale face and pink jowls. A conservative mustache, maybe, thick but well kept. Eyes flat like silver dollars.

"The only snag is," I said, "our friend Barton does not deal in runners. Not him and not his church. Not anyone he's ever met. He was shocked by the very idea."

"He's lying."

"Yeah. No shit."

"He's sniffing you out."

"Let him sniff."

"You'll get to him."

"I'll try."

Bridge repeated himself. Not insistent, not chastising, just a statement of fact. "You'll get to him."

This was how the man talked: clear pronouncements of uncomplicated truth. Never in our years of working together had I detected a note of sarcasm or subtlety. His tone was always the same, cold and unbending, like iron, the hint of a southern accent coming up off his voice like the whisper of smoke from a gun barrel. *You'll get to him.*

My arrangement with Mr. Bridge was simple. Clear as a searchlight. Strong as the law.

Under the Fugitive Persons Act, those who escape from service are to be captured and returned, anywhere they are found in the United States, slave state or free. All law enforcement agencies are obliged to assist in these operations when called upon (as, indeed, "all good citizens" are so obliged), but it is the US Marshals Service that is specifically charged with the job. This law was passed in the ancient year of 1793 under its old name, but it's been updated repeatedly: strengthened in 1850, reinforced in 1861, revised and strengthened a half dozen times since. When, in 1875, Congress at last ended slavery in the nation's capital, the slaveholding powers were appeased by the raising of fees for obstruction. When President Roosevelt, in 1935, proposed the creation of a "comprehensive regulatory framework" for the plantations (and the Bureau of Labor Practices to enforce it), he quieted howling southern senators with a sweeping immunity bill, shielding US marshals from zealous northern prosecutors.

Tit for tat. Give and take. Negotiation and conciliation. Compromise. It's how the Union survives.

People still find ways to evade the burdens of the FPA, though. Local sheriffs sandbag investigations; state legislatures pass thinly veiled personal liberty laws, no matter how many times the Supreme Court sends them back stamped *Unconstitutional*. Plenty of "good citizens" go to jail every year rather than lift a finger to assist a slave-hunting marshal. Since 1970, African American law enforcement officers are allowed to claim nonparticipation under the Moore amendment.

The US Marshals Service, therefore, has needed to find other means of pursuing its mission.

That was me. I was "other means." A man with no name, a quasi-employee of a clandestine branch, moving from city to city, job to job, under the supervision of a voice on a Maryland telephone. Bridge assigned me my cases, but my tactics were up to me. I pursued my cases efficiently and effectively, and as long as I did that, my own past remained buried. I remained in the North and free. Give and take. Negotiation and conciliation. Compromise.

When we were done on the phone I was feeling low and mean, which is how I always felt after talking to Mr. Bridge. Certain emotions were bubbling up in my stomach, close to my throat. Certain kinds of memories were rattling their chains. As always. I flicked away the butt of the shitty Pakistani cigarette and stared out from the darkness of the balcony into the greater darkness of the parking lot, feeling as if I barely existed at all.

I did, though. I was real, and the case was real. Somewhere in this city there was a lonesome runner, terrified and tired and overwhelmed by the sights and the lights of the free world, and I was going to find him. Have him dragged home. Home.

The full file would come tomorrow, like Bridge said. Tomorrow my search would begin in earnest.

5.

It is remarkable, when you consider it, all the complicated works we construct to avoid anything that might disturb us or cause us pain. The bulwarks and baffles we build up, the moats and the mazes.

When I got down to the lobby the next morning, Thursday morning, my head was clear, and I felt focused and calm. I had slept well. It was just before 7:30 a.m., and I was the only one in the complimentary breakfast area off the main lobby of the Crossroads Hotel. That's how I like it. I like to get down to these free breakfasts after they've set everything out but before the crowds of folks come in, smiling and chattering and buttering their toast. I'm not a man for small talk in the mornings. I found a seat by the window and set down my newspaper on the table to claim it. I always try to stay at hotels that have these kinds of free breakfasts: warming trays brimming with bacon and herbed diced potatoes, bottomless cups of coffee, sweet muffins in paper wrappers. It is my practice to savor whatever is there to be savored, whatever is available, whatever they just put out for you to take.

I scanned the front page of the *Indianapolis Star,* which was all about Donatella Batlisch, she of the firestorm, the one who had struck the match. She was the president's nominee to chair the Securities and Exchange Commission, and someone had dug up her master's thesis, which highlighted the "range of instruments available under existing law" to punish investment companies that trade in plantation profit. Then Batlisch gave an interview, *Time* or *U.S. News,* one of those, refusing to disavow her views, saying only that she'd discharge the duties of the office without prejudice. And then the president, an avowed "centrist" on the Old Question—as you had to be to get to be president—had surprised everybody by declining to withdraw her nomination.

Is this a watershed moment? said the page 1 editorial I was staring at now, chewing on my bagel. *Is this a moment when things begin to change?*

"No," I said to the paper. "It's not." I took another bite. I turned the page.

A girl came in, a white girl in blue jeans and a blue-jean jacket and massively scuffed black Doc Martens–type shoes. She had an oversize leather pocketbook, this young lady, and as I watched she began casually dropping items into the bag's big maw. This little white lady needed to refine her thievery skills, that was for sure. With each act of petty pilferage she looked first right and then left, like a cartoon mouse about to grab a hunk of cheese, before dropping whatever it was—a banana, a single-serving box of muesli—into the big purse.

A hotel man came in, khaki pants and polo shirt, treading silently enough on the thick carpeting to escape the girl's attention—although I, a great noticer of small sounds, heard him fine. He waited, watching, arms folded across his chest, as the girl helped herself to one of the paper cups stacked beside the coffee machine and began to fill it with the two-percent milk meant for cereal.

"Miss?" he said suddenly, loudly. "May I help you?"

"What?" The woman turned quickly, jerked the paper cup from the milk dispenser, sloshed some over the sides. "No. No, you're fine. I'm good. Thanks."

The hotel man walked over to her, brisk and self-important in his slacks and magenta shirt with CROSSROADS HOTEL sewn on the breast pocket. I turned my eyes back to my newspaper, studied the headlines. The Batlisch hearings. The Pacers win a close one. Wilmington joins Syracuse and Detroit in bankruptcy, and what cities will be next?

"The food set out for breakfast is intended for use during the breakfast hour only."

"Oh—wait." The girl tried on a smile, looked around. She couldn't even figure out a lie for it. "I mean, yes. Oh. Of course."

The man studied her. "I'm sorry—would you remind me what room you are staying in?" He had that voice that hotel managers must learn in hotel-manager school, smooth and fussy and disapproving. The girl's smile was flickering, fading.

"Ah. Okay," she said. She fiddled with a barrette she had in her hair, a bright yellow butterfly. "I'm not—I'm not remembering right this second."

"Well, perhaps if you showed me your key card?"

The manager's clipped-on name tag said MR. PAULSEN, but I already knew his name. I recognized him, a gleaming bald scalp and small features—too small for his big head—that made him look blandly sinister. He was the guy who'd checked me in yesterday, given me my key card, and had me sign the register for "guests of color." "Just go ahead and jot down your full name and date of birth and Social Security number, if you don't mind." Giving me the old standby, "It's the corporate policy, but if it were up to me . . ." I didn't take offense. I was very used to it. I stayed at a lot of hotels.

"Okay, so . . . I don't have a key card," the white girl was saying, shifting from foot to foot on her big shoes. "See, so, we are staying here, or I mean, we are *going* to be." Before the first of the *we*'s she stumbled, just a little bit.

"I'm sorry?" said Paulsen. "You're *going* to be staying here?"

I was paying close attention, half hidden behind the paper, eating my bagel. It was a novelty, I suppose, hearing that kind of petty authoritarian bullying, that ugly, half-threatening tone, used against a white person. She was a small thing, this young lady, girlish in her form and her face, with warm brown circles for eyes and thin pink lips and a lot of messy brown hair pinned up with the plastic yellow butterfly. And here's this manager hectoring, and the woman just nodding like a schoolkid taking a scolding, tears coming into her eyes and her cheeks flushing and her eyes slowly widening.

"Yeah. See, okay, I'm up from Evansville. For the job fair. Medical job fair? You know? I'm a—I was a medical assistant. A home health aide, actually. I'm looking for a new, uh—whatever. The point is, my sister said her place was cool to crash, but then I guess her boyfriend is around or—I don't know. Something or other." She grinned, sheepish, at Paulsen, who moved not a muscle on his face. Gave her nothing. "Sorry. Too much information, right? But I'm gonna need the room tonight, swear to God." She shrugged, smiled one more time. "Room comes with breakfast, right?"

"Breakfast is complimentary, yes. And you will be entitled to one once you are a guest."

Other guests had filled the dining area: a pair of pale businessmen, overweight and ruddily jowled, napkins tucked into dress shirts; a trio of college-age kids, all girls, in long prairie skirts, looking like evangelicals. Everyone working hard at not noticing the showdown at the buffet line. And then there was a little boy, tugging on my sleeve. I looked down at him, and he grinned up at me. "Hey. What's that say?"

The boy was black. Face full of happy mischief, round cheeks, skin a handsome high yellow, eyes deep, beautiful pools. His shirt had a picture of Captain America on it. He had scooted in next to my elbow and was trying to read the front page, upside down. The situation came into sharp focus, all at once: the white woman's "we," Mr. Paulsen giving her the business. Young white mother with her black son, trying to live in the world. This world.

"You couldn't, like, front me a breakfast?" she was saying. "Like, advance it to me?"

"No," said Mr. Paulsen. "Our policy does not allow for that," the word *policy* like a gate coming down, and the next thing would be *I am afraid I will have to call security if . . .*

Her son, meanwhile, who was maybe six or seven, had eased up beside me with no reservations and was peering at my paper, up on his tiptoes. "What word's that?"

"Controversy," I told him. Pointed to the capital *C*.

He nodded. "Oh." Bothering me without qualm, the brave, sweet boy. I wondered that nobody had told him not to talk to strangers. Maybe black strangers were okay. The kid moved his mouth, squinting at the word. "Controversy."

"Ma'am. If you please . . ."

"Hey, you know what? It's fine."

Slowly and with exaggerated dignity the white girl removed her contraband from her pocketbook: three muffins, one by one; the cereal box; the banana and two oranges; then two plastic spoons and a yogurt. These items she placed in a line along the buffet table, like sacrificial offerings, while her nemesis in his magenta shirt stood with arms crossed.

And as she came over to my table to retrieve her son, the girl caught my eye and gave me this fleeting, rueful look, the meaning perfectly clear: "This guy, huh? What a dickhead."

It is a marker of the kind of relationship I had with white people in general and with white women in particular—having to do not only with the caution that adheres to my profession but also with my upbringing, the way I was raised—that I did not return her look. I made myself busy, reaching across the table for a fresh napkin, and while I was busy she scooped up her boy and bore him away, the front section of my *Star* dangling from his forefingers across her back like a cape.

I sat there feeling that for a beat or two, then I folded up what was left of my paper.

Fussy little Mr. Paulsen strode self-importantly from the breakfast nook, not bothering to apologize for the scene—not to the likes of me.

The white girl's car was not hard to find in the parking lot: a beat-up South African shitbox with a dented driver's-side door and a bright pink paint job that was peeling and rust-splotched. The automotive analogue of the denim jacket and scuffed Doc Martens. She was in the driver's seat filling out the top application on a whole stack of them, the stack balanced atop a hardcover book that was in turn balanced on her lap. She wore a look of troubled concentration, her eyes screwed up, a strand of her hair tucked into the corner of her mouth. Her boy was in the shotgun seat, one leg lodged against the glove compartment, playing some sort of hand-held electronic game.

I thought about rapping on the window, but then I didn't. I left the food I had gathered up, still on its tray, on the ground just outside the driver's side and went off to work.

6.

I parked my car on the street beside a graveyard about a quarter mile west of the address and walked the long couple of blocks as the day got itself going, the sun spreading out slowly onto the black-top. It wasn't raining, but it felt like it wanted to, clouds glowering, crowded, low down in the sky.

As I walked toward Mapleton–Fall Creek I crossed Central Avenue, and looking south I could see what appeared to be the smoke from a dozen small fires, rising up and mingling from campsites and cookouts, clustered tents. That had to be Freedman Town, another five miles downtown and a universe away. Maybe it was as simple as that: maybe the man I sought was lying desperate under a torn blanket somewhere in Freedman Town, crammed in among second cousins in an unheated efficiency. The classic move, the fool's move, the move of a desperate runner.

It wouldn't be that easy, though. If Bridge's office thought it was as easy as creeping into Freedman Town and knocking on a couple of doors, that's what I'd be doing. Or, actually, my services would not have been thought necessary. The white vans could roll up on Freedman Town with no help from me.

Mapleton–Fall Creek, by contrast, looked to be a tidy little neighborhood of one-story aluminum-sided bungalows, their trim green front yards like welcome mats. The homes were old but well tended, their small wooden porches cluttered with outdoor furniture — rocking chairs and love seats. Every house was painted some bright color, and it looked like the block association had gotten together to make sure nobody came dressed to the party

28

the same: a powder-blue house, a chipper yellow house, one of green, and one of pink. One house had a black-and-white dog yipping behind a short chain-link fence; the next place had a string of Christmas lights dangling from the gutters, put up either early or way too late.

Up on one of these porches was a very old black woman, her hair in curlers for the day to come, rocking slowly on her rocking chair. She waved, and I waved back. A nice little neighborhood was the vibe that I was getting, a black neighborhood, working people, poor but proud. The kind of place a white person might drive through with the doors locked, thinking it's dangerous for no reason except for the color of its occupants.

I came out onto 38th and turned right, passed a run of businesses, everything closed up tight this early morning. A clothing shop called The Big & The Tall; a barbershop called Men & Ladies; a steak-and-lemonade place called just Steak & Lemonade. One sad liquor store with the paint peeling from around the door frame, with a solitary drunk smoking in an oversize warm-up jacket, playing it cool, dying for the place to open. This is where he had come, cherry-cheeked Father Barton, on Sunday afternoon. He was down in this unlikely neighborhood for some reason, and he had stopped at that bank right over there—the one next to the gas station that's next to Captain D's Fish Fry—to take out a couple hundred bucks, which was gone from his wallet by suppertime last night.

The ATM stood under a little green awning, just to the right of the front door of the bank proper. As I ambled toward it I felt my body take on the young father's spirit, the righteous white man, walking upright and unafraid in a black neighborhood, a man of the people, wearing his serious, sacred expression. I stood at the cash machine a second, then I did a slow 360, even going so far as to mime the action of taking out a wallet, tucking bills inside it, putting it away again. Halfway through my turn, I was looking down the cross street, Central Avenue, toward the south. Down there, a block down, a streetlight was blinking, reflecting itself back murkily in a pothole full of rainwater. On one side of the road was a weedy vacant lot, and across the street was a small white-painted building with a wooden cross hanging above the door. The sign beneath the cross said SAINT ANSELM'S CATHOLIC PROMISE: COMMUNITY WELCOME.

"All right, now," I said, hastening my step, bobbing my head. "All right, all right."

Approaching the building, I heard the rush and roar of a small engine, and then I saw him: a groundskeeper, hunched over and focused, working a leaf blower in an even line along the curb, throwing clouds of dirt and detritus off the sidewalk into the road.

"Hey, hey, man," I said, waving my hands as I came up the sidewalk. "Hold up a sec."

The groundskeeper looked up, weary and wary, but he killed the engine.

"Oh, yeah, hey man. Hey." I rolled into the character as I came up on him, taking on a little decrepitude, a little stagger in my walk, a little grit in my eyes. Drifter, knucklehead, working on that good early-morning drunk. "How you feeling, brother?"

"What can I help you with?"

The gardener was a tired middle-aged black man, a dozen lifetimes of this kind of yard-work bullshit already behind him. Not old, but getting there fast. Tired this morning, bones and fingers tired. Wanting to get this job done, get back in his truck before the rain came, if it was coming.

"Yeah, yeah," I said, talking quickly, licking my lips, addled and rapid. "Yeah, I tell ya, man, I been *wandering*. You feel me? Been *wandering* today."

He raised his eyebrows just the tiniest bit. He wore forest-green coveralls with the name RUBEN stitched into a white oval above the breast pocket and CIRCLE CITY LAWNSCAPING in big stenciled block letters on the back.

I hustled out my words. "Yeah, so I saw this was a church, okay, and I just felt like I had to come on down here. 'Cause listen, man, it just happens I been hearing the angels, man, and they been saying I need to get right. Get right with God. Angels been saying what I need to do is go on and get right *today*."

"Well, you won't be doing it here, man." Ruben turned his cracked lips up for a brief smile. "This is not a church. It's a community center."

"What? *Oh*."

"Church own it, but it ain't a church. And it's closed, man."

"Well, *shit*."

Ruben liked that. He ground out a laugh, gravelly and low. "Sorry, boss. The what-you-call-it — you know, the diocese — they closed this place up a while back. Six months ago, something? They got us coming by once a week to keep it from getting overgrown and all. That's it."

"Oh, wow. Wow, wow. Guess my angels got they wires crossed."

"I guess they did."

We both laughed a little then, me and my man Ruben, and I stood and swayed in my drunkenness and shook my head and took a good hard look at that building. Not so grand a structure as Saint Catherine's up there on Meridian Street, not by a long shot: old, wood-sided, one-storied, a flat black roof. The front of the building had but one door, up a short walkway lined with box hedges and ivy. One of the windows was broken, a shatter scar down the middle of it like an unhealed wound. At the door handle, though, was a bright glint of gold.

I held my eyes to that door for a second, squinting hopefully, as if to open it by force of will and get the salvation I was seeking.

"All right, well." Ruben raised his leaf blower. "I better get back to it."

"Hold up a sec," I said, in a burst of inspiration. "Y'all hiring?"

His brows arched with fresh skepticism. "I dunno. You gotta ask Rick about that."

"Rick?"

"Yeah. Rick or I guess—Rick or Tiny."

"Tiny?"

"That's right."

"You got a number?"

"It's on the truck, man."

Ruben was done with me. He turned away and fired up his leaf blower and called "Good luck" over its roar as I tippled over to that truck, a Pakistani pickup on high wheels towing an enclosed flatbed trailer cluttered with mowers and rakes and shit. Both the truck and the trailer had CIRCLE CITY LAWNSCAPING painted on the side, and under the name was the number.

The whole community center was about as big as a Monopoly house, and it looked older than sin, older than Adam and Eve the sinners.

Except for the lock on the door. That lock was brass, and it looked shiny and new.

I smiled to myself as I got the number off the side of the truck, feeling pretty pleased at having noticed that detail. Happy about having gotten—guided by the ATM receipt—to the bank, to the Catholic community center, to Ruben, to the door. Happy with all I'd done even before Bridge and his people managed to get me the full file. I was feeling the pleasure of discovery, the pleasure of the job.

That's the problem with doing the devil's work. It can be pretty satisfying now and again. Pretty goddamn satisfying.

I had with me in Indianapolis all my usual equipment. Some of it was in my room at the Capital City Crossroads, some of it was stashed in the trunk of the car. A variety of costume pieces—some wigs, some fake jewelry, and various basic elements of facial camouflage: a tube of spirit gum, a few shades of foundation, an eyebrow pencil. I had six different pairs of clear-glass spectacles and six different sets of colored contact lenses. Other tools, too: a set of picks and rakes for cracking locks, plus a backup set. Lanyards with name tags, fake badges in fake badge holders. Clothes and shoes. My phone and its charger and its various accessories; the computer. Paperwork for Jim Dirkson, and three more complete sets on three other names, all of it comprehensively backstopped, every phone number connected to a real phone, a real person who knew what to say if somebody called. Cash, too, of course—rolls of bills in rubber bands, available for my use for incidental expenses, all of which were to be reported at the completion of each assignment.

I had a gun, but it stayed in the hotel. Almost all the time, that's where I kept it. I am an undercover operative in a dangerous line of work, but understand that I am also an African American male living in the United States of America. There are *going* to be checkpoints. I am *going* to get stopped. Every once in a while I'm going to have to dump out my bag under the watchful eye of some kind of lawman. Sheriff's deputy, patrol officer, state trooper, what have you. Might just be some shopping-center wage-slave shithead rolling up on his Segway, flashing his costume-shop tin, wanting to prove his cock size to the girl at the sunglasses kiosk.

When that sort of BS happened I had no choice but to submit. I had no badge, no ID. I was true undercover, right down the line. If you saw the way I traveled, if you went through my suitcase or the trunk of my car, you'd think I was a thief, some kind of con man.

Which I was, of course. Really, that's exactly what I was. I was a thief. I was some kind of con man.

When I got back outside, I found a police car parked right alongside my Altima, just outside the cemetery gate. I stopped and I stared at it for a second: an IMPD black-and-white, with the stenciled letters on the side and the sirens on the roof and the long radio antenna sticking up stiff and proud from the rear. I glanced up and down the street to see if the owner was around, but it was just as quiet as it had been before. Even the sky, still gray and cool, the clouds right where I had left them. Everything same as it was, except for the marked car.

I bounced on my heels a couple times, as if my body were getting ready to take off running. But I didn't do that. I didn't do anything. I just stood there, looking at the rear bumper of that police vehicle, looking at the gravestones, at the houses down the street, an uneasy feeling gathering and drifting in me like mist.

I was thinking that there had been two cops in the Fountain Diner last night, a black one and a white one, a couple tables over from the priest and me, looking at something on one of their phones, laughing and carrying on. Slowly I approached the parked police vehicle, listening to the distant, indistinct sounds of the city. Someone honking somewhere. A doorway gate rattling up, maybe Steak & Lemonade or The Big & The Tall opening for the day.

I committed the number to memory. Car number 101097. Big city, I was thinking. Big city, full of cops. That's all.

7.

"What is this? What is this, now?"

I was standing on the hotel room's rickety wooden chair so the top of my head grazed the ceiling. I had a halfway decent printer, government-issue and portable, but it worked just fine, and when a file came in it was my practice to print it and lay the sheets out on the hotel bedspread in a grid and study them from above, as though I were doing helicopter surveillance on a city block.

The full file was a goddamn mess, and I was not pleased. I hate mess. I hate unevenness and uncertainty, and that's what the full file was—it was uneven and uncertain.

It was midafternoon already. The file had appeared on the second server by noon, as promised, and I'd been staring at its ugly sheets since then, scowling at them, drinking water from the cheap hotel-room tumbler, puzzling over the nine pages of closely typed text and illustrations, and thinking the same thing: *What a goddamn mess.*

The first three pages of the file concerned Father Barton and his cell of the Underground Airlines, and this section was short on details and long on conjecture, pure search-engine bullshit. Some intern in Bridge's office had strung it together from old arrest warrants and radical abolition chat rooms: Barton's birth date, town of origin, known and suspected associates. His close ties to the International Canaan Organization (ICO) and Les Bénévoles Blackburn, his loose ties to the Black Panthers and two other "domestic terror organizations." His name in connection with a nasty incident twenty-two months ago: a body found in a crate in a Cincinnati

FedEx routing center, never delivered, substantially decayed. This corpse was eventually ID'd with a PIN and a service name—a runner from Boone County, Carolina, who'd gotten himself crated and sent to "Saint Catherine's Cathedral, Indiana." The FedEx employee who'd facilitated this Hail Mary maneuver, an abbo sympathizer working freelance, was in federal prison but could not be persuaded to admit he'd been acting on Barton's behest—at least, that is, not according to this useless, messy, bullshit file.

All these first few pages did was tell me what I already knew—that despite his claims of innocence, the parish priest was a prolific smuggler of runaways, directly or indirectly responsible for dozens of illegal manumissions over the last several years. Bridge or Bridge's intern had "a high degree of certainty" (whatever the fuck that meant) that it was Barton and his group who'd pulled Jackdaw off the plantation and/or gotten him across the Fence. They were equally certain it was Barton's people shielding the boy till he could be moved across the 49th parallel to permanent freedom.

I scowled. I shifted my weight. My eyes flickered past the hole in my grid, a gap like a vacant lot in a row of homes. That was page 7, and I hadn't printed it. I wasn't ready to look at it. Not yet.

The section about Garments of the Greater South, Incorporated, wasn't much more useful. Nothing that any mope couldn't have pulled from public records. Total acreage; acreage devoted to production; total annual yield; yield of upland, yield of American pima. Gross annual revenue, gross annual profit, projected future revenue. Every time I read about one of these places, they'd gotten bigger, more modern, larger in scope, and more sophisticated in their operations. This one, this GGSI, boasted of having customers in seventy-two countries around the world for its "durable, high-fineness fibers" and its "premium-rated seeds and seed oils." GGSI housed the Institute for Agricultural Innovation, with support from the state of Alabama and the American Cotton Council, performing "cutting-edge research on new technologies in the production of pest- and drought-resistant cotton strains." GGSI had 4,232 Persons Bound to Labor on its sprawling campus—in its fields, in its factories, in its offices.

Four thousand, two hundred and thirty-one, I thought. *As of Sunday night, 4,231.*

There was an aerial photograph of the facility in there, too, a smudged satellite image with every blurry rectangle numbered and labeled. Thirty-two separate structures. I let my finger move from rectangle to rectangle. I traced the lines between the buildings, along the service roads and gravel paths connecting them, fighting off a burst of dread imagination, me down in there, running in slave grays from building to building, from shipping and receiving to facilities maintenance, bare feet slapping the paths.

The population center was five buildings arranged in a semicircle around a courtyard labeled RECREATION, five grim rectangles of identical dimensions, arrayed like soldiers. Past the pop center was building 20, labeled DETENTION/RECONDITIONING, which would have been known in the land of my own youth as the shed.

I paused, just a second, just a half second, my forefinger pressed into building 20 until the blood had left it and it was white as the fingernail.

Some things on the map I could not understand, and I noted them all, put them aside to discuss with Mr. Bridge later on. One building, just behind the Institute for Agricultural Innovation, was unlabeled and blacked out, a redacted rectangle, hidden from the eye of God. And there was a whole set of lines on the map I could not explain, a broken black line making a loop around the periphery of the campus, just inside the line of the fence. Was it an extra line of fencing? A kind of shock collar around the whole place? I didn't like it, that line. I felt sure it was connected to the PB population. Some new innovation in the control of men.

I wondered. I clenched my jaw. I memorized the map and moved on.

Not to page 7, though. Not yet.

My eye slid over the gap in my grid where page 7 should have been and arrived at the relative safety of page 8, a dry recitation of facts, detailing the events of the escape as presently known. The runner, service name Jackdaw, registry PIN 78312-99, had been roused from the pop center on Sunday morning, marked present at muster (confirmation from multiple sources). He was scanned into stitch house 2 (building 27) at 7:30 a.m. (visual confirmation from two PB overseers and a Free White Worker on the floor). Jackdaw had performed his shift, twelve hours on a stool, trimming stray threads from collars. GGSI ran its PB population on the eight-twelve-three system, in accordance with the Labor Practices Act: eight hours in population for every twelve on the floor, with a mandated job change every three years at the minimum. BLP agents regulated the shifts, checking everyone in and out, enforcing all the rules: breaks to be taken as scheduled; punishments to be humane and proportional to infraction. Violent slavery is against the law.

The file didn't say how deep Jackdaw was into his rotation, because the file was a goddamn mess.

I put myself in the man's shoes, imagined the man's day. Jackdaw perched on a backless stool; Jackdaw at his small steel table with his tiny pair of scissors; Jackdaw, squinting through a magnifying glass, clipping the impossibly small and delicate threads, tidying up the black or red or blue collars, collar after collar, thread upon thread. Jackdaw's cramped fingers and tired eyes. His pile slowly shrinking until the moment, every half hour or so, when the buzzer shrieked and a warehouse forklift would arrive from receiving, and the PB or the Free White behind the wheel would dump out a new load of collars.

I turned the page.

> 7:30 p.m.: 78312-99 shift ends, scanned out (multiple sources), returned to Pop Center B
>
> 7:47 p.m.: 78312-99 self-reporting "stomach pains." Responsible on-call party admins 750 mg NSAID in situ
>
> 8:17 p.m.: 78312-99 self-reporting stomach pains + vomiting + diarrhea. ROCP transports TM to worker care

I nodded to myself a few times. I closed my eyes. The scenes came in to me as red flashes, summoning themselves from between the words of the file.

The boy in his cot, adrenaline flooding his veins. Jamming on the red button for the trusty: "I'm sick, man; I'm real sick. . . ." Thirty minutes later, 8:17, calling again: now he's puking. Now there's shit on the floor.

8:35 p.m.: 78312-99 admitted to worker care (building 47) for treatment by staff on call

And on and on. PIN 78312-99, taken from his bunk in "heavy restraining garments" (per protocol), moved in a one-man mesh transport containment unit (TCU) to the worker-care facility in the western section of the campus. Brought up via the elevator, gravely ill, removed from the TCU and restrained (per protocol) with zip ties to the examination table, and left in the care of the on-call nurses: Monica Smith, age twenty-four, and Angelina Croth, age twenty-seven. When the guard returns an hour later (protocol, protocol, a small contained universe of protocols), he discovers a horrifying tableau. Blood splattered on the floor of the worker-care unit; blood on the walls; blood on the rear wall in two descending smears, as if the helpless nurses had been slammed into the wall, then left to slide down slowly. The four zip ties that had been used to bind the patient to the bed by the wrist and ankle were snapped, as if by violent strength. Not just one but all the windows in the examination room were shattered, presumably by the wheeled examination cart, which was found upended in the hedges six stories below.

The subsequent fate of the nurses, or their bodies, was not noted. Also not noted was how the perpetrator of this ferocious act had managed subsequently to disappear. A very sick man, two nurses attacked, then poof. Thin air. The invisible man.

I got down off the chair and paced the room a little. I thought about going out onto the balcony and smoking a cigarette, but then I decided not to. I was boxing page 7. It was daring me to look at it, and I was turning away. I was going to have to look at it sooner or later. I skimmed the last part of the file, and it was just the usual paper-chase bullshit. Even that, though, even the basic paperwork, the warrant and the authorization, the judge-signature pages . . . all that was a mess, too, a mess of potholes and question marks and uncleanlinesses. I recorded these to bring to Bridge's attention later on. If I was going to do my job, he could do his, for God's sake.

This was how I fooled myself, you see? That was *one* of the ways I fooled myself. *If I was going to do my job, he could do his!* The righteous, wry refrain of a long-suffering employee, rolling his eyes at the incompetent desk jockey higher up the food chain. I understand why I did it, hard as it is now to admit, hard as it is to reconcile, as shameful.

As if he and I were—what? Coworkers? As though I were just some harried but ultimately steadfast employee, rolling my eyes at the frustrating flaws of my thick-skulled but ultimately lovable employer?

And then at last, after there were no more pages to review, and after I had steeled myself by sitting perfectly still for five minutes, seated with my hands in my lap, looking at nothing, seated in the uncomfortable armchair and staring at the white wall of the hotel room—when I had no other options, I connected the laptop back to my portable printer and printed out page 7.

I laid it on the grid. I climbed back on the chair and observed it from a distance, looking down. And I swayed atop my chair. Somehow I had known. Somehow I had known how hard it would be. How the man's picture would make me feel.

Granted, all PB file photos are disturbing in one way or another. Typically the subjects are coldly furious, hatred burning from their eyes toward the lens, or else they're sapped out, dead-eyed, staring straight ahead into nothing. I had seen some smiling, seen the wolfish, defiant grins of those unwilling to be bowed, and I had seen the lunatic, lopsided smiles of those who had slipped into an alternate dimension, who had let go the hand of reality. And who, after all, would deny them that mercy? I swear to God, man, anyone gives you the old "better-off" line, about the natural state of the Person Bound, about slaves actually preferring their lot and the simplicity of a circumscribed life, well, you just dare them to look at a few of those pictures, or a few hundred of them, as I have looked at a few hundred or more.

This man, though, Jackdaw, PIN 78312-99. His picture was something different. Jackdaw was a handsome man, almost perversely handsome, like when you see a movie star playing a tramp or a wastrel and the face is not only so familiar but also so obviously well cared for, and it just doesn't ring true. He was thin, with slender cheeks and a slender nose, with something almost feminine in the delicacy of his features. In the picture he looked straight ahead, following instructions, but the eyebrows were half raised and the mouth just barely open, as if the camera had caught him about to speak. His eyes had sadness in them, and sensitivity, and some other thing hard to name. Nervousness? Questioning? *There must be some sort of mistake,* the eyes seemed to be saying. *Some lines got crossed here. I've ended up in the wrong room.*

I tried to correlate this delicate and sensitive face with the horror show described in the full file. The smears of blood, the broken glass. There seemed to be some Incredible Hulk shit going on here; some Jekyll-and-Hyde kind of shit.

He was tattooed, of course, with the letters GGSI stylized into a logo: three little letters, *G* and *S* and *I*, safe under the curling roof of a sturdy and paternal capital *G*. This emblem was etched at the root of his neck, just above the low hollow of the collarbone. Beside it were two other boxes, squares of pure black: the logos of previous owners, now covered over.

On my own collarbone was a single black box where there once had been the bell-and-cow logo of my birthplace, long since filled in. This would be a telltale sign of my former status, except that a lot of people marked themselves this way—in some parts of the North, almost every black person did, freeborn and manumitted and runners alike. A mark of solidarity: if we are all former slaves, then none of us is.

I flipped the picture facedown on the bedspread, coward that I was, but the paper was printed on both sides. Jackdaw was on the back of it, too, deaggregated into his stats and identifiers: "PIN 78312-99 ('Jackdaw'), p.l. unknown, m.l. unknown. Age 23. Height 5'8", weight 153 lbs (BMI = 23.3)." Shoe size and shirt size, waist and chest. Marks and scars, bumps and moles. A man as a map of his dermatological idiosyncrasies. His pigmentation was given as "late-summer honey, warm tone, #76."

That was enough. I collected the papers off the bedspread and locked them away. Closed the clamshell lid of the laptop.

I heard car doors slamming beneath my window. The white girl and her black son, making their way across the parking lot, dragging suitcases. The kid, in rumpled jeans and a white sleeveless undershirt, was bent forward at the waist, dragging a giant purple suitcase twice as big as he was, a determined expression like a hunter returning from the kill.

"Boo-boo, come on," his mom said over her shoulder. "I can take it."

"I got it, Mama."

"Yeah, but Lionel, you're scraping it all up."

"Mama. I *got* it."

I turned the woman over a minute, trying to figure if she'd really been planning to stay here tonight or if she'd shown up just to give Mr. Paulsen the stick. Fifty-fifty, I figured, watching Lionel drag the suitcase. I revised my estimation of Lionel's age—he was seven at least, maybe even eight. He wore scuffed-up sneakers with yellow stars. His Afro was grown out, more than most kids grew it out these days, a gold halo of curls. Jackdaw was waiting for me, back in the room; waiting for me, somewhere in the city. The kid stopped, right outside the door of the hotel, looked over his shoulder, and saw me, and I saw him, and for some reason—whatever reason it is that little kids do anything—he let the handle of the suitcase fall and struck a funny muscleman pose, raising both scrawny brown arms and flexing. I smiled, then the mom turned around and I ducked back into the room. The last thing I needed, with Jackdaw's tender, baffled, frightened face floating around, stirred up in me, was some kind of awkward conversation—thanks for the fruit, what have you—with the child's white mother.

The photo page was still on the bed. That description, "late-summer honey," you know, that sounds like poetry, but it's not. "Late-summer honey, warm tone, #76" is one of 172 varietals of African American skin tone delineated in the US Marshals Service field guide in a chart called "Pigmentation Taxonomies," located in chapter 9 ("Identifiers/Descriptors"). I, myself, am "moderate charcoal, brass highlights, #41."

8.

"Hoo, shit! What is *this?*"

"Hey, yo—stop, man. Hey, yo, slave. Stop, slave."

I stopped. I turned, but slowly, slowly. I didn't turn my whole body: just my head.

"Come on, now, PB, slow it down." The boy said the letters with singsong double emphasis, *Pee-bee; pee,* then *bee.* There were two of them, two boys hollering from the top step of a wooden porch. I was back down in the same neighborhood, a few blocks from Catholic Promise, in uniform, ready to go. Getting on now toward twilight. The same no-weather weather it had been all day: it was cloudless, or maybe there was just one large cloud, a blanket across the whole of the sky.

"Slavey be rushin', man."

"Shit, yeah, he be rushin'. Get back to the field before Massa scan him in late."

They howled. They bumped fists. Hip-hop music blasted from a portable stereo beside them.

I ground my teeth and fought back a rush of bad, bad memories, my life behind the Fence coming up all together in a red flash: dangling flesh and blood guttering down into the drains. I pushed it down. I choked it back.

"Y'all talkin' to me?" I said to the boys, very slowly, very mildly, palming my chest.

"Yeah, man."

"Yeah, son."

They prowled down from the steps they'd been sitting on, a pack

44

of two, and flanked me. I stood military straight. There was nothing to be concerned about here. They hadn't seen through me, no way. Not these two. These were just boys, mischievous children of good, hardworking free people, a couple teenagers throwing poses, pants down around their nuts, playing at gangster. There were wind chimes tinkling on that porch behind my tormentors. This was some long-suffering mama's porch.

But one of them, skinny with bare arms and a head shaped like a peanut, hitched up his T-shirt to show me the handle of a Saturday night special. I stood quietly between them at the foot of the wooden stairs. The rap song on the stereo ended, and another one began, a shouted lyric and a ropy bass line snaking between beats. It was not a song I knew, but I don't listen to a lot of rap. It's that power in it—that danger that scares a lot of white people, that's gotten it banned outright in some places—that power that's right up there on the surface. It's too much for me sometimes. It batters at me. It catches me in the rib cage.

"I am afraid you fellas have me mistaken," I said, still mild, even smiling slightly. "I have never even *been* behind the line."

"Oh, yeah?" said the other of the two boys. He was larger, dense, thickly muscled arms in a sleeveless Colts T-shirt. He had beady little eyes. Medium-red pigment, somewhere in the mahogany range; his friend, with the peanut head, he was brighter-skinned, almost Caucasian. "I think you lyin'," said the thick one, but then turned, uncertain, to his boy. "He lyin', right?"

Peanut Head ignored him, pushed a flat hand into the center of my chest. I didn't flinch. I kept my cool.

"You a hardworking man, PB?" he demanded. "You got good years in you, yeah? How much you think you worth?"

"Yeah," said the other. "How much we earn, we call you ass in?"

"Call it *in?*" Peanut Head turned to his friend, incredulous. "Shit, Bernard. We ain't calling the fucking *tip* line. We call Elron, he call his cousin what's-his-name, that snatcher. We make some real bread on this fucking runner."

I contemplated my options. I wondered about Elron, about the cousin. There *are* real snatchers, of course, man takers cruising the back alleys of black neighborhoods and Freedman Towns, looking for men to peel off the fringes of life: parolees, the homeless, sex offenders living low—anyone who can be thrown in an SUV, shorn of papers, and sold to some bargain-hunting middler who'll turn him around on a no-auction sale. It happens rarely, but it happens. Everything happens.

"Hold 'em," said the littler one to his friend, but Bernard hesitated. "Grab him, son, go on."

Bernard cornered me against the porch rail, wide body blocking my exit, and I thought about my move. If it came to it, I'd catch them both before either could draw. Quick, easy martial-arts throat chops to bring them down, slam their heads together to make them still. Drag them down the stairs quickly and put them in the trunk of the Altima. Drive back north toward the hotel, call Bridge from the car. There was a man he used, I knew, to handle these kinds of situations. His name was Ferdinand. He was a Cuban. I didn't have the number, but I would call Bridge, and Bridge would call Ferdinand. *Unavoidable,* I would say. *Nothing I could do.*

"Go on, Bernard," said Peanut, one hand on the butt of his gun, the other calling Elron with his phone. "Grab that bitch."

Bernard raised his hands as if to seize me, but he wasn't quite sure on this thing, not quite yet. I took the moment. I spoke, slow and low and clear. "I would not do that."

Bernard's hands came down. He could hear it, the cold ancient strangeness in my voice, all that cow's blood and knife heat pulsing in my eyes.

Peanut Head wasn't there yet. He lowered his phone and turned back to glare at me. Yanked out the gun. Bernard winced. He didn't like this at all.

"Put it down," I told him. "Put down the weapon."

"Or what, slave?"

"I am no runner. I am no slave."

"What?"

I kept going. I told them the truth.

"But neither am I a man."

"What?"

"I am a monster in the shape of a man. I am a man with the skin of a snake and the feet of a wolf."

"Fuck you talkin' about?" said Peanut, starting to get a little bit of Bernard's nervous eyes. His fingers dancing on the gun butt. Bernard, for his part, was *done*. "Come on, man," he said, tugging on his boy's sleeve. "Come *on*."

"I do not walk the world, son, but stalk it," I said. "With the scent of blood in my nostrils, my flanks a mess of scars." I started down the street, still talking. "I am not a slave. But neither am I a man."

"That ain't no PB," I heard Bernard say behind me. "That dude's just fucking *crazy*."

The problem was that those old bad times, once they got keyed up, were hard to quiet. It was all around me in the air now, all those miserable fucking memories, the terrified lowing of the cattle and the ka-thunk of the bolt gun. The heat and stench of the workroom, my cramped grip on the saw, the cows' slow turning in the air, bloated and dripping gore. My brother Castle, his big eyes in the darkness. I was trying to go along now and get on with my work, and all these snatches of vision hovered like bits of ash or motes of dust, flickering glimpses of an old world, my old world, floating around me and settling on my skin as I came out onto Central Avenue, breathing hard.

"All right, now, honey," I whispered, talking to myself, nice and soft. "All right."

It was twilight. Streetlamps blinked to life. I just breathed. Nice and easy.

Once I got back to the spot, I was fine. I was cool. I ambled slowly up to the community center in a pair of heavy black work shoes and

47

the CIRCLE CITY LAWNSCAPING coveralls I had boosted off the back of Ruben's truck. The tag above the breast pocket said in cursive letters that my name was Albie, and I liked that name. I murmured it twice, thinking maybe I'd put it to use sometime in the future.

I stood outside the community center at dusk with my hat tilted back, taking in the building, scratching my head, and I knew exactly what I looked like: I looked like a gardener. Albie the lawn man at the end of the day. Maybe trying to puzzle out the location of the hose connection, maybe going back to pull out this one particular dead rosebush the boss man said to be sure to pull. I had gloves on, tight latex, thin as skin. I walked down the hedge-flanked walkway with a workingman's purpose, peered in the windows, and tested the handles.

I hummed and whistled and crouched and took a sounding of that big brass front-door lock, running my fingers gently across its surface, feeling for nicks and scratches that would show that some-one else had been here before me. My humming built its way up to a crescendo as I opened my slim black case and found the right rake and the right tension bar and stuck them in there and wiggled and poked at the lock's invisible insides. As I tested that hardware-store lock I considered which way I would run if this turned out to be the moment when I ran. Highway overpass was one mile west. I would move as fast as I could without running. Chuck the lock-pick kit into the bushes, peel off Albie's uniform, stuff it into a garbage can, and head away on foot, due west on 38th Street. One mile, then I would hustle up the on-ramp on foot and flag down a car and get myself gone.

I shooed the idea away. I always shooed it away. I wasn't going anywhere. I was tethered tight. There was a device inside of me, right up at the place where the top of the spine meets the base of the brain. Screwed in by government doctors, sending out coor-dinates on me all day every day to Bridge, to whoever sits beside Bridge. Smaller than a grain of rice, that little device, or so they'd told me. Smaller than the head of a pin.

They also told me I would not feel it, but I could feel it, I always felt it, I always heard it, though it made no sound. When I was too quiet for too long I heard it singing in me: humming, taunting, burning. A hook. An anchor. A leash.

It didn't take more than a minute to persuade the lock of Saint Anselm's Catholic Promise to let go. I straightened up, cracked my knuckles, nodded approvingly—nice work, Albie the gardener—and nudged open the door with my foot.

I moved quickly through the empty quiet of the community center. Most of it was taken up by the one room, a big room, with a dozen beige folding chairs arranged in a circle and a coffee service set up in the back, as if for a meeting of drug addicts or drunks. I crouched down to examine one of these folding-chair seats and found no dust on it at all. I looked for gaps in wallpaper. I looked for loose tiles on the floor. I counted entrances and exits. Doing this part of a job, straight breaking and entering, covering a room, sniffing for holes and hideaways, I really was not a person. I was neither black nor white. Just action. Just work. A machine. I dropped down onto my hands and knees to feel my way across the floor.

I turned on my flashlight and pointed it one way, then another, watching the line of light pick out stains on the floor, dust balls, a couple of cigarette butts, bent like tiny broken bones. I didn't imagine I'd be finding the PB himself in here, alone in the darkness, behind a stack of boxes or under loose floorboards. I gave smooth young Father Barton more credit than that. Although it had, at least once, been just that easy. In Buffalo once—or Burlington, or Baltimore, some northern city—the poor son of a bitch I was looking for had been in a child's tree house in the backyard. Some foolish dilettante abolitionist, a software engineer or some other kind of workaday white man, had volunteered to serve as an attendant on the Airlines, told himself that he could hide a rabbit for six days until the man could get put on a connecting flight to Ontario.

But then this software man had gone and stuck the hapless runner in his kid's damn tree house. I guess a secret attic was too risky. Or maybe, however righteous he was, he didn't care for the idea of a dark-skinned stranger actually living in his house for a week.

That slave, whatever his name was, never knew what happened to him. I spotted a candy wrapper, fluttering down from that tree like a shining silver leaf, and I took pictures of him up there with a telephoto lens and put the pictures on the secure server, and Mr. Bridge made his calls. I never even got out of my car.

It wasn't going to be that easy this time. Barton was too smart a customer to have his runaway slave squirreled away on church property.

I was looking not for a man but for information, a broken twig in the underbrush, some scar-barked tree that would turn me in his direction. And that's what I found. I had known that I would, and I did. There was a small kitchen behind the meeting room, and in the small kitchen a small refrigerator, and hidden behind the small refrigerator was a small door. There was no point in getting my rakes and tension bars back out, not for the chintzy lock that secured that secret door. I found a paper clip on the ground, and I unfolded it and bent the edge and hummed to myself, eight bars, twelve bars, then I had that lock open, and in I went.

The PB in the software engineer's tree house, that man's service name was Hand. A common-enough slave name. He had fled, like Jackdaw, from a textile factory — Clearwater Cotton Products, somewhere in eastern Mississippi. And the tree house I dragged him out of wasn't in Buffalo or Burlington or Baltimore. It was in Monclova, Ohio, nineteen miles outside of Toledo.

I do it even now, you see? I play false, I dance and dance. I murmur the stories in shadow or half shadow; I pretend to myself that I don't remember the names, the details, when in fact I do. I did and I do—I remember all their names.

I left Saint Anselm's and walked back to the car, not even checking for my new friends on the porch. All around me, all inside me, was a feeling of unease, of incipience. A murky sky, holding the possibility but not the promise of rain.

9.

"She's fine, thanks," I said, stepping out onto the cold and narrow balcony, frisking myself for cigarettes. "How's *your* mother?"

Mr. Bridge gave me his patient, neutral silence, as he always did. He had called precisely at 9:50, as always, and asked after my progress, same as always.

"My progress is good," I told him. "But first I got some questions about this file."

"Oh?"

"Yeah." I lit a Baba and talked through clenched teeth. "File's a goddamn mess."

Mr. Bridge didn't agree or disagree. He breathed evenly, waiting for me to explain. I did it without thinking, after all these years, measured Bridge's silences, held each one to feel its specific weight and texture, each silence a certain kind of stone. This one here, this was tolerant silence. He wasn't interested in my questions and certainly not in my feedback, but he would suffer them to get the goods.

"Let's start with these nurses," I said. "They find their bodies?"

"I do not know."

"Might be worth finding out."

"I agree. And I will find out."

I sighed, my sarcasm sliding off of Bridge like water parting around the prow of a battleship. "Do that. Bodies don't disappear. They don't disintegrate. And there's gotta be accomplices—they know that, right?"

"I presume so."

"You presume so?"

"What I need for you to do, Victor, is to focus on your end."

"Oh, all right, then. That's great. Let's look at my end. You got the file open over there?"

I knew he did. I heard his fingers clicking on the keys, scrolling through the pages while I talked. "Okay, so on page nine. We get the date and time of GGSI's statement, we get the judge's order, but not the judge's name. All it says is"—I spoke from memory; the papers were inside the room, spread out on the bed—"all it says is, 'So ordered by a judge of the Alabama district court.'"

"And?"

"What judge is it?"

"What judge?" Bridge's tolerant silence was darkening now with irritation. "The owner attests to an escape and gives a detailed description of the escapee. The judge records the proceeding, orders a transcript produced, and issues his writ."

"His or her."

"Fine."

"His, her, or its."

"Victor. Why does it matter?"

I hissed out smoke, watched it spread over the parking lot. Mr. Bridge was right—as far as our side of the thing was concerned, as far as running the man down was concerned, it couldn't matter any less what fucking judge it was. It only bothered me because it was sloppy work, and sloppy work never felt right, not when a man's life hung in the goddamn balance. Still, I pressed on. The shadows of impatience were growing longer over Bridge's silence now, and I was aware that there was a limit to how much of this pushback he would tolerate. I leapfrogged to the part that was bothering me most, the part that really did matter.

"How do we even know this boy's in Indianapolis?"

"Because it says so."

"Well, no, it doesn't."

I stepped back inside the room. I left the balcony door open, and the room was just small enough for me to leave my cigarette hand back out on the balcony while I craned my neck to look down at the pages on the bed.

"What it says is, 'The subject is known to have intended to remove himself to Indianapolis, Indiana.'"

"Exactly."

"What do you mean, exactly?"

"I mean—what?"

"Listen." I took an irritated drag, and ash tumbled down on the bedspread, snowing gray onto the pages of the file. Damn it. Sloppy. "It doesn't say he's in Indy. It says he is known to have intended to remove himself there. Now, what does that even *mean?*"

I could hear his inhale. He was about to answer, but then he didn't; instead he gave me a new silence, one I'd never heard before. Something hesitant in it. Something uncertain. I slipped back outside.

"You there?"

"It says what it says. It says he's in Indianapolis."

I read the sentence to him again, struck—as I had been the first time I read it and each time since—by its obscurity, the ugliness of the construction. Even for government grammar, it was a nasty and clotted run of words. *The subject is known to have intended to remove himself to Indianapolis, Indiana.* And then, at the end, there was a strange little mark. A dagger.

"You see that it's footnoted?" I asked Bridge. "Is it footnoted on yours?"

"It is."

"So?"

"I don't know."

I stared at that sentence. At the footnote marker. There wasn't any footnote at the bottom of the page to go with it. No amendments or addenda at the end, either, no page of notes the dagger was telling the reader to go and look at. I heard Bridge's fingers clicking away, so I knew he was looking, so I asked him, and he said yes, it was the same in his copy: a reference with no referent, a dagger pointing to nothing.

"Okay," he said. "I'll look into it."

"All right. Good."

"Victor. How is your progress?"

That was it: question time was over. I lit a new cigarette with the end of the old one, and I gave Mr. Bridge what he was waiting for.

"I followed Barton's bread crumbs to a church facility in a colored neighborhood on the west side of the city," I said. "Place is all closed up, but the good father is coming and going, probably other folks, too. Someone at the diocese level had it shuttered a few months ago, but there's a new lock on the place. My money says this is the new temporary HQ for an ongoing operation. Permanent floating craps game."

"Okay. And?"

I sighed. Mr. Bridge did not give pats on the back. No chucks on the chin.

"Victor?"

"I cracked the lock in about a minute."

"And?"

"I had a look around."

"Did you find the runner?"

"Yeah, Bridge. I got him. He's here. We got fried chicken and watermelon from room service."

But you couldn't get a rise out of Mr. Bridge. You couldn't make him jump. So I just went on, staring down at the cars in the lamplit parking lot. I pried away for Mr. Bridge the plywood panel over the hidden doorway at Saint Anselm's Catholic Promise; I led him into Father Barton's crawl space, and showed off for him a variety of distinctly nonclerical objects I had discovered therein. Six guns of a variety of manufacture and caliber, none with serial numbers; three bulletproof vests; a shoe box full of driver's licenses, displaying a wide array of black and white faces, issued by the states of

Indiana, Illinois, and Pennsylvania. A locked chest that had yielded to the attention of my picks and rakes and turned out to be full of money—small and large bills, rolled up in tight circles, the better to be passed into waiting hands.

What was most interesting, though, was a single photograph, which I had found taped to the underside of a small wooden schoolboy desk, pushed up against the wall in one corner of the crawl space. The photograph was of excellent quality, seemingly the result of high-quality macro-lens photography. The faces of the two causasian gentlemen in the photograph were crystal clear, and there could be no doubt as to the activity in which they were vigorously engaged.

"Fucking?" said Bridge.

"Yes, sir. Fucking."

Discomfort. Embarrassment. A rare species of silence, to be prized. I smiled.

"Are you suggesting," said Barton at last, "that Father Barton is a pornographer?"

"No," I said, rolling my eyes. No worldly sense on Bridge at all; a desk man, right down to the floor. "Not a pornographer. A blackmailer."

I spelled it out for poor, dense Bridge. Of the two gentlemen captured in the photograph, one was in his socks, but the other had had the poor judgment to remain in his green work shirt, the corporate logo of which was displayed to the lens: a purple-and-green globe emblazoned with speed lines. Visible behind the happy couple, painted on a gray tiled wall below a row of clocks, was the same logo. Before Bridge's call I had figured out where they were: Whole Wide World Logistics, a third-party transport company, short haul and long haul, mostly small freight, with a regional headquarters and "client relationship center" in Indianapolis.

"So maybe lover boy is married," I told Bridge. "Maybe he doesn't want his boss knowing what's going on in the office after hours. Either way, they're leaning on this mope to arrange special deliveries."

"Do you have a name?" Bridge's voice had recovered its customary composure.

"Winston Bibb. He's the assistant regional manager."

"And have you paid him a visit yet?"

I said no, and Bridge said why not, and I drew in a lungful of poison and said because I was done with this approximation of a human existence, with bending not only my abilities but my real human soul to the sinister will of an authoritarian state, and that one day I would transform my flesh to metal and become a sword aimed at his heart.

Bridge didn't laugh. He waited in silence until, in the same even tone, I said no, I hadn't gone to Whole Wide World yet, because it was nighttime and they weren't open, and I doubted I would gain much ground by B and E. In daylight I would go over there and find out what special shipment poor Winston was forced to arrange so Jackdaw could be put on it. From there I could find out who took delivery, find out where—find out and find out until I found out the man himself, found him out and called him in, and then Bridge's white vans would roll up in their rough government splendor and bear him away.

As I gave my report and we laid our plans I could hear Bridge's fingers rattling on his keyboard, and I could feel his happiness buzzing and popping, crackling along the cables and down the invisible waves between us. His pink bureaucratic heart was alive with pleasure. Another file, almost ready to be closed.

"Okay," he said, "very good," getting ready to be done, and I said, "I got one more question about the file."

"Do you?"

"Where'd he come from?"

"What do you mean?"

"There's nothing here on the record of acquisition. It says he's been in service for nineteen and a half months. So what about before that? He's twenty-three years old. His patrimonial and matrimonial lines are question marks. All his stamps before the current one are blacked out."

Bridge didn't answer right away. Somewhere in the darkness below me, a car stuttered and started. I tried to guess what kind of car it was based on the tenor of the engine noise and the shape of the lights: the high whine of the engine said it was something cheap, subcontinental. Bridge, in his office, was frowning at his screen, scrolling through his own copy, seeking out the relevant portion of the record.

"Perhaps he was inherited," he said finally. "Maybe he was a gift. Maybe he was won in a card game."

I finished my Baba and flicked it out into the lot. "Does that still happen?"

"Everything happens."

I scowled. A dark feeling was fighting up in me like a living thing, clawing up from my stomach, pushing its way from the inside out. "Well, can we find out?"

"I will look into it."

"What does that mean?"

"It means that I will look *into* it."

And there it was: for the first time in the years I had known him — except of course I had never known him at all — Mr. Bridge had raised his voice. A change in tone, almost but not quite below the level of notice. He had . . . insisted. He had *emphasized*.

Castle's eyes would get so wide in the dark.

Castle's bright and beautiful white eyes, like twin planets. His eyes were all I could see when it was just Castle and me under our shared blanket, on our shared cot, in our cabin, which was the one closest to the northernmost chain fence. There was no light in the cabin except the moonlight coming from one high window, but even under the blanket I could always see Castle's eyes. He was my brother. He'd wake me up when the other ones were all sleeping. The Old Man and the others of us as well. In the middle of the night, almost every night, he would shake my shoulder till I woke. This is starting when I was . . . God, I don't know—six years old? Seven? It feels like I was so little, except I was on the pile already when he started it, which means I was done with the school, so I had to be eight or more, and Castle was off the pile—he was indoors, on the kill floor. One step up from where I was. Same thing had happened when we were babies: when I was done with the breed lot and into the school, he was already done with school and on the pile.

"Carburetor."

"What?"

My sleepy little head. I remember how it felt to be so tired, looking up into Castle's eyes, big and white, like I was dreaming them.

"Go on. Try and say it. Carburetor."

"Carburetor."

He was ten, and I was eight. We were little boys. I don't know how he trained his body to wake, but he did, and he'd shake me till I woke up, too, and then he'd tell me stories and teach me words.

The dead-to-life breathing of the other ones, a darkness filled with sleep. The fat, shuddering snores of the Old Man. Just me and Castle, alive together in the dark.

"Good, honey. Right on. A carburetor is a little part of a car, or of a tractor. Or of one of the small carts, you know, them the working whites putter around on. It's a little part in the engine, helps get it started."

"Oh." My head drifting back toward the pillow, Castle flicking me with his fingers, going, "No, love. No, honey, no. Eyes open, now. I got more for you."

I huddled together with him underneath our scratchy blanket, sleep swimming in and out of my head. Murmuring car parts and cities.

"Montreal."

"Montreal."

"Chicago."

"Chicago."

From the near distance, on the opposite side of the farm, came the mournful night songs of the cows, mooing in their lairages.

Castle told me stories, too: a man who got eaten by a whale and came swimming out fine. A boy and a girl who fell in love and killed a witch and ate her.

We had to be real quiet, of course, whispering back and forth so soft it was almost like just thinking. Obviously lying there talking in bunk you could get charged: Theft of Rest. Bad Use of Time. There had been a man in our Family named Bones, one of the older of the youngers, a skinny broomstick of a man with sharp elbows. Someone flagged him for being a masturbator—Theft of Rest; Bad Use of Time; Act Against God; Act Against Mr. Bell. We all got woke in the dead of night from him hollering as they were dragging him out for it. They charged him right there and took two witness statements in the presence of a Franklin, who certified the verdict, then they hauled him to the shed. The shed was just a few yards from where our cabin was along the fence, and you could hear Bones in there weeping and whatnot, right till morning.

"Betcha he ain't playing with his little thing about now," said Harbor. "Not with his hands bound up behind him." Harbor had a hard smile like a knife slit that showed up when others were suffering. "No, I betcha he is not." I never wondered who had whispered against poor Bones.

But we kept nice and quiet, Castle and me, and we were all right. Our

Old Man in those early years, he was a heavy kind of sleeper, and once he was down he was down till the rooster. Harbor never heard us, I guess, and no one else did, either. We were charmed in some way: just me and Castle in a private world, beneath the blankets, with only the dimmest glow of moonlight in there with us, like we were somewhere under the sea.

There were certainly many of those nights when I did not care to be woke. By the end of the day I ached all over from tending that pile. Head aching from the sun, back aching from crouching, arms aching from the hauling: dung buckets, rumen buckets, hay, and straw. Raking it and raking it. Last thing I wanted sometimes was to be shook awake, feel all the ache of my body again while Castle whispered me words. His wide white eyes hovering in the dark above me were unwelcome as searchlights, sometimes, and I'd complain bitterly, whisper hotly at him to leave me be.

"Listen, honey," he would say when I moaned. Never getting cross. Never even the littlest bit. Only one of us I knew who never did. "Listen, love. Deep nighttime is the only time we got. This is our opportunity."

"Our opportunity." My tongue was thick with exhaustion.

"That's right. We crazy we don't take it."

"What about all these, then?" I blinked, gummy-eyed in my tiredness, looked around the room at the other ones.

"What about 'em?"

"They crazy?"

"No, no." He wouldn't ever say that. He would never talk down on any man. "They just — my love, you know, they not us."

That always got me. It was nice to be us. I'd ease myself up on my aching elbow, blink furious till I came full awake, and listen to my good, good brother talk.

I was six months on the pile, a year, maybe, when I saw a pale gleam of yellow in there. You would see things, of course, in the pile. A lot of times. Cows'll eat things, or goats will, and it'll pass right in and through and they'll never know. Stones; glass; once, I swear, a bedspring. Now this, though, now this, peeking and winking out from the pile, in among all the mud browns and dull vegetable reds: a tiny plastic sheath, smaller than a thumb and bright yellow like a bird's beak. I nearly didn't see it, but then I did, and it called to me and I lifted it and felt there was something inside.

I popped it out. A single piece of paper, folded and folded and folded again until it was a tiny hard rock. I hunched in the shadow of the pile, crouched like a goblin and unfolded the paper.

There were no words on it, only pictures, black figures with their hands raised in fists, tugging apart their chains. Black figures seizing guns from white figures, white figures with their heads cut off, perfect black teardrops of blood spurting up out of their necks. I couldn't read the words, only the punctuation: a big red exclamation point. Exclamation points were on signs all over Bell's Farm: don't go in there, must wear masks in here, only overseers and staff may pass. I knew what exclamation points meant, and I knew about blood, and I did not know what the paper meant, but I stared at it and felt from it a queer power, a sparkling panic passing over me, like something melting.

I folded it back up carefully, jammed it back into the balloon how it had been, hid it in my cuff, and hurried back to my labor, busied my fingers and bent my back for the rest of the day. Someone fed that balloon to one of our cows. Someone did it on purpose. I was stunned by that purposefulness. I carried the paper in my cuff all day and brought it to Castle, and I gasped with grief later on, in the johns, when he told me he'd destroyed it.

"You gotta be crazy, boy" is what he said, and though his voice was still kind, I had never heard him say anything like it. It was in the supper line that I had slipped it to him sly, out of my cuff and into his palm. "Could you read it?" I asked him in the johns, and he didn't say whether he had or not. He told me only that I was crazy. He told me he had taken that piece of paper and flushed it away and never to bring him nothing crazy like that again.

Castle forgot to wake me that night, but my body woke itself, and I saw him. I never told him that I had seen him, but I did. I saw him like a vision, clinging to that single sheet of goldenrod, staring at it in the darkness with his big white eyes.

I don't know if it was ten minutes after I got off the phone with Bridge or five hours, but when I came around out of it I was in the middle of the room with my hand clamped over my mouth, breathing hard and heavy through my nose.

Castle! Jesus Christ, what was I doing thinking about Castle? I had not thought about him, not the man or even the name, had not wondered about where he had ended up—not in years. In years.

But here I was, all of a sudden; I was just surrounded by those memories. Just swarmed, man, just absolutely fucking fly-bit, like I was right back there, hip deep in that stinking fucking pile. When usually I was able never to think of it at all. When I wasn't thinking on my cases, turning over the pages of files, I kept myself busy with enjoying the world, with savoring freedom, breakfast buffets and hotel sheets and birdsong and my MJ tapes in the Altima. Even though I knew they were down there in me, all those scenes and feelings, beating just behind my heartbeats, rushing through my veins behind my blood. Like all I had to do was get cut and they'd come oozing out, a thick pulp of bad memories.

I worked so hard to keep everything inside, but now here I was. A poor boy at the Crossroads Hotel, pacing the thin flowered carpeting, feeling the squish of old blood beneath my feet, feeling blisters on my toes burning in my boots.

I don't know when or how I fell asleep. I must have at some point, but I know I lay awake in my bed a long hour, many long hours, just working that shit out of my system.

10.

"Mr. Dirkson? You better get up. Come on and wake up now."

I opened my eyes, and there he was, legs kicked up on the rickety hotel desk, eyes bright with laughter. The cop from the restaurant. The black one. Car number 101097.

He saw that I was up and he raised his eyebrows and his smile widened, crocodile wide. "You're mumbling in your sleep there, man," he said. "You having some bad dreams?"

I found Mr. Dirkson's voice before I opened my mouth: timid fellow, nervous, waking up confused from a restless slumber. "Oh, my goodness," he said. I said. Fumbled for the spectacles that he wore, which I'd kept folded by the bedside clock. "Officer? What—what seems to be the problem?"

The cop chuckled and swung his legs off the desk, planted his sturdy brown patrolman's shoes on the carpet. He palmed his chin and leaned forward. I slipped the glasses onto my nose and pushed them up, my eyes darting from his eyes down to his belt, to the service pistol snug against his hip. A Glock. A lot of major metro forces, they carry Glocks.

His skin was moderate chestnut, sunflower highlights, number 145. When my eyes found his face again, he was smiling, but his eyes were no longer laughing.

"Now, Mr. Dirkson," he said calmly. "We need to have us a little talk, don't we?"

I thought, *Goddamn it all to hell,* but what I said was, "Goodness gracious." In Mr. Dirkson's mouse voice, eyes widening with surprise. "Am I in some kind of trouble?"

"Funny thing about that question," said the cop. "Any time anybody ask if they in some kind of trouble, they know that they are. And they usually know what kinda trouble they in, too."

He laughed; I could tell from his face that the man liked to laugh. He was a handsome devil, this grinning young cop. Nice nut-brown skin and nice white teeth, nice big, expressive eyes, nice neat Afro, short and sharp. He sat tipped back on the chair, fingers laced behind his head, amused as all heck, waiting for me to say something. I wondered how far he had gotten. Did he know simply that I was not Jim Dirkson and that I had no wife? Or had he gotten as far as Mr. Bridge? As far as Gaithersburg, Maryland? Had he cracked the trunk of the Nissan, broken into the double-locked false bottom, and found the bag of fake IDs and hundred-dollar bills?

I wondered, too, if there was a silencer on the Glock. That wasn't standard equipment for a policeman's gun, but there are plenty of cops who put 'em on.

Car number 101097 stood up and scratched the back of his neck, advanced casually toward me across the room. On the notepad on the bedside table was a ballpoint pen, and there was a way to drive it through a man's trachea, but he would drop me first with the Glock. He had reflexes. I could see it in his movements, graceful and self-controlled, like a ballplayer.

"I'm sorry, Officer, but I'm uh . . . well, I'm a bit confused. What is it that I can do for you?"

I half rose out of the bed, and he motioned with two hands, palms down, stay where you are. He sat right next to me.

"You had supper a couple nights ago with Father Patrick Barton, the parish priest of Saint Catherine's Church on Meridian Street."

He said this as a grand announcement, like I was supposed to be amazed already by how much he knew, and so I took it that way, letting my mouth drop open.

"You ate down at the Fountain." He winked. "I do believe you had the fish."

"Oh, my goodness," I said. "How did you—"

"I was there, brother." He grinned, his face practically glowing with satisfaction. "Love that place." He patted his stomach. "Love it a little *too* much, I think. Anyway, I caught the basic gist of your conversation, know what I'm saying?"

"I don't understand," I said. "Are you—are you watching Father Barton?" Then I furrowed my brow and leaned in, catching a hunch, trusting a feeling. "Are you *with* Father Barton?"

"You got it." The grin widened. "Fact, you might say I'm more with Barton than Barton is."

My racing heart slowed a little. Poor old Jim Dirkson remained flummoxed and uncertain, licking his lips and adjusting his glasses, but inside I was performing a series of recalibrations. Thinking that what was emerging here might, in fact, be a positive development.

"So you're like a, a what—a bodyguard?"

"Bodyguard? *Shit*." The cop made a sour face. "Let's say I keep an eye on the man, okay? Keep the shepherd from coming into any harm while he's doing the work of the Lord."

"Wait, wait." I snapped my fingers, scratched my chin, put up a little playlet called *Man Remembering Something*. "There was another officer . . ."

"White man? Big thick neck? That's Officer Morris. He's my shift partner sometimes. We have dinner most nights, so I take him along when I'm babysitting, 'cause he's a simple man. If I begged off, he might get his feelings hurt. Start asking questions."

"So he doesn't know that you're . . . you're . . . ?" I left it there, wide-eyed and tentative.

"That I'm moonlighting with a flight crew? Running peebs up out of the Hard Four? *Shit*." This time he slow-danced with the word, pulling the vowel sound out like taffy: *Shiiiiiit*. "Officer Morris wouldn't know he was on fire 'less a pretty girl told him so."

"So—so, I'm sorry, Officer," I said and shrugged meekly. "I don't understand."

This cop got up suddenly from the bed and stared down at me. The grin shut down to a tight line, the eyes stopped twinkling.

"I heard your whole pitch, man, and I know that the padre shot you down. 'You got the wrong man, nuthin' I can do for you,' the whole dog and pony. And he's just being cautious, is all, because that's how we do. Especially because . . ." He hunched forward and raised his brows. "Especially because we just *did* one."

My Dirkson eyes grew big and wide, but behind them was me thinking, *I know that, brother, I know that you just did one.* There's a poor suffering child of God named Jackdaw, and he managed to drop through the floor of an Alabama cotton house on Sunday night, and y'all scooped him up and brought him north on an invisible plane, and now he's stashed somewhere in this proud, busted northern city. And I've got Barton, and I've got Barton's workroom, and I've got Winston Bibb and Whole Wide World Logistics, and now I've got you, you laughing idiot, and I know we will find him. Bridge and me. Goddamn Bridge and goddamn me.

The smug cop just kept on talking. On his feet now, moving around the room, working himself up.

"Usually, see, priest's rule is, we do one, then we hang back. Hang back in the cut awhile. You can't be too careful. More things we got going on, more chance there is for the soul catchers to find us." He paced around the room, making tight circles like a tiger in a cage. "But me, see, I got a different way of thinking. I think people need help, people like *you,* you know, and if we're set up, we're set up, and we should do as much as we can. Get out the whole three million if we can. Now, this here, your woman—what's her name?"

A half second I hesitated before I found the name. "Gentle."

"Right, Gentle. In Carolina, right?"

"Yes."

"Carolina. Bauxite. Yeah, see, that's all different. Different part of the country. Different kind of job. And you know, I want to do more, to be honest with you. In our organization. And I feel like Barton was hearing you, but he wasn't really hearing you, you know?"

He glanced over, and I gave him what he wanted. I nodded vigorously. I was still in the bed. Still had to piss and everything.

"But Barton, you know, he don't listen to me. I could plan the whole thing, I could run it myself, but I'm not the one with the purse strings. He's got the donors, he's got the cash box, he's the one running the show." He puffed up his cheeks, blew out air. "Plus, you know, look at me, right? Look at us. The way he sees it, whites are the ones do the saving. Black folks best hang tight and wait on getting saved. He's got what I call a *Mockingbird* mentality."

He was talking about that novel: the Alabama runner hiding in a small Tennessee town, the courageous white lawyer who saves him from a vicious racist deputy marshal. That book was one of a hundred or more I read in a Chicago library basement, in the tender, terrified early months of my own freedom, trying to teach myself the world, and I remember how it moved me. The point, though, was that the hero of the book, the hero and the heart, is that good lawyer: the white man is the saver, the black man gets saved.

"So I'm thinking, I bring you back to the father, I push you on him a little bit. We're gonna get your wife free and move me up the ranks a little. Show the man what a brother can do, you feel me?"

"I feel you," I said. "I feel you, brother."

For some reason that caught him by surprise, Jim Dirkson all nervous and confused, saying "I feel you" like that. The cop laughed loudly, and I saw the little pink glob of chewing gum moving around in the dark of his mouth.

I was startled by a red flash of last night's dream, Castle's hovering eyes, the reek of the pile. I shoved it all away with a violent act of mind. I thought instead of my poor, dear, imaginary Gentle, in headlamp and coveralls, shackled to the cart she pushed through the darkness of the mine.

"All right, so get up, man," he said. "Let's get moving."

"Oh, my goodness," I said. "Oh, my goodness, thank you."

I came off the bed and clasped the cop's hands in my hands, and he looked away still chuckling while I kept on saying "Thank you" and "My goodness" and "Thank you," while I was thinking *I'm sorry* and then *I'm sorry, Jackdaw, I'm sorry,* and something was giving way inside me, and Mr. Dirkson and me, we couldn't hold it in anymore, and out came tears, my face just collapsed into trembling.

"Aw, come on, now," said the cop, shaking his head, lifting me up off my knees. "No need for all that. Let's go."

But I kept right on saying "Thank you," I said it over and over while he waited by the door for me to gather myself together, get dressed, use the toilet, brush my teeth. His hand still resting on his gun belt, amused at Jim Dirkson's puppy-dog earnestness.

"Now, wait," I said when I was ready. "Now—I don't even know your name. What is your name?"

"Cook," he said, and pulled open the door. "I'm Willie Cook. Now, come on. We got a meeting to get to."

11.

Officer Willie Cook drove us south in his IMPD cruiser, tapping his fingers lightly on the steering wheel and chewing on his gum. I sat in silence, uneasy in the shotgun seat, while his eyes danced back and forth between the road and the dashboard computer, where crimes in progress scrolled by in alphanumeric cop code. As we crossed Broad Ripple Avenue we passed a small knot of black kids, laughing and walking together on the narrow sidewalk; one of them, a short kid pushing a bike, wore a hoodie pulled low over his eyes. Cook slowed down and gave a blurp of the siren, gestured at the kid to make sure his face was showing. His friends laughed while the boy obeyed, slowly, muttering curses, pissed as hell.

"Dumb son of a bitch," said Cook, shaking his head, sighing. I caught the kid in the mirror with his middle finger aloft, a miniature of impotent rage frozen in the side-view as we drove away. "Right now they calling me a Tom, but these kids know the rules. Face has gotta be visible, that's all. Better he get a warning from me than have one of these crackers roll up on him." He pointed at the screen of the dashboard computer, where his fellow officers were represented by white numbers on a green screen. "Officer Peele is out here today. Peele'd knock that kid's head off, hoodie and all, put handcuffs on the corpse. Resisting arrest, no fucking joke."

I nodded. I murmured my agreement. I noticed things. The in-car data-communication system, I noticed, was called DPSC. Indiana's warrant-database system, I noticed, was called IDACS, and it was linked to NCIC, the national system, and to the Marshals Service's fugitive-database system. I watched that Marshals Service scroll for a moment, waiting for Jackdaw's profile to come up, until Cook saw me watching.

"They could reset it, take that feed off of there," he said, "but I told 'em don't even worry about it. Shit kinda comes in handy, actually."

He winked, and I marveled at Officer Cook: double life, complicated game. He wasn't obligated to have the names and aliases of runners coming up on his screen because black cops were exempt from enforcing the Fugitive Persons Act under the Moore amendment. But Officer Cook liked having the info so he could push it to his pals in the Airlines. He wasn't the only one, and plenty of white officers did the same, and plenty of police chiefs and public safety directors were if not sympathetic to abolition at least neutral. One of many reasons why the marshals had more or less stopped relying on local law enforcement. Why they had begun instead to use people like me. Complicated game.

Officer Cook moved his gum around in his mouth and tapped his fingers on the wheel. He had a big flat gold ring on one finger, catching the sunlight. Class ring. A whole life behind him.

"So—can I ask you, Officer . . ." I let my voice, Dirkson's voice, come out in a reedy tremble. "Where exactly are we heading?"

"Monument Circle. Old Abe. I texted Father Barton to meet us."

"About me?"

He gave me a look. "I told you, man, we gotta play a little smart on this. I told him I got new information on our open case. The kid is stashed just fine for now, but we're working on getting him on a connecting flight. Getting him squared away up in Côte Saint-Luc." He took a stab at the proper French pronunciation, but it sounded silly, and he snorted. "Whatever you want to call it. *Little America*. We've been waiting for word from some folks we work with, some snowmen, and we don't know how they're planning to get in touch. So I told Barton I had news on that front."

I nodded. I noticed all the details. Jackdaw's anticipated itinerary (Little America; suburbs of Montreal; a new life); I noticed the off-hand status update on him (stashed just fine for now; waiting for a Canadian connection to come through). I knew more than Cook thought I knew. I knew more than *he* did. I nodded meekly. The wiper blades pushed thin lines of rain off the windshield.

I framed my questions with care. "So is that how it works, usually? Get a person settled in the North? Would that be—that would be for a woman, too?"

I readjusted my posture in the seat, sat as Dirkson would sit, thinking about his beloved Gentle, imagining her in a parka and winter gloves in the snowy reaches of Little America.

"Yeah, usually." He frowned. "Well, I think so. Not my department."

"Barton handles that part?"

"No." Cook rolled his eyes. "Father Barton does a whole lot of nothing, most of the time. A lot of speeches. A lot of passing the fucking hat. But other folks do the rescues, other folks run 'em north, other folks sit on 'em till they ready to move 'em on. See? Nobody talks to nobody."

I nodded. This was classic underground: distinct, discontinuous cells. Cutout operations. Everything clean and careful and strictly need-to-know. The road turned into an overpass, spanning a muddy tributary down below, then back into a road, with fast-food chains and small office buildings slipping past my window. Homeless people on bus-stop benches. Storefronts available for lease. Same thing everywhere. Every northern city.

"And this poor young brother," I said, hushed and hesitant. "The one y'all just took. How is he adjusting to his freedom?"

"Ah . . . well." Cook gritted his teeth, gave his head a quick shake. A passing pain or a reflection of pain. "He's a special case, that one. A special kind of kid."

"Oh, yes?" I said, but Cook didn't seem to want to elaborate, and I didn't want to push.

We parked downtown, across from a tall monument that sat at the center of a traffic circle. It was an imposing white obelisk topped with a statue of a man in an old-fashioned long coat, standing slender and erect, with his arms extended. The man was tall and made taller by his long face and long top hat, and he was surrounded by shorter white columns and tiers of white steps. A nine-foot-tall, bearded, rail-thin white man, stone-faced and stoic, staring out over the downtown, hands out with palms up, as if imploring.

Oh, Jesus, I thought, studying the statue. Oh, God. That's right—Indianapolis. Indiana. It was *here.* This is where they killed the poor bastard.

"This spot right here is the exact center of the state," Officer Cook was saying, talking over his shoulder as we crossed the circle and approached the man on his high marble pedestal. "Indy is smack dab in the middle of Indiana, see, and Monument Circle's the center of the city, and the statue of Old Abe—you get the idea. Plus, of course, the state's in the middle of nowhere. So there you have it: right now we're in the exact geographical middle of fucking nowhere."

Cook walked briskly up the steps, and I trotted up behind him. Pathetic, desperate little Jim Dirkson, scrabbling and shifting, trailing after tall, striding, confident Officer Willie Cook. He'd told me that Barton would never *get it,* because Barton's white, but I knew that Cook would never get it, either. A northern man, a black man who had never been a slave—we were like creatures of a different species. I was as different from him as I was from Barton or from Bridge because of what I had seen, because of what moved still beneath my skin.

As I thought about it, it came up again, heaving up, and I felt my hand rushing up to my mouth to clamp it shut, keep everything back. The old loud sounds and the stink that always clouded my nostrils, sounds that only I could hear. All I wanted was silence, so I could listen to this cocky young officer and gather up the details he was dropping like fruit from a tree. All I wanted was silence. Silence to do my work. What the slave wants

73

but can never have is not only freedom from the chains but also from their memory.

We got to the top of the steps, Cook and me. We stood beside each other looking across the traffic circle at the surrounding storefronts: a sandwich shop, a big pretty Presbyterian church, the entrance to the symphony hall. A couple of friends walked into the Starbucks, a black girl and a white girl, both of them in nurse's scrubs, their arms linked together, giggling.

The first-thing sun was wavering and uneasy behind a thick bank of clouds. Glimmers of blue making a faint effort around it. I felt the sour acid of anticipation in my gut. I felt the cool mist of rain on my face.

"Be a few minutes," said Willie Cook. He tugged out a fresh piece of gum, leaned back on the base of the statue, stuck the dead wad into the foil. A former smoker; traces of old habits in the new.

Running around the base of the obelisk was a series of bas-reliefs, starting with Lincoln in knee pants, splitting rails.

I wandered slowly around, tracing the lines with my fingers. I remembered it dimly, all the history I had crammed into my head during my wilderness years, my time in Chicago learning to be human, memorizing the world. It was all here, illustrated in stone, the whole story of Old Abe's assassination—the martyrdom that saved the union, the murder that remade the country. Here he was, hands raised in humble farewell to the adoring crowd around his train car, the president-elect leaving Springfield for Washington. Here he was on a hotel balcony, eyes wide as he fell backwards from the fatal shot into the arms of his son Robert. Here was Lincoln with a halo, the good angel hovering over the hastily reconvened Congress. Even the members who had thrown down their commissions, who had resigned and stomped off to form the Confederacy in the preceding months—they had returned, moved by the death of a president, wary but willing, ready to start anew.

They had found a speech in his pocket, sticky with blood, the address he had planned to give that fateful morning, February 12, before the pistol shot laid him low. Secretary Seward read it aloud to Congress, and they wept—even the Confederates wept—when Seward got to the words I traced now with my forefinger, words chiseled into the stone at the base of the statue. I HOPE THAT WE MAY MEET AGAIN UNDER ONE FLAG OF UNION.

What emerged from that fraught session of Congress, in the spring of 1861, was a revised version of Senator Crittenden's complicated compromise, one of the last-ditch failed union-saving efforts from the year before, seen in fresh light and taken up with fresh energy, while the new Confederate government was suspended, then abandoned.

Six amendments and four resolutions, preserving slavery where it was, preventing its extension elsewhere; balancing northern sentiment and southern interest, northern principles and southern economic welfare. And the clincher, inscribed here in marble as it is inscribed in the Constitution: the Eighteenth Amendment, making the whole rest of them permanent and everlasting. Eternal compromise. The great legislative Hail Mary: *No future amendment of the Constitution shall affect the five preceding articles...*

I read it in Lincoln's shadow that early morning, and it seemed as it always did to me: impossible, illegal—childish, even, like the child who wishes for infinite wishes. And yet it has worked, so far. It has held.

Cook yawned. The nurses came out of the Starbucks, chatting happily, steam rising from their cup lids. I craned my neck and stared up at him, at Old Abe, Honest Abe, Abraham the Martyr. Big hands palms up, long fingers outstretched, his homely features solemn and beatified, looking south down Meridian Street.

"You see how they posed him, looking down the street? *That's where the hotel was.*" Willie Cook pointed south on Meridian Street, then jerked his handsome face up at Old Abe. "Poor guy's gonna stand there forever with birds shitting on his head, looking at where he got killed."

I mustered a hollow laugh, but Officer Cook wasn't paying

attention: he was watching the man who was coming now, a power-fully built black man crossing Market Street with his hands jammed in the pockets of gray slacks.

"All right," murmured Officer Cook. "Here we go now."

He stood up straight as the man came up the steps toward us. He was very tall and very dark-skinned—midnight, I calculated automatically, offhandedly: midnight, purple tone, a number 121 or 122. His eyes were bright and yellow, hidden deep in his head, shifting questioningly back and forth from Cook to me, me to Cook, taking us in. I read the man as muscle, a body man; what was called, in Airlines slang, a baggage handler. I looked down Market to see what kind of car he'd come out of, but wherever he had parked was out of view.

Cook raised his hand cheerfully, but the newcomer spoke first.

"Who is this?"

"This here's Jim. Jim's new business. Jim, meet Mr. Maris."

Maris nodded at me once, not impolitely, then turned back to Cook, repeating the words *new business* in mildly accented English. I couldn't tell if he was upset or uncertain of the expression or what. My mind chewed on the accent. African. West African? He wore a cheap blue work shirt with the sleeves rolled up, and he had the thick forearms of a prizefighter. I've known tall men before, but there was something about this Maris's tallness that made you want to turn around and run.

"You must spread your legs and raise your arms, Jim."

Cook looked with amusement at me, soft-bellied Jim Dirkson, then back at Maris. "Does he look like he's carrying a gun to you?"

Maris stepped forward into the shadow of the statue and effi-ciently ran his big hands over my body. "I am sorry," he said. "It is necessary." I shrugged. "Oh. It's okay. I understand."

Right as I said it, though, he came out of my back pocket with my butterfly knife, which at the last minute before leaving the hotel I had taken out of my toiletries bag and jammed into my back pocket. Maris held it up to me with a grave expression, then showed it to Cook, who looked at me with eyebrows raised. I blushed, looked down.

"I've uh—I'm sorry. I've been advised to be careful."

Cook looked steadily at me for a second, but then he laughed. Maris did not laugh. Wordlessly he slipped the knife inside his breast pocket, then cocked his head, considering me.

"And what of Jim, if anything, is known by our favorite?"

Maris delivered this inquiry to Officer Cook with a solemn expression, pronouncing the word *favorite* with three syllables: fave-o-writ. The slight lilt in Maris's voice contrasted pleasantly with the formality of his speaking style, like violet flowers in rich, dark soil. Definitely West African. I wondered if his prints were on file somewhere, if his name or alias was on a watch list. In Bridge's building in Gaithersburg or in Washington, at Counterterrorism. A Liberian; a friend to the cause.

"Oh, he knows, he knows," said Cook. He smiled at Maris, who did not smile back. "Father Sunshine's just being a little particular. You know how he gets."

Maris's eyes narrowed, and his nostrils flared. His dislike for Officer Cook rose off of him like steam. "He does not like to take on new projects until old projects have been completed."

"Right," said Cook. "He don't *like* to, but he *will*. He's done it before."

"I don't like to, either."

"No disrespect, brother, but I could give a shit what you like."

Maris glowered. I bore silent witness, thinking, *There is no army of abolition*. This is what the world has for heroes. Ordinary men, squabbling and prideful. Hassling each other, doing their best, busting the world free. And men like me, behind fake papers and clear-glass spectacles, keeping it chained.

"This man's got a woman he loves and nowhere else to turn," said Cook. "And the other thing is just about put to bed, right?"

"No, it is not yet . . ." A minor hesitation as Maris furrowed his brow, decoding the idiom. "It is not put to bed."

"How's he holding up, by the way?" said Cook. "Our boy? What's the word from Dr. V?"

I kept my eyes blank while I listened to their conversation with radiological intensity. I noticed "How's he holding up?" I noticed "Dr. V." I stood silently just behind Officer Cook, noticing things.

They were done talking before long, and the three of us stood and waited. Cook leaned on Lincoln's pillar, but Maris crossed his arms and stood erect, his big forearms bulging. He darted out his tongue and licked his lips, and the tip of his tongue was bright pink, like a bit of fruit. And then at last came Father Barton in civilian drag, no collar, just a black overcoat and blue jeans, slightly hunched forward, floating like a shadow up the white steps.

Maris descended one step, raised his hand to the priest.

Barton saw Maris, then he saw Cook.

Then Barton saw me, stopped walking, and turned and went back down the steps.

"Oh, for fuck's sake," said Officer Cook.

Maris hustled down the steps after Father Barton, raising one arm, literally giving Cook and me the back of his hand.

"Fuck's sake!" Cook called again, and chased after them both. "Hey—hey, come on. Hey—"

I was left at the top step, alone with ugly Abraham Lincoln, with his grim hawk nose and gloomy face, forever president-elect, looking out over his world.

12.

Back in the hotel room, I'd found a long, spidery crack in the corner behind the rickety desk they give you for writing on, and I sat and stared at that crack for a while, clutching my chest at heart level, holding myself still. I had all these leads, the case was wide open, I had Cook and Maris and their conversation leaky as an old boat, I had Whole Wide World to get to, but here all the old stuff was rising up in me like swamp water, the Old Man and the Franklins and Castle and Mr. Reedy and a swamp full of black red blood, all of it coming up until the mud filled the back of my throat, until I was choking—when I had work to do. Castle, Castle's big eyes in the darkness—so much fucking work to do.

With a slow, careful motion I opened the laptop and turned it on. While it was starting up I set up my cassette player and put on a mix tape I had. It wasn't all MJ on that one, but quite a lot of it was, and the first song was "Ben," nice and easy, gentle and tender. I let that song work its magic a second, let it cool me out, then I opened my laptop to look for Dr. V.

There was no shortage of doctors in Indianapolis, it looked like. It looked, actually, like medicine was one of a handful of bright spots in a dark economic landscape. Like a lot of big midwestern cities, this one had spent the second half of the twentieth century stumbling in and out of recessions, trying to make the best of America's fucked-up, piecemeal economy: all that proud but self-defeating unwillingness to do business with the Hard Four; all the blood and treasure wasted in the Texas War; all the industries, from cars to coal to computers, that had bloomed and then wilted in the face of international boycotts and sanctions (while, funnily enough, the slave states prospered, protected by the economic insulation of permanently deflated labor costs).

Everything's changing in the twenty-first century, of course, thanks to emerging global markets—various former Communist states and economically insurgent African nations wanting nothing to do with the European Consensus—but that tide seemed not yet to have hit Indianapolis. The city, as I saw it from that rickety desk in that cheap hotel room, was a place with a lot of former glories: a used-to-be publishing industry, a used-to-be rail hub, a used-to-be powerhouse in coal and steel. What remained were services: a convention trade, a marketing trade, a handful of technology "start-ups"... and health care. Lots and lots of health care. Drug companies and medical device companies, ophthalmology centers and optometry centers and cancer centers. I counted five general hospitals, three private and two public, plus two children's hospitals and a vast constellation of outpatient clinics.

I sat at the computer, listening to my music, drilling deeper in. Within the city's vast population of doctors was a certain number with surnames beginning with the letter *V*; within that group was a much smaller group, those with *V* names long enough or unusual enough to be shorthanded down to "Dr. V."

I pecked at the keyboard. I typed in instructions.

At first I excluded the outlying areas—Carmel, Fishers, Zionsville, Plainfield—but then I reincluded them, expanding my lists, narrowing my lists, playing with my lists. I eliminated psychiatrists and psychologists. I eliminated pediatricians and obstetrician-gynecologists. I did not, after some reflection, eliminate dentists and orthodontists. Who could say? I did not know what I was looking for. I was just looking.

And meanwhile I had my map application open and was keeping one eye on it, watching a blue blip move block by block through the city. That was Mr. Maris, still carrying my butterfly knife in his pocket. Embedded in the handle of the knife was a tidy little GPS tracking unit, throwing up location signals to some satellite, which was then throwing them back down to me.

I watched Mr. Maris drive south on Meridian Street away from Abraham the Martyr, then cut right on West South Street, then left on Capitol.

Planting the bug on Maris was an old trick. An easy one. I had done four months of training after they picked me up, in a desert in Arizona, before they sent me out on my first file. I had learned picks and rakes, footprints and fingerprints, fighting and following, database infiltration, encryption and de-encryption.

And then after all that, a doctor with no name and a cold room, two unconscious hours. The hook, the anchor, the leash.

It was funny to think about. Not that funny. Me tracking Maris, Gaithersburg tracking me.

MJ was doing "Everybody's Somebody's Fool," and I took that as a good sign. I just listened to that a second, just that, shoo-bop, shoo-bop, swelling strings in the chorus. After that there was a James Brown song, which made me smile—they didn't play a lot of James on the radio. He'd been the leader of one of those god-awful "family bands" that toured the North in the fifties and sixties, talented slaves brought north to sing to sold-out northern audiences, living proof of how happy everybody was down there. But James defected—snuck out of his Buffalo hotel room and turned up in Quebec City, making beautiful music and touring the world, except for America.

"Just look at me!" he used to crow from European concert stages, palming his pompadour, braggadocious in his spangled cape and boots. "Look at what they robbin' themselves of!"

Sort of thing used to happen all the time. There was an Olympic gold medalist from Alabama, boy named Jesse Owens, who took a mess of world records in Berlin in 1936 and then defected to the Soviet Union. For the next half century he was one of the evil empire's prize possessions, turning up in *Pravda* every once in a while to denounce degenerate slave-state capitalism.

When I felt ready, I got back into it, making notes on Maris's route, jotting it all down, toggling back and forth between his journey and my slow search-driven encircling of the mysterious Dr. V.

After I was satisfied with my initial list of doctors, I closed out the pages full of hospitals and clinics and started opening the donor rolls of every abolitionist organization active in the city and state. There were local organizations called Total Freedom Now! (pure abolitionist) and Indy FreedomWorks (gradualist); there was a central Indiana chapter of the Fire Bell Society, and there was the Indianapolis chapter of the Black Panthers. The membership rolls and the donor lists were all public information, except for those of the Panthers, which was officially classified as a terrorist organization, but I got their names by hacking the IMPD.

Maris, meanwhile, had gotten on the highway. He moved south by southeast on 465, tracing the city's outskirts. While I watched him I rehearsed his distinctive African cadences in my mind, replayed what he had said to Cook about the "old business." *No, it is not yet . . . it is not yet put to bed.*

Seized by an impulse, I said the words out loud, drew myself up to stand at full height, as Maris did, making my face solemn, as he had. "No, it is not yet . . ." I said to myself, to the computer, to the cracks in the wall. "No, it is not yet put to bed."

Then I eased back down into the chair, relaxed my limbs, grinned to show my teeth. What had Cook said, Officer Cook, complicated Cook? *How is he adjusting to his freedom?* I said, and what was the officer's reply? I spoke it in his smooth voice: "He's a special case, that one. A special kind of kid."

Then I was myself again. As much myself as I ever was. I popped out of the chair, pulled out the full-file pages from their locked box, and read again my favorite part, my least favorite part, the baffling run of words: *Known to have intended to remove himself to Indianapolis.*

There was something in all of it. What was it? Something buried in all those bits and scraps, scratching to get out.

I did the next piece. Cross-referenced names with names,

circled some, and crossed out the others. When I was done I had a list of four complicated surnames written carefully in pencil on the hotel notepad: Vasilevsky, Vorshonsky, Venezia-Karbach, and Vishaparatham. Ten minutes later I was reading a magazine profile, two years old, from a special issue of *Indianapolis Monthly* celebrating "Indy's Unsung Heroes," about a lauded general practitioner who had closed a thriving suburban practice to open a storefront clinic in Haughville, a historic working-class African American neighborhood north of Freedman Town. This doctor accepted all health plans and dedicated one-third of her appointment slots to the uninsured.

"Health care," declared Dr. Elizabeta Venezia-Karbach in the article, "is a basic human right."

"All right," I said, toggling back over to my other screen. "All right, all right."

Mr. Maris, it seemed, was still on the move. His blue dot had come off the highway on the near east side. I watched him cruise 42nd Street, past the fairgrounds, then turn right to come south on Keystone.

I was still watching him while the phone rang, but then when Dr. Venezia-Karbach's receptionist answered I stood up and found my voice, said, "Yes, ma'am, how are you, sweetheart?" A little growly and weary, a cough in the back of my throat, a man in need of a doctor. My name, I said, was Kenny Morton—sliding open the balcony doors now, staring again at the parking lot—and yes, I would be a new patient, that's right, ma'am, and no, ma'am, I had no health insurance at this time, and I had to confess I was of limited means, but if there was some way I could—yes, tomorrow morning would be fine—Saturday, right, I know, that'll do for me just fine, and oh, my, thank you so much, that's just wonderful, ma'am, and I really do appreciate it so much, and thank you, and while I turned in this small, workmanlike performance, leaning into the balcony threshold, growling over the phone, I could see the memories coming for me, swelling over the horizon, charging across the parking lot between the cars like bloody horses.

"There he is. Mystery man. My savior."

She was out of her jean jacket, and she'd changed into some sort of short-sleeved dress, but the Doc Martens were still on. She had winding tattoos, dark ink on the strawberry flesh of her calves: summer flowers, peonies and roses. Her boy was in a bathing suit, with a Spider-Man towel slung over his shoulder. The white girl fell into step beside me, walking down the second-floor hallway, with the boy trailing behind.

"I'm Martha, by the way."

"How do you do? I'm Jim Dirkson."

"Oh, okay, Jim Dirkson. Sorry. I didn't know we were doing last names." She was in her late twenties, early thirties, but she was tiny and laughed like a teenager, big and unself-conscious. "Martha Flowers. And this here is Lionel, like the trains."

"Mama!" The kid scowled and bumped into his mom, accidentally on purpose. "Like the *lion*."

Martha rolled her eyes. "Do you know that cartoon? *Lionel the Lion*? It's terrible."

"It's—no, it's not. Mama!" said Lionel. "It's badass."

"Whoa! Hey!" Martha, playfully shocked, knocking her son gently on his shoulder. "Don't say *badass*."

"You say it!"

"I'm allowed to say it."

I smiled at all this, the teasing and admonishment, the affectionate banter. I had learned about the love between parents and children the way I had learned so many other things, by observation. By skulking, by paying attention through what I came to call in retrospect my shadow years: years out of slavery but not yet in civilization. Saving up to buy solid papers, living underground. In Naperville in a church basement; under a train bridge on Chicago's west side. I'd spend whole days in the reading room of the big library downtown, a shadow in the corner; reading the great slave narratives, reading Ellison, Baldwin, Wright. Learning my own history. I read Zora Neale Hurston's masterpiece, the one that had, legendarily, been smuggled page by page out of a Florida cane plantation two decades before that state went free.

Slowly drinking water in coffee shops, perching on corners, watching people interact, learning free American language. The way people laughed when they were allowed to laugh out loud. *Ha ha ha,* I said to myself on the basement floor in the middle of the night. *Ha ha ha.*

The elevator door binged. "Well, come on, Jim Dirkson," said Martha. "Come on down to the pool and chat a minute."

It wasn't much of a pool they had down there, fifty square feet, maybe, a shallow end and a deep end and no diving board or anything. A list of rules, painted on a wooden sign. No diving. No horseplay. No lifeguard on duty. At the far end of the room was a glass wall revealing the "fitness center"—a couple treadmills and a bowl of fruit and a wall-mounted TV set to CNN.

Lionel dropped his towel and leaped unceremoniously into the pool, cannonballing in, disappearing and then splashing back up a second later, sputtering and grinning, water dewdropping on his brow.

"Hoo, my God," he shouted. "It's so cold. Mama, you gotta come in. It's so cold."

"No way."

"Come *on.*"

"I didn't even wear a suit."

Lionel blew her a raspberry and wheeled back under the surface, flashed around, a streak beneath the chlorine blue. A second later his feet jutted up from the surface and kicked back and forth.

"Kid's amazing," said Martha softly, then, abruptly, "Thanks for the food yesterday morning, by the way. Very decent of you. Extremely human."

I shrugged. "How was the job fair?"

"Great." She pushed at her hair. "Really great. Really, really, really great." She smiled sardonically, but her eyes were anxious and scared, staring into some kind of bad future. "It was the sort of thing, the first day is all applications, meeting the people, then people call you back on the second day if they want you to come in and interview." I remembered the stack of paperwork on her lap, dog-eared photocopies, ballpoint pen smearing everywhere. "So, you know, anyway," she said. "Here I am at the pool."

Well. I had my own thing going. I had my own problems.

A clutch of new kids came in, white kids, shrieking. A girl maybe thirteen plus two twin brothers just about Lionel's age, the girl with freckles and the boys with flat midwestern crew cuts. They all splashed on in there, and the boys immediately got into some kind of tussle with Lionel, the way kids that age do, making themselves into animals, sliding around each other, surfacing on each other's shoulders.

"So what's your story?" Martha asked me, and I lingered, polite as Dirkson was polite. "Business or pleasure? I'm going to guess business."

"Why do you guess that?"

"Oh, well, you know. A gentleman traveling alone? In Indianapolis? It's a nice town, but it's not, like, I don't know." She laughed. "Cancun. Right?"

"Right." I smiled. "Yes. I travel quite a bit for business."

As soon as I said it, I wished I had held my tongue. It was a foolish thing to say. Unnecessary. Martha was interested, too. "Cool," she said. "God. I wish *I* traveled a lot. What do you do? Why are you here?"

"I work for a company called Sulawesi Digital as a site analyst." She blinked. I smiled. "It's a cellular service provider. Based in Indonesia."

"What was it? Sula—*what* was it?"

"Right, well"—I smiled, apologetic site-analyst smile—"see, that's what we're working on changing. The company's wanting

86

to start opening some American locations. Raise brand awareness. So I've been traveling to some cities, investigating available retail properties in storefronts and shopping centers, and then what I'll do is submit an analysis to Jakarta as to the relative desirability of each potential location."

I had delivered this short speech, with the same dull Dirksonian earnestness, ten or twelve times in the past. Most people, you could watch them glaze over the minute you said words like *analyst,* words like *relative desirability*. But this girl, this Martha—her eyes were open to the story. She was nodding with fascination, as if I'd announced that I was a contract killer.

She even asked a follow-up question, asked what makes a location suitable or unsuitable, and I gave her the combination of factors: pedestrian traffic, neighborhood demographics, competition, while Lionel shrieked and giggled with his new friends. I could keep this up all day if she wanted to. My identity was researched: backed up, backstopped, and double-backstopped.

Martha sighed. "I've been to, like—Vincennes. That's *my* world travels." Her eyes were far away. "What's the best place you've ever been?"

"Best?"

"Yeah, best. You know. Most interesting."

Bell's Farm. Bell's Farm was interesting. "Chicago," I said.

"Aw! Chicago! I would love to go to Chicago. Have you been there a lot?"

"I actually—" My throat felt rusty. The room breathed chlorine. How long had it been since I spoke to anyone this way? "I lived there for some time."

Lake Shore Drive, the first time, skyscrapers lordly and glass-walled, hovering magisterially above Lake Michigan, reflecting gloriously at one another. My astonishing, terrifying sentinels of liberty.

"I've never been," Martha said. Her shoes were off. Her toes were in the water. Among her tattoos were twin butterflies, one on each ankle, perfectly symmetrical. I noticed. I notice everything.

"You believe that? I've lived in Indiana my whole life. I even lived in Gary for six months once. And I never got up there."

"That does seem like a shame."

"You're telling me!"

She closed her eyes, like she was picturing it: picturing herself in Chicago. I pictured myself there, too, eating a hot dog. I pictured Castle. I opened my eyes again.

"I don't know," Martha was saying. "I never got hold of the right weekend, I guess. And then the kid happened, and—well. You don't have kids, huh?"

"No, ma'am."

"Well, they're great." She leaned into me, gave me a big stage whisper. "But they fuck everything up."

Martha laughed, and her eyes found her boy, goofing around with these white kids, trying to dunk one under, his sleek body spangled with droplets. Another woman had come in, meanwhile, a middle-aged white lady in a black bathing suit, freckle-specked cleavage and sandy hair and big midwestern arms, with a towel wrapped around her waist. She took a look at us, at me and Martha sitting there talking. Then she looked at the pool.

"Watch this," Martha said. "Just watch."

"What?"

"Just watch."

But I knew; I knew what Martha knew. The woman put her hands on her hips. We knew what was coming. Even Jim Dirkson knew.

"Marcus? Dylan? Jamie?" The woman waved her kids in, like a lifeguard when there was a shark. "Time for lunch."

"What?" squealed one of the white children.

"We just *got* here," said another.

The boys treaded water, their freckled faces twisted at the injustice. Lionel bobbed beside them. The teen, sitting on the pool steps, wrinkled her nose. "I thought we were gonna swim first."

"Nope," said the mom. "After. Come on. Now."

The family climbed out, and the woman toweled them off and hustled them out. Lionel was left alone, treading water, a solitary buoy. Martha raised both middle fingers and pointed them at the lady like guns. We heard the children, their complaining voices growing dimmer as they disappeared down the corridor.

Lionel went under and then came up, crested the blue surface with a harvest of sparkling droplets across his curls, his mouth a small disappointed line, watching the other kids trudge away.

"Do we have to go, too?" he said softly.

"No, sweetness. We're good. You're good. I'm just chatting with Mr. — God, I forgot it."

"Dirkson," I said quietly.

"Right, right. It's a nice name."

"Thanks." I muttered it. Murmured it. I didn't know where the name Dirkson came from. It came from Bridge, or from Bridge's people. It probably came from a Gaithersburg phone book. Martha was still talking, small talk, talking about the Batlisch hearings. "Have you been watching my girl Donatella, by the way? Squaring off up there? She is my *hero*."

"Well, anyway," I said suddenly and stood up. "Anyway."

I was walking fast. Behind me I heard Martha saying "Jim . . ." and the boy, too, I heard him calling after me from the water's edge, giving me back the word I gave him — "Controversy!" — but I was gone.

13.

Day three of the investigation, and possibilities were fanned out in front of me like playing cards. At some point, Cook would make contact with me again, or maybe I with him. I had his car number, after all, and his badge number. I had his face emblazoned in my mind, a row of white teeth and a wink and a smirk. I had an appointment for tomorrow morning, the first available slot, with the famous Dr. V. And there was Mr. Maris, freedom fighter, soldier, a blip on my screen, a man on the move. I drove with my laptop open on the shotgun seat, so as I cruised the city I could watch him cruising it, too. At some point he'd stop his car, and maybe that would just be that. Maybe Maris was the body man, the baggage handler, and I would go where he was and there would be the boy.

Get this done. Get out of here. On to some other northern city.

Whole Wide World Logistics was in an office park off Binford Boulevard in an industrial section of the northeastern part of the city; one in a row of identically unimpressive gray storefronts lined up like prisoners, with smudged plate-glass windows and doors of streaky glass. Across the parking lot, casting its vast shadow over this dingy arrangement, was a massive converted warehouse painted with bright jungle murals and a cheerful cartoon sign: COME AND PLAY IN INDY'S BIGGEST INDOOR TRAMPOLINE PARK.

I got out of the Altima already working, crossing the lot in a hustle with my face anxious and my body tense. A rush of noise washed over me from behind my back, a laugh and a delighted squeal and the celebratory ding-ding-ding of an arcade game. Someone had opened the door of the trampoline park, let its noise filter out across the parking lot, from a universe away.

I pushed into Whole Wide World and got right to work, thinking, *Here we go,* breathing hard, saying "Hey, I'm sorry, hey," as the door made its little bing-bong noise and eased closed behind me.

The woman behind the long counter was looking at me, already skeptical. She checked me out, and I checked out the room, the tottering stacks of papers and file folders all along the counter, the window letting in smudged sallow light, the tile floor in need of a sweep and a mop. High on the wall was a row of clocks, Manila and Mumbai, San Francisco and Paris. Distant cities, foreign lands. Under the clocks was the globe logo I'd seen in the picture, purple and green and radiating lines of speed. Closest to the door was a giant dry-erase board cluttered with handwriting, different colors, a crosshatch of numbers, dates, account numbers, and order numbers—and in the lower left-hand corner, a little purple heart and the words DEAR DAY SHIFT: HAVE A GREAT DAY! LOVE, NIGHT SHIFT.

"Yes?" The day shift was a middle-aged round-cheeked black woman, a glossy magazine open on the counter in front of her.

"Yeah, hey," I said, talking quickly, slightly out of breath. "Winston around?"

"Nope," she said. "He's sick."

"Sick?"

"Yeah. He called in."

Sick. Could that just be a coincidence—just bad luck? Or had my man Winston smelled something coming?

This woman, meanwhile, was looking at me, fingering the pages of her magazine, waiting for me to split. I could appreciate that. I was back in Albie's rumpled gardener's outfit, stained grass-green at the knees, bits of soil clinging to the cuffs. I was putting on a full show here, huffing and puffing, wiping sweat off my brow, drumming my fingers on the counter. "Just my luck, boy. Sick! Boy."

"Yes." She shrugged. Obviously she was supposed to say *Can I help you with something,* but it was equally obvious that she did not want to help me. "Do you want to leave him a message?"

"Naw," I said. "No, thanks."

Still I didn't leave. She cast a longing glance at her magazine. Thin white celebrities in swimsuits, lying like famine victims on a scorched beach. Winston Bibb's colleague was dark-eyed and plumpish, her hair elaborately woven, her forehead high and gleaming under the fluorescents. Her skin was coffee, light-toned, in the number 120 range. I did this evaluation by reflex, then found that just doing that quick calculation, for some reason, made me sick. My stomach rolled. This here was a free woman, after all, a northern woman, a vested citizen. What right had I to look at her that way, to size her up, mark her down for a Gaithersburg file?

"Well..." she said. Poor girl: I had given her no choice. "Maybe I can help."

"Oh, I don't know; I hope so. I don't know. I really don't know."

At last she closed her magazine and looked straight on at my face, and her expression softened. I saw it happen, and I doubled down. I tilted my head a certain way I had, and I grinned a soft grin of mine, narrowed my eyes in a way that I knew put light in them and crinkles at their corners.

"My name's Angie, by the way." She slipped the magazine under the counter. "Tell me what you need."

"Okay, well," I said, "it's a little complicated."

For Angie I rolled out a long story, one with several twists and turns in it. My boy Sully, see, had gotten me a gig not two dang weeks ago, driving a light truck, just around the city, nothing long-haul, nothing complicated! 'Cause you know I just last year got my CDL, see, and Sully'd hooked me up, man, a nice gig driving for this garden supply place, loading a pickup with different kinds of supplies, you know, mulch, topsoil, garden rocks—I ticked it off on my fingers—all that kinda shit. Sorry, Angie, that kinda *stuff*—

she smiled, waved it off, go on. Part of the gig was to meet up with the long-hauls coming from outta town, help 'em unload at the company warehouse down there off Troy Avenue.

Angie nodded sure. Her cousin Addy, as it turned out, lived near there. Near Troy Avenue.

"Oh, yeah?" I said. "No kidding."

The warehouse address I'd pulled off my mapping software. Everything else was pure spun sugar, a song I was singing, finding the tune as I went. I talked as quickly as I could, gesturing a lot, charging my voice with exasperation. Angie was nodding, magazine forgotten. On the clock above her head, it became midnight in Abu Dhabi.

"Anyway," I went on. "Easy gig. Just load it up, drop it off, nothing to it, you know?"

When I said that I gave Angie a smart look, like, *Yeah, right,* there's *always* more to it, whatever *it* is, and she returned the look with a smart one of her own, shaking her head, *Yeah, right.* Angie and me, we were no dummies. We knew the score.

"Oh, hey, look at that," I announced suddenly. "Loving those nails."

She beamed, held 'em up. This stray compliment was just icing, just a little conversational texture, although I did mean it sincerely. Each fingernail was painted a different color, and together they formed a sparkling ten-finger rainbow across the faded yellow of the countertop. She spread her fingers for further inspection, which I supplied, whistling admiringly before getting to the heart of the matter.

"But so Monday morning Sully tells me about a job. Truck left the supplier sometime Sunday night, and now I'm supposed to go and do the pickup at a vacant lot on Twelfth Street, maybe two miles past the Speedway, almost out in Hendricks. Paperwork ain't come in yet, he says, but I better get moving. Two barrels of pit-run gravel, two cubic yards to the barrel, we're talking, like, a couple tons of this shit—sorry, Angie, there I go *again*."

Angie cased my hand for a wedding ring when she thought I wasn't looking.

"But so I pulled up the light truck Monday morning, to this lot, and guess what?"

"No rocks," said Angie.

I slapped the counter. "No rocks! You believe that?"

She shook her head. She clucked her tongue. "Your boy messed you up."

"That's right."

I tugged out my handkerchief and wiped my forehead, laying it on thick for sure at this point, but sometimes this is how you gotta do it. You make yourself an open face of need, you send out need like smoke signals. You let need billow out and fill up the room.

"Because now the boss," I said, "Sully's boss, Mr. Coleman, who is now my boss, he's saying this is on *me*. He's saying I better find out what happened to that shipment or it's coming out of my check."

Angie guffawed, incredulous. "And you haven't even been paid yet."

"That's right!" I slapped the counter again, both hands this time. "That's right!"

Angie smiled. I smiled. We smiled at each other.

"So I been going crazy, this is four days now," I said. "All Sully knows is the name of the supplier, and I called them, can't get a straight answer. Sully does not know the name of the truck company. Between you and me, Angie, my man Sully, we're not talking about Albert Einstein here, all right?"

"I'm getting that."

"So I been going around to the different shippers, you know, because I gotta figure this out or I ain't even getting my first paycheck. I'm supposed to be Sherlock Holmes or something. I'm the dang pea-gravel police all a sudden!"

Angie laughed. I laughed. We laughed with each other.

"You got a packing slip number?" she said, coming down off the laughter.

"No."

"Client account number?"

"No. Like I told you."

"You got nothing."

"Zip."

I leaned forward on the counter, let my golden eyes brim with need. I pushed the cap back so she could see my whole sad, handsome face. I was a weary and sorry soul, but nice to look at. I knew exactly how I looked.

"Well, let's see," said Angie, and then, bless her beautiful free heart, she turned to her computer. "So Sunday . . ." she said and started typing. "What's the name of the place?"

"Okay, now, that's another little problem."

Angie reared her head back and clucked, gave me a look: *Are you serious?* I grinned, sheepish.

"It's Garden something," I said, "I know that. Garden Store? Gardens of—oh, I don't know. Garden *something.*"

"And you know where it's coming *from?* Of course you don't."

"Alabama, maybe?"

Angie gave me a different kind of look, sharp and serious. Angry, even.

"Not Alabama. Not with us. We do south-south, and we do north-north. We do a little bit of north to south, but we usually contract those out. We do zero south to north. You want south to north you need a specialty shipper to make sure you're clearing all the regulations and whatnot. Most S-N places, they *only* do S-N, because the other customers, they do *not* want to be dealing with that shit." Angie did not apologize for the word. "Best believe I would not be sitting here shipping south to north."

"Oh, right. Right."

"Best believe it."

Angie clucked. The very *idea.* Meanwhile, I was processing this. I had assumed, and Bridge had assumed along with me, that Barton had chosen Winston Bibb to blackmail because Whole Wide World

95

could arrange a truck to go all the way—to bring Jackdaw from GGSI up to Indy. But this company didn't move shipments north out of the Four: Angie was leaving little doubt about that. She was back to the computer, still shaking her head, typing rapidly without breaking her masterpiece fingernails.

"So look," she said. "I can just look for shipments starting with Garden, that's all. Anything coming out of anywhere, Sunday afternoon, starting with Garden. I can do that."

"You can do that?"

"Oh, baby, there's a *lot* of things I can do."

Totally deadpan, just the tiniest shadow of a smile, not even looking up from the screen. "Don't tease me now, Angie," I said. "Don't you mess with me."

Angie typed a while, then told me to give her just a second more, and I did. I drummed on her counter with my fingertips and flashed her sweet smiles, pulsing with anxiety and flirtatious energy, while inside I thought with a certain indistinct longing of the kids in the indoor trampoline park on the other side of the parking lot, white kids and black kids, hurling themselves up and down, up and down. I pictured them in slow motion, smiling from ear to ear, howling their glee.

"Here," said Angie. "Here we go."

She turned the screen so I could see, and I slapped the counter, one last time, loud and hard enough to make the dry-erase board shiver on the wall and the little bell above the door ring.

"Oh, Angie," I said. "Oh, Angie!"

She leaned back in her chair.

"You just tell your man Sully I said not to be jerking you around again."

"I surely will, Angie, I surely will." She beamed. A nice girl like Angie, she'd tangled with a Sully or two in her day. "Hey—listen," I said at last. "You think you could print this screen out for me?"

14.

Only very rarely is there a real plane involved. Every once in a while you'll hear about some damn fool thing: some billionaire thinks he's God, hires a daredevil pilot to swoop into the airspace of the Four, land hard and dark in a clear-cut Alabama hollow, try and get back with a hold full of refugees. Never ends well. A plane is big and hard to hide, and defending the sovereign airspace of the several states is an enumerated responsibility of the Air National Guard. Rich boy ends up in court and the pilot in jail. Peebs go back where they came from, if they're lucky.

No, man—Underground Airlines is a figure of speech: it's the root of a grand, extended metaphor, "pilots" and "stewards" and "baggage handlers" and "gate agents." Connecting flights and airport security. The Airlines flies on the ground, in package trucks and unmarked vans and stolen tractor-trailers. It flies in the illicit adjustment of numbers on packing slips, in the suborning of plantation guards and the bribing of border security agents, in the small arts of persuasion: by threat or cashier's check or blow job. The Airlines is orders placed by imaginary corporations for unneeded items to be shipped to such-and-such a place at such-and-such a time.

Once, for a month or more, I was Jean-Claude Cisse, a.k.a. Café au Lait, a Montreal-born mulatto and a member of a French-Canadian biker gang called Les Bénévoles Blackburn, which specializes in transporting runaways from their temporary and dangerous quarters in northern cities to *la vraie liberté* in Côte Saint-Luc. Among that crew was a woman named Cherie, who had herself escaped from Louisiana and then dedicated her adult life to the Cause. Most of their work, Cherie liked to say, was done at a desk. Forget the glory of the predawn raid. Smashing in the face of the system and pulling free the enslaved was mostly a matter of paperwork. The opening of bank accounts, the forging of documents. The creation of routes and backup routes and backups to the backups. *"La liberté,"* Cherie was fond of saying, in that charming Montreal accent of hers, *"est une question de logistique."* Freedom is a matter of logistics.

The other thing to remember, of course, is that most people get no help at all. I sure didn't, oh, no: it was just me and Castle, charging, desperate, through the country darkness, and that's how it is for most folks who dare to run—no help from no Airlines, no help from *no one*. They just go, man, after years of planning or in the heat of a sudden moment they *go,* hurl their skinny bodies over a cyclone fence or plunge themselves into a moat, break free of a chain line or a guard's hard grip and *run,* brother, *run,* sister, run along back roads and through forests. No planes and no cars or trucks, either. Just brave souls darting across open fields and wading in and out of rivers and stumbling along deer paths through dark woods. Find the star and follow it, as runners have done all the way back to the days of Old Slavery.

I was turning all this over. I was turning over the whole world. I was sitting in a restaurant called Hamburger Stand, a chain place they got all over Indianapolis, waiting for my waitress to bring me coffee. I was staring with glass eyes through the window, looking at the restaurant parking lot, where a grimy old white dude in a knitted cap was slumped against the curb, dressed in black garbage bags, with another black garbage bag draped across his body like a blanket. Nothing I hadn't seen a thousand times before—every poor city, every northern city—but it hit me this time as bizarre, somehow, a human body just lying there like that, people stepping past him on their way to Keystone Avenue as though he were a corpse.

The lady brought me my coffee, and I asked her for a hamburger, then I turned my eyes down to the document that had come off Angie's printer. Row 6 showed a delivery leaving from Gardens of Paradise in Clayton, Ohio, and Angie had highlighted it in bright pink, because that's the shipment poor rattled Albie was after. But me, down there inside Albie's skin—my interest was in row 7, the next one down in the alphabetical list: the shipment that had left Garments of the Greater South, Incorporated, in Pine Woods, Alabama, at 8:49 on Sunday night.

According to the full file, Jackdaw had fetched up in worker care at 8:35. And now here was a truck, put into motion by Winston Bibb, to rattle out of the gates of shipping and receiving at 8:49.

I traced the row from left to right; I moved my finger slowly across it, like a man reading a Bible verse, memorized the numbers and the facts the numbers represented, and then I dragged my finger back over and did it again. The shipment bore internal identifier number 49-09-5442. The hauling vehicle was a forty-five-foot semitrailer pulled by a midroof tractor unit, VIN number 6ZRFL1622CJ287765. Behind the wheel was driver number HR59.

The truck was bound for Hartsfield-Jackson International Airport laden with "4,200 raw bolts for export" along with "six tons misc. supply/waste" and twenty-six pallets of cotton T-shirts: forty boxes to the pallet, seventy-five shirts to a box.

That made 78,000 T-shirts, plus—I was now sure, I was pretty goddamn sure—one brave, scared, sick, and desperate man. One human being tacked in there, among all the numbers. *La liberté est une question de logistique.*

I looked at the sidewalk again, the old man shifting around, people walking past, in and out of the parking lot. Wherever I looked in this city, all I saw was parking lots. That's what it felt like, anyway. Bleached sidewalks and a grim, sunless horizon. Something about this job was washing out the world. Taking the weather out of the sky.

Jackdaw left GGSI at 8:49 on a tractor-trailer bound for Harts-field airport. Pine Woods to Hartsfield. South to south.

Georgia abolished slavery by statute in the year 1944, same as Kentucky. It was President Truman's great victory, achieved by dangling the prize of wartime contracts, a huge economic incentive for states to go free. But the Georgia legislature, in its wisdom, and under pressure from Alabama and the newly united state of Carolina, had kept its airport quasi-southern—half slave and half free. The same with the Red Highway—US Highway 20—like an open wound, east to west across the state, keeping its neighbors connected to its airport and to the international market for cotton and cattle and corn.

According to the very last column on the chart, all those cotton T-shirts were bound, ultimately, for Shanghai Pudong International Airport.

But Jackdaw hadn't been flown to China, had he? He was here. He was *known to have intended to remove himself to Indianapolis*. Right?

When the girl brought my hamburger, I murmured "Thank you" and ate it slowly, purposefully, enjoying each bite as I had trained myself to enjoy such things. I chewed and swallowed and cleaned my chin with my napkin, not thinking about the smells and sights of my childhood, imagining Jackdaw as a blue dot moving east and not as a man, folded up inside a forty-five-foot trailer, dying from having to piss, his delicate face wilting and sweat-soaked, his eyes big in the darkness of whatever box or pallet he was crated up in. What was he thinking about? Did he know how he was going to get from there to here? Had Barton's proxies briefed him on the plan, or had he simply cast his lot with strangers? Was he just waiting to find out what would happen to him, as I was waiting to find out now?

When I was done with the burger I pushed away my plate. I kept on staring at the printout from Whole Wide World, but all that was left to be discovered was on the back, where Angie had drawn a smiley face and her phone number in pink highlighter.

*   *   *

In the car I turned on my laptop and saw right away that Mr. Maris was no longer driving around. The dot, which had been making Pac-Man patterns around the map of the city, had now settled on 30th Street, a mile and a half past Keystone. Maybe Maris had realized he was still carrying around old Jim's butterfly knife and tossed the thing out the window—or maybe he was there now with Jackdaw the slave, and all my searching and cross-checking were moot, and all I had to do was go and scoop him up.

15.

When I got there, though, there was no sign of Mr. Maris.

I got out of the Altima at the address the map had given me, in yet another gray parking lot on East 30th Street. This lot was little more than a widening of the road shoulder—an oval of rough gravel with parking spaces haphazardly painted on.

The businesses arranged around the lot, all apparently part of the same fiefdom, were of a ramshackle, third-world quality. There was Slim's Market, an unpainted small building, wide and low as a log cabin, the front door propped open with a phone book, a few rows of fruit and vegetable bins haphazardly arrayed outside on staggered wooden platforms. Opposite the market was Slim's Garage, an auto-body shop with its doorway nearly obscured by a half dozen teetering columns of tires. And then there was a rickety unsanded picnic table, and behind the picnic table a flimsy copper archway, hammered into the dirt like a croquet wicket at the head of a rough path winding down into the woods. Following this path, said the sign, would take you to Slim's Trailer Court.

No Maris, no sign of Maris. No sign of anyone. Mine was the only car in the lot. I opened the shotgun door and checked my laptop again. Lo and behold, the dot had disappeared, and no new location was being shown. Mr. Maris had dropped clean off the map.

"Goddamn it," I said out loud. I looked around. "Fuck."

A single bird, small and dark-winged, lit on the copper arch and then flitted away again.

I walked a few paces on the dirt path, down toward the trailer park, until I could make out the shapes of the parked RVs and Winnebagos, shadowy under the bare trees. There were a dozen or more down there, ringed around a bank of water hookups. Most were up on concrete blocks, the wheels long gone, trailer homes more home than trailer. The whole scene had a quiet, dirty beauty: the pockmarked gravel lane between these tin-can houses, the cheap clothes hung up to air-dry in the chill air. Behind the cluster of RVs was a leaky twist of muddy brown water flowing tiredly out of a drainage pipe that emerged from a shallow hill. More than one of the campers was festooned with a red pennant, and these identical fluttering flags had numbers on them—I looked closer, peered in the dusk gloom. Four red numbers on a white background: 1819.

A dog barked inside one of the trailers; barked, then growled. Then a squat white lady in sweats came out, her hair in curlers, talking on her phone. She saw me, squinted in confusion a minute, then went back inside. The screen door slammed behind her.

I tried to imagine Mr. Maris inside one of those tin cans, sitting motionless in the darkness, watching me through slatted blinds with his bright golden eyes. I imagined Jackdaw under a bed; I pictured him in the narrow space between a refrigerator and a wall. I would have to go from house to house, trailer to trailer, knocking on doors or climbing in windows.

It was getting along toward twilight, and I squinted in the growing darkness at the bank of parked vehicles. The sky was dense, low, heavy with rain that wasn't yet ready to come down.

Not right. Something wasn't right. I turned and walked back up the lane.

"You need something?"

"Let me guess," I said, raising a hand to the man now standing at the door of the market. "You're Slim."

He didn't answer. He watched me as I walked over. Slim had a long, droopy brown mustache, and his eyes were droopy, too, coming down at the corners like he was born sleeping and never quite woke up. Slim bent his head slightly and spat. My shoe heels crunched on the gravel.

"I asked what you needed, boy."

I flinched and hid my flinching. I felt my mouth turning up into a scowl, and I ordered it not to do that. The little one-syllable insult, *boy*, it worked as it always did, like a little chunk of gravel, a pointy rock of disgust and contempt.

I smiled. God forgive me, I did. The word hit the side of my face, and I smiled. I was working. "Not meaning to bother you, sir," I said. "I'm just looking for a friend of mine."

"I ain't seen him," said Slim immediately. Before I could answer there was a short, blaring shriek, like two pieces of sheet metal scraping together, from inside the body shop behind me. Slim didn't turn his head, so I didn't, either.

"Due respect, sir," I said, nice and calm, "but how do you know you haven't seen him? Can I tell you what he looks like?"

"Due respect," he said, "does he look like *you*?"

I required of my smile that it widen. That it broaden and harden and glaze, become a smile that was like a shield. The answer to the question was no, of course. Mr. Maris wasn't even close to looking like me. Maris was built like a boxer, and he had metallic skin and distinctly African features, a long nose and wide nostrils, bright golden eyes. He didn't look shit like me.

"If you're asking is he black, then yes. He's black."

"Like I said. I ain't seen him."

"You mind if I come in the store a minute, have a look around?"

"We're closed."

My smile was having trouble. I could feel it flickering.

"It'll just take a second," I said. "I'd just like to have a quick look. This friend of mine, see, I'm trying to find him. He said he was coming down here."

"Did you not hear the man?" I turned around and saw a dump truck in mechanic's overalls. "He said *git*."

The man who'd come out of the garage to join us was burly and bearded, with streaks and smears of oil on his chest and fat stomach. Slim sniffed and spat again, while the big fella snorted. They could have been a goddamn vaudeville team, these two, except that the big one was holding not a microphone but a long rifle. He had it clutched across his chest, minuteman style. My smile gave up. It extinguished. Fuck it.

"I don't know what I've done to upset you fellas," I said. "But I don't want any trouble."

"He don't want any trouble," said the mechanic over my shoulder to Slim, who harrumphed and stroked his mustache. I turned at the sound of gravel, as fat boy took a step forward and brandished the rifle.

I steeled my jaw. Jim Dirkson wasn't going to cut it, and I found inside myself a hard man, a stone-cold antihero from one of those 1970s black revenge pictures, from *Jim Blackmon's Slaveland Vengeance* or one of its many sequels.

"Drop the weapon, shitheel," I said. My voice was down half an octave. I was cold and keen-eyed and hard in my shell.

"Or what?"

"Or I'll wrap it around your fat white neck."

This was dialogue, I was doing lines, but goddamn if I didn't mean it. This bearded sack of crap dropped into some kind of firing-range stance, but man, I was just one step too close and he didn't know what I was and I had gravel in my hand and I was flinging it in his piggy eyes and then I was leaping at him, one big panther leap. I had him by the hair and the gun on the ground and I slapped him with my big open hand—once, twice, then three times, slapped his face back and forth like a cruel father hitting his boy because he hates himself.

The mechanic was down on the ground, his hands feebly defending himself against my superior strength, the rifle at his feet in the gravel. I heard movement on the porch and without turning, still holding fat boy, I said: "Stay where you are, Slim."

"Hey," said the mechanic, and I kicked him in the face and his mouth blew open with blood and he turned and started to curl away. I grabbed the gun and wheeled around and was glad to see Slim rooted to his place as instructed. A drool of tobacco spit ran from the corner of his mouth. I came at him now with the rifle, one step, two steps.

"You seen my friend?"

"I seen no black men."

I fired. The glass behind Slim shattered, and the whole door jumped and shuddered in the jamb. Slim's old coyote face convulsed with fear. It felt good; it all felt good. I took another step forward and raised the muzzle to his eyes.

"You seen him?"

"No." He kept his hands where I could see them, raised them slowly and laced his fingers behind his head, like a man who'd been trained. The interrogation was over. I believed him. He hadn't seen Maris or anybody else. But I—I don't know. I wasn't done.

"You military, Slim?"

"What?"

"Were you in the army?"

"Yes."

"You see action?"

"Yes. In the gulf. In Texas."

"Oh, yeah? What side?"

He stopped talking. He stared at me. "America. Our side."

"So what were you fighting for?" His eyes went down to the gun, then back to my face; my face was set and cruel. He knew where I was going. So did I. I couldn't stop. "I said, what were you fighting for, Slim?"

"For—for America. For the Union."

"Yeah, but Texas didn't want none of the Union. Right? They didn't want nothing to do with it. With us. With *slavery*. They just wanted to be done with it. Remember?" He tried to move his head, but I had the gun pressed between his eyes, really grinding in hard between his eyes. "But you went and fought to keep the Union together."

106

"I got drafted."

"Coulda run. Plenty ran. They still up there."

"I was fighting for my country."

"Bullshit."

"All right."

He closed his eyes. He thought I was gonna kill him right there. I was glad. I was tight with rage. My rib cage was a fist clenched around my heart. The sun had gone down. There were no lights in the parking lot. The moon was coming up, pale and disinterested.

"What were you fighting for, Slim?"

He looked down. Mustache drooping down. He whispered. "Slavery."

I shot him in the knee. While he wailed, while the fat one moaned, I wiped my prints off the rifle with the sleeve of my shirt and threw it in the dirt and drove away.

16.

I drove away trembling.

What the hell was I doing?

What did I care?

Texas was the Lone Star miracle, the success story of early-twentieth-century activist abolitionism: in an orchestrated campaign, migrant manumissionists from all over the country flooded in, along with tens of thousands of Catholic-abolitionist Mexicans, drawn by the come one, come all immigration policy shortsightedly enacted by a state eager for oil-field hands. Hence the miracle, *el milagro*: the largest state in the union, free by statute in 1939. It wasn't till twenty-five years later, under the first Mexican-American governor in that or any other state, that they went further, declared their intention to secede, and Washington said, the fuck you will. There was a Texan in the White House by then, one who'd been a schoolteacher, who'd had some of these Mexican sumbitches in his classroom. He took it personally. These folks needs to read their history books, said President Johnson. Secession is illegal under the Constitution—and by the way, that's American oil under all that sand.

Eleven years of fighting. Battleships in the Gulf of Mexico, swift boats on the Rio Grande. Mexican partisans fighting hicks like Slim on the shores of Corpus Christi.

Not my war. A useless, nasty war, and nothing to do with me.

Eleven years of grueling, bitter combat, ending in nothing. Uneasy detente. Contested status. They call themselves the Republic of Texas, but we keep their star on our flag. We created the

Special Economic Zone to protect our oil interests in the Gulf of Mexico, and they formed the Gulf Irregulars to protect theirs. Status quo antebellum.

I was shaking. My arms were shaking. I drove back slowly to the hotel, my hands at ten and two, not even putting in a tape. Eyes on the road, deep breaths, hoping and praying for no checkpoints. I didn't know what I would do.

Putting a bullet in a man's leg. Leaving carnage behind me. In the hotel parking lot I sat in the car a minute or more, hands on my knees, trying to get my head right. *Work your case,* I said to myself. *Solve your goddamn case.*

Someone was on the phone in the horseshoe driveway of the Capital City Crossroads. There was a copse of tall hedges to the right side of the door, out of range of the streetlights, and someone was hidden by one of them, talking loudly and with emotion into a cellular phone.

I could hear this private conversation as I came across the parking lot, and my instinct was to veer to the right, keep my head down, get to my room as soon as I could. It was 9:20. I had half an hour until Bridge called, and I wanted that time. I needed it. I needed to sit in the room with my hands on the desk until my body quit the shivering it had started up with. The tension of the confrontation at Slim's—the buck and kick of the firearm. I wanted time for all of it to sluice out of me and leave me empty.

"No, but that's just not—" said the voice. It was Martha. My white friend from the breakfast area, from the pool. "That makes it very difficult for me to—no—wait, what? No. Wait . . ."

I had walked past her. She had not seen me. I stopped at the threshold of the building, and the automatic door sensed my approach and whooshed open.

"Fuck!" Martha shouted. She had not seen me. "God fucking damn it."

I stepped back, let the door whoosh closed again. No. Fuck this.

Come on. I stepped forward, and the door whooshed open, then back again. Whoosh.

"You okay?" I said, and she smiled, stepping out from behind the hedges.

"Well, that's — good question." She stuffed the phone in her pocket. She was wearing the same jean jacket, the same jeans. She did not look as if she had slept. She twisted her small mouth into a wry grimace. "Are you okay? That's the million-dollar question, right? My mother always told me to watch out. For that question, I mean. Because, like, are you or aren't you, right? It's not usually one or the other, you know?"

"Oh," I said. "Sure. That makes sense."

"But no. Not really." She tugged the phone out again and looked at it, and I studied the side of her face. I had been thinking of her as a girl, a sassy kid who'd become a mother much too early. Now — sighing, frustrated, anxious, in the moonlight outside the hotel — she looked like what she probably was: a woman in the first years of her thirties, with a few worry lines at the corners of her mouth, with some of life's grief already in her eyes.

"Everything all right with your boy?"

"Lionel, remember? Like the train."

I remembered. I remember everything. "Oh, yes, of course. Lionel."

A long, rolling shudder passed through me, and I held myself still till it was gone. I had put a bullet in that man without thinking. Without hesitation or regret. *What were you fighting for?* What was I doing?

"The kid is fine." She gestured inside. "Sleeping like the proverbial . . . whatever. Do you have kids, Jim?"

"Nope," I said. "Nope. I never went down that route somehow. Never went down that road."

"Right. I asked you that. Your traveling."

"Yes," I said. "Well, that's just it."

The door whooshed, and a couple came out, a man and a

110

woman, arm in arm, whispering together. The man lifted his keys, and we heard the bloop-bloop of a car door unlocking somewhere out in the darkness of the lot.

When I looked back at Martha, her head was tilted back, and she was studying the stars.

"I'm just trying hard. You know? Real hard."

"I'm sure you are."

"Trying so hard."

I saw myself again an hour earlier at Slim's, wielding that rifle like a lightning bolt. That was a different person who had done all that. Now, this, here—this was Jim Dirkson, speaking softly to a distressed stranger in the parking lot of a hotel. Jim, kind and calm, lending a comforting presence, and me underneath, searching, hunting, pushing. Doing my thing.

"I think you said . . ." I began, and when she jumped I said, "Sorry, sorry. But I think you said you were from here originally. Like, you grew up here?"

"I'm from Indiana. Not Indy. My sister lives up here, though. Sometimes we come and visit."

"But not this time."

"No. This time it's—" She held up the phone. "Business."

"All right. Well, I have a question for you. It's just a number: 1819," I said. "A year, I'm guessing. Does the year 1819 have any kind of special meaning around here?"

Martha's expression changed, sharply, completely. She dropped her eyes down to the gravel of the lot, then she looked back up, unsmiling, and spoke in a sad hush. "Where did you see that number?"

"Oh . . ." I said. "You know . . ."

It wasn't right, dragging my problems in front of this innocent bystander, who clearly had problems of her own. I was pretty sure I already knew the goddamn answer anyway.

"Just something I spotted hung up outside somebody's house."

"Hung up how?"

"On a flag. A number of 'em, actually. Like pennants. But you know what? It doesn't matter. It's fine."

"It's not fine." Something like anger was choking Martha's face. "Because it just gets into everything."

"What does?"

"It. All this shit."

"What shit?"

Martha shook her head. "Where did you see them? Downtown? Southside?"

"East side." All the questions were making me a little uneasy. I felt the need to reinforce my ID, duck under my cover for a moment. "I was at a potential retail location, kind of poking around the area."

"Oh, all right," she said. "I see."

"You know what?" I said, regretting the whole line. It was 9:30. Bridge would be calling in twenty minutes. "Don't worry about it. The business with the number. I'm sorry to have bothered you."

"No," she said. "No, you're fine." She gave her head a little shake, took a deep breath, preparing to bear up to unpleasantness. "It's the year before . . . what's his name?" She squeezed shut her eyes, remembering hard, then popped them back open. "*Lasselle*. The Indiana Supreme Court, 1820." She closed her eyes again. She looked older with her eyes closed. "'The framers of our Constitution intended a total and entire prohibition of slavery in this State.' So 1820 is the year Indiana was officially and fully free."

I smiled sadly. "Gotcha."

"So 1819, for these dickwads, that's the good old days. See?"

"I see."

She looked at me head-on, tears standing in her eyes. The people with the flags were reversionists—people who as a matter of politics or personal taste regretted that their state had ever adopted its constitution and thereby abolished the practice of slavery. And it made Slim's Trailer Court, Slim's Market, and Slim's Garage the unlikeliest possible place for Mr. Maris to have

112

landed, the unlikeliest possible place for Jackdaw the runner to be squirreled away.

"Mr. Dirkson, I'm sorry you had to see that."

"Call me Jim. And it's okay."

"It's not. My state is a really nice state, for the most part. It really, really is."

"Oh, I get that. That's the feeling I get for sure."

Mr. Bridge would be calling in fifteen minutes. But here was young, kind Martha in her cheap denim jacket and her long brown ponytail tied back with a pink rubber band standing out here in the parking lot suffering whatever it was she was suffering. She reached up to neaten the ponytail, and the motion caused the top of her white dress shirt to open slightly, and I saw just below the root of her neck a black box, inked in all the way. Not a lot of white people got them, but some did. A mark of solidarity or empathy or guilt.

Martha saw me looking, blushed, and brought her shirt collar together.

"God," she said. "People think it's far away, but it's not. It's here. It's everywhere. Clouding over everything. Hanging over everything. Don't you just feel that way sometimes?"

"I do," I said. "I guess I do."

With an effort of will, she made herself smile, made her eyes get hopeful. "But you know what? Maybe this thing with Batlisch, you know, the president sticking up for her and all . . . maybe it's the beginning of some real change."

I smiled. I nodded. I'd read the same article. It had been in my own newspaper. "Sure," I said. Thinking, *Shit does not change*. Thinking, *It will never change*. "You never know."

"Listen, Jim," she said. "Hey. Would you ever . . ."

She paused. She looked down at her phone, considering something, gathering some kind of quick courage. My heart was a tight, high knot; there was some keening emotion making itself felt that I had never felt before while I stood in the invisible light of those words, hanging and spinning between us, *Would you ever . . .*

Then her phone rang. She opened it, and it rang again, and then we both realized together it wasn't her phone ringing, it was mine.

I looked at the incoming number and at the time. It was 9:36.

"Mr. Dirkson?"

My phone rang again. Bridge was calling, fourteen minutes ahead of schedule.

"I should get this."

"Oh. Sure."

"I need to get this."

The world was a confused clamor. Bridge ringing in my hand, those 1819 flags flapping in my brain, Jackdaw trembling inside a box, the rifle bucking against my shoulder, and Martha, *Would you ever*—would I ever what?

"It's . . ." She gave a little toss of her head. "It's nothing. Seriously. Take your call."

I answered as I turned away, and the doors whooshed open, and Bridge said "Victor," short and sharp, his voice charged with some energy I did not immediately recognize.

"Oh, yes, hello," I said, still in Dirkson voice, walking fast, not liking to talk to him out in the bright no-man's-land of the hotel lobby. It was like I had conjured a demon to rise up out of the patterned carpet, right where everyone could see it. "Hey, could you hang on just a sec?"

I kept the phone pressed against my chest until I was back in the room, out on the balcony, with a cigarette clenched in my teeth.

Would you ever . . . what? Would I ever—

"Victor."

"You caught me in the middle of something."

"And is that a problem for some reason?" A current running through his voice like rogue electricity. "I will call when I call, Victor. Do you understand? I will call when I want to."

I took the phone away from my ear and studied it. Maybe it had connected me by accident to the wrong man. Some other Victor, somewhere else.

"How's your progress?"

I skipped the jokes. I gave the man a whirlwind tour of the day's adventures. I gave him Officer Cook and Maris on the steps, I gave him the pin I had put on Maris; I gave him the name of the doctor; I gave him the printout from Whole Wide World Logistics with the route of escape. I told him about Slim's, but not about shooting Slim.

The whole time I was providing this debrief, I was measuring the short, cool silences that breathed between my sentences. Something was off—something was way off. Some new weather, a heaviness in the atmosphere, was brooding over our call like a storm system, darkening the color of the sky.

Like a good employee, I wrapped up my report with next steps. Tomorrow morning I would feel out the doctor, try again to pick up Maris's trail, seek out Cook the cop if I had to, prevail upon him to make another run at the recalcitrant priest.

Another half step of menacing silence from Mr. Bridge. Then he said something that blew a hole in my understanding of the world, like a cannonball smashing through the high wood sides of a ship. "You holding out on me, boy?"

"Am I—what?"

But it wasn't even the question. That word—that word again—that *word*. I sucked in poison from the cigarette and felt my cheeks tremble. Felt my neck get hot.

"If you are dragging your feet, I will know it."

"I'm not."

"What I'm hearing from you, Victor, is a list of half-completed tasks. Bullshit leads. This is day three on this."

"Three days is nothing," I said. "Remember Milwaukee? Fuck, man, remember Carlisle?"

"If you can't get this over with—"

"If I—what?"

"If you can't find the man—"

I was staring at the phone again, holding it at arm's length and shaking my head. We were upside down. We were in a shadow land. Bridge's aggression was way, way out of character. He was my handler, and he was handling me poorly. I noticed his uncharacteristic inarticulateness, the strange doubling back, how he had arrived at "If you can't find the man" only after "If you can't get this over with," which has a whole different character.

"If you're slow playing this, Victor, I will know that. Do you understand?"

"Yes," I said. "I do."

"You understand what that means."

I stood in silence, simmering in the implication of the question. The violence gleaming cold behind it.

Looking back, I don't know why I was surprised. All that'd happened was that the truth of Bridge, of me and him, had unexpectedly shown itself right up close where I could see it. It had always been violence. For six years it had been violence: behind our professional exchanges and collegial banter, there had always been violence. For six years I'd spoken to him on secure lines, from comfortable hotel rooms, smoking my cigarettes, breathing night air, playing at freedom. But the first time I spoke to him I was shackled in a Chicago basement, hands tied to a table and feet to a chair, and he was a cold unfamiliar voice spooling out from a speakerphone like a length of wire, the voice of my doom until he offered me a choice that was no choice.

After all those years in the shadows I had gotten it together, gotten papers, gotten myself a job, loading and unloading trucks at Townes Stores, just north of the Chicago city limits. Two years, two normal, happy human years, then one night I came off shift at dawn and it was behind me, a silver car was idling on Monroe Street with no plates, and I didn't even fucking think about it. I dropped the hot dog I was eating and ran, looking with wild instinct for the North Star and finding only the egg-yellow glow of streetlamps.

I made it maybe thirty feet before they tackled me and brought me down. While they dragged me to the car thrashing and wailing, I thought crazily that I should have turned right instead of left, should have gone up the alley instead of down the sidewalk. As if it mattered, as if there were any direction I could have run to escape the unforgetting world.

Next thing I knew I was in a basement. Federal building, downtown Chicago. I was still in my work shirt, still in my nice clean Adidas, in my blue jeans. All that peace and safety draining away, all my new life sloughing off onto the concrete floor. I was already feeling the cold steel of the chains drawing down between my shoulder blades, running in lengths around my ankles.

Somebody came in and put a phone down on the table, and I stared at it, confused, until it beeped two times and a voice came on the line.

"My name is Bridge," said the voice. "I am a deputy marshal in the United States Marshals Service. I trust you appreciate the gravity of your situation. Your instructions now are simply to listen to my proposal and answer when I'm done. Your answer will be either yes or no." Listening to his cold voice, I was thinking about cows' heads, cows' necks, bloodied flanks. Thinking of the hours and the days. Bridge said again, yes or no, and I would have done anything, yes, anything, I would have said anything, anything, forever, anything.

When he was done talking, I said yes. Right away I said yes, of course I did, I said yes.

And now Bridge, his same voice after all these years: *You understand what that means.* It means I was there in Indianapolis, in that northern hotel room, but a trap could open in the floor and crash me down into that federal building basement; the walls could fall away and show how all along I'd been at Bell's, in the stink and blood haze and weariness of Bell's Farm.

You understand what that means, he said, and I did. Violence had always been behind our conversations. What's behind everything, what's under everything. Violence.

"Sir," I said, very slowly, very calm. "I am pursuing the case to the best of my ability."

Bridge didn't answer. No more silences, brooding or angry or anything. He just hung up.

Maybe there was something going on with the man I didn't know about. Maybe it was another case. Maybe it was Batlisch, the hearings, adding some tension to the air of those government hallways. But I didn't think so. Something was going on with this—with Bridge, with me. With this case.

I was going to have to sleep, but I didn't even try it yet. I stood out on the balcony for a long time, for what might have been hours.

All of it cycling through, rutting me up. Cook in the car, "A special kind of kid . . ." and Bridge on the phone, "get this over with . . ." and Martha Flowers, "Would you ever . . ." All of it. All of this life.

Something was piercing through me, some kind of heat burning the raw layer under the skin. Something I couldn't then explain and that even now I have trouble transforming from thought into words. But *something* was happening. A dial was turning.

You can imagine a compass needle twitching to life—the smallest pulse—the barest movement—struggling for north.

Twice a year a group was graduated off the pile and moved inside, and soon enough it was my turn. It was something of an occasion: work halted inside and outside; everybody circled around the flagpoles. The only kind of time like it was church, or when one of us died or when someone was sold.

Mr. Bell came out and walked down the line of us. I think it was nine other boys and three girls who came off the pile along with me. We stood with our chests stuck out. We had on the yellow suits we'd just been issued, and the respirator headgear, those fancy magic face masks that you had to wear on most shifts inside.

The ceremony only took ten minutes after all that—for us to be lined up and for Mr. Bell to kiss us each one time on the top of our heads and tighten the straps of our masks with tender ceremony. And then the buzzer sounded for our very first kill-floor shift, and he said, "All right, y'all, get to it," and we marched inside.

By the time that first day ended my yellow suit was no longer clean.

"So?" said Castle when he found me in the johns. "You all right?"

"Course I am."

I didn't want Castle to know how I really felt after that first long day inside the cutting house. I had been very close all day to vomiting. Not from the work itself, I guess—that first day all I did was throw the lever of the downpuller machine, over and over and over, align the mechanical jaws, press the button, and watch them tug off the cattle hide. One swift motion and the full skin came off, like taking off a shirt. I guess the sight of it, over and over. The glistening black and red of the insides. I don't know. But I did—I had felt all day on the brink of vomiting, and I still did even then in the johns, but I didn't want Castle to know that. I didn't want him to lose his pride in me.

"I'm fine," I told him, and I smiled weak and watery. When I looked at him I felt like I could see his insides, like his skin'd been pulled away.

"You'll be all right," he said, like he hadn't heard me say I was fine. He put his hand on my shoulder, which made me jump. You didn't want the Old Man seeing that, talking close and confidential. The Old Man or anyone who might tell him. "What's next is what matters," he said.

Sure enough, there was Harbor, looking at Castle's hand on me, looking at us whispering all together like that.

"What you mean, what's next?" said Harbor with his hard, slit-face smile.

"You mind your own, how about, son?" said Castle.

"My own what? Everything's everybody's." Harbor smiled. "Right?"

That was one of the mottoes. Everything's everybody's. Eyes on the prize. For you and me and Bell's Farm!

Harbor ignored Castle then and talked right to me. Harbor was between my age and Castle's age, but he talked just like a grown man. Talked almost like an Old Man, actually, like he was in charge of something. "Your man here talking about what's next. Lemme tell you what's next. Today they fit on that mask. Tomorrow you work on the carving line. Then the kill floor. Till they put you on the block or put you in the ground. That's what's next."

Castle shook me awake that night. Not to tell me any words or stories. His big eyes wider than ever but serious. Focused.

"You remember what I told you?"

I blinked. He had told me so many things.

"They not us," he said, so quiet I could hardly hear him. "Not Harbor, not anyone. Something'll come for you and me."

"What?" I said. "What'll come?"

He wasn't even making noise anymore. He just mouthed the word. "Opportunity."

Pretty soon I decided that inside was worse than the pile.

That was punishable, of course: to think of any kind of work as worse or worst or bad. Thoughts Against Good Work. I kept my thoughts to myself. Out on the pile there was some music in the air, kind of: there was the distant rush and honk of the highway; there was the caw of crows and even on occasion the merry chirrup of a songbird. Inside the only sounds were work sounds: the chunk-chunk of the bolt gun and the chug-chug of the ramp, the dull, ignorant lowing of the cows, the buzz and rattle of the hot machines. And the nervous click-clack of boot heels all around you: the Old Men and the guards strolling with their hands on their holsters, the Franklins with their clipboards, the USDA in their lab coats, with their instruments.

I got through it by telling myself Castle's stories, all the ones he had told me over all those years: the man who slipped into the water and was eaten by a whale and spat out again; the leopard who cannot change his spots; and the one (my favorite one) about the man who built another man from parts he had found, brought him to life with lightning for magic.

Other times I told myself the words. Doing my tasks, again and again and again: cracking skulls, pulling out viscera, carving out tongues by their thick roots. Repeating Castle's old words from under our blanket together:

Carburetor.

Chicago.

Opportunity.

Six or eight months after I moved in to the cutting floor, Castle shook me awake one night, and I was as mad as I'd ever been.

"Getting too old for this," I said, grumpy.

"No, love," he said. "Don't say that."

My hands hurt so much. I had been moved from the downpuller onto a straight carving station, and in sleep my hands stayed cramped in the shape that held the knife.

"Too old."

"I know, dear. I know. But listen. I have to give you something."

And always, Castle knew what I didn't know yet, because he had seen it happen with the olders. Soon they would come and read his number out and move him to another cabin. He was the oldest of the younger ones, and soon they'd need the room for the new littlest coming out of the breed lot. He'd go to cabin 9, and after a year, on from there to breeding.

That night while he waited for me to wake and listen, his big eyes were full of tears. I think they were. I wish I could remember.

"I got a secret to give you. You gotta listen. This matters."

"Huh?"

"You listening?"

I allowed with a shrug that I was.

"We are from the future."

"Man, what?" That had woken me all the way. "The future? Castle, come on."

But his face was serious. So, so serious.

"We are from the future, my sweet brother. We are future boys. Okay?" He was talking too loud. He was all worked up. I put my finger across his lips. He brushed it away. "We look like we're here, with all this, but we're really somewhere else. In the future we got somewhere else. Some other time."

"What place you mean?"

"I don't know, honey. Someplace. Chicago, maybe. Future place." He had told me stories about that city he got from somewhere. It was a city on the other side of America. Buildings upright and proud. "I'm in Chicago, and I'm eating a hot dog."

I had to put my cramped hand over my mouth to keep from laughing out loud.

Castle had never eaten any hot dogs, and neither had I, but we knew what they were well enough. There was a dancing hot dog on the trucks that rumbled in and out unceasingly from the loading dock on the north side of the kill house. But for our food we had mostly the loaves, dense and filling. Carrot loaves and sorghum loaves and vanilla loaves for a treat.

"We live in two places at once, you and me." Castle's eyes shone with pleasure, with real, true electric pleasure, and I felt it arcing between us like starlight. "You live here, you live there. You live now, you live later. You live in this place, you live in the other place. There's two of you. Do you understand?"

I nodded. I wasn't sure that I did, but I wanted him to know that I did.

Castle held up two fingers in the dark, and from then on that was our sign. Two fingers, raised and spread apart. It meant—you and me—two of us. It meant him and me, but also it meant me and me and it also meant him and him. Me now, me later. Castle now, Castle later.

This place and the other place, here and there, now and later on.

17.

In the morning, in the silence of the waiting room, in the bright light of the small examination room of Dr. Venezia-Karbach, I felt the uneasy and unwelcome sensation of being completely alone in the presence of myself. I had spent so much of my life costumed and posing, turning and turning myself, like changing the channels on a television set, that sometimes when I was caught as I was now, in a silent moment, just waiting, nothing to do but sit and wait and think in a white and airless room, I felt like a blank screen. I felt like a dead television. I was myself. I was nothing. I sat there in the thin paper robe. My ass was freezing on the steel of the table.

The one piece of artwork in Dr. Venezia-Karbach's office was a framed print of a Norman Rockwell painting, *First-Day Jitters:* little black girl in a plain white dress, handing up an apple to her pretty black teacher, and both of them looking shy and aw-shucks nervous. That was a famous painting, the first day of class at Little Rock School for Negro Children, 1954, seven years after Arkansas became free, nine months after the Supreme Court ruled that freedom wasn't enough—there had to be schools. There had to be a chance.

I stared at that schoolteacher now, her wide excited eyes, her worry, the white bows in her hair. I had read some sort of magazine feature about her recently, the real person, about the way the rest of her life had turned out. I tried to remember where I had read it. Tried to remember how she was doing.

"Good morning, Mr. Morton. I understand you're here for a checkup—is that correct?"

"Yes, Doc, you got it," I said, snapping right into it. "That's right."

"Let's have a look."

Dr. Venezia-Karbach was a white woman in her late fifties or early sixties, not unfriendly but not friendly, either. Her hair was short and spiked up, boxy and sexless. On her instructions I removed the robe and sat in my underpants, hands laced in my lap, while she conducted her examination with brisk efficiency. Her fingertips lit on the various regions of my anatomy—torso and limbs, eyes and ears, pulse points and glands. I breathed deeply while she pressed my chest with the cold flat face of the stethoscope. I opened my mouth and said "Ah" and flinched a little while she inspected my throat with the funneled light of the laryngoscope.

She started a chart and asked me some questions. Mr. Kenny Morton, it turned out, was the type of old-fashioned amiable cat who called the doctor Doc, who probably called cops Chief, and who called fat strangers Big Guy. He was the kind of fella who scratched his head with theatrical uncertainty when asked where his previous physician's practice was located and when his last appointment had taken place. Dr. Venezia-Karbach registered no surprise to hear that Mr. Morton had no insurance or current place of employment.

I imagined for one sharp second Dr. V's tidy white examination room as the tidy white examination room at the worker-care facility in the western section of the GGSI campus: imagined it splattered with gore, covered with an exuberance of blood. Two dead nurses. Jackdaw on the loose.

Dr. V wrote everything down on her chart and told me that for a man of my age and height and weight I seemed to be in fine shape. When she asked what it was that had brought me to the doctor today, I figured that was enough of that. "Well," I said, emotion coming hot into my voice, choking me up, "well . . ." and I slid off the examination table and exploded with need. "That *boy!*"

"What?" Dr. Venezia-Karbach stepped backward in startlement

while I fought back a sob. I advanced across the small room and grasped her roughly by the shoulders. "That boy y'all got!"

There were more graceful ways I could have gone about this. More circumspect methods, more careful. But I was feeling half off the horse that morning. I was feeling like a battering ram, just wanting to shove and smash through this thing. What had Bridge said, in that unwonted casualism—I wanted to get it over with.

"What on earth are you talking about?" said Dr. V, furrowing her brow, playing at confused, putting on a nice show of her own. "What *boy?*"

"Come on," I said. "Come on, now. They brought you a boy. The Airlines, a boy, Sunday night. Monday morning?"

"*Sir.*" Without turning around, Dr. V extended a leg behind her and kicked the door shut.

"The boy!"

"Sir, *please.*"

I waited for some stammering excuse—what are you talking about, I don't understand. But it was too late, and she knew it— her eyes had betrayed her, her neat physician's mask had slipped to reveal not fear, or not just fear, but also the shock of having been discovered. In a fluid gesture she turned around, locked the door, and turned back around. She smoothed her white coat with both hands, adjusted the stethoscope that had been jostled, ran thin fingers through her hair.

"Okay," she said. "What about him?"

"Well . . ." What the hell, I figured. "Where's he at?"

"I do not know, and I could not tell you if I did." She nodded once, a quick birdlike gesture. "Now, as I've said, your checkup shows no areas of concern. Have a good day."

She unlocked the door and opened it, and I was across the room, reaching past her and pushing it closed again. Dr. V's shoulders tensed as she turned to face me, the two of us separated by inches. This was a fine line I was walking here. I'm big, even for a man, and she was small, even for a woman, and the room was small and close.

"He's my brother," I told her quietly, damn near whispering now. "What?"

I took two deep breaths. The space between us was ruffled by a drift of warm air from the heating system, riffling Dr. V's short, spiky hair and making it look like white grass.

"I don't mean he's my biological brother; I mean he's my *brother*." It was a southern voice, PB voice, the blood traces of my old real voice tasting like dirt in my mouth. "You know what that means down there? Raised up together, eyes on each other. Family." I was careful not to say what kind of place it'd been, this plantation or mine or rig where Mr. Morton and Jackdaw had been bound together as boys. The full file was empty on Jackdaw's history, and I guessed that Barton and company didn't know any more and that, regardless, they wouldn't have shared anything with a physician brought in on a freelance basis to tend to him. But this was dangerous territory, and I moved past it quickly.

"We come up together ten years, him and me, but then he gets sold. No warning, no good-bye. That's how it goes, you know?"

Dr. V was watching me warily, arms crossed, eyes darting back and forth in the small room. I charged on.

"I stay up in Wisconsin. I got people up there. And I been trying to find him all these years, writing letters to manumits from our old place, then with the Internet, you know, everything's easier and harder, too. I'm looking at forums, typing his name in search engines. Looking for anyone matching his age, description, you know? Saving up my money and all, like somehow I'm gonna put together enough scratch to buy him out." I looked down, shook my head self-mockingly, as if a poor freedman like Kenny Morton could ever earn enough to buy a man out of slavery. As if there weren't laws against it. "And then, suddenly, jackpot, you know? A decade of nothing, and then one day, up pops the name! Boy called Jackdaw, gone ghost from some Alabama stitch house. Well, first thing I think is he's here. He was always talking about Indianapolis. Don't know how he got it in his head. Don't know how he even heard of this place. But that was it—*I ever get out of here*—you know, just talk. Night talk."

Castle and I, talking under the blanket, telling stories. Imagining made-up futures. Whispering *Chicago* to each other. And we did, didn't we? We did make it out, did we not? Opportunity came— one, two, three, like horseshoes ringing onto the post—and we flew away.

"But so I came up here, and someone down Freedman Town, they told me you the doc who sees to runners, least sometimes."

Dr. Venezia-Karbach's eyes flashed, and her arms uncrossed from her chest so she could plant her fists on her hips. She didn't like that the word was out on her. I had rattled the woman for sure. I stared at her pleadingly, and she looked back, and behind her the 1954 schoolteacher waited for her students to arrive, an unlikely hero in Salvation Army shoes, surrounded by her uncertain future.

"All right. I understand." The sternness in Dr. V's eyes softened, and her mouth twisted at the corners. She was keeping her voice firm, but with effort now. Something else was trying to find its way out, pity or empathy or kindness. "And what is it that you want?"

"All I want to do is see him," I said. "That's all. Just—before y'all spirit him away. Up north. I just gotta see him one time. I need him to know I never did forget about him."

And there were tears in my eyes now, of course. Seems like one thing I could always manage was to conjure up some tears into my eyes. I was still nearly naked, just in my underpants, and it only added to the awkward urgency of our exchange, that we bore this relation to each other—doctor and patient, woman and man. "I just want him to know I never let him out of my heart. I never did. I just want to see him and tell him that. That's all that I want."

She should have simply said, "I'm sorry." She should have said there was nothing she could do. I could only imagine the firm instructions she got from Father Barton, the sternness with which his admonitions of silence were delivered. But the ripples were passing over her, the ripples of want. She *wanted* to help me. She *needed* to. It was the flip side of the reflexive hatred of Slim and Slim's fat pal—someone like Dr. V, white and liberal and a child of her era: she wanted and needed for the poor black man in her office, he of humble circumstance and simple hopes, to see that she was *not* like the sneering bigots and whiphands of the world, that she was a person of conscience. She was different.

Barton would demand that she keep her peace, do as he did in the diner and disclaim all knowledge. But Barton wasn't there— he was an abstraction, and I was there in her office. Mr. Morton was real, hands knitted together, eyes wide with need.

"The problem is," she said slowly, "that I don't actually know his location."

"Look, I don't want to hurt him," I said, "or take him or nothing. I just want to see his face. I want to hold him one more time."

"You're not hearing me. I don't know his location."

"But—but you went to him. I thought—you didn't help him?"

She nodded minutely, bird head popping down, then up. "Yes. But I don't know where."

Goddamn it. Fucking priest. Shifty, snake-eyed, base-covering little hypocrite.

"What do you mean?"

"Look, okay." Her hand ran again through her hair. "I never know much with these—these situations. I get a call from someone. I don't know who it is. It's a different number every time. Okay? That's how this goes. I have a phone they give me, and it rings and I answer it and they tell me where to go."

"Where?"

"Downtown."

"Where?'

"The mall. Circle Centre Mall."

I nodded. I knew it. Right downtown. You could see its parking garage from the statue of Abe the Martyr.

"But that's not where I met him. That's just where the car picked me up. It was a taxicab, but not—it wasn't in service. It was just for me."

Barton at work: cutout operation, prepaid phones, wheels within wheels.

"So where'd the car take you? It take you to him?"

"Yes, but. Blindfolded."

They packed her into the car, drove her for at least an hour, drove her around and around in circles, north and then south, until she could have no idea where she was, and then they guided her out of the car and down a path. Rough beneath her feet. Slipping some. Still blindfolded. When they took off the mask, it was dark, totally dark, then someone turned on a flashlight, and there he was.

"There he was," I repeated softly, remembering the delicate, intelligent face I had seen in the photograph. Dr. V was remembering it, too, standing before me quiet and thoughtful, reliving the moment when she saw him. She gathered some strength, stepped forward, and laid her small hands on mine. "You should be happy, Mr. Morton. I have never seen anyone like that young man. Never. And now he's going to be free. He's going to be fine."

No, he's not, I thought. Because I'm not any damn Mr. Morton, and I'm getting closer. Because I'm a wolf and I'll find him, today, because Bridge said *if you can't find the man....* I offered Dr. Venezia-Karbach a weak, watery smile. "Is he all right, though? What kind of place is this they holding the man?"

"I don't know, really." She shook her head softly. "It was a room. I don't know. There was a generator of some kind, but it kept cutting out, and the lights would flicker on and off."

"So like a—like some kinda empty building?"

My mind turned. Sprinted out in different directions—warehouse district, abandoned homes, unfinished building projects. "What about all your things?" I gestured around the room—stethoscope, laryngoscope, tongue depressors, gauze. "What about all the doctor things?"

"Oh, no," she said. "No. My supplies I brought with me. There wasn't any . . . no, nothing like that."

In her mind, she was *there*. The place. Lair. Hideaway. I could see her seeing it. Smelling it. I leaned in.

"What is it?" I asked. Simple and quiet. "What?"

"There was . . ." She nodded. Her small bird eyes narrowed, remembering. "Kind of a noise, an odd noise. A whooshing. Like pipes. Like water flowing through pipes."

"Pipes?" I said. "So . . . a basement? Some sort of cellar, or—"

"Maybe. It might have been. I don't know. That's—I think that's what I know. Okay? I think that's all I can tell you."

The doctor was done. She was casting more and more anxious glances over her shoulder at the door, as if any moment the next patient would come in, or her nurse, or Father Barton himself, glaring with those pale eyes, floating a foot off the floor, leveling a finger at her, denouncing her as a betrayer of the Cause.

"Well, listen," I said. "I thank you so much. I really do. If I can just see his face . . ."

She nodded rapidly, said, "Yes, yes," and something in the rapidness of her nodding and the way she darted her lips in and out made me wonder if it wasn't just guilt she was feeling but *fear*. Who is this Barton, anyway? What kind of vengeful Old Testament father are we talking about here? I said thank you about a million times. Humbly I thanked her. Humbly I assured Dr. Venezia-Karbach that her confidence would not be betrayed. She smiled sadly, smoothed her lab coat, and put her face back on.

"Oh, actually, though," I said, when she was almost out the door, when she had almost escaped me. "I just have one more quick question, if that's all right."

"No, Mr. Morton, I'm sorry. I don't—"

"Please."

"No more questions."

"Ma'am? It's just—why did he need to *see* a doctor?"

*　　*　　*

I did test the leash one time. Very early on, I tested it. Years ago. I suppose I had convinced myself, staring at some hotel-room ceiling in an insomniac stupor, as I had lain unsleeping so many of those early nights, almost every night in the first year of it, that the whole thing was a hoax, a con. They had drugged me, put me in a thick opioid haze for two hours, then told me on waking about the tiny computer chip they'd injected in my nervous system, right where the spine touches the brain, that it would be singing out my location from there on out.

Ain't no way, I told myself. That shit's impossible, and I'm a fool to believe it. So I refused to believe it.

I remember it was the first time that Bridge put me on to a woman. The service name was Darling. I traced poor Darling to goddamn Idaho City, Idaho, and I was supposed to be staking out the home of a relative, a second cousin, I believe, and instead I shoplifted a change of clothes from a department store and boarded a bus to Oregon, with a vague notion of hitching north to Port Angeles, stowing away on the ferry to Victoria. But when I got off the bus in downtown Portland, what did I see but three men in dark suits drinking coffee. All three stood up at once, and I turned around and got back on the bus and went back to Idaho and finished that job and the one that came after it. Mr. Bridge never mentioned it. Never said, "How was your trip?" That was not his way.

The chip was no joke. No hoax. Everything is possible. Everything is real.

That woman Darling, in Idaho, she wasn't a woman. She was just a girl. She was all of twelve years old.

I remember them all.

18.

A curl of smoke was coming up out of my car. I could see it from across two lanes of 12th Street, between the spreading leafless arms of an elm tree and the bent trunk of a streetlamp. A tendril of smoke, rising from somewhere in the hood, rising and spreading and dissipating into the wan daylight like an exorcised spirit. I hustled across the street, thinking for one crazy second that something had happened inside the engine of the sweet little Altima— it had given out and burst into flames and now was sitting there smoldering.

But no, of course not. Halfway across the potholed street I slowed up. Cigarette smoke. That's all. Of course. Someone was leaning against the car on the opposite side, smoking a butt, waiting on me.

Had to be Maris. He'd done some digging, or Barton had; they'd pushed through my backstops and figured out that there was no Gentle in Carolina, no Dirkson at all. I looked up and down the street—was it too late to run? I looked for witnesses and hiding places. I was in the middle of the street. I willed myself some courage, willed myself a gun, imagined the heavy loose weight of a Colt in the front pocket of my overcoat, jostling against my hip like a deck of cards.

It was the girl, the white girl. Martha. She had a chopstick in her hair, holding it together. She looked hesitant, half hopeful.

I was so relieved I almost laughed. It was almost good to see her—and the kid, too, Lionel in a tracksuit a size or two too big, athletic stripes on top and bottom, plugged into his music, grooving his head back and forth like a snake, bouncing on his heels beside the car. He didn't see me coming, but Martha did, and she gave me a funny self-knowing wave and a cringing sort of smile. She was smoking one of those ugly little hand-rolled hipster cigarettes, "sourced" free-labor tobacco and all that.

"My goodness," I said. "How are you?"

"This is crazy," she said. "I know. I know this is crazy."

"What's crazy?"

"Well. Okay. So—I need to ask you a favor."

What could I say? What would Dirkson say? What did I *want* to say? I said sure. She pulled out a booster seat from the backseat of her boxy pink SA hatchback, which we left parked on Meridian Street. Away we went, Lionel settled in the backseat and Martha up front beside me, her fingers laced in her lap.

"Where are we headed?"

"Uh, this way, I guess," said Martha softly, and I went the way she pointed, straight south down Meridian Street.

"So," I said, and she smiled, bright but quick.

"So," she said, as if this was all perfectly normal, as if we did this every day. "You had a doctor's appointment?"

"Yes," I said. "I did."

"Is everything okay?"

"Oh, yes, thank you. Just fine." I was Dirkson. I had my glasses on. I held my hands at ten and two on the wheel. "Just a little thing. Slipped is all. Out last night working, and I just plumb slipped on the sidewalk and twisted my ankle. Not a big deal, but the folks in Jakarta, you know, any little thing . . . insurance and all . . ."

I was talking too much, polishing my stupid lie until it practically glowed. She'd stopped listening anyway. She gazed out the window. She had on cheap sunglasses, cat's eyes, which went perfectly, somehow, with the plastic chopstick in her hair. A vintage day dress, paisleys against midnight blue. Martha also had on this ring, a cheap little shopping-mall band of fake gold, and while I drove she was twisting it on and off, on and off, moving it restlessly from finger to finger, like she was running a shell game on herself. One thing I was used to seeing from young white people, it was confidence, an easy sense that the world belonged to them. This Martha, she had that, too—even now she was going through my glove compartment, examining my tapes, no big deal—but it was only a thin layer, only on the top. Underneath was all kinds of nervousness and fear.

"Do you mind?" said Martha, the tape already half pushed into the player.

"Not at all."

The Jackson 5 sang "Who's Lovin' You," MJ out front, his four older brothers doing tight, high harmony in the back.

I glanced at Martha, her head turned to look out the shotgun window, and I saw it again, the black box tatted on her neck, and below it a glimpse of cream-white skin and pale pink bra. I flushed, confused and obscurely angry. Lionel danced his head like a robot in the backseat. Storefronts rushed past the window. Medical supply; Oriental rugs; buildings available for lease.

"Okay," I said. "I guess at some point I'll need to know where it is we're going."

"Of course," she said. "Yeah."

Martha took a quick look at Lionel—tuned out, grooving to Michael, a world of his own—and launched in. "Okay, so what I need," she said, "is, like, like a—an escort, I guess. Like . . . just—a friend, I mean. I gotta do this errand, kind of meet this lady . . . it's—just this thing I gotta do. I thought she was gonna come up to the hotel, but now she said I need to come down to her."

Straitlaced Mr. Dirkson frowned a little bit. "Is this in relation to a health-care position?" and Martha said, "No, not exactly," while my mind clicked through possibilities. Drugs? Guns? Easy to imagine Martha, single mother in thrift-shop clothes, lugging around some wagon of debt she was trying to get shed of.

Martha still wasn't telling me where we were going; we were just going. I turned right on 16th Street. I stopped for a red at North Capitol.

"And I've been advised—God, Jesus, that sounds so fancy." Martha made a fancy voice, uptown lawyer, mock snooty. "I have been *advised* not to go by myself. You know, as a . . ." She looked over at me. The light turned green. "As a girl."

She didn't say *as a white girl,* but there it was with us in the car anyway. I nodded.

"But—so . . . you just . . . you're a helper. You're obviously one of the good guys. So I thought . . ."

I said nothing, and my silence I knew she would attribute to shyness or modesty when in fact I was muzzled by the horror of it, the dark, grieving irony of the idea that I would be a good person— that I would *obviously* be such a person. I blinked back to life and turned left on Dr. Martin Luther King Jr. Street. I had an idea already of where we were going. I could feel it coming. Michael came into the last chorus, soared right up into it like a little angel.

"I am not going to even offer to pay you. I have, like, zero dollars. But I could owe you. I'll pay you—maybe even later today. Maybe even after the meeting." She took a breath. She looked at me, plucky and anxious, over the rims of the cat's eyes. "So what do you think?"

The only logical answer was no. I was hot on my case. I was within sight of the finish line. I had Bridge breathing down my neck, I had old ghosts making howling circles in my mind.

"So?" I asked. "Where to?"

She had it on a piece of paper. She dug it out from the pocket of her jeans. She had the address on the silver foil of a gum wrapper. "Here. Uh. Tenth and Belmont."

I nodded. Yeah. I was already on my way. "Freedman Town."

I knew what it was like to get a person to do something and they're not sure why. To coerce. Give over some information; help you find an address. I did it all the days of my life. I didn't know what I was stumbling into here, doing some kind of downtown deal or maybe bringing money to some rough boys so they'd teach a lesson to an ex-boyfriend. None of that seemed likely, just from my read on this girl, but people have layers in them. People go down deep. They go all the way down.

We got to the bridge to Freedman Town, a shabby two-lane span running over the slow brown churn of the White River. I was glad to be running Martha Flowers's mysterious errand. All we do all day long is deal with our own problems, handle our shit some way or other. It felt nice, for a little while, to be dealing with someone else's shit instead of my own.

"Wow," said Martha. "God."

I drove carefully through the streets down here—you had to. Potholes wide as craters, rocks and bottles in the street. The blasted apocalyptic acreage of Freedman Town.

Lionel craned up in his booster seat and peered with wonder out the windows.

I'd been here before. Not to this Freedman Town, but to plenty of others. I've been all over the North, and every northern city has a Freedman Town. New York City's got a few, and Chicago's got more than a few. Baltimore, Washington. The manumitted have got to go somewhere, and the world doesn't give them a lot of options. The details are different—some of 'em are built on a high-rise model, bent towers clustered around courtyards, crammed to the gills with the poorest of the poor, living hard, the forgotten children of forgotten children. Some are like this one, blocks and blocks of small ramshackle homes, no sidewalks along narrow roads with the concrete worn and blasted through, the yards between the houses as weed-choked as vacant lots. Ivy growing in wild overlapping networks, engulfing the lower stories and sending menacing tendrils into upstairs windows. Gutters dangling or cracked, porches falling.

Martha, I could tell, had not been here before. Martha had never seen anything like it.

"Here," said Martha. "Will you just—can we just stop here?"

"Are you okay?"

"Yeah." She gnawed at her pinkie. We were a block, still, from the address she had given me. "Just give me one sec, I think."

Her anxiety was a living thing, thrumming in the air between us, traveling through the recycled air of the Altima. She fiddled with the nearer stem of her sunglasses, sort of snapping it along the side of her head. A kid rolled slowly past the car on a skateboard, balancing a bucket on his head, while another kid taunted him not to drop it—"Careful, boy . . . careful, now . . . nice and easy"—then brayed laughter. There was a woman pushing a stroller, somehow keeping it in motion though she was on the phone and smoking a cigarette; the two- or three-year-old in the stroller was playing happily with a closed bottle of soda. A knot of tough boys sat on a stoop, smoking and staring hard at the street—the real thing, what my friends in Mapleton–Fall Creek had been aspiring to. As we watched, a man approached at a shuffle, opened a shoe box to them, offering whatever was in it for sale, and they shooed him away like they were kings.

A big nasty dog, tall as a wolf, wandered zigzag from side to side, trailing its leash.

"You can't believe it," Martha said darkly. "You can't even fucking believe it."

"Watch your mouth, Mama."

"Sorry, bear." She reached into the backseat and patted her boy on the knee, but Lionel was off on his own trip, staring out the window, tapping his nose with his finger, like a kid concentrating on a math problem.

I didn't feel it anymore. I had long since stopped feeling it, that feeling you get coming into Freedman Town the first time, the surreal astonishment that such a place can exist. A not inconsiderable swath of a major city, in a wealthy industrialized country, in the twenty-first century, in such a grievous state of disrepair. An invisible city, floating like a dead island, in the wide water of civilization.

A police cruiser made its slow way along the avenue, windows rolled up and tinted. The siren was off but the light was on, slowly flashing red and blue, red and blue. Not going to any particular emergency, just rolling through. Someone had spray-painted on the hood THE POLICE IS THE PATROL.

"You know what?" said Martha. "Forget it."

"Forget what?"

"Just—let's forget it. I don't want to . . ." She looked back at Lionel, who was staring back at her. He had on his uneasy kid face, trying to read his mom, trying to figure out how serious this situation was.

The cop car had sharked past, turned right, and disappeared.

"All right," I said, thinking, and started the car. "Sure."

A knock at the driver's-side window, three knocks, bang bang bang. A massive midsection was filling up the window, blocking out the daylight. Outside Martha's window was another man, as big as the one on my side, who was now gesturing for me to roll down the window.

I didn't have my gun. I couldn't have brought it to my doctor's appointment. I could see it, imagine the size of it, in the room safe at the Capital City Crossroads. I buzzed down the window and squinted out. A gigantic black man in a golf visor, a leather jacket over a tight T-shirt, his face acne-pitted and moon large. He leaned into the car and talked across me, addressing Martha.

"You Wanda?"

"Yes," she said. She darted a glance at me—phony name—and said, "Do you work with Mrs. Walker?"

"Sure do," said the mountain of a man, his voice a heavy rumble. "She's my mama."

"Oh. Okay. Well, listen, will you just tell her I'm really sorry, but I actually was thinking forget it? I changed my mind. Okay?"

The dude in the golf visor looked amused. "Sure. Okay."

"So you'll tell her?"

"You can tell her." He yanked open my door, and the other big man, the same size and dressed identically to the first, opened Martha's. "C'mon, now," said the new one. The new giant's voice, not surprisingly, was the same distant-thunder bass. He had two chipped front teeth, the new brother — that was the only difference between them.

Martha nodded rapidly, sure, no problem, and licked her lips. "Hey, Jim?" she said, and put her hand on my knee. "Do you actually think you can stay here and keep an eye—"

"Uh-uh," said big man number 1. "Everybody comin'. Everybody out the car." He tugged open the back door and pointed at Lionel. "You, too, little man."

My manager way back in Chicago, at that Townes store where I worked, was a good-hearted black man named Derrick, and sometimes he would give me a ride home. Every time he drove me, we would be going south on Lake Shore and they'd come into view, the jumbled ugly towers of Freedman Town, and Derrick would shake his head and say, "I wish I understood. I wish I understood why they can't tear them places down. There has got to be something better we could do for those folks. Don't you think?"

"Of course" is what I said to Derrick, and I meant it.

Now I see things differently. It took me some time, but I know the secret now. Freedman Town serves a good purpose — not for the people who live there, Lord knows; people stuck there by poverty, by prejudice, by laws that keep them from moving or working. Freedman Town's purpose is for the rest of the world. The world that sits, like Martha, with dark glasses on, staring from a distance, scared but safe. Create a pen like that, give people no choice but to live like animals, and then people get to point at them and say *Will you look at those animals? That's what kind of people those people are.* And that idea drifts up and out of Freedman Town like chimney smoke, black gets to mean poor and poor to mean dangerous and all the words get murked together and become one dark idea, a cloud of smoke, the smokestack fumes drifting like filthy air across the rest of the nation.

*　　*　　*

We proceeded in a slow parade, one of Mrs. Walker's big boys in the front and the other in the back, the two of them escorting our strange family, herding us down the wide, rutted street, past graffitied doorways, past broken-down cars and plywood shanties, fire pits with smoke tendrils crawling up, raggedy hammocks strung between trees.

To look at him, Lionel gave no signs of being frightened—he bounced on the balls of his feet, looking every way at once. But about halfway down the block he grabbed my hand, and I held his, awkwardly at first, feeling his tiny fingers moving like curious animals inside my closed fist.

19.

"**Now, tell** me how I know you again, baby?"

"You don't," said Martha. "Not really. My friend Anika, she knows your grandson Wayne."

"Wayne in Gary?"

"No, ma'am. Wayne down in New Albany."

The woman seated regally at the end of the long dining room table snorted and held up a wagging finger. "Grandson? *Please,* baby. That boy Wayne ain't no kin to me. *Godson.* He my godson." She took a long drag of her skinny cigarette and ashed it out in the juice cup at her elbow. "He still down there?"

"He's in Louisville now, I think."

"Well, you keep well clear of him. He dumb. Dumb and small-minded, too. There's a difference, but he both. Stay clear."

"Okay, ma'am. I will. I'll do that."

"Stop calling me ma'am, baby," said the old lady. "Everybody call me Mama."

"Okay, then."

Martha smiled, barely, her face and her body rigid. She didn't call the woman Mama. She wasn't comfortable with that—she didn't seem comfortable with any of this. Her sunglasses were folded neatly beside her at the table, like she was playing cards and this is what she was ready to bet with, if she had to. The room was small and stuffed with greenery, potted plants and vases full of flowers, all miraculously thriving in the low-hanging choke of smoke from Mama's contraband Camels and the dope being enjoyed by her sons, who'd walked us up.

Mama Walker was middle-aged, but no telling how middle: somewhere north of forty-five and south of sixty. She'd been beautiful once and was beautiful now, in a way, an older lady's leathery beauty. She was dark-skinned, and her face was lined, especially at the edges of her mouth. Her eyes were alert and alive, glittering with awareness, darting every which way at once. Noticing everything.

"Them two are my babies," she said suddenly, swiveling to me, pointing with her smoke hand at the pair of men. "Twins. Believe that?"

I looked at them, and Mama's babies nodded in unison from the love seat, two giants side by side, a couple of defensive linemen five years out of the game, old musculature hidden deep within layers of fat. In the apartment's back room were a bunch of other kids, much younger, arrayed on and around a heavy sofa. Lionel, at Mama Walker's encouragement, had fitted himself down among them, become instantly absorbed in whatever cartoon garbage was playing on the plasma screen across from Mama's sofa.

Mama Walker stubbed out her Camel, pulled a new one.

"Misery sticks, I know. But I can't smoke them Indian things. I feel bad about it and all, but them things taste like cow shit. So how old are you, baby?" The riff on slavery smokes was directed to me; the question was for Martha.

"Thirty-two."

"Thirty-two. Thirty-two." She looked at Martha carefully, critically, like a fine piece of jewelry. "Tricky age for us women, ain't it?"

"Yeah. Sure."

"Different for white girls, I guess."

Martha shrugged uncomfortably. "I guess."

"Everything different for white girls."

I wondered again what the hell was going on here. I wondered, too, how I had managed to get myself implanted in it.

"And just so I'm straight on it," said Mama, tilting her long head toward the back room, toward Lionel on the sofa. "Little man's yours."

"He is," said Martha, looking yearningly toward the boy. "That's right."

Mama nodded slowly. She was looking at the kid, judging his complexion, casting as keen an appraising eye over the boy's color as I had over Jackdaw's—as I had over every runner I'd ever gone after. Mama Walker, I decided without thinking about it, without wanting to think about it, was moderate pine, red tone, number 211 or 212.

"So you what?" Mama Walker turned her eyes on me. "You Daddy?"

"No, ma'am," I said quietly, and Martha rushed in: "He's just a friend."

"Just a friend," she said, her voice low and easy, almost a whisper. "Just a friend." She leaned forward, blew smoke out of the side of her mouth, and patted me on the knee. "Nice to meet you, Just-a-Friend."

The Walker boys, over by the door, were sharing a one-hitter, silently trading hits.

"So where *is* Daddy?"

"Well . . ." Martha gave her head a tiny shake. "I don't want to talk about that."

"You don't?" Mama's smile fell away. "And why not?"

"I really just want to uh, to, you know—to cover our business."

"Oh, all right," said Mama Walker. "Of course."

There was the click-click of a lighter by the door, and I glanced over at the sons: son number 2 refiring the skinny pipe, son number 1 staring into space. A cartoon punch line blared from the television, one animated electric eel zinging another one, and the kids all roared. Lionel laughed along with them, perfectly at ease.

"But you know what, I *do* want to talk about it, just for a second. You don't mind, do you?" She stared at Martha. "How about I just guess what happened to him?"

"Well..." Martha wrung her hands together. Her face was agonized. "I guess."

"I'mma guess white men killed him." Mama Walker said this without trouble, almost cheerfully. "'Cause of you. That it? Am I close on that?"

Martha didn't answer, but Mama said, "I thought so," as if she had. "That's how they do, you know. You gotta be careful. North or no north, some things you just gotta be careful about. White man don't play, you know? Right, Just-a-Friend?"

"Right," I said.

"I'll give you a little example, okay? All this shit hole here?" She pointed outside, at the trash-strewn street. "This all used to be green. Verdant. That the word, Marv?"

"Yes, Mama," said one of her sons, in his thick voice.

Martha suddenly stood up. "I am so sorry that we bothered you," she said, her voice thick with tears. "Hey, Lionel, honey?"

Lionel looked over from the couch, but meanwhile one of the big Walker boys had gotten up, too—not Marv, the other one. "Have a seat, little girl," he said. "Mama talking."

Martha sat. Lionel's head swiveled back around to the screen. Mama gave no sign of having been interrupted. "It was verdant down here, back in the day. That's what they say. I'm talking 'bout before I was born, understand. Before my mama was and hers was. There was a stream here. Little creek. I got a map, somewhere, somewhere in here, but you can see it, too, you go hunting through the dog shit and the broken glass out there, you can see, like, the traces of it, where it ran once, all those years ago. But see, the white men who were planning out the city, they didn't like it where it was. The little river. So they just"—she made a quick gesture with her hands, sweeping the air—"ran it under the ground. Built right over it. You understand? You see?"

She waited. She wanted an answer. Martha whispered, "Yes." I took off my glasses and wiped them on my shirt. Dope smoke wafted over from the love seat.

"They sent that little river underground, and they built their fucking ugly city over it. *That's* how they do. Anything they don't care for, anything that does not please, they use it up or they kill it or bury it, and they never think of it again. You see?"

Martha's eyes were shut now. "I see."

"So that's what they did—open your eyes, sweetheart. Open." Martha obeyed. "That's what they did to your boy's father. Them. White people."

"I'm sorry." Martha closed her eyes. She was sorry she'd come here. She was sorry she was white. But there was no undoing either of those things. "I just need some help."

"Yeah. No shit, baby. Everybody come here need help. Everybody in the *world* need some kinda help, right? Ain't that right, Just-a-Friend?"

For once Jim Dirkson and I were all synced up, my alias and I equally perplexed. I smiled carefully for both of us. "That's right."

"Question being for you, then, okay, what kind of help you need? I'm looking at you, pretty white girl. Pretty white girl don't come downtown to get something up her nose." Martha nodded, trembling a little, her hands fussing at the hair at the nape of her neck. "Pretty white girl don't come downtown to get something in her arm. Sure as fuck don't need passing papers. Don't need pussy. Or . . ." She raised her eyebrows, and Martha shook her head quickly. "No. So pretty white girl ain't here to get fucked or get high or get free. So what she need?"

I wished I knew Martha well enough to take her hand; to pat her knee reassuringly under the table. I couldn't do it—I didn't really know her at all was the thing. I was a passenger.

"It's gotta be money that baby needs. Right, boys?" The Walker brothers nodded in unison, right on cue. It was all performance; this was part of the performance, every time. "So the question is— how much money does baby need?"

Martha placed her hands flat on the table, to steady herself. Past her, out the window, I caught a glimpse of movement—the cop car was rolling past again, slow lights flashing.

"Twenty-nine thousand, five hundred."

Mama's thin-line eyebrows arched higher. "Twenty-nine thousand, five hundred dollars?"

Martha nodded, the tiniest mouse motion of a nod. Mama raised her voice, addressed the boys like they were a studio audience. "Twenty-nine thousand, five hundred. Can you all believe that?"

They could not; they shook their heads in shared astonishment, real slow, back and forth. I couldn't quite believe it, either. I tilted my head to one side, looking with fresh eyes at this girl—this Martha, or Wanda, or whatever her name might have been. Mama leaned back and pulled out a new long Camel.

"Twenty-nine thousand, five hundred," she said, lighting her cigarette. "That number is very—what is the word I want, Elton?"

"Specific," said Elton through a mouthful of smoke. Elton was the one with the knocked teeth.

"That's a lot of dollars." Mama looked at me. "Ain't that a lot of dollars, Just-a-Friend?"

"Yes," I said. "I guess so."

"Question being, baby—you white. What about you get a job?"

"Well, I . . ." Martha looked down, then away, pained. "I'm working on it. I was actually just at this job fair thing, at the convention center, that's what I was doing all week . . ." She looked at me for confirmation, and I nodded, although of course I had no idea what she'd been doing all week. Of course I knew nothing about her. "I'm trained as a medical assistant."

"Medical assistant." Mama shook her head and smoked and clucked.

"Yeah. And—and a couple other things. I work. I do. I have money. It's just—not enough. I have my son, you know. I have bills. I can't hardly save nothing."

"Times is tough," said Mama Walker, waving faintly at the abandoned house visible through the kitchen window. "Times is real tough. And we still haven't heard what you need it for, anyway, this very specific twenty-nine thousand, five hundred dollars."

Martha answered right away. "I can't tell you."

"You can't tell me?" Mama Walker's eyes glittered. "She can't tell me! Marvin, baby, you hear that? It's a secret!"

"Look—come on, ma'am. I mean, Mrs. Walker." Martha steeled herself, looked the older woman straight in the eye. "Is it going to be possible to borrow the money or not? It doesn't have to be the whole twenty-nine five, okay? Whatever you can do, I will take. And I can pay it back. With interest."

"Goddamn right you will!" said Mama Walker. She stood up, and a long circle of ash fell from her smoke down to the table. "Obviously you would fucking pay interest. This isn't fucking Goodwill. I'm not running some charity shop for desperate white girls."

"Sorry," said Martha. "Sorry." More apologizing. I had known this girl Martha for three days and all I'd seen her do is say she was sorry. Abashed before fussy white men and flinty black women alike.

"All right, well, listen, baby," said Mama Walker, and Martha smiled hopefully, but it was over. Mama wasn't sitting down again. The boys had shifted their weight. There was a change in temperature, and I knew what it was—I had sat in rooms like this: I had observed negotiations. Gun runners, bent cops, border bribers, slave traders, snatchers. I could tell a no-go when I was sitting with one at the table.

"Listen to me very carefully: when I give out money, I give it on return. I give it on terms."

"I know," said Martha. "I said—"

"I know—you're going to pay it back with interest. Well, how I guarantee that, baby? You won't tell me what you want it for; I barely know how I know you. You come in here, a black boyfriend, a black son, like I might get mixed up, start thinking you something you not. Like I'm gonna trust you then."

"But I—I would promise! You would have my word on it!"

Mama Walker didn't even bother to answer that. She stubbed out her cigarette with hard meaning, and the boys at the door opened it. At last Martha saw that this wasn't happening, and immediately she switched modes; immediately she was ready to get out, out of Freedman Town, as fast as feet could go. "Lionel," she called, and when he didn't come at once, captivated by the cartoon show, climaxing in a blur of flash and sound, she said it again, sharp— "Lionel!"—and he bounced over.

"Real nice to meet you," said Mama Walker. "Real nice to meet all of you."

The big men stepped aside, then Mama Walker said—so low you almost couldn't hear her—"I'll give you the money you give me the boy."

"What?" said Martha. I pulled her out by the arm. "What did you say?"

I pulled her down the stairs. "What did she say?"

I hustled her and her child along the block, her eyes wild. I stuffed her in the car. I drove her away.

20.

The TV was on at the Fountain Diner. It played with the sound off, attached to the end of a jointed mechanical arm jutting out over the counter. Everybody in the place was watching or half watching the hearings, the special Saturday session of the Senate finance committee: customers with eyes locked on the screen, ignoring their pancakes, busboys rubbing the same spot of dirty table over and over. Our waitress set down our plates in the wrong spots, gazing up at the TV. Batlisch, unflappable, staring back at her tormentors. Her thumb tucked between forefinger and middle finger, her eyes narrowed and stern, and the crawl below the screen: "If the question, Senator, is do I think that my opinions . . . or my, my ideology, as you put it, although I don't think that's necessarily . . . no, excuse me. If I may finish? If the question is, do those ideas put me outside the mainstream of American opinion, then I think the answer is no. I think the answer is a resounding no."

The busboy at the next table, a young guy, shaved bald, he liked that answer. He nodded to himself with satisfaction and walked back toward the kitchen, smiling.

Even Lionel, seated across from me at our booth, was rapt: maybe not totally understanding, but thinking somehow, as everybody thought, that this was some big deal. Some kind of watershed moment, as they like to call them. He was coloring on the back of the menu, but he kept stopping, staring for a beat or two at the tough white lady on the screen. I stared at the TV, too, trying to gin up some feeling of excitement, trying to feel what the busboy was feeling, the cooks. Let's say she did get confirmed. Maybe she does what she says—maybe she brings new vigor to the prosecution of financial firms that trade in blood money. But the firms would find ways around it. The Southern Regional Lobbying Association would send in their K Street shock troops, white papers in hand, and the floors of Congress would ring with the old refrains of popular sovereignty and imperishable tradition. Nothing would change.

Martha was the only person in the place ignoring the TV. She sat very still, staring straight ahead, steam rising off the cup of coffee that was all she ordered.

"You all right?" I said, and she exhaled.

"I guess so." She shook her head. Her hair had fallen down. The chopstick that had pinned it all together had disappeared, maybe into her cavernous purse, maybe onto Mama Walker's floor. "I mean, no. This is weird. I dragged you into this thing, and now— I mean, it's just weird. Aren't you even gonna ask?"

"Ask what?"

"Are you serious?" Martha peered at me, at Jim Dirkson, trying to figure out this good, gentle businessman, too polite or too dense for this universe. "About twenty-nine thousand, five hundred dollars."

"Oh," I said. "Sure. Well, I guess I did wonder."

"I'll bet."

She'd wanted lunch, asked for us to go, and here she was not eating. She'd picked the restaurant, too, and I was keenly conscious the whole time we sat there of Officer Willie Cook. It was his favorite spot, after all, and right there was the table where he'd been seated with his white partner, I could see it from where we were sitting, and it was having an effect on me. I felt jittery and unsafe. I kept seeing that overfriendly smile, that knowing expression of his. While Martha sat and stared into whatever dark vistas her life gave her to stare at, I wondered how I might explain to Officer Cook what I was doing here, what bereft, wifeless Jim Dirkson was doing enjoying lunch with his new white ladyfriend—and the other way around, of course. "Oh, yes, Martha, this is Officer Cook—he's a police officer I know and also an agent of the Airlines..."

On television, Donatella Batlisch finished a point—"considering each issue on its merits, absent any kind of prejudice"—and lifted her water and sipped it and set it down again. C-SPAN then turned the camera on a pair of richly jowled southern senators huddled together, whispering with grave expressions, conscious of the cameras.

What the hell was I doing, anyway? I was in the middle of a case. I had a man I had to find. I had Bridge biting at my heels.

"Honey?" said Martha. Lionel had put his head down on the table. He was crying. "Baby—baby, *what?*"

It was just the maze, though. He'd been trying to work the maze on the back of the menu, a sea-creature theme, and he couldn't crack the fucker, and it was making him weep. This was right— this was good. With all that was happening in his mama's world, all that was happening in the whole world, he was stymied by the maze. A baby octopus, trying to find the way home to his cave.

I leaned across the table and pointed, and he started, hesitated. I put my finger beside his and showed him.

"Oh," he said. "Duh."

"This is a tricky one," I said. "Just take your time, now. Take your time."

He went slowly, cautiously, started down a path following the line I proposed, and wound his way out. He circled where it said END a couple times, and I said, "There you go," and we took a look at each other for a second or two.

"What do you say, Lionel?"

"Thanks, Mr. Jim."

"Well, you're very welcome."

There was no question that I was feeling something toward Martha and her son, some softening. But there was a sense of danger, too, a caution flag whipping way in the back of my mind. I could have gotten up anytime, said it was nice to meet y'all, and gotten back to work. What was I *doing?*

"There is this man I met," said Martha, looking through me—past me.

"What, now?"

"A man in Ohio. Steubenville." She said the town name one syllable at a time, as though it were make-believe. "Steubenville. I didn't meet him. I met him on the Internet."

Her voice was distant, quiet, but full of force. She needed to be telling this to me—to someone. The whole rest of the restaurant was watching TV. Lionel was back in Lionel world, drawing a castle in a blank space on the menu.

"He said that for twenty-nine thousand, five hundred dollars, this guy, he could . . . well." She took a deep breath, looked at me head-on. "So apparently there's a . . . like a, a database."

"A—what, now?"

But I knew immediately. Immediately, much had become clear.

"A database. It says where they all are." She leaned across the table. She was fidgeting with her fingers, twisting them together. "All the slaves, you know? And this guy says if I pay him, he can—he can get into that for me."

"Huh," I said, soft and uncertain, as if I didn't know precisely what she was talking about.

The database was TorchLight, a comprehensive listing of every person who is or who has ever been held by any of the plantations, factories, mines, "working prisons," home systems, oil rigs, all the endless variety of places where Persons Bound to Labor are bound. All slaveholding corporations and individuals are obligated under the laws of their various states to report to TorchLight every purchase or sale or escape, every birth and every death, every injury resulting in a scar. Every piece of data to be stored and cataloged.

All the information crucial to the southern man-owning class—those with the vested interest in the health, current value, and projected depreciated value of their workforce.

I was profoundly skeptical of Martha's mysterious database hacker from Steubenville. I had tried over the years, on various assignments, to find my way into the TorchLight database. It would have been handy for all kinds of reasons. But TorchLight was protected by law, protected by internal security, protected by proprietary software. You damn near had to be sitting at a computer in some whiphand's back office to open the thing up.

"But who——" I started, and Martha turned her gaze very quickly to her son, then back to me, and even old Jim Dirkson understood. And just at that moment, of course, the lady came, my sandwich and the boy's pancake platter and the carafe to refill Martha's coffee. Martha said "Hey, Liney? You want to hear something crazy?"

"What?" Lionel looked up. "What's crazy?"

"You want to listen to music while you're eating?" She dug out from her pocketbook a pair of big headphones, and she plugged him in to some sort of thin handheld device, no bigger than a slice of bread, one of the marvelous new Japanese imports——her sister had gotten it for him for his birthday. When he was inside the cocoon, when I was eating, she told me about his father.

"His name was Samson. Sam."

"That's an unusual, uh, what do they call it? An unusual service name."

Martha's eyes flashed darkly. "That wasn't his service name. He had one, but we don't need to talk about it. He wouldn't have—— he doesn't like to talk about it. His name was Sam, okay? Sammy, sometimes. He had been on a shrimp boat."

"Louisiana?"

"Alabama. Bayou La Batre."

I had no experience of shrimp-boat slavery, only the stories: hot work, sweat work, the boiling sea, and the roll of the waves.

"There was some kind of crazy rescue," Martha said. "The Mexicans. With the boats. I forget what they call them."

"*Los emprendedores,* I think," I said as if I didn't know for sure. As if I didn't have in my head a catalog of every kind of South American or Central American or Canadian partisans, all the alien freelancers. There had been a movie called *Los Emprendedores,* actually, and I happened to have seen it—it came out during my Chicago years, and I snuck into a theater on Halsted Street and watched it twice in a row. Edward James Olmos as the pirate jefe, Denzel Washington as the stoic peeb. James Woods, maybe, someone like that, as the noble but conflicted Coast Guard captain running them down. There's a famous scene at the end, the two exiles leaping overboard, choosing to face the sharks.

Martha told me that Samson had been a tackle-box rescue, belowdecks, tumbled by waves, washed up in Jacksonville, fetched up somehow in New Albany, where she had been living at the time, as arbitrary a locale for him as it had been for her.

A UPS driver, a thick-armed white man who delivered to the outpatient clinic where Martha was working, had whispered to her after work one day: *We're tryna get help together for this boy. Can you help?* "I thought he was hitting on me," Martha remembered. "The UPS guy!" She went to the meeting, though, and there was this boy—this man. With all the marks of his journey: fingers blistered from the mast, his back a mass of half-healed scars. One eye burned out from six sun-bright weeks at sea.

"He was so beautiful," she said quietly. "I don't know what I was expecting. I didn't know what to expect. Some, like, skinny, ignorant, bald...thing. Like, not a human. Like a monster or something. But he was..." She shivered a little, a shiver of memory, a shiver of awe. "He was beautiful."

"Did you know?" I said softly. "It is illegal for peebs to be shaved bald."

"Oh?" Absent. Lost in memory.

"Yeah. State law. All four. Without hair, sometimes, it's hard to tell who is black and who is white."

"Oh."

She turned and looked at her son, who was ignoring his pancakes, dancing back and forth with the headphones on. She mouthed to him: "Eat, honey. You gotta eat."

He gave her a thumbs-up, kept on grooving.

Martha and Samson fell in love, she and the runaway. It's so cheesy, she told me now. It's so stupid. But it wasn't even love, she said. It was: whatever is next up from love.

"I mean, just, straight up. Hard-core. Love, love, love. Have you ever been in love?"

Castle. Big eyes in the dark, his long arm thrown across my chest. My brother.

And Alix. One woman. In Chicago, during the good years. Alix. A stock girl at Townes Stores. Complicated, gorgeous black woman, fierce and political and romantic. I never told her the truth about me. Never even came close.

"No," I said. Jim Dirkson was a lifelong bachelor. A mama's boy. "Not really. Nothing to speak of."

Martha's coffee was cold. On TV, the hearings were on a break. Pundits were huffing at each other in a studio, the DC skyline behind them.

Dirkson was listening to Martha with warmth and kindness, his head tilted and his eyes wet with empathy, and I was listening, too, in there under Dirkson, alert and anxious, my heart beating rabbit fast. Waiting for Officer Cook to come in and take his favorite seat, waiting—absurdly—to spot Mr. Bridge in the spectators' gallery at the Batlisch hearing, although why would he be there? And how would I know his face?

While I listened attentively to the story of Samson's recapture— how a very clever hidey-hole had been constructed for him above a public men's restroom, how Martha and the UPS man and the UPS man's roommate were so, so, so careful to bring Samson food without being seen, how they worked with utter discretion to find a connecting flight—I thought of the faceless man who had been working the file. A man in a New Albany hotel room, listening to phone conversations on headphones, tracking data points from satellite software, a man with no face but my same heart.

"And . . ." I had to clear my throat. "What happened to him?"

Martha glanced at Lionel before she answered, but he was eating in earnest now, bobbing his head while he shoveled in mouthfuls of pancakes. "I was at the clinic; I was working, you know."

I could see how this killed her, that she had been at work. She'd been spending every extra moment with Samson, but this wasn't an extra moment. She was at work, and the UPS man called, talking fast, crying on the phone: there was this van, this white van, and they were dragging him . . .

I put my hand on her hand.

"Oh, God," I said. "Oh, Lord."

It is a very specific skill, pretending to be okay. Pretending to behave as one ought to in a particular situation, leaning forward, giving a small smile of earnest empathy, hiding, meanwhile, a storm of terrible feeling, patting the hand of a friend. "I'm terribly sorry."

"Not your fault."

No, not mine, I thought. Not mine personally.

And meanwhile, all the while, my mind was alive. I could not stop it. I was thinking about one or maybe two things I had noticed during the last three days. Thinking about Mama Walker's apartment, what Dr. V had said about water. Retracing my steps. The whole time she was telling her story, there I was, I was working my case. I was in my world.

Lionel screamed—"Ah!"—and I jumped. Martha shrieked, turned to him. "Ah!" he said again, but he was laughing and laughing, pounding the table. They had used strips of bacon and two strawberries to build a smile and eyes on Lionel's pancakes, and he was lifting the features up one by one, de-facing the pancake man. "Ah! My face!"

"Come on, honey," said Martha, halfhearted, tender. "Be good . . ."

Lionel ate at last and, having eaten, fell promptly asleep in the car, smudges of maple syrup on both his cheeks. I drove us back to Martha's car and unbuckled the boy, lifting him up carefully so as not to wake him. Sometimes it's possible, just barely possible, to imagine a version of this world different from the existing one, a world in which there is true justice, heroic honesty, a clear perception possessed by each individual about how to treat all the others. Sometimes I swear I could see it, glittering in the pavement, glowing between the words in a stranger's sentence, a green, impossible vision—the world as it was meant to be, like a mist around the world as it is.

The real world was a trap, though, and I couldn't escape it. I knew this, and because I knew this I knew where Jackdaw was. I had worked it out. Not on purpose, but that's how it happens a lot of times—my mind does the work while I'm busy with something else.

I'd always known I would crack it, because I always do, and I had.

"Jimmy?"

I don't know where the nickname came from. Lionel's face had appeared at the driver's-side window, and he was looking right in at me, concerned, peering at my face as if through aquarium glass. "Are you okay?"

I guess maybe I had been moaning or something. I don't know what all I was doing, but I was doing something. But he said it, like, three more times, instead of good-bye, suddenly racked with anxiety: "Are you okay? Are you okay? Are you okay?"

21.

The rain had started. Fat dark drops, relentless out of a dark sky. I watched it come down from the balcony of the room.

It would have been nice to be able to say *Sorry, boss, no idea.* I can't crack it. Move me on, I guess, or make good on your threat and send a van to pack me up and haul my ass back home to Bell's.

But I knew. Goddamn me, I did.

The photograph was locked away with the rest of the file, but I could see it clear as looking at it: the delicate face, bemused expression, grief-stricken, scared. Oh, Jackdaw; oh, son; oh, poor lonely boy.

The rain was rushing down outside. Making up for all its timidity and teasing over the last few days. Coming down in sheets, in crashing torrents, pounding down onto the parking lot outside. Thunder rippled in a distant corner of the sky.

I took out my cell phone and took off Jim Dirkson's glasses and folded them arm over arm and put them away, then I settled on the edge of the bed, holding my phone between my hands. One phone call.

The rain was a wall of gray.

This case had been building up in me, pushing against the barricades like rushing water, not only the case but the town, the girl, the memories, all these red-and-black memories, crashing in and pushing in on me since I got here, too. And why were these visions returning now, my old story flashing back to life, coming down out of the gray Indiana sky? Why now? Why—

I told myself I didn't know, but I did; I had some inkling. I had some idea.

And now all of it would be over. One call to Maryland. Just make the fucking call.

I stood up. The phone was a hard flat square in my hand, a dislocated thing, an alien artifact. It was heavy as a ship's anchor; it was a barb sunk into the meat of my palm. I imagined what it would feel like to open one of those balcony doors and hurl the thin object out into the rain-flooded parking lot. I imagined it borne away on a rivulet, taken down to the White River, and ending up in the depths of some sewer, some sea. I imagined myself lying on my back, my arms and legs splayed out, carried by the furious current from the blacktop parking lot to the ugliness of 86th Street, making no resistance, until some fierce roll of water turned me over, took me under, swallowed me whole.

What happened when I called would all be according to procedure, specific steps dictated by statute. I would give my considered opinion as to the whereabouts of the missing man, based on the evidence I had accumulated, and then I in the field and Bridge at his desk would collaborate on a plan of capture. Bridge's office would file notice with his superiors down the hall in Gaithersburg, and when I was directed to do so I would take a field position, and Bridge would initiate the plan we'd agreed upon.

The swarm of white vans, the whoop of sirens, the truncheon and the Taser; then a fugitive court, a commissioner, a court-appointed attorney, a comparison of the runner's features with the features enumerated by the complainant, the fingerprints run against the fingerprints on file.

I found that I had pressed the button. The phone was ringing. I was making the call I had made already a thousand times in my career.

(And see what I do? *A thousand times in my career,* as if the actual number is lost in the blur of memory. I had made the call, before that day, 209 times. Some of those times I had sent a text message. But my conscience was stained with 209 positive identifications.)

The phone rang in my ear while it rang in Gaithersburg.

I was ready for it to be over, and it was over. I knew where the man was, and fuck Barton and fuck Cook and fuck Dr. Venezia-Karbach: I was ready. The words were poised on my tongue, ready to be said: It is all done. It is all set.

"Marshals Service. This is Bridge's office."

It was a woman's voice, bright and cheerful. It was Janice. Bridge's assistant. When she answered it meant he was out in the field. In the field or in a meeting.

Opportunity. It was Castle. Castle whispering in the dark. *Opportunity.*

Janice, patient, cheerful: "Hello?"

"Yes," I said. "Hello." There was no voice I could have done better. Cold as steel, flat as dirt ground, a smoky whisper of a southern accent. "It's me."

The rain lashed against the flimsy balcony doors, and they rattled in their grooves. My number would have come up blank—a field number—but so, too, I suspected, would Mr. Bridge's own cellphone number, blank, masked, agent-to-base communication, the same as mine. From Janice's POV, a blank is a blank. It was a wild risk to try out such an assumption in these circumstances. This was just one of many risks I was taking, about to take.

"Well, my goodness. Are you calling from your meeting?" Janice had a little southern accent of her own, a late-modern southern accent, more Atlanta than Little Rock. I put her in her late twenties. Red lipstick, sensible shoes. A dog at home, something cute and loyal.

"Yes," I said carefully. "That's right. Still here."

"And are you checking up on me, sir?"

Janice's tone was sugary, chipper, borderline flirtatious. In response I tried out a noise, something I had never heard performed but imagined must exist, a matching of tone with tone: I chuckled. A gruff Bridge-style chuckle.

"No, my dear. I am not checking up on you."

"Well, sir, maybe you *should* be."

I wondered if he ever called her Jan. I wondered if she called him Lou. I wondered if Lou saw Jan at the office Christmas party. I wondered if he brought his wife, sipped eggnog, made toasts, got tipsy, took a cab home, coached soccer, saved for college, took the minivan to the minivan place when the brakes were squealing. I wondered about the whole normal human world.

"What is it I can do for you, sir?"

What *could* she do for me? Having come this far, what happened now? I focused on the voice, the manner, the best way to get what I needed rather than thinking about what I was doing and why. Had I stopped to think, I might have asked myself the very logical question: Was I out of my goddamn mind?

What was I hoping to get, giving Janice that cold, slow, mild accent, I was not yet entirely sure, nor did I know why I'd done it.

Because of a dagger on a file? Because of some sloppy grammar? Because of an unusual pattern of fact?

It was none of those. I had seen messy files before. I had seen strange facts in cases before, and sometimes they had been reconciled and other times not. What was different this time, what had driven me to my unusual action, was Bridge's voice. The way he had sounded in our last call, tight and tense as a bent wire. His voice on the phone at 9:36, calling early for the first time ever.

My hand drummed on the desk, as my hands were always doing.

"I just had a quick question for you. About the case." I had dropped back into an all-business tone: *Fun time is over, Janice.*

"And which case is that?"

My mind reeled momentarily. How many cases? How many runners? How many Jackdaws? How many of me?

I gave her the case number, and she said, "What?"

I gave it to her again. I read it slow, digit by digit, and she repeated it back and said she was sorry but she just did *not* know which case I was referring to. "That number is just not coming up."

"The boy," I started, and almost gave the name, then I stopped. I held my breath. *That number is just not coming up.*

"Should I ask Marlena?"

"No—no, that's not . . . forget it. Forget I called."

I didn't smoke or pace around in tight circles. I didn't even think, really. I hung up the phone and went onto the balcony and stood and listened to the distant howl of sirens while the rain blew around me in curtains. It was weird how calming it was, how it gave me this—I won't say peace, not peace, exactly, but a peaceful sense of the irreversible. I was a stone that was falling. I had jumped, and there was no way to jump back.

That number is just not coming up, she said. *Not coming up.*

The thing is, there *had* to be a file. If there was a runner, there was a file. The service didn't freelance. That's how it worked, by custom and by law. Plantation loses someone, they file with a local magistrate who issues a transcript and requests the participation of federal law enforcement. It's the judge's chambers that notifies the marshals. That's how it works—that's how it's been working since 1787.

There had to be a file, but there was no file.

Mr. Bridge knew facts I didn't know; he always did. That's how it worked. But I knew with a sudden certainty that behind every fact of this case there was an unknown fact, felt but not seen, like a kidnapper with his rough arm wrapped around a victim's neck.

Now I could feel it, I could feel the storm rain slick and warm against my skin, and *now* my heart began to race, *now* it began to slam, now the adrenaline was galloping along in my veins.

An official case had never been opened. No home-state judge had issued a transcript certifying the claimant's description. No slave commissioner in the Southern District of Indiana had been put on alert. There was no real hunt. There was no case. There was only a file.

If the marshals weren't hunting Jackdaw so he could be returned—if *we* weren't hunting him so he could be returned—then why were we hunting him? What would happen to Jackdaw when we found him?

That was the easiest question to answer.

* * *

I was a monster, but way down underneath I was good. Wasn't I? Wasn't I good? Didn't I have some good part of me, buried deep underground, beneath Jim Dirkson and Kenny Morton and Albie the gardener and whoever and whatever else I was? I was good below it. I was, and I am. Good underground. In the buried parts of me are good things.

A still picture, me and Castle, whispering joy, telling stories, cabin by the northernmost fence, making plans, whispering quiet crazy hopeful.

I started moving quickly. I toweled off the rain I'd let fall onto my head and my face. While the computer was turning on I changed my shirt, then I spent five minutes on basic research, old-fashioned digging, three paragraphs of history, ten minutes of tracing lines on the map with my finger.

Then I gathered up my flashlight and what all else I thought I might need. Bridge wouldn't be long in knowing what I had done. I could almost hear the stop-start conversation, Bridge and Janice, Jan and Lou: hey, I went ahead and asked Marlena about it for you after all, and . . . asked her what . . . what . . .

As soon as I was ready to go, I got going. I knew where Jackdaw was, and I knew I better get down to him soon.

22.

By the time I got back to Slim's roadside fiefdom the storm had spent itself and the clouds had cleared away, but somewhere in there it had become nighttime. Darkness giving way to another kind of darkness. The pale face of the moon, a scattering of stars.

The grocery store was closed up and shuttered, and the body shop, too. All right by me. I parked across the street and hustled across the parking lot in the gloom, walked swiftly under the copper arch and down the shadowy little lane, head down, heart beating, man on a mission, going to the creek.

I had barely noticed it before. And if I did, I guess I figured it was drainage: a hole in the foot of a small hill, just barely visible between and behind the cluster of motor homes, dribbling over-run out into the shallow brown creek that wound behind the trailer park.

I moved swiftly past the tin-can palaces with their tribal flags, ignoring the sure, strong sense I had of dozens of eyes watching me, small beady eyes in pink piggy faces, peering from behind slat blinds, staring at my dark body moving unfamiliar and un-welcome through their cloister. Any one of those pigs could come out with a shotgun, and I wondered what I would do, but no one did.

I cleared the trailer park and passed a jumble of picnic benches and playground equipment and stepped carefully down the slope of the ravine and swung the heavy beam of my flashlight along the creek. Now it was clear, with the water swollen by the rains, the direction the brown water was flowing. The black mouth in the base of the shallow hill was an entrance, not an exit. This low little trickle of mud water was a kind of rivulet, a poor cousin of a creek, and this spot behind the motor court is where some long-ago engineer had diverted it.

This creek was called Pogue's Run. I'd found it on the map. I'd looked up the story. This small waterway was discovered at the turn of the century — the eighteenth turning into the nineteenth — discovered and named and recorded, penciled in on early maps, when the city was not yet a city — when it was a gathering of huts, a stopping place on the way to other places. The small river was inconvenient for the city fathers and the grid they'd drawn. So they did just as Mama Walker said: they ran it underground.

I walked up to the creek, my shoe heels making slippy track marks in the muck.

Mr. Maris had never, after all, discovered he was being traced. He'd never found Jim Dirkson's clunky butterfly knife in his pocket and tossed it overboard. He'd gone down to the creek, that's all. Disappeared into a tunnel. He'd gone underground.

The water in the creek was shallow, but it was rushing, pulsing a little as it rose with the rain. I walked slowly, picking out individual rocks to stand on, till I got to the mouth of the tunnel. There I got down on all fours, feeling the creek water rush around me, swallowing my hands up to the wrists and surging around my knees and feet, and looked with narrowed eyes up that infinite darkness of pipe. A cold, wet animal smell breathed back out at me.

There was nothing left to do, right? This was it.

I shivered, fighting off a wave and then another wave of memory. They called it the shed, but it was more like a chamber. An underground compartment. More like a coffin, really, is what it was, concrete and narrow. Four hours in there for hygiene violations on the kill floor. Six hours for spillage. Overnight for Thoughts Against Good Work. Every hour on the hour a Franklin would crack the lid, shine the light in your eyes, listen for your breathing, close the lid again.

There was nothing to be done. This was it. I leaned forward and hunched my shoulders together, pushed the upper part of my body carefully forward, as a circus performer gingerly places his head into the lion's mouth. I eased back and forth, back and forth, getting a sense for the width. Jackdaw at five eight and a buck fifty could fit in here, no problem. For a bruiser like Mr. Maris, I thought, it would be tight. But not impossible.

I got in there okay myself. Turned off my light, stuck it back in my jacket, and eased my body all the way into the hole. I splashed in the dirty rush of water, hunched forward, keeping my upper body small and bent. I walked with my hands stretched out on either side, fingertips scraping along the roughly textured walls. I walked a long time that way, bent almost parallel with the ground, genuflecting as I went, until the ceiling tapered back down and I was forced onto all fours and went awhile that way, soaking my kneecaps and my palms.

Time passed, and I didn't know how much time, either. I just walked, an invisible man moving through the darkness.

That makes it sound like I was cool, cool as the water, level-headed, nice and easy, but my stomach was clutching at me. This was the part of it I never had to do. This wasn't part of my job description. My deal was, I tracked him down—him or her or they—I found the lair, and then I called in the cavalry. My job was the following of bread crumbs: I had tracked men across miles of prairie, down crooked Freedman Town alleyways, along boardwalks, out onto beaches. And every time I called Bridge to put the rest in motion, and every time I turned back into smoke and drifted away. The final part I never had to see.

One time I decided to force myself to stay. I must have been in some kind of mood. Some foul place. Because I decided I needed, for once, to force myself after calling it in to hang around and watch the denouement.

It was in Massachusetts. It was in February. A small college in the cold far west of the state, where I had followed the thread of a man to a fraternity house. They'd put him in a room in the attic, had been bringing him beer and dining-hall cereal for three days, trying to figure out a connecting flight. But there were way too many girl-friends and study buddies and drunk pledges wandering in and out of there, too many people brought up to the attic after swearing se-crecy, and word was out—all over campus. All over town. Easiest file I ever closed.

But I don't know. I was down. I was feeling foul. Something about the season, the ease of the work. I forced myself to stay. I made myself up as a professor, bow tie and tweed, sat sipping cof-fee at a rickety table in the residential quad with a view of that frat house. I prepped a whole story about being an adjunct in the racial history department in case anyone asked, but no one asked. I watched the vans roll up and I watched the men charge in and I watched the milling, baffled, outraged frat boys, watched them watch their charity project bundled and taken hand over hand by the marshals out of the house and van. I saw the boy's face, his stricken, humiliated, terrified expression, blinking snow-blind in the brightness of the quad, crying out, confused. To have come so far and to be returning—his new friends in their Greek-lettered sweatshirts feebly shouting support, promising aid, announcing in righteous tones that their dads were lawyers, while the USMs shackled the poor peeb's arms behind him as though he were a madman, strapped him to a gurney inside the van. The last I saw of that boy was his feet, kicking desperately against the reinforced glass of the van's rear window, a thrashing barrage of kicks as they drove him away.

Eventually the tunnel gained some headroom, and I was able to draw up to full height. My feet echoed with wet clicks on the slimy concrete. I turned my flashlight on and followed the light, the beam wavering into strange patterns on the irregular, parabolic surfaces of the tunnel. Above my head was its thick stone shell and above that there was clay and river rock and then a thin layer of topsoil and then the streets and sidewalks of the living city.

I walked the tunnel murmuring something to myself, some old weird scrabbly lyric from my bone-hard childhood. Somewhere up ahead he was there, Jackdaw gone runner, cocooned in his bandages, waiting to get sent up to Canada. I wondered if anyone was down there with him—a flight attendant, someone to give him comfort, hold his hand in the darkness. Would it be Maris? Big, tough Maris? Or Officer Cook? Or young, pale-faced Father Barton himself?

I shook my head in the darkness. I don't know why, but I knew that they would not be there with him. No flight attendant. No steward. I was picturing Jackdaw alone.

Alone and swathed and mired in pain. After what Dr. V had told me when I asked her that last question, what she had told me in a quick nervous rush about the extent of his injuries: the usual, she had said—exhaustion and dehydration, scar tissue new and old. And, less usually, symptoms consistent with acute toxicity.

"Now, what is *that*?" I said, playing baffled Kenny Morton, playing him to the hilt. "What does *that* mean?"

"It means he'd ingested some substance or combination of substances," the doctor told Kenny. "It means he was poisoned."

I made my careful way along the dark tunnel. I contemplated the man I was coming to see, all that he had undertaken and what he still had to face. What he still had to face was me, the monster coming slowly down the pipe to find him and do . . . do what, exactly, I still did not know. It was too late to ping Bridge and disappear. Like they say, I knew too much. But I didn't know enough, either. Not yet.

I'd walked at least two miles. The tunnel was tilting slightly downslope, and it was getting colder, too. The air was heavy and damp, thick with uncirculated oxygen and the dank smell of the water.

I was getting closer. I took out the gun I hardly ever carried but was carrying tonight. Soon I'd find it, whatever it was—the dangling padlock, the walled-off chamber, the rock rolled in front of the mouth of the cave.

But when I got there, when I found the locked door, there was no lock. There was no door, even. I was sliding my palms roughly along either side of the tunnel, feeling for the narrow crack of a hung door or the bulge of a handle, when the left-side wall just opened up. I turned and crouched and held up the flashlight and found a narrow gap in the tunnel wall, like a secret left there for a child to find. I got down on my knees and turned off my light, although of course if he was in there—and I knew that he was, I knew that he was—he'd already have seen me, seen my light bobbling down the tunnel as I came, seen it shining into this hidey-hole on which there was no lock and no door.

They could have gotten in there, if they needed to. Bridge's men, I mean; the recovery team. They're ex–armed forces, those guys, big bastards. They'd roll in here with flash grenades, barking orders, they'd pull this shivering boy out and have him bundled in thirty seconds or less. Bridge's men wouldn't care what kind of shape he was in. They would come and take him. All I had to do was call. I'd explain myself to Bridge, about calling Janice and borrowing his voice, ha-ha, just having some fun. Maybe just maybe I was too valuable an asset to be thrown in that van next to Jackdaw.

Maybe I should have just turned around. Done my job. The one I had agreed to do six years ago. All I had to do was go back up there and make the call.

I passed into this new chamber, into deeper darkness, and empathy rose up in me. I was him. I was that man huddled in there, waiting, holding his breath, terrified by the small approaching light. My heart hammered, as his was likely to be hammering. I felt the sweat of fear on my brow that was the sweat of his fear.

An investigation feels so permanent, even after only a couple days. It starts to feel like its own state. You almost forget that every search is directed at a goal, and at the end of the search, if you're good, you find the one you're looking for. The part is always coming when you open the door or the lid or you unzip the bag or pry open the crate or you yank open the trapdoor or pull down on the tug and let the ladder drop down.

The ground in this narrower passage turned into a short stone staircase, three shallow steps going down. I was both of us. I was myself, and I was also the person at the end of the path, seeing my own shadow grow larger. I was the person hearing me coming. The sound was ancient and reverberant, the click and scrape of heels on stone steps.

I was him, seeing that light cutting into his world. I was me, and I was him, struck with terror at the sound of this invader. I felt my own fear increase. I felt not the keen anxiety of the predator but the panicking fear of his prey.

The flashlight beam struck a wall and made a pale radius, started to creep across a small room.

I'd call out now. I wouldn't be able to stand it anymore.

"Who's that?" he said, a desperate small rasp. "Who's here?"

I didn't answer. I didn't know what to say. I moved the beam around the room and found him staring back at me. Huddled under a blanket, staring up at me with quavering cheeks. The little concrete room he huddled in was lit by one emergency-exit light, gleaming dully against the slickened packed-mud walls. He moaned and I kept coming, and it grew stronger, this dissociated feeling of watching myself approach, a looming menace in the darkness, the reaching evil hand. I saw myself as he saw me, coming in slow, step by step, my sidearm in my fist; him cornered and terrified, treed like a wounded bear, cocooned in blankets, lost in shadow.

Jackdaw looked like shit. Sallow and unwholesome, bunched up on the ground, a discarded thing. Someone had left a bottle of water beside his bed with a straw poking out at a steep angle; in the other corner of the room was a bedpan, a dribble of piss at the bottom of it. Jackdaw's eyes were half closed, squinting from the dim light, like moles' eyes; his skin was marked by lesions, yellow halos of bruise and discoloration. He was crumpled atop some sort of cot or pallet, covered in blankets, and—there—Mr. Maris's blazer, one added layer against the underground cold, no doubt with my butterfly knife still in the pocket. The kid was twisted up in all those damn layers, half in, half out, like a child who's not sleeping, like Castle, like me. It was only later, when I saw the place again in my mind, that I recalled the semicircle of candles beside him, blown out or burned out, drowning at their bases in their own spent wax.

Beneath his miseries he looked just as he did in the picture: handsome and fine-boned, a movie star trapped in a nightmare. No one who ever killed any two nurses, that was for sure, no one who ever battered them to death and leaped out of a window to run. A thin face and delicate eyes, face bruised and worn, but still, still he was a beautiful child. Too beautiful for this world for sure.

I stood in the dark staring and saying nothing, and then it was Jackdaw who started us talking.

"So you him, huh?"

I stayed back against the wall. In the shadow.

"Who?" I said. "Who am I?"

"Come on." Jackdaw shifting his body under his mass of sheets, drawing himself back till he had pulled up against the wall. He made his delicate face tough: squared off his jaw. Jutted out his lower lip. "Go on, then. Let's go. Where's it start? Fingernails or what?"

"What?"

"You work on the legs, that it? You got a bat? A blowtorch. I know how y'all do. I seen the movies. Y'all with the bats and the pliers and shit. Listen. I ain't telling you where it is, so you do what you have to do."

His voice was like his face, grim and terrified and strained with the effort to be strong.

"What is it that I have to do?" I said, doing my own pretending,

pretending I knew what was going on. I was baffled. The darkness was between us. *I ain't telling you where it is. I seen the movies.*

"What movies?" I said. "What movies have you seen?"

"What?"

The truth was washing through me, phrases and scraps, small ideas, understanding—Cook: *A special kind of kid;* Janice: *That number is just not coming up*—and I drew in breath and came over and knelt beside the shivering boy. "You're not a real slave."

Jackdaw coughed, looked at me like I was crazy. "I'm not, and you know I'm not."

"I don't know anything," I said, and I meant it. Jesus, did I mean it.

"I'm a free man, you asshole." He gathered up some spirit in his eyes, and he stared at me and declared it: "Free man. Born and raised."

23.

I picked him up, and I carried him away.

Half-dead boy, he weighed nothing at all. However long behind the Fence and nearly a week down here, buried alive by his rescuers. Worn and tired as I was, I still could carry him with no trouble, and that's what I did—threw him over my shoulder like he was a troublesome child. He struggled, but not much. He was weak. I moved as fast as I could.

When the space was too tight for carrying I put him down, and I pulled him and pushed him. I might have fucking rolled the kid. I went the other way, opposite the way I came in, following the underground creek where it flowed back, away from the trailer park and Slim's decrepit little dynasty, figuring there had to be an exit to this tunnel somewhere, and I dragged Jackdaw until I found it.

We popped out on the other end, where the water spilled itself out into the muddy roll of the White River, south of downtown. I scrabbled with the boy down the swampy banks till we fell together by the river. There was no promenade, no sidewalk, just the embankment, just patchy scrub grass and loose stones covering fifty feet of graded slope from the water's edge up to the roadway above.

The scene was lit, barely, by a sliver of moonlight and a pair of dim streetlights on an overpass bridge some distance downstream. I laid him gently by the water's edge and hunched over to breathe and to think.

I didn't know what I was doing—I didn't know if I was bringing him in or rescuing him and if I was rescuing him what I'd be rescuing him from.

He crawled over onto all fours and spat a long trail of yellow spit, and it clung to his lower lip. He bent forward and gagged.

"Go on, then. Get it over with."

"I am not here to torture you."

"So," he said. "So shoot. Shoot me, nigga. Just—" His bravado wavered. A tremor ran through him. "Just . . . just not in the face, okay? Don't—and just . . . tell my parents I'm sorry. Okay? Can you do that?"

"Listen to me."

"They're in Brightmoor, okay, in Detroit? That's where I came up, and they're still up there. Okay?"

"Jackdaw."

"My name is Kevin," he said. "It's Kevin."

I wanted to slap him. I wanted to embrace him. This poor boy, pleading with me under the sliver of moonlight. The river was swollen from the rain, and it churned beside us. "You tell my parents I was tryna do good, okay? Tryna—" He was weeping again now, big tears rolling down his cheeks. "Just tell 'em. Charles and Chandra, okay? In Brightmoor, in Detroit. Tell them—"

"Stop it," I said. "Stop. I'm not here to kill you."

He looked up and gaped at me.

"So what, then? What? *What?*"

And I had no answer. I looked at him with imploring grief, like it was for *him* to tell *me* what the fuck to do, and we gaped at each other like that, like two dumb fish. But it was already late, too late already. Somewhere on the roadway above a car screeched and stopped, and I could hear the doors slamming closed, hear fast footsteps on the scrub grass, coming down fast.

It was Cook. I saw the brown of his cop's shoes, and I grabbed the boy. Monster that I am, instinct kicked in, and I leaned into the one thing I knew, which was that this kid, whatever he was, whatever had happened, he knew something these people were after, and they weren't going to kill him till they had it. I seized him and dance-stepped him backwards, one step, and my feet splashed in the river as I hung him before me as a shield.

"Stop there," I yelled, and Cook—gun out as he tripped down the slope—he did as I said, and I kept it going: "Throw down your gun and raise your hands."

I could barely see him, but I saw a flash of white teeth as he snarled, and I saw the gun where he tossed it, between us, into the bush.

Jackdaw was frozen in my arms. His heart was beating, a rabbit against my body. Slowly I took out my own gun and held it to his temple.

The others were already coming. First big Maris, then Barton, too, gliding through the darkness, and they arrayed themselves around us in a semicircle, halfway up the slope, looking down at us standing in the water. Barton was the smallest of the three, small and pale and ghostly, black cassock on black night. But it was Barton who made Jackdaw terrified and brave. When he saw the priest he became a tight wire in my arms, fearful and defiant and taut.

"It's okay," I heard myself tell him, murmuring brotherly in his ear, even as I held the gun to his head. "It's gonna be all right." And then, to Maris, "Weapons on the ground, please."

"I do not carry a weapon," he said forcefully, coldly, meaning he did not need a weapon. Would not need one to kill the likes of me.

"How do you sleep? How do you fucking sleep, *Jim?*" said Officer Cook, sneering on the name.

But I did as Bridge did. I answered his question with a question.

"Who is this boy?"

"Go to hell," said Cook.

But I was the one with the gun. I was the one with the hostage. I directed myself to Father Barton.

"Tell me who this is."

"The young man can tell you himself," said Barton, and Jackdaw— Kevin—reacted to his voice with a fresh jolt of energy, jerking in my arms. I purred "Hush" in his ear and said to Barton, "No." I said, "You tell me."

"He is a soldier in the army of the Lord."

"What does that mean?"

"Ask him," said Father Barton, and just as my own eyes had not left the priest, the priest's eyes had not left Kevin. "Ask the boy."

"Goddamn it," I said. "I'm asking *you*."

Mr. Maris, meanwhile, his face bronze in the dim light, was still playing catch-up. "Who is this man?" he said.

Cook turned to him, incredulous. "He's a nigger stealer." Then, back to me, with a taunting grin. "Ain't that right? Nigger stealer. Soul catcher."

Maris looked astonished. He looked me up and down like I was a ghost, an ogre of myth. "He's from the government?" he said.

"Yeah," said Cook. "He's from the fucking government."

I felt Kevin feel this new information. Felt his body change as he understood what kind of salvation he had fallen into this time.

"He is an undercover agent," Father Barton said quietly, sadly, a wise parent explaining wickedness to a child. And then, to me, with sympathy: "What miseries you have seen . . . what grief you have encountered on this earth."

Maris took a step toward me, his big fists clenched and half raised—ready, now that he knew what I was, to tear my head off my body. I pivoted a quarter turn, made sure he saw how tightly I was holding their precious cargo.

"Now," I said. "Tell me about this boy. *Now*."

Barton nodded very slightly. The sun was just starting to come up, washing our desperate scene in a hazy yellow light. There was a railroad bridge fifty yards to the south, the underside of it marked with graffiti, like petroglyphs. Barton stepped toward me as he started to speak. Looked me dead in the eye, me with my gun and my hostage. A man used to breathing God's true word even into the face of monsters.

"Five years ago our organization was made aware of certain actions being undertaken by this particular plantation. Garments of the Greater South. We had information from multiple sources. We worked out a way for evidence of these activities to be gathered. Brought north. And made public." As he spoke, Barton's clerical calm melted off of him, and his voice rose, and he began to nod as if from the altar, and his hands slowly came up, like he was delivering an invocation. "And in this way we can shake the very foundations, bring down not just this plantation but all the plantations . . . in this way we can strike at the very heart of the old evil. In this way the scales will fall from the eyes of the world . . ."

He had changed entirely, a hellfire evangelical emerged from the shell of the inward young priest. What was he like, I wondered, on the other side of the confessional curtain, murmuring God's forgiveness? What was he like in a meeting of abolitionist donors, pressing flesh, demurely tucking folded checks inside his cassock? He was many men. He suited the need. He was like me.

"So all right," I said. "So you recruited him. You sent him down there."

"That's right," said Cook. "And the boy was perfect. He was goddamn perfect."

Barton nodded, posed, arms extended and palms raised, breathing. Now he spoke to Kevin, who looked back at him, face frozen with repulsion.

"I remember that night. I remember how proud I felt to have met you, to have found you. How inspired we were. How excited we both were for this undertaking."

"He came to my school," said Jackdaw suddenly, and I jerked him closer to me. "This man here. In plainclothes, you know, jeans and a shirt and the collar. All fucking cool. My sophomore year, Earlham College. He shows up at a black students' meeting, talking all hot about taking responsibility. Saying, hey, who's tired of signing petitions? Whose feet are tired from marching? Who's ready to do something *real*? And I said . . ." Kevin spoke faintly, mockingly, contemptuous of his former self. "I said me. I said *me*. I was all fired up." He closed his eyes, energy spent, and hung limp as a doll in my arms.

"How much time?" I asked Barton. "How long did he have to work down there before risking his life to get your—whatever it is."

Barton raised a single finger, thin as a bone. "One year."

I felt Jackdaw's heart pulsing warmth where I held him. I felt the sacrifice of this, for this kid from Detroit, a kid growing up with his pals in the free world, playing basketball, going to school. College sophomore, liberal arts, textbooks and term papers, bumping fists on the quad, and then a year behind the Fence. I could not imagine it, except that I could; I could imagine it exactly. Mine had been a livestock slavery, the blood knife and the dirt, and his had been a glass-wall slavery, stitch-house slavery, needle and thread, but the baseline is the same. The bare facts are always the same.

"And he performed..." Barton trailed off into a smile, took another step toward us, held out his hands to Jackdaw. "He performed perfectly. Kevin? Are you listening to me, Kevin? You performed beautifully."

Jackdaw cleared his throat and shot a thick wad of spit onto the priest's face. Barton did not flinch; very gently he raised one arm and wiped the spit away. I kept one eye, meanwhile, on the other men, still up there on the slope. Cook with his arms crossed, eyes narrow. Mr. Maris, hulking and furious, brow furrowed with concentration, waiting for his moment. Waiting for a chance to separate us, to push the boy out of the way so he could tear me to bits.

"So where is it?" Silence from everyone. River rush, distant traffic. Someone honking on southbound 65. "Come on. The boy goes down, performs beautifully, gathers up the evidence. Where is it?"

"Ask the boy," said Barton, and I said, "I'm asking you."

"This crazy motherfucker didn't bring it," said Cook. He took one step down the slope toward us, and I tightened my grip and he stepped back. "He says he got it out, but he stashed it somewhere on the way up."

"Why?"

"Because he is confused," said Barton softly. "He is tired and confused."

"Because of Luna," said Jackdaw—not Jackdaw . . . said Kevin the sophomore, and he didn't sound tired or confused. He snapped to life again inside the threatening curl of my arm, taking over his own story. "There's a girl named Luna, a PB, and she was the one who got your precious evidence. She took all the fucking risks, this girl who was born a slave and was a slave her whole life." His voice was a hot rush, rough with tears, rising with passion, as Barton's voice had risen. "I told that girl that if she helped me we would get her out, too. But then your people—"

"They ain't *our* people," Cook said.

"Your people—"

Barton shook his head. "We work with various entities—"

"They *left* her. Left her behind. So I told them . . ." He rolled his head backwards, and it pushed against my chest. "I told them, go and get that girl and I tell you where I put your fucking envelope."

Silence. The sun was rising. The ugly water lapped at our feet. Barton stood with his eyes closed, some of that spit still making its slow way down his cheek, over an expression of agony and forbearance.

And then Barton took another step, and I said, "Stop," but he ignored me. He knelt in the muddy water at our feet, and the brown ripples lapped the hem of his robe, his shoes, his thin brown socks. He spoke with a voice that was soft and charged and urgent, as if he were administering a rite.

"You must reconsider, Kevin. You *must*. We are talking here about the fate of three million people."

"I don't care about three million people. I care about one. You go and get her, and I tell you where it is."

"We can't do it," said Barton. "That plan was years in the making. Years. We can't just wander into places—"

"She's dead," said Officer Cook suddenly. "Okay? Your girl is dead."

Barton turned to look at the cop, and Maris was looking at him, too. There was a long, brutal stillness. None of them spoke, but in the gloom of the sunrise I could read their silent communion— they hadn't planned to tell him, afraid of how he would react, what he would do, but now there was nothing left. No other choice. The government had arrived, a monster was in their midst, the situation was at crisis, and so he had been told.

Kevin's face, meanwhile, had gone slack with astonishment and grief. I felt his narrow rib cage next to mine, felt his grief jump like an electric arc from his heart into mine, and then at last he wailed. The sound that was coming out of poor Kevin was low and long, an animal's trapped holler. "No," he was saying, more sound than word. "No . . ."

Barton, without expression, watched him scream. His pale eyes were lasered in on suffering Kevin: X-raying, filleting, dissecting. I believe that if he could have he would have cut into that boy and torn his secret out by hand.

Cook kept going, sighing, sad. "They found out she helped you get out, and they went and put her down. They made it look like an accident. You know how they do."

Kevin shook his head, pain evident on his face. Cook's choice of words was brutal: they put her down. Like a dog—a wolf. Something wild.

"No, see, no," said Kevin. "They can't do that. She can get punished, but—no, capital punishment . . . no. There's laws. Laws . . ."

Wishful thinking. I thought it but did not say it. There are laws. There are rules. Violent slavery is against the law. But rules are forever being broken. Guards get carried away. Workloads get dangerous. Franklins get bribed; Franklins are sloppy; Franklins don't give a shit. A surprising number are former guards. When I was ten or eleven years old I knew a PB called Cat's Eye who used to call a certain working white, whose name was Dickie, he used to call him

Dickweed and say, "Oops, sorry 'bout that," and every time he got punished, and then he'd do it again. Then one time he was working in the tannery, and he fell into the vat. Industrial accident; these things happen. Working whites somehow missed him going in, and so did the guards, and even the Franklins—three yellow jumpsuits in the room and nobody noticed until it was time to fish out what was left of him with the long curved stick they kept hung on the wall in there. The stink of it filled the building so severely that the first three Families who worked that room afterward had to work it with rags tied around their mouths, even after it had been closed for a week for fumigation.

"Yes," said Cook. "Sucks, man, I know. It sucks."

"Yeah," said Maris.

"It is God's will," said Barton, "because now you are free . . . free to tell us—"

But Kevin had had enough after "It is God's will." God's will was more than he could bear, and he thrashed and brought his knee up into me, which I was not expecting, and maybe I didn't want to stop him, maybe that's why he had the chance to twist around, knee me in the side of my leg, grab the gun from my hand, and aim it at Father Barton.

"Monster," he shouted, and Barton said, "I am not the monster, son, I—"

A pair of pops, one after the other, pop pop, barely audible over the river rush—pop pop—ricocheting and overlapping each other, and everybody was moving at once in every direction. Barton jerked as if hit, but he had not been hit, only me, a sudden appearance of pain in my shoulder. I saw as I fell backwards with the bullet that it was Maris who'd fired, Maris, with Cook's gun, scrabbled up from the ground, and Kevin had taken the other shot, right through the chest: I fell, and he fell on top of me, and he was dead.

*　　*　　*

He should not have died, but he had died, and there I still was.

I should have died.

I should have died in Bell's Farm in a rainstorm and a swamp of blood, and I should have died on a Chicago sidewalk. I should have fought against the men from the vans until they were forced to shoot to kill.

And now here beside this gray churning river I should have been the one who got shot, but there I still stood, and still I wanted life.

The sun continued on its rise. A wash across the scene, blood splatter on the shallow rocks, scuff marks on the scrub. And all the anger and confusion turned upon me. Maris and Cook wheeled toward me, and Maris was still holding the gun.

"Gimme my gun back," said the cop. The sun caught his class ring. Class president, homecoming king. All of us just a bunch of people out here, stumbling around down by the river.

"I will return it to you when I'm through," Maris said to him, and then to me, steely-voiced, cool: "Stand up."

I stood up.

"Raise your hands in the air."

Barton was kneeling in the low run of the water, with Kevin's head cradled in his lap, praying. Or silently cursing. Or, as he stroked the side of that dead child's face, trying to bring out the information that he wanted so desperately, bring it up to the surface by conjure or caress. Maris advanced toward me. It seemed wild to me that they would do it here, here with the morning traffic already rumbling past within earshot. Barton was holding the boy, and Maris was coming closer with Cook's service pistol.

"Wait; wait." Cook was in motion, moving fast. Putting himself between Maris and me. "Hold up."

The cop crouched down by the priest, and they huddled together, their heads just touching, the two of them an arch spanning Kevin where he lay, in and out of the water. Cook was whispering into Barton's neck, and the priest began to nod, fire coming into his eyes.

"What?" said Maris, and then louder. "What?" Impatient, nostrils flaring. Anger fuming off his forehead. This monster, this government man, me—I needed to die, right then. It was so clear.

But the other two men kept talking, a minute or more, with Maris frozen out and Kevin dead and me just waiting, until Cook pulled back and stood up. "All right?"

Barton rose also, laid Kevin's head down gently, and rose slowly, too, saying "Yes" again and again, and I saw how pleased Cook was with himself that he had made this sale, whatever it was. Even as the arrogant priest swooped in to seize his idea, swoop in and take it over: *Mockingbird* mentality. "Here is what we are going to do." His voice was steady now, steely. The murmuring priest was gone, the fiery preacher was gone; here now was the field commander, leader of men, decisive and determined. "You will go and make these arrangements," he said to Cook. "But first you need to deal with the body. Do you have a way to handle it?"

"Yeah," said Cook. "I do." He looked down at Kevin, and so did I, and we saw the water wash over the boy's face, his eyes staring up at the sun.

Barton next addressed Mr. Maris. "You will take the government man to the place and wait. Do you understand me? You are to *wait*." The priest did not wait for Maris's answer. He turned and walked up the slope to the road, water dripping from the fringes of his cassock. "Now," he said. "It is Sunday. I'm going to Mass."

Maris did as he was told.

He drove me to Saint Anselm's Catholic Promise, where I had been before, and we sat in that dusty main room, in the circle of fold-up chairs.

We listened to church bells ringing, listened to the boastful revving of motorcycle engines, listened to the rattle and thump of hip-hop bass lines coming out of SUVs on Central Avenue. I longed for a radio, longed to ask my captor if he might put on something to pass the time. Something sweet and easy. Some Smokey Robinson; some MJ. But there was no engaging Mr. Maris. He sat across from me with his legs spread wide, staring at me evenly, a shotgun between his legs. I sat woozy while my shoulder burned and bled. My hands were tied together behind the back of the chair. I was offered no first aid, no water.

"Were it me," said Maris at one point, very softly, still staring, "I would make it hard for you. Slow. Do you understand my meaning?"

I didn't answer him. I was thinking about Kevin.

Thinking about his old neighborhood: Brightmoor, in Detroit.

Thinking about his parents: Charles and Chandra.

Thinking about what he had done, what he had tried to do, and how he had died. I yearned for music, to separate me from these thoughts.

"Were it me," said Maris, "it would not be pleasant. Do you understand?"

Still I said nothing. Maris was not done. He scraped his chair out of the circle, moved it closer to mine, keeping the shotgun between his legs. I considered ways I might have disarmed him, even with my hands tied to the chair as they were. Things I had learned.

"How many has it been? How many have you brought in, in your hunt? How many?"

When still I said nothing, Maris flared his nostrils, narrowed his gaze.

"You do not even know. Is that it? More than you can count? More than you think of?"

Two hundred ten. I could have told him if I wanted to. Two hundred ten since Chicago, since Bridge in the basement of the federal building, since my training in the Arizona desert. Two hundred ten, including this most recent: Jackdaw. Kevin. Son of Charles and Chandra.

Kevin of the Brightmoor section of Detroit, Michigan.

I held my hands and felt the blood creep out of my shoulder.

It was nearly nightfall before the door of that old abandoned community center creaked open and Barton came in, with Cook behind him.

Barton, out of clerical costume and in jeans and a shirt, carried a laptop under one arm. Cook leaned against the wall and chewed his gum while Barton pulled a chair out of the circle and dragged it by the back until he was sitting across from me.

He opened the laptop and turned it so I could see the screen. Maris stayed where he was, the shotgun balanced across his knees.

Barton clicked on a familiar icon, and a map opened up on his screen. The map showed the world, then it zoomed in, a sickening, rapid descent, until it showed the United States, then Indiana, then the city. There was a red dot, midcity, and it flashed on and off, on and off.

"Do you know what that is?" said the priest.

"I do."

"Tell me what it is."

I stared at the dot. I was transfixed. "It's me."

"Correct." He shut the computer and stood up. "It's you."

"How is this possible?" I said, as if that mattered. As if that were the important thing. I was trying to figure out what was happening here — what was next.

"As you know, this man is a law enforcement officer. There are certain channels to which he has access."

Cook waved his hand. "A man owed me a favor."

I took a new look at Officer Cook, and he returned my gaze steadily, slight smile, eyebrows raised. *No big deal,* his face was saying, but we both knew — if perhaps Barton did not — that this was a very big deal indeed. I imagined Mr. Bridge's reaction if he were to discover this pinhole leak in the steel sides of the US Marshals Service Information Technology Division.

Barton kept his eyes on me.

"You are a tracker, and you are an investigator. What you are going to do now is track and investigate. The package Kevin was supposed to bring us, containing items of crucial importance, is still within the Four."

"How do you know that?"

Barton grimaced, and Cook answered for him. "Well, it ain't here, is it?"

"The point is"—Barton again—"you are going to find what Kevin left behind and bring it to us." He pointed to the laptop. "We will be watching where you go. We will watch you go south, watch you come north again. When you do, you will come here directly and hand over what you have found. If you do not do this, we will find you." Again, he gestured to the computer. "And we will kill you."

There was no use pretending I didn't understand. No use asking why. Barton understood exactly what I was, exactly how this worked. I had no fingerprints. I had no permanent identity. I had the training and the resources of the United States government behind me. And of course if I was caught, if I was tortured or beaten, if I were to be murdered or sold south, then no one would miss me. No one would care. An invisible man is an expendable man.

I let my eyes rest a moment more on the blinking dot on the screen.

I turned back to Cook. "I don't understand something here. You're tracking me, but my handler—my boss—he's tracking me, too. So—"

Cook started to answer, but Barton raised one hand, palm out, gesturing him to silence, as he had done to me at the Fountain Diner. Then he lowered his voice, cocked his head, and dropped into an impression of me, of someone like me, the cool, tough undercover agent calling in: "Hell of a thing," he said, "but what I'm hearing is, this runner never made it past the Fence. He's still down there, it looks like. If I'm gonna find him for you, that's where I gotta go."

I closed my eyes and nodded. This was my life; this was my destiny—to be someone's tool, someone or other.

"When you have found what we are looking for," added

Cook, "you call and tell boss man no luck. You couldn't find the boy."

"Hell of a thing," I murmured.

"Then you bring us our package," said Barton. "And that's it. We're done."

"Done?" I said.

"Yeah," said Cook. "Done."

This was too much for Maris. "No," he said. "No—" but now it was his turn to be hushed by Barton's imperious hand. "Yes," said the priest. "Succeed in this. Make this right. And we will arrange a connecting flight to Canada for you."

Maris stood and laid his shotgun on the ground and stomped out of the circle of chairs, took a sullen distance on the far side of the room, leaning in the doorjamb with arms crossed. Barton did not move. Kept his glowing eyes on me.

"All right," I said. "So what am I looking for?"

"It's a package. Small. An envelope, padded and sealed. Kevin's instructions when he had it were to mark it on the back with his initials, so we would know it for sure. We do not know if he did that or not. But on the front it will bear the insignia of Garments of the Greater South. Do you know that insignia?"

I nodded. I knew it. I knew it from where it had been emblazoned on the collarbone of Jackdaw the slave, Kevin the sophomore. I knew it from the full file.

"So it's a sealed envelope from GGSI. Thick envelope. Marked on the back." Barton nodded. "But what's inside?"

"Evidence. Powerful evidence that will bring down the very foundations of slavery."

I almost laughed: the willful obscurantism, the curtain of mystery. "So I go down into the Four, I chase down this thing, I don't even know what it is?"

"You will do," said Maris from his new remove on the far side of the room, "as we have told you to do." And for once, he and Cook were in agreement.

"Or," said the cop, "we'll kill ya."

But Barton looked at me thoughtfully as he rose. "No, we'll tell him. We will tell you. Mr. Maris and Mr. Cook, you will tell our friend how to make contact with the lawyer. And you will explain to him what it is he is recovering." He laid his hand on my head and let it rest there a moment. "Let him understand why it matters so much that he succeed. Not just for his life but for the lives of us all."

Barton bowed his blond head toward me. "This is a hard situation we are putting you in. But you *must* see it"—he emphasized the same word he had used with Kevin, that soft and powerful word, *must,* soft and hard at once, like a hammer wrapped in velvet— "you *must* see this as your opportunity to undo the evils that you have done. To put a mark in the other column. Here you can be a soldier—you can be good, my son. You can do good."

24.

It was another hour that I sat there with the Underground Airlines, in the cold company of Mr. Maris and Willie Cook.

I was told everything I would need to know. Told me about the lawyer, where and how to find him, everything I needed to get started chasing down what Kevin had left behind.

They told me all about it, too, the shocking evidence, what was going to shake the very foundations. And I had to work hard, pretending to be impressed with it all. With the enormity of the crime, with the scandal that was to be exposed.

It was Cook who broke it down; Maris was still angry, seething at me from the back corner of the room like lurking death. Garments of the Greater South, Incorporated, was in violation—long-term, systematic violation—of the Clean Hands laws.

Beginning as early as 1994, GGSI had set up a cluster of shell companies in Kuala Lumpur through which they were annually channeling millions of dollars' worth of cotton goods. Their Alabama plantation exported finished textiles to the Malaysian companies; the companies changed the labels and resold them to a stateside retailer. Even after the shells took their cut, even after the costs of shipping, even after the costs of bribery and permit forging and logistical workarounds, this operation was massively profitable for both sides.

But the kicker—the part that required me to be most impressed—was the identity of the criminal partner on the American side. This ain't no small potatoes we're talking about, was how Cook put it. No mom-and-pop operation. GGSI's partner was none other than Townes Stores, the single largest retailer in the United States: shops in thirty-six states, selling everything from refrigerators to perfume, from small electronics to coloring books. And clothes, of course—aisles and aisles of cheap cotton clothes.

"You believe that, man?" said Cook, but of course I could. He was a city policeman who was secretly moonlighting for the Airlines; I was a retail site analyst and secretly an enforcer of the FPA. I believe anything. Everything happens.

It was Massachusetts that passed the first Clean Hands law, back in the day. Good old radical Mass., where crazy John Brown had passed the hat for his crusades, where Nell and Morris's League of Freedom was born in the 1850s and reborn in the 1910s. The hunting ground of the Boston Vigilance Committee, hunting for slave catchers till the slave catchers left town.

In 1927 the commonwealth's legislature declared that the possession, sale, or consumption of slave-made goods within its borders would thenceforth be a criminal act.

Southern interests—in their genteel and eloquent southern manner—said no fucking way. Why, this was an illegal regulation of trade! Why, this was protectionism! American citizens were being robbed of their God-given and constitutionally protected right to spend their money however they liked! This clash of virtues landed in the Supreme Court in the form of *Amalgamated Products v. Hendricks*. The attorney general of Massachusetts argued that it was within the police powers of the individual states to safeguard the moral fitness of their respective citizens. Wearing clothing that had been plantation-picked and plantation-sewn did grave harm to the people of the commonwealth. And the Supreme Court, surprise surprise, endorsed this point of view.

Other northern states hurried to pass Clean Hands laws of their own, and Roosevelt's Democratic majority sealed the deal with the federal version in 1934. If your company wanted to do business in *any* Clean Hands state, you were required to follow those rules everywhere you operated. Since then, Clean Hands has been an article of faith. All right, says the Righteous North: so we must live with the grievous reality of slavery, we must live with official state racism within our borders. So we are bound up economically and politically with the evil behind the Fence, tied to it and even enriched by it: southern tax dollars go to the national treasury, and southern profits go to Wall Street. And of course Clean Hands only goes one way—there are no laws preventing *southern* consumers from enjoying the fruits of *northern* manufacturing.

But at least there is this great conscience-soothing balm: when you go to the store in Milwaukee or Peoria, you are not coming home with blood on your hands.

It was exactly that consolation, that comfort, that Father Barton was intending to tear away.

He had sent in Kevin, and Kevin had come out with evidence of the collusion between GGSI and Townes Stores: a hard drive bristling with incriminating information, six months' worth of internal data—shipment tracking records, transaction records, the numbers of bank accounts in four different countries. All documenting a commercial connection between a massive retailer and a slave-state factory that would (Barton thought...Barton hoped...Barton dreamed...and Barton had persuaded Kevin to dream, too) scandalize northern sensibilities. It would demonstrate the fecklessness of the federal regulatory scheme. It would prove the whole edifice of compromise to be rotten to its very foundation. It would show northerners who liked to believe, who *needed* to believe, that they were not personally touched by the cruel hand of slavery that they were in fact touched by it every day. Were wearing it on their feet, were lining up for it the day after Thanksgiving.

He would splash his evidence on the front page of every northern newspaper, deliver it himself to prosecutors in the Southern District of Illinois, which had jurisdiction over Townes's headquarters, and the world would change.

This was the idea that had so gripped Kevin when first he heard it, the plan he had agreed to with a rapidity that was like a fever. It was this possibility that had persuaded him to take the hideous risk, allow himself to be costumed and tattooed and sold.

Barton thought the world would change, and his lieutenants thought so, and Kevin had thought so, too.

I didn't believe it for a second. I could see the future. I knew what would happen, and what would happen was nothing.

They'd been talking about freedom in Old Abe's time, but then they shot Old Abe, and what changed? Nothing changed.

A hundred years later Dr. King was dreaming his dream, telling America it was time to finish its unfinished business. Northerners, black and white, went south for Freedom Summer, crisscrossing the remaining slave states, bearing witness. A huge crowd of abolitionists gathered in newly free Georgia and marched all the way to Selma, Alabama. A brave slave woman in Montgomery refused to eat until conditions were improved, sparking hunger strikes all over the South. The president got on board: the Voting Rights Act, the New Agenda, "abolition in our time."

And then what? Then the BLP officially condoned the force-feeding of Persons Bound to Labor. Then LBJ got distracted from the New Agenda, drawn deeper and deeper into the swamp of the Texas War. The movement cut itself up, violence versus nonviolence, "rights for us" versus "freedom for them." The Panthers were declared a terrorist organization. Dr. King, celebrating his great victory — legislated abolition in Tennessee — was shot outside his hotel room.

Nothing changed, not really. The Eighteenth Amendment remained the Eighteenth Amendment. America stayed America.

So what was he thinking now, this zealous priest, this radical child, wild with self-delusion? All of them, Maris glowering and righteous, Cook talking about the new era that they were about to bust loose. I knew better. I knew what would happen. Of course it would be shocking if all those Iowans and Idahoans found out that the cheap T-shirts they've been buying have blood on them. It would grab some headlines. The chairman of Townes would give a press conference, shake his head and purse his lips and say, "I accept full responsibility." GGSI would be shuttered—maybe, maybe not, or maybe just temporarily—while an inspection could be undertaken. Townes Stores would pay a big fine, and they'd have a bad quarter.

In time, people would go back to Townes, because their shit is pretty cheap, wherever it's coming from. It's pretty cheap, and it's pretty good. Nothing would change. People shaking their heads, shrugging their shoulders, slaves suffering somewhere far away, the earth turning around the sun.

And that, honey, is how I justified what I did next. That's how I thought it through to myself as I drove back to the Capital City Crossroads, even then, even with Kevin's broken, bleeding body lying fresh in my memory like a chastisement.

I believed—I truly believed; I allowed myself to believe—that if I found that envelope filled with stolen data and turned it over to Father Barton, that not a goddamn thing would change. The three million would not be set free.

But there was a way that envelope could get *one* person free, and that one person was me.

I went out onto my hotel-room balcony and lit a cigarette. And then I called Mr. Bridge.

25.

"**I don't** know what you thought you were doing, son. I don't know what you thought you were up to."

Mr. Bridge spoke slowly but firmly, projecting control. I listened to him, standing out on my balcony, smoking my cigarette, waiting for him to get it out of his system. I thought about other things. I saw the streetlamps blink on. I gazed at the faded twilight ghost of the sun.

"By placing that call to my office, and by playing false with a federal law enforcement official, you have committed a serious violation of the law. Not to mention a serious violation of our agreement."

Mr. Bridge, scolding a wayward child. Mr. Bridge, enumerating my sins. *Federal law enforcement official* took me a second. Janice — he meant Janice.

"Impersonation of an agent. Illegal possession of classified information."

This bill of indictment I didn't even bother to answer. I didn't even take the time to say, "Fuck you." Sunday sunset had brought something like a peaceful calm to the gray city, a wan beauty. I was exhausted. The pain in my shoulder was a buried throb. I still had dirt on my boots, on the palms of my hands, on my knees — the mud stains of the underground.

Poor Bridge was assuming that I was a couple of steps behind him, trying to keep up. But I was way out ahead. I was so far out ahead that he could barely see me.

"Quiet, man," I said finally. "Hush up a minute."

"What?"

"I said hush. Listen. Okay? Because you're a dead man."

"Are you—" A silence I hadn't heard before: genuine shock. "Was that a threat?"

"Nope. It was a statement of fact. True fact. I'm not telling you nothing you don't already know. You're fucked, but I'm gonna help you. We're gonna help each other out. Okay?"

"I..."

Mr. Bridge let the word dissolve into silence. A silence that was easy to read. Slow and thick, gummy with fear.

"Here's what's next," I told him, and he didn't even bother with another stammering interruption: he just listened. I told him to hang up, leave his office, and call me back from the pay phone just inside the baggage claim area, door 7, at Baltimore-Washington International Airport. The pay phones, I told him, were across from the bank of courtesy phones that got you a rental car or a motel room.

"Write this down," I told him, and I gave him the number of a new phone, a disposable phone I had purchased for this purpose, at a place on 38th Street, on my way from Saint Anselm's. "Forty-five minutes."

There was one more silence while he considered whether to lodge a fresh objection, but then he clicked off.

I stood in the stillness of the balcony, watching spotty Sunday evening traffic go down 86th: first one car, then two, then one more. If I had misread Bridge's last silence, if he had been grinning cruelly in that last instant, relishing the last time he'd ever have to take bullshit from this smartass nigger, then the vans would be screeching up any minute.

They did not. He was reading the situation correctly: he was in a bad spot, and if anyone could get him out of it, I could.

I pictured him, middle-aged Bridge, hustling down the stairs of the Marshals Service building to the parking garage, pushing the speed limit in whatever poky American four-door he could afford on his government pay, all the way to BWI.

This, for me, at the end of a long and difficult twenty-four hours, should have been a moment to relish. Cherish, even. Slowly showing Bridge what was going to happen. After so many years in his power, forcing him inch by inch to do what I wanted. Clawing out from under Bridge. Lifting him up, shaking him upside down.

But the moment of Kevin's death kept on ricocheting through my body. Over and over again. Flying backwards, and he flying backwards on top of me. The blood from my shoulder mingling with the blood of his chest. That had changed everything—a bell that rang in me. A crack in the firmament of the world.

I should have felt good, but I only felt weary. I only felt sad. My shot shoulder sang with a low hurt, the bullet in there burning, a smoldering fire buried inside a pit.

Like moving through the tunnel—you only keep going. Whatever happened next, it was going to happen quickly, and it was either going to work or it wasn't.

Thirty-four minutes later the phone rang.

"Hang up," I said.

"What?"

"Go upstairs," I said. "Call me back from the phone between gate B13 and gate B14. By the men's restroom."

"If you want me to call you from a gate area, then I'm going to have to buy a ticket."

"Well, then, you better buy a ticket."

Mr. Bridge called back right on time, from the phone between gates B27 and B28. I didn't say hello. I just started talking.

"This boy Jackdaw, this slave we been following, he was a mule. When he—"

"Where did you get this information?"

"Don't interrupt. When he left GGSI he took something with him. An envelope."

I didn't tell Bridge what was in that padded envelope, because

I didn't know if he knew what it was. I didn't say to Bridge that Jackdaw the slave was actually Kevin the college boy. I didn't know if he knew that, and if he did know, I didn't know if *he* knew that *I* knew, and anyway, fuck him. I wasn't handing Bridge any piece of information he didn't already have unless it would be beneficial to me.

I skipped to the meat of it. The pivot point of my discourse. The wedge that I was going to drive between him and me.

"This material the boy is carrying, you all are mixed up in it. Right? I mean the marshals. If this comes to light, what he's got, your agency is implicated. Is that right?"

I waited. There was a strange quality to the silence, and I realized it was because I was holding my breath, keeping myself totally still. I exhaled.

"Bridge?"

"Yes?"

"Are you not answering because you don't know the details, either, or because I told you not to interrupt?"

A thread of silence, then: "Both."

I was making him sweat—that was good; I needed him nervous—but in truth it didn't matter how the marshals were implicated, it only mattered that they were. Maybe the marshals were acting as facilitators or as muscle, or maybe they were just looking the other way at some crucial juncture in the customs approval process. It was one of the above. It was all of the above. What mattered to me was that Bridge's ass was in the fire, and so were the asses of whoever was further up the chain of command.

All that mattered was that he wanted what was missing—what Kevin had hidden. For whatever reason, the marshals wanted it as badly as Barton did, and I was now in a position to deliver it.

Bridge remained quiet, and I heard the burble of the airport behind him. Gate announcements; a baby yelping; the muted beep beep of some kind of small vehicle in reverse.

I kept talking. "So when this man escaped, it created a special problem. For the Marshals Service. He couldn't just be caught, because if he's caught, whatever he's carrying ends up in Canada or in front of a judge."

More silence.

"You still not interrupting because I'm right, right?"

"Right."

"Okay, well, now you gotta answer. Now I got a question." I didn't really. I actually knew the answer. But I needed to hear him say it.

"Where it said Jackdaw was *known to have intended to remove himself to Indianapolis* . . . that's torture. Right? That little 'known to have'? That's some Franklin who's persuaded to look the other way while Jackdaw's accomplice got hung up or buried till she told what she knew."

Silence.

"Answer me."

"Yes."

"Yes?"

"Yes."

I had to hold the phone away from me. I bared my teeth. I tilted my head back. Tortured, then, before she was killed. Of course. I knew there was something behind it all along, and what's always behind everything? When you scrape away the sticky cobweb of euphemisms like *known to have intended to remove himself,* you always find something hiding underneath it, and it is always violence. It's always some kind of violence.

I said the girl's name to myself, the name Kevin had called out to the sky. Luna. The sun was all the way gone now. The sky was dark, and the moon had crept up, shrouded in clouds.

"The one thing . . ." Bridge started, then stopped.

"What?"

"I didn't know."

"What didn't you know?"

"Anything. When I delivered that file to you, I thought it was real. I promise you that, Victor."

Jesus Christ. He wanted me to care. He wanted me to know that he cared, for God's sake.

"I agreed with you from the beginning about the quality of the file. I also felt there was something off there. I told you to do your job because that's *my* job. But you had—numerous concerns, and you were vocal about them. You were persistent about those."

"I told you to look into it."

"And I looked into it." He cleared his throat. "Correct."

A sensation welled up in me, of tenderness. Empathy. This feeling I strangled. I tightened my grip on the phone. I focused on sorting out the timeline.

"So you called your boss and asked him about the file."

"Her."

"Fine. Her. And she called you back when? Friday morning?"

"Yes. And she told me there was nothing to be concerned about. But that—I was not satisfied with that. I pushed her. She hung up. She called me back Friday night."

"Seven thirty."

"Yes. Right. She told me..." A fumbling half-second silence, a search for language. "She gave me the backstory on this."

"She told you that members of your agency have been participating in a massive fraud on the American people." I was in a mood now to have my suspicions explicitly confirmed. "Bridge?"

"Yes."

"And she told you the real job here was to find this kid so he could be killed and this evidence could be collected and destroyed."

Silence. Total silence. Dead and sad.

"Bridge? She explained to you that the real job here was to find this kid so he could be murdered and his magic envelope tossed on a fire. Yes or no?"

"Yes."

"And why didn't you tell her to go fuck herself?"

"It's just...that's not—that wasn't an option for me."

Not an option for him. I marveled at the phrase. I wondered

in shades of furious red what the shackles were that he imagined himself to be wearing: loyalty? Some tawdry piece of information she was holding, this boss, maybe about some malfeasance of *his* some years ago? Was it—the word choked in me—love? Were they *fucking,* Bridge and this mysterious *her?* I held the phone down to my stomach for a second, twisted the cheap piece of plastic like it was someone's neck, and then I put it back to my ear.

"—you want, Victor?"

"It's very simple. That boy is dead."

"Dead . . . how—"

"They killed him by accident."

I didn't give him time to be happy about it. I ground my teeth. I bore down. "But the package never made it out of the Four. He left it behind. Somewhere."

"Why?"

"Just listen. He left it behind. He felt betrayed by the Airlines, and he stashed it. It's still behind the Fence. And no one can get it. And they are sending me there to get it. Do you understand? I have been subverted. I am a double agent now. I work for the enemy."

At last Bridge did not ask why or say, "What?" At last he simply understood.

"You work for the enemy, except you are telling me that you do."

"I've got layers, Mr. Bridge. I go way down."

Darkness was rising all around me like black water. Darkness was subsuming me; darkness *was* me. I focused instead on the distant light, high and far above me, the glittering promise I had glimpsed when Barton set me to my new task.

"I'm going to go get this thing for these people," I told Bridge. "And then I'm going to bring it to you. And in exchange, you're going to give me what I want."

"Which is?"

"Which is freedom. I bring it back, and you pull out my pin. You unclip me, and I go to Canada, and I never hear from you again."

*　　*　　*

I caught up to Martha coming out of her room, halfway down the first-floor hallway, a duffel bag strung over her arm. I was holding a bag, too, the thin plastic bag they give you for dirty laundry.

"Martha," I said, and she turned around, and I didn't have my glasses on and my clothes were a rumpled mess. There was blood on my sleeve, blood down the length of my arm.

"Jim?" she said, but even as she said it she knew that Jim was gone—I had left Jim behind; he had melted into mud in the bed of the White River.

"My name's not Jim," I said. "It's Victor."

"What?"

"And it's not even Victor."

"What—what's in the bag?"

We went into her room, where we could be alone. The same as my room, but with two double beds instead of one king. One of the beds, Martha's bed, was spotless, made, and Lionel's was a mess of kid stuff—comic books, small garbagey plastic toys, spacemen and soldier-men and superheroes. Lionel was waiting in the lobby, she said, while she packed up the car. Except I told her that she couldn't go.

"No. What? We're—I checked out. We're leaving."

I took her hands—I squeezed them.

"Listen," I said, and goddamn it if I wasn't crying—crying for Kevin, crying for me, for Castle. "I need help," I said. "I need a lot of help."

I had never been on the blood sump because the blood sump was not a station. In your first two years inside they moved you every three months, and in two years I had worked the lairage, the chiller, hooves and horns, the downpuller, every stop along the rail. But the blood sump was not a regular station because it did not need to be tended regularly.

It tended to itself. Excess blood from the kill floor guttered through the drain and filled up the sump outside, and two times a year a truck came with a pipe and sucked it out.

But it was raining. The Chinese were on-site, that was the first thing, and the second thing was the rain, and then there was fat Reedy getting sick like he did.

Opportunity came like that: one, two, three. Castle had been telling me it would come, and it came like that, like horseshoes ringing on the pole, one, two, three. Did Castle know that opportunity would come, or did opportunity come because Castle said it? Anyway, it came.

I had heard about the Chinese before but never seen them. On this day in the morning we got woke before even the rooster, and the Old Men had all been woken before that, and they were all clapping and shouting: Tianjin Jiachu! Tianjin Jiachu! That was the name of the company, our biggest customer, but to me then those words were just like magic words, and all the Old Men and the guards were fussy or furious, barking orders, and all the working whites were walking double-time, talking loud. Get down to work. Eyes on the ball. Do it for each other. For Mr. Bell.

I was cutting out intestines on that day, pulling out the thick ropes of stomach and winding them into careful piles, and I was at it but fifteen minutes when they swept in, a crowd of curious Chinese, appearing on the floor all together and then scattering into every corner: bowing, peering into stations. I kept on working. Everybody did. The men and women from Tianjin Jiachu had knee pads on, and they crawled under the machines and murmured. They had clipboards tucked neatly under their arms. The Franklins made way for them, and so did the working whites.

And then in came Mr. Bell, in his big brown boots and his sharp white shirt and deep red tie, shaking the hands of the Chinese, answering the questions as they got translated, waiting and smiling, stroking his mustache, while his answers got translated back. He smiled at every one of us he saw, smiled and rubbed us on our heads, then the Chinese did, too, as if in wonder. They felt inside our mouths with the tips of their fingers. One of them pinched the flesh of my upper arms and smiled, as if he were pleased with the feel of me, and I remember how odd I felt, odd and proud.

That's what was first. And then there was the rain. A late-summer storm like we had never seen, not in my days, cascades of rain pounding the tin roof of the kill house, soaking the poor littlest ones out there on the pile . . . and overflowing the blood pump. I was holding my knife; I was slicing into the heavy belly of the skinless cow that hung shackled before me. A working white raced in, water weeping off his cuffs and sleeves, and he whispered something frantic to a guard, and the guard made a face and came over and pulled at Mr. Bell, and Mr. Bell crooked a finger at fat Reedy.

Mr. Bell smiled, untroubled, at the worried-looking Chinese, who were writing on their clipboards and muttering things that were not being translated. Mr. Bell laid a hand on big Reedy and said, "Take one of 'em. Bail it out."

Mr. Bell picked Reedy and Reedy picked Castle and Castle picked me.

I have always wondered if Castle understood. Did Castle see opportunity in this moment, Reedy laying his doughy hand on his shoulder? Did he know—this is it? The other world is seeping through—the other world, our future world? Or did he only think, I am being granted a half hour off the line, and let me give that to my brother, too?

Because Reedy just said, "You, boy." And it was Castle who dared to question his judgment on that. Castle who said, "Respect, sir, I think I need another one."

Castle must have known—or did he know?—he must have known,

which I did not know, that the blood pump, by the primitive, premodern design of Bell's Farm, was sandwiched into a strip of muddy land between the kill house and the fence. Castle must have guessed — or could he have? — that the presence of the Chinese would be consuming the attention of the staff and that these facts combined with the rainstorm darkness and the flickering old electrics would make it more likely than ever that we could take the chance that we had been waiting for, find the story Castle had never needed, in all those years, to tell me. And all that stood between us and that story was old Reedy, fat Reedy, sad Reedy.

Reedy was an easy one. There were hard ones, and there were easy ones — among the guards, among the working whites, among the Old Men, and among the Franklins, even. Reedy wore glasses. Reedy was worn down. He had white in his hair and red on his cheeks. Once, watching us march in our line from kill house to bunkhouse, once I had seen him shake his head and look to the ground. Sadness.

"All right, son," he said to Castle. "So pick one."

So Castle picked me, and we squatted at the door of the kill house and tugged on our thick galoshes, and we were bailing that blood pool and we couldn't keep up with it. The rain was too fast, and it was backed up, clotted at all the drains, and Castle and me were working as quick as we could, but it was rising and rising, swamping our ankles and creeping to our knees, a thickening mass around our bodies.

"Ah, hell," Reedy was saying, watching us uneasily from the lip of the sump, shifting in his boots, rubbing storm water off his glasses for the hundredth time. He looked around in the rain. He didn't want to be down in no blood pit with no two boys. But even worse would be going in there and telling Mr. Bell the job wasn't done.

"Ah, hell," he said again and peeled off his overcoat and holstered his gun and came down into the sump with the two of us, Castle and me.

The rain flooded down. It crashed around us. Two black boys and one white guard, bailing like crazy, buckets and barrels, and from the corner of my eye I was watching those fence posts. We were always talking about how high they went, those fence posts, high wood pillars connected by sheets of mesh with cyclone wire at the top, always talking about how high they were, but never *how low they went. That was another question — how deeply those posts were rooted. I had never thought of it, but now the rain was turning the dirt to mud, and you could see where the roots of the posts were leaning, shifting in that mud, just a little, starting just a little bit to shift and lean.*

"We're doing it, fellas," shouted Reedy, forgetting himself entirely. "We're doing it! Keep on, now."

But he was wrong. As furious as we were bailing we weren't keeping up with it, not even close, not now with the rain filling up the blood hole as fast as we could pump it. Reedy was maybe working the hardest of the three of us, going faster and faster, until he was grunting and sweating, and I was watching the ground beneath that fence post getting muddier and muddier, the post coming looser in the mud. But Castle was watching Reedy, who wasn't just grunting but moaning now, who had dropped his bucket and collapsed onto his knees, splashing and falling into the mud and lurching forward.

"Oh, Lord," he said, and then something else that wasn't words at all. Just a long animal groan.

"Mr. Reedy," I shouted, and he said something like "Get — " and then stopped talking. His mouth hung open, frozen, like the word had thickened in his throat and stopped him up.

Get help. Get someone. Get me up. But Reedy was past words. His face was dark, choked, and red; all his body's blood had come up into his cheeks and his neck, and I was wet with fear and the rain in wild sheets. Reedy staring at us helpless, arms flapping, eyes wide, like a great fish.

"It's okay now, sir," I said, talking automatically, and I stepped toward him through the waist-high thickness of blood water, and Castle grabbed me hard and pulled me close and slapped me. Castle's big eyes, wide in the rainstorm, Castle shaking me by the arms — by both arms.

"Turn around, boy," he said. "Turn and run to that fence. Go!"

I did it — I ran to the fence and bent to its foundation and was tugging at it when I heard the shot behind me, one hollow shot swallowed in the rain. I had the post up already. I had the chain down.

"Come on!" said Castle, still holding Reedy's pistol, and we ran. There was no time, but I looked back once and saw Reedy's body as it slipped down and was swallowed in all that blood.

Part Two

SOUTH

Obviously there will be disagreements within any such body, and the United States of America does not shrink from disagreement. But every nation has her traditions, and America shall not relinquish its traditions as a prerequisite to participation in any institution.

— Secretary of State Henry Kissinger at a press conference to announce the United States' withdrawal from the United Nations, December 11, 1973

Good riddance.

— Sir Colin Crowe, British permanent representative to the United Nations, quoted in the London Times, *December 12, 1973*

1.

We drove south all day Monday, Martha and me.

We drove in a white Toyota with Wisconsin plates, an Airlines junker that had been waiting in a Southside parking lot, just where Cook had said it would be, with the keys duct-taped in the wheel well. The Toyota rattled at speeds over sixty miles per hour, so I kept it at fifty-five all the way through southern Indiana and the western part of Kentucky. Route 65 down there behaved more like a country two-lane than a big interstate, winding and gentle, running like a brook. We drove up and then down the Blue Ridge Mountains, into the clear blue air of Tennessee. The ugly weather burned away as we went. We passed red barns and green fields and acres of swaying corn. The sky was all porcelain blue and gentle white clouds, the whole curve of heaven like painted pottery. Every town had its steeple and its water tower, and the shoulder was dotted with wooden signs advertising pies and antiques.

It all made me weary and anxious. I took it all, all the sugar-sweet beauty of the sky and the charm of the landscape, as a taunt: a haughty sneer from the venerable southland as we drew nearer. *Purty down here, ain't it? Well, come on, now, 'n' sit a spell...*

We listened to Michael all the way down. We started with *Thriller,* then we jumped back in time, did *Ben,* MJ with the big Afro on the cover, looking mournful.

His tragedy was always in his face, even from the beginning. You could see it in his eyes.

We listened to "Take Care of Our Brothers," the charity single that caused poor Michael so much grief. It raised a ton of money for relief, but half his fans called him a sucker, said it was an amelioration anthem—so he disclaimed it, and then the other half of his fans said he was letting himself get pushed around, boxed in, politicized.

Sometimes I think he never recovered from that. Sometimes I think he spent the rest of his life trying to escape from all that shit, from what our country is, but of course he couldn't do it. Of course you can't.

God, those songs, though. That voice. It carried us all the way down.

"Evenin'. What can I do for y'all?"

This man wore no name tag. Either this motel, the Rambler's Roost, did not provide uniforms for its employees or the desk clerk was happier in his rumpled plaid button-down shirt, worn unbuttoned to show off a beer-company T-shirt. He surveyed us warily from behind the desk.

"We just need a room, thanks," Martha told him.

I hung back, hovered in the shadows of the dark, unpleasant lobby of the Rambler's Roost, with the mismatched armchairs and the smell of burned coffee.

"Just the one room, eh?" said the old cracker.

"Yes," said Martha.

"And how many beds?"

His eyes were moving slowly back and forth between the two of us: me and Martha, Martha and me. The Rambler's Roost was in Pulaski, Tennessee, fifty miles north of the Fence, but of course it got thicker the farther south you went, that coefficient of difficulty involved in doing even the simplest tasks. I think of it sometimes as a pressure in the atmosphere, like walking under water: the extra effort required to get served at a restaurant, make a purchase at a store. Check in to a motel.

"Whatever you got is fine." Martha spoke through clenched teeth. "Do you have a room or don't you?"

"Oh, I reckon I might."

The clerk turned with his hands on his hips to look at the pigeonholes on the wall, nearly every one of which had a key inside. He pulled out number 12 and placed it on the counter, but when Martha reached for it, he put his flat, heavy hand on top of hers and whispered.

"Listen, hon." Hoarse, plenty loud for me to hear. "Everything all right here?"

Martha didn't answer. She pulled her hand free from under the old man's, as though she were escaping from a trap. He shrugged, pushed her the key.

"Okay, then," he said. "Checkout is at ten thirty."

Room 12 was no improvement from the lobby. An indistinct and unpleasant smell; tattered curtains over a streaked window; a thin rug spattered with a grim archipelago of stains. There was one bed, a twin, and a rollaway cot on the floor beside it. Martha grimly lifted one corner of the bedspread, looking for bugs, I figured, and I felt a jolt of regret for bringing her here—for bringing myself here—for all this. Martha disappeared into the tiny bathroom, and I watched the door shut. I had no choice. I had a mission here—a goal. But this girl . . .

There was a mirror tacked to the wall above the dresser. I looked into it. I told myself it was okay. It was all going to be okay. This time tomorrow, Martha would be back in Indianapolis, picking up Lionel from her sister's place. By this time tomorrow, all this would be a strange dream—in twenty-four hours I would be a dream she had woken from.

Our deal was simple: clean and clear. Money for service.

The money had come from my petty cash, all the unmarked money Bridge provided me with for incidentals, money that— after the next couple days—I would never need again. I'd had twenty grand in a lockbox within the safe of the hotel room. I'd had five thousand in a false bottom of my rolling suitcase. Another

$5,200 in the glove compartment of the Altima. Four hundred-dollar bills from one wallet and two hundred-dollar bills from a second wallet; a final two thousand sewn into the lining of a tan sport coat.

From this I'd counted out Martha's $29,500 and brought it to her in the laundry bag.

I told her the truth—a version of it. A portion, calved off from the whole. I was an agent of the Underground Airlines. I was going down into the Four to recover something that had been lost, a weapon in the battle against the old foe. All true; no lies. All true.

And no black was permitted to travel into any of the states of the Hard Four without a white companion to vouch for his whereabouts and be responsible for his conduct.

I needed a white person.

"I know this is a lot to take in," I told her.

"It's okay," she said. "It's okay." I kept going. I spoke quickly.

"I will provide you with a false identification for the border crossing," I told her. "When we're across, clear of the border, you will reenter the North with your real ID and burn the false one. Then you're done. You go back to Indy and get your money and you're done. You can do what you had intended with it, or you can—I don't know. Take your boy and get out of the country. Go to Europe. So—"

"Yes," she said.

She wasn't listening to what I was saying about Europe. About leaving. I could see the option sliding past her, untouched. She was going to hand my money over to the clown from Steubenville, Ohio, who claimed he could get her into TorchLight, and that was a foolish move, but that was not my concern. She was an adult, and I was making her an offer, and all I needed was for her to take it, and she took it. She was in.

I handed her the laundry bag. She didn't look inside. She didn't count the money. She held the bag carelessly by its thin plastic strap, looking with new interest at my face. "I have one condition."

"What?"

"You have to tell me your name. Your real name. That's my only condition."

It took me a minute. I had to fish around to find it. Castle called me honey and Bridge called me Victor. I've hung so many names on myself, one after another. And I actually have a name, a real human name that my mother whispered in my ear when I was four years old, before I was taken from the breed lot and put into the school. Sweet and secret private name.

I almost told it to Martha, but then I decided to give her my service name instead. My Bell's name. That was fine. That was close enough.

"Brother," I told her. "My name is Brother."

That was last night. Now here we were, five hundred miles away, and I was staring out the window, standing in my pants and undershirt, watching red taillights stack up in the darkness. Martha came out of the bathroom.

"Whoa."

"What?"

She was squinting, coming closer, looking concerned. "Your shoulder." I realized I was holding on to it, clutching the spot where bands of pain were radiating out into my neck and upper back. "That needs to come out."

I took my hand away, and it was slick and glittering with pus. "Shit."

"Yeah. Shit. That is definitely infected." Martha took a step closer and squinted at the wound.

"Let's get it out," I said. "Now."

We had no extra time tomorrow. No time tonight for a fever, no time for the course of illness. A hospital, obviously, was out of the question.

And Martha, as it turned out, a frequent traveler and an unemployed medical assistant, had with her everything she needed, more or less, to pull a piece of battered metal out of my flesh. Suture kit and bandages, aspirin and gauze, even a small scalpel.

"The only thing I don't have," she said, "is any kind of anesthetic. But in the morning I'm sure we could get to a pharmacy—"

"No," I said. "Now."

She shook her head and looked at me, a wounded stranger in the dim hotel room. A long way from Jim Dirkson.

"All right, Brother. Go ahead and lie down on the bed."

She fetched ice from the vending machine, and she wrapped some in a washcloth and held it on my shoulder till it was numb.

"Well, that oughta do *something*," said Martha, and I couldn't say if it did or not: her knife slid into my shoulder, and it hurt like hell.

I winced. I held my breath. My shoulder was on fire; my shoulder and my back.

"You're doing great," Martha said in the soft, coaxing tone I'd heard her use with her boy. "You're doing just fine. Just hang tight."

She breathed carefully while making her careful incisions, and then I felt her fingers working on and in my flesh, burrowing, sentient things, insects crawling around. I clutched the edge of the thin mattress with both hands and squeezed. I wasn't born for this, I was thinking. I wasn't born to be any kind of soldier or spy. This was all a mistake.

"I see it," she said gently. "I see it already. It's close to the surface. Just hold tight, Brother. Just hold on."

Martha began to tug, carefully at first, and then quickly, and I felt the bullet wriggling loose, pulling free. I wondered if this was what it would be like with Bridge. Bridge's doctor, taking out the chip. That was part of it, part of the deal we had made, the deal I had forced him into. It was deeper down than the bullet, of course, deeper down and more tightly interwoven. Tied in to the base of my brain with a million tiny fibers. Tucked tightly between the two upmost vertebrae.

Then, with one last intake of breath, Martha pulled it out. "Got it!" I craned my head around and saw her grinning. "There! Got the little fucker."

Her fingers in their thin gloves were covered in my blood. Her face was exultant. I smiled, weakly, and struggled up in the bed. She dropped the bullet into my outstretched palm, and it was small and ugly, smeared with blood and tissue, its black copper head flattened by force. When Martha laid it in my hand it was warm, like a grub or the end of a tongue. I put it on the night table, under the shade of the lamp, and lay back down so she could sew me up.

Somehow this hurt less—the stitching. Maybe I was already feeling better from the bullet being gone. Maybe I was getting used to it, another person's hands inside my body. Maybe being put back together just hurt less than coming apart.

"You're like a different person," I told Martha as she finished up, pulled the black thread through me one last time. "Doing this."

"What do you mean?"

"I just mean—steady."

"What do you mean, steady?"

My answer was interrupted by a gunshot, outside, somewhere close. Loud and unmistakable. I yanked the bedside light out of the wall, rolled over onto Martha in the darkness and covered her on the ground, lay there panting on top of her, my shoulder throbbing and burning. There was a second shot, then a third.

"What do you think—"

"Stay here," I said and crawled to the door. I crept, hunched over, down the hallway to the front office, my gun tucked into the waistband of my pants, blood oozing from my wound. I went down that narrow hotel hallway in the middle of the night with the sure dark feeling that something new and terrible had happened. Something bad was happening.

"Well, hey there, boy," said the cracker at the desk. "You coming to join the party?"

Another gunshot outside, then loud cheering: shouts, applause. A celebration. They weren't shooting in anger, they were shooting in the air. I glanced at the man's TV screen, where CNN had put up a still photograph of Donatella Batlisch, a file photo, a head shot, frozen.

"Was she—" I don't know why I asked. I already knew. "Did she get confirmed?"

"No, and she won't be. She got taken care of is what she got." He mimed the shape of a gun, mimed the squeezing of the trigger. "One shot. Back of the neck. Some boy did his mama proud tonight, that's for damn sure."

I didn't have to tell it to Martha. When I got back to the room the lights were still off, but the TV was on, and she was sitting on the edge of the bed, her face bathed in the glow of the bad news.

I closed the door behind me, and she stood up quietly and turned it off.

I stood at the window with my right hand reached across to my left shoulder, my hand tight on the wound. I wasn't feeling sorrow, not exactly. Not surprise, certainly. I was feeling again like I wasn't made for all this. That's what I was thinking. Born into the wrong life, somehow. Wrong body. Blood seeped from my shoulder, drying in the thin cotton fabric of my undershirt. The celebration was growing outside, a crowd of happy Tennesseans clustered in the moonlight around the tailgate of a dull white pickup truck, handing out bottles of beer.

Beyond them, traffic had eased up on I-65, and cars were rushing south toward the Fence.

Martha's face was set, grim and hard. "Have you ever been down there?" she said.

"Never," I said. "Never in all my life."

2.

We cleared the Border House with no problem.

There were six wide lanes of traffic, six guard stations, six mechanical arms rising and falling to let vehicles in one at a time. There was a lane for WHITE (ALABAMA CITIZEN) and a lane for WHITE (OTHER UNITED STATES CITIZEN), and a lane for COLORED IN CAR (ALABAMA PERMIT) and the lane we took: COLORED IN CAR (OTHER UNITED STATES PERMIT).

They're federal at the Fence, agents of a special division of the Department of Homeland Security called Internal Border and Regulation. IBR is black boots and yellow jackets and mirrored glasses, automatic pistols in shoulder holsters. It was one of these IBR men, deeply tan and sandy-haired, stone-faced and courteous, who motioned for me to roll down the window of the Toyota, who leaned over me to address Martha in the backseat, who flipped cursorily through our papers—papers furnished for me by Mr. Bridge, sterling papers, papers made of solid gold. Who then said politely to Martha, "If you would ask your Negro to step out of the car, please," who then walked me through a bank of scanners, who ran his gloved fingers under my tongue, passed hands over my scalp, who shined a light up my asshole and lifted my balls, who ran flat palms over all the inches of my flesh. Who removed my body momentarily and completely from my control and then returned it to me with a grunt: "You folks are just fine." He said it to Martha, not to me. "Go ahead."

The IBR is federal, but on the other side of the Fence are three more agencies, each its own brick building, bristling with flags and radio antennae: the Alabama Highway Division, the Limestone County Sheriff's Office, and the Alabama branch of the Interstate Colored Persons Patrol. Each one of these agencies has the statutory right to stop any of the vehicles leaving the custody of the IBR, but none of them chose for whatever reason to stop us that morning in our white Toyota.

There was a Latin motto on the far side of the Border House— AUDEMAS JURA NOSTRA DEFENDERE—bright white on a lavender background, then a cheerful sign in roadway green: WELCOME TO ALABAMA THE BEAUTIFUL.

I drove, and Martha rode in the back. They were watching me; I pictured them watching. Bridge in Maryland, Barton and company in Indy, glued to their screens. My dot moving south, crossing the line.

My own eyes were wide open, waiting to see all the ways the world would change now that we had crossed through, past the limit of civilization and into the dark land, where whites keep their rule by savagery and fear. I waited for the sky to darken, for the crows that would wheel across the clouds. But it was the same winding road, the same spreading green countryside, the same taffy-blue sky. Same on either side of the Fence.

"Hey," Martha said. Was saying. Leaning forward between the seats. "Brother?" I guess she had been talking for a while. I turned slightly toward her, and it hurt my shoulder.

"You all right?" she said.

"Don't worry," I said. "You did it. You're done." I turned back, kept my eyes on the road. Careful driving, nice and easy. "We're fifty-seven miles now from Green Hollow. We'll pull up, like we said, in the town square. Then you're going to turn around. Find a shoulder you can pull off on and burn those papers, like I showed you. Then you get on back to your boy. Park the Toyota in that Townes Stores lot."

"Southport and Emerson."

"That's right. And you know where the money is."

Martha didn't say anything. Black highway rushed beneath us; streetlamps passed us; trees.

"Okay," she said.

"And thank you, Martha," I said. "Thank you."

Two hours later I was walking on a sunlit sidewalk with my head down through the bustling small-town square of Green Hollow, Alabama, looking for a man on a horse, looking for the lawyer.

It was as if I had arrived not just in another part of the country but in another part of the century. Men in fedora hats and mustaches, ladies in short-sleeved flower-pattern dresses pushing big perambulators, smiling. Everybody smiling. The gentle ting-a-ting of welcome bells as these gentlefolk pushed into stores under multicolored awnings that fluttered in the wind. Folks tipping their hats, holding the door for one another as they went in and out of a diner called the Cotyledon Café, a tidy little freestanding pink building with a window box full of peonies along its front glass and a sign with proud curly-cursive lettering: THIS IS A PREJUDICED ESTABLISHMENT.

The other restaurant on the square was General Bobby's, a fried-chicken chain that, I happened to know, was owned by the same conglomerate that owns Hamburger Stand in Indianapolis, where I'd just eaten a few days ago. That's how they do it, these big chains that don't want their customers to know how much business they're doing behind the Fence: subsidiary companies, parent companies, diversified holdings.

I made my way around the square, beneath the sky of daydream blue, the pure white clouds like drifts of cotton. I passed a couple of white men in hats, men of the world conversing in somber tones about what one of them called "last night's unfortunate incident."

"What else could be done is the question," said the other, while both nodded their heads with solemnity, men of the world. "Oh, yes, I know. What else could be done?"

And while they discussed in their somber tones the tragic necessity of ready assassination, their Negroes stood behind them staring at the sidewalk, unseen and unspeaking. And behind a white lady pushing a carriage was a black woman, much older, lugging a diaper caddy and an armful of boutique shopping bags. And there I was, moving through this watercolor world like a ghost. It was like there were two realities out here, overlaid one on top of the other, like transparencies on an overhead projector.

Where was the lawyer, though? Where were the man and his horse?

"So how do we make these arrangements?" I had asked Mr. Maris back in Indianapolis, back at Saint Anselm's, in the shabby headquarters. After Barton was gone again, when it was just me and the lieutenants. Cook gave me the backstory, and then he and Maris briefed me on the connection I was to make.

"Arrangements?" he said. "No. Listen. Understand."

"We don't make arrangements, man," Cook put in, leaning in the doorway, working at his teeth with a toothpick, listening closely. "We make connections."

"What does that mean?"

Maris didn't turn his head. He kept his cold eyes on my face while Cook talked. "What Mr. Friendly Sunshine here is gonna do is tell you where to go and how to find the lawyer. What happens after that is up to you and the lawyer. You understand?"

Maris, then, very slow and very low. "We only know what we know."

"All right," I said. "All right. And who's the lawyer?"

Maris said it again: "We only know what we know," which wasn't exactly the same as saying he didn't know who the lawyer was. Mr. Maris, of all those I had met, was the hardest to read. His sharp features a perfect mask. "The town is called Green Hollow," he said. "Twenty miles northwest of Birmingham. There you find a statue. In the square."

"What square?"

"It's a small town, man," said Cook. "Just the one square."

222

"You go to the square. Weekday. Any weekday. Between eleven twenty-five and eleven thirty-five in the morning. You stand beneath the man and his horse. You wait for the lawyer there."

So here I was: it was 11:28 in Green Hollow, Alabama, in the one square in town. I was sweating now. My papers were good, solid rock, but there had to be a limit to how long you could wander around in public, unaccompanied, in your black skin, papers or no papers. Law enforcement on the square was in two forms: the friendly neighborhood cop from the Town of Green Hollow Police Department, with his hands behind his back, a bright silver whistle around his neck, smiling at children and nodding to passersby; and up on the rooftops an officer of the Alabama branch of the Interstate Colored Persons Patrol, in all-black, body armor, rifle, and helmet. He was either trying to be inconspicuous and failing up there or, more likely, making absolutely sure that his presence was registered by every person on the square—the black ones especially.

I, at least, had a keen awareness of him as I searched that square looking for a goddamn statue of a man and a horse. The only statues I could find, though, were wrong: the first was an ugly gray statue of a man on the prow of a swift boat, a Texas War veteran, stabbing his forefinger aloft as if commanding unseen troops but receiving only the attention of a flock of sickly pigeons roosting on the brim of his hat. The other statue was of a short bespectacled man in a midcentury suit, waving gaily, trailed by a beagle. I had circled the square three times looking for the man and his horse without finding it.

I took another pass around the square. Outside the Cotyledon was a small crowd of blacks, talking quietly, waiting, I figured, for their masters to finish lunch. And inside, alone at a table for two, was Martha Flowers.

What the hell? I thought, feeling a queer surge of anger and—what? Relief? *What the hell?*

We had said our good-byes on the outskirts of town, in the parking lot of a Qatar Star gas station. All I said was "Say good-bye to that kid for me," and all she said was "I sure will," and then I got out of the car and went around the back to use the colored persons' restroom, and when I came back she was gone, just as we had planned it.

She should have been at the Border House by now, digging her real actual Indiana driver's license out of her big messy pocketbook.

Instead she was in there, studying the menu of the Cotyledon Café, legs crossed at the ankles like a proper belle, like her own evil twin. I looked twice, making sure it was Martha, and then I stopped looking, not knowing how many times you could look through the plate glass of a restaurant at a white woman before the patrolman up on the roof noticed you looking.

I took another turn around the square. There was a good film of sweat on me now: desperation, confusion, some sour combination of fury and fear. Martha Flowers was enjoying a slice of pie on the town square, and meanwhile where the fuck is this horse? Where the fuck is this lawyer?

I stumbled on an uneven patch of sidewalk and very nearly bumped into the broad back of a slow-walking white man with a cane. I breathed. I slowed my pace. Passed carefully beneath the oak trees and the black lampposts. Passed the general store, the movie house, the Internet café. I saw that, scattered across the lawn of the park, clustered together, were a dozen or more dark-skinned men and women lying about in small groups, dozing and talking and drinking out of paper bags.

And then, finally, for the third time, I walked around that stupid statue before I decided to read the plaque beneath it: HENRY SMITH, TOWN FATHER, AND HIS LOYAL COMPANION, HORSE.

Horse. A dog named Horse. Somewhere, Willie Cook was having a good long laugh on me.

I leaned against the fence that ran around the statue, then immediately thought better of it and straightened up. The clock on the courthouse said 11:35 — was it too late? Had I messed this up already?

I rehearsed in my mind the call and response, the password and echo, that Maris had given me.

"Some fine day, ain't it?" this mysterious lawyer would say when he spotted me, and I then would say: "Fine and dandy, like sugar candy."

Three times we had practiced it. Maris: "Some fine day, ain't it?"— the country slang made mildly comical by his African accent—and me: "Fine and dandy."

The lawyer will spot you, Maris said. He will know you by where you stand and when. You will know him by what he says. Now say it again. We practiced it three times, simple as it was: "Some fine day, ain't it?" "Fine and dandy, like sugar candy."

I stood beside the statue and waited for the lawyer. I couldn't see Martha from here. The diner was on the other side of the square. I thought of my future. I thought of a home in Canada, a small fairy-tale house, smoke coming up from a cookstove chimney. Snow on the eaves and on the branches of maple trees. A view across a frozen lake.

I did not try to calculate how close or far I was from Bell's Farm, neither as the crow flies nor on the roadways that could be crossed by a transport van.

When I looked up again at the people of Green Hollow, going about their bustling midday business, shopping and eating and chatting, I did not see the white people, only the black: and as I watched I swore I could see fumes rising from their mouths— fumes rolling out of their mouths like exhaust, and I could see that every black person had the same small cloud of angry smoke coming out of his or her mouth and nose, a haze rolling up off the street like exhaust, filling the air, the white people breathing all that and not knowing it.

Someone tapped me on the shoulder, and I turned. He was black, wiry, wearing overalls, carrying a shovel.

"Some fine day, ain't it?" said the man with the shovel, and I said, "Fine and—" and he caught me on the side with the handle of the shovel, a hard smash that knocked me right off my feet. I reeled back into the arms of a second man, a man I hadn't seen, who caught me and held me tightly by the arms.

"What the fuck?" I said, or started to say, but the first man said, "Shut up, boy," while he dropped the shovel and punched me in the stomach.

I would have doubled over, but I was held too tight. The fresh gash in my shoulder threw up a hot flash of pain, and my guts hurt where I'd been hammered. I kicked my legs out and wriggled like a bug in the air while the first man danced backwards, fists clenched, and the huge man holding me whispered, "Almost done."

"What?" I said.

"Shut yo mouth, nigger," the first one shouted and punched me on the side of the head.

Through a haze of pain I saw the Alabama patrolman, up on the roof, watching us impassively.

"Hey," I said, but then they were all in on me, punching me again, throwing me down, landing their boots in my chest. I convulsed, moaning, closing in on myself like a fetus, and from the far corner of my eye I saw the merry beat cop on the other side of the square taking this all in with mild amusement, shaking his head as though I and the men beating me were rambunctious kids on a playground. I saw two white men in fedoras in front of the pharmacy, murmuring to each other and laughing. I saw all of them, all the good people of Green Hollow, the men and the women and the kids; all the fine folks had stopped to take in the show.

They kicked at me a few more times, though I writhed enough, wrenching my body this way and that, to take most of their shots in the shins or in the back, on the hard surfaces of my spine. I spat pink into the dirt and hauled up onto my haunches, steadying myself on my arms with my hands palm-planted in the scrabble grass. Above me the two men stood with fists balled, staring down.

I wondered if a rumor was flying around town. I wondered if it had reached Martha's table at the Cotyledon. I hoped she'd have the

226

sense to stay where she was. Not to give herself away, not to rush out and cry my name—Jim, or Brother, any name at all.

"Stay *down*," the bigger of the two men hissed, and I did, I stayed down, and the two of them leaned over me glowering and godlike.

The one who hissed at me had a fierce, cold look about him, like he was wrought from iron. I let the strength of my arms go slack and fluttered my eyes shut and the two men heaved me bodily out of that dirt. I was carried between them like a bag of soil, aft and end, my head lolling back to one side. My ears were ringing, and a thick knot of pain was gathering in my stomach where the one man's boot had first connected.

They bore me that way, body slack and head hanging backwards, across the patchy courthouse lawn toward a big car waiting, pulled up to the sidewalk. A woman fell into the pack, walking along with us, a pace or two behind. Her hair was wrapped in a tight-fitting orange cloth. She had thick arms, a powerful striding body. She scowled at me as we progressed across the lawn, her hands clenched into fists, her eyes like two stones deep in her head.

"Are you the lawyer?" I said to her.

"Do I *look* like a fucking lawyer to you?"

She stepped close to me. To me, being carried as I was with my head thrown back, she was upside down. With swift, precise movements, she took out a hypodermic needle and a small vial. I struggled, but there was nothing to be done—the men held me tight while she filled the needle and jabbed it into a vein in the side of my neck. My vision swayed. They dropped me into the trunk of the car.

"Welcome to the Hard Four," said one of the voices, gruff and full of laughter, while the world slipped away from me. "It don't get a lot better."

227

3.

When the world and I found each other again I was swimming through some kind of pink-hued southern sea. I was a gone goose. I was flying, but I was underground, too. I was under the city of Indianapolis, back in Jackdaw's miserable tunnel, surrounded by dripping clay walls, by darkness and illness and cold. I was in Bell's Farm; I was in the shed buried underneath the earth, a Franklin's black government boots just visible through the slit, and I had done something, but what had I done? And I was also at the Capital City Crossroads Hotel, in the basement, where the pool and the gym were, and I was on that planet that Castle used to murmur in my ear, the planet called the future.

I got up, and I fell down. First onto my knees, and then, after a moment's consideration, the rest of the way, down onto my back. I felt something alien on my thigh and looked down and it was my dick, flopped over like a scrap of rope. I was bare-ass naked, which was hilarious, and some people were laughing, so I went ahead and laughed, too. My voice was a creepy giggle, unfamiliar to me, so I stopped.

"Get back up on the chair now," said a woman's voice, stern but not unkind. A little tremor of humor in the voice. "Go on. Come on."

I obeyed instructions as best I could. First I put my forearms onto the seat of the chair, then I heaved myself up and twisted myself around. I had to stop halfway through and get a couple breaths in me, paused with my ass in the air, gulping the smell of basement—what the hell basement was I in?—and hearing more laughter swimming all around the corners of my brain.

The jab and the sting. That vial, that stubby little pot full of poison. Someone caught me with a shot of something. Whatever it was had me all cooked up for sure. I was out on the ice—I was out on the dance floor no question.

"Siddown, honey," said the voice, then the face that belonged to it came into focus—it was the woman from the square there, the one who had poked me. The orange head wrap was gone: her hair was short dreadlocks, a bristle of corks. She was crouching now in front of me. She had cagey eyes and ruby lips and her skin was smooth. She lifted a red bath towel that had fallen off my lap and pooled at my feet. It must have been covering my nakedness while I dozed in the chair—I lifted it up and covered myself up again.

"Now, listen," I began.

"Shush, man. You're in no state."

"Ah, he all right," called someone else, a man, from the far side of the room, and someone else said, "He's just fine," and then a third voice, a woman's voice: "Fine and dandy," and then all the voices were laughing. Not me, not this time. "Now, look," I said, and the woman told me to shush again, firmly, and I shushed again. The kitchen was crowded with people. A kitchen! I was in a kitchen, in a basement, unfinished and unfancy. One of the men was sitting on a counter, swinging his legs. Another was leaning against a refrigerator, with a girl wrapped up in his arms like they were old-time sweethearts.

Everybody was in black. Everybody was wearing overalls, with a logo at the breast. Everybody was either barefoot or in sandals.

There was music playing. It had taken a while to reach me, but now I could hear it, and it was like sugar. Horns. Trumpets. Saxophones? And drums: snares and cymbals. It was fast and sweet, and it rolled around the room. I tasted that music. It was like hard candy.

"Sorry about the violence out in the square," said the woman with the dreads. "Two black folks slipping in a car together is a conspiracy. Couple black boys beating the shit out of another one, that ain't nothing. That nobody cares about. Black folks scrapping, cops ain't looking. Patrol, neither. They turning away."

"Turning away?" said the man on the counter. "C'mon, Ada. Placing bets, more like."

"Yeah," said Ada. She reached forward, touched the side of my head, and I winced. My head *hurt*. "But anyway. It's gotta look real. So. Sorry 'bout that."

"So okay," I said. Blinking my eyes and trying to get this lady to come into focus. "Are you the lawyer?"

"Damn. You all business, huh?"

"Are you?"

"No," she said. "I am not."

Ada stood up. She was a girl, really—twenty-two, maybe? Twenty-three? She was a slave. They were all slaves. Overalls, shoes or no shoes. House slaves. My body was lurching around inside me. The music was rushing, dazzling: high, squeaking horn lines and rat-a-tats on the drums.

"Who is the lawyer?" I said.

"Listen. Shut up," she said. "That was a pretty heavy kiss of olanzapine I gave you. You in no state yet to be talking business, fella."

I shook my head, insistent. I started to stand again and wobbled, and the woman called Ada placed me firmly back in the chair. Close up I saw the logo stitched on one strap of her overalls: a gavel wound with a snake. A peach dangling from a bow.

"Sit, all right?" She turned away. "Someone get the poor boy a glass of water."

"I—"

"I got it, Ada." One of the others. How many people were down here?

"Listen—"

"*Sit.*"

It was a party of sorts, down there in the basement, and I sat amid it for an hour, maybe for two hours, people walking past and around me, these beautiful black people in their overalls and sandals, grown-out scruffed-up Afros or dreadlocks, figures in a dream, while my head swam and swam. There were unlabeled boxes of wine stacked beside a tub full of cold water. A plate of cookies was being passed around, and there was a bucket full of peanuts in one corner, another bucket for shells.

I swayed to the music awhile, tried to catch up to its rhythm. Someone put a glass of water in my hand and I drank it and needed more and someone brought me more.

"You should try to relax," said the girl who brought me the water, looking at me shyly. I laughed—just the idea, the idea of relaxing. It made me laugh. I tried to think of the last time I had done that: done nothing. Acted *without* purpose. Barton, Bridge, everybody waiting on me. Indianapolis; Gaithersburg. The whole world waiting.

But I did. I relaxed. I spent the next hour, or it might have been a few, trying to count how many other people were in the room. I had an impression of people coming and going, everybody friendly, laughing loud. Slapping palms. Punch lines hollered, good-natured, grooving laughter. Aw, man, you *know* that's true. She ain't say that! She *ain't* say that!

It felt like I was among a huge crowd, a happy, bustling infinity of black folks, but it was only five of them in the room—or at least, only five by the time I got my head straight enough to count. Two women, besides Ada: Maryellen, short and puckish, with very long thick hair hanging in one big braid between her shoulder blades. She was the one who brought me the water. And Shai, a little older, narrow-eyed and observant. The bigger of the men was Otis, very dark, heavily muscled. The last of them was Marlon, who wore a scruffy kind of billy-goat beard. He was the one who had hit me, but he was also the one who came over now with a couple pieces of ice wrapped in a thin paper towel, held it tenderly to the bruise above my ear, hidden in my hair. "I'm a hard-hitting dude," he said, adjusting the ice pack. "Can't hardly help it."

"You all don't have service names?" I asked Marlon, but it was Maryellen who answered, from way over on the other side of the room, where I wouldn't have thought she could hear. "Oh, we got 'em. We don't use 'em is all."

I smiled. I looked at Maryellen, and I found that my mind would not assign her skin a value. Wild honey, light tones, all that shit. I couldn't even call it up in my mind, the pigmentation chart that had first been thrust before me in Arizona six years ago. If this didn't work, all this adventuring, and I ended up back in Bridge's command, I'd be in some difficulty, and to that I said, "Thank fucking God," and Marlon said, "For what?"

"Nothing," I said. Gingerly I removed the ice pack from my head and thanked him again.

"You straight?" he said, and I said, "I'm straight," and he chunked the ice into the sink.

The music stopped, briefly, while someone flipped the tape, and when it came on it got bigger. Multiple voices singing, sometimes words and sometimes just sounds. Rough, uneven melodies with high harmonies, then fast overlapping chopping passages. Big drumbeats, hand claps, and whistles. I had been missing it forever, whatever music this was. I longed to have known it before—I longed to have known this music all my life.

I felt myself come back into myself, drop by drop, like a drained well filling back up. I stood up, and everybody clapped for me, then they died laughing when I offered an ironic bow. I think I may have done some dancing. I politely declined the fat rolled joint that Maryellen offered to me, not wanting to find out how cannabis would interact with olanzapine.

When I was sitting again it was at the kitchen table, and for the first time I noticed a very old white man. I could have sworn he hadn't been there before, that I would have seen him, but on the other hand he looked like he'd been there forever, for centuries: pulled up close to the table in a wheelchair, dressed for a funeral, dark suit and thin black tie. Everybody else was drinking from cans and bottles, but his crooked fingers were splayed around a rocks glass containing only ice and the last clinging droplets of something dark and brown.

"Is that glass empty, son?"

"Sorry?" I had been looking out the window—the basement had a pair of high garden windows, letting in a peek of dirt-colored sky. I was wondering where exactly I was.

"It is rather dark in here, but I do believe my glass is empty." His voice was a decayed whisper, still carrying its ancient and decorous southern accent. "I do believe that it is. Would you be so kind as to fill up that glass? You will find a bottle of Johnnie Walker Red in a cabinet beside the icebox."

His watery eye was fixed on me. I found the whiskey and poured him out his glass.

"I appreciate it, young man. I do very much appreciate it." The old white man sipped slowly and licked his thin, cracked lips. "I do not believe I have had the pleasure."

"This man is named Elijah, sir." It was Ada. She had materialized at my side, one hand on my shoulder. He craned his thin neck around to peer at her.

"Elijah?" he said, looking back at me slowly.

"That's right, Counselor." Ada looked at me carefully, and I said, "Yes, sir. Elijah." And then, because it seemed like the thing to say, I said, "It's an honor to meet you."

"The honor . . ." He cleared his throat with effort. "The honor belongs entirely to me."

His body had been incapacitated at some point, probably by a stroke. Half of him was slumped and slurred like a melting candle. He's a hundred, I thought. He's a thousand. He had the look of eternal old age, like he had been old forever, sitting pale and wraithlike in his old-fashioned wheelchair.

"Now, Elijah." He gazed at me, licked the tips of his yellow teeth. "Now. You have embarked upon your journey. You are finding your way to freedom. The bad times are behind you, Elijah, but much uncertainty lies ahead. I cannot imagine..." Another pause, another elaborate throat clearing. "Cannot imagine how you must feel. But please know that *here*, boy, *here* in this home you are welcome. Here, there is..." He spread his arthritic fingers as wide as they would go. "Sanctuary."

"Well," I said, and then—what else was there to say?—"Thank you."

"Yes, sir, Counselor," said Ada on my behalf. "Elijah is on his way. On his way to the promised land."

"God bless you, boy," said the lawyer. "God protect you."

And then just like that he fell asleep: tilted his head to one side, and his eyes clicked shut like a doll's.

"Sir?" said Ada. "Mr. Russell?"

"Oh, he *out*," said Marlon, easing past, a beer bottle in his fist.

"Yeah." Ada patted the old man on his hand. "Think you're right."

"One of these times, you know, he gonna just die."

"Hush your mouth," said Ada. She smiled with undeniable tenderness at the lawyer as Marlon wandered away. "He's right, though. He comes and goes. One of these days he won't come back."

The group was getting quieter around us: people talking in low voices, murmuring. Big Otis and little Maryellen had settled into the chair I was in before, she on his lap, cuddling close.

"We just tell him everybody's named Elijah. Makes things easier is all."

I scratched my forehead. "I'm supposed to be talking to him. That's what they told me."

"Well, go on," Ada said. "Talk."

I looked at the lawyer, then at her, and I saw that she was laughing, and I laughed, too.

"Yeah, how about that, huh?" Ada shook her head. She draped a blanket across the old man's lap, eased a few strands of white hair out of his eyes. "But you try telling the Holy Ghost up there it's a bunch of Negroes running the show."

Cook had said much the same thing, laughing but not smiling, as we drove down Meridian Street to the monument: that *Mockingbird* mentality.

"So he . . ." I looked warily at the sleeping old man. "He owns you."

She laughed again. She had a deep, musical laugh. "Yes, he does, Elijah. The house and the yard, everything and everyone in it."

"You trust him."

"Oh, we got to. Got to. Him more'n anyone. You heard of something called the *Gulliver* case?"

I had. It rang a bell. I knew this stuff. I looked at the old man again, trying to find familiar features under the layers of age. For a time I had become obsessed with the history of slavery law, studied all the Supreme Court arguments, memorized long chunks of decisions and dissents. *Hospital Corporation v. Mississippi*. *Schools of Florida*. *Conroy v. Wilson*.

Ada refreshed my memory on the *Gulliver* case. The PB in question, service name Gulliver, had been a Louisiana slave in service to a small farmer named Peabody, who took him to New York State for the wedding of a Peabody cousin. Gulliver was threatened by some local boys outside the nightclub, waiting for the wedding reception to end, and defended himself — ended up in federal prison on a gun charge. After he served his eight months, a local abolitionist group showed up to claim him before Peabody could, and then they sued for his freedom, making the sly argument that federal prisons were free territory, like national parks and landmarks, and that being housed in one for more than six months triggered the domicile clause: under the law, the boy had relocated, so the boy was free.

The New York circuit court agreed, and the Supreme Court might have, too, if not for the efforts of a silver-tongued lawyer from Alabama. One of these graceful southern gentlemen of the bar, with goatee and white suit and red suspenders — nothing like this haunted old husk across from me at the little table, withered hands clawed around his rocks glass.

"It was looking to be one of the landmark cases, you know?" Ada said. "A major blow to the possessor-travel rules. But then this firecracker lawyer rolls up out of the slave lands, talking about how—ah, what was it, now?—how it's not the *duration* of the trip that matters but the..." She snapped her fingers, trying to remember. "Marlon? Hey, what—"

"Intent," said the lawyer softly, opening one eye. "Not the duration of possession but the intent of the possessor that is determinative under the statute."

"That's right. That's right, Counselor."

The one eye fluttered shut again. The old man breathed softly, slowly, in and out.

"That did it. Supreme Court liked that," said Ada. "Gulliver came home in chains. Peabody turned around and sold the man offshore."

This thought brought me to a blur of sadness, a sour taste of regret. Everybody ends up somewhere. I thought of Martha, sitting primly at the Cotyledon Café. She must be gone by now. Long gone. I hoped so, and I hoped not.

Both of the lawyer's eyes opened, small and inky and wet. He raised his glass. "To Gulliver."

The slaves all raised their bottles, too, all together, and spoke in unison. "To Gulliver!" Then they drank and went right back to their conversations while the lawyer's eyes slipped back closed.

"I gotta say, Ada, I don't get it," I said, watching the old man, his chin slipping slowly forward onto his chest. "I don't quite understand."

"Let me guess." Ada laughed. "You don't understand why we don't get the fuck out."

"Yeah. I mean..." I pointed at the shrunken figure of the lawyer, half drunk, half sleeping. No dogs around, so far as I could see. No guards.

"Get out and do what?" She patted the lawyer on top of his head, went over to the counter, and started to fix coffee. "Go north? Put my life in the hands of that crazy-ass priest of yours? Get followed around in stores the rest of my life? Otis, baby, we got milk?"

Otis lumbered over, cracked open the fridge, while Ada scooped coffee into the machine.

"Get pulled over every time I'm driving? Get shot by some cop, walking down the street?"

"Or in your house," said Otis.

Ada nodded. "Y'all hear shit about down here," she said. "We hear shit about up there."

She flicked on the coffeepot, and it bubbled away, doing its thing. Ada leaned on the edge of the counter. "Listen: of all the lives I could have led, all the places I coulda been born? Born here, into this household? Massa, this deaf old cracker, a hundred years old already when I got born, so sick with guilt he can't sleep one sober night. Shit-ton of money, big old mansion, perfect hideout for runners on the way. Yeah, man, yeah. We could walk anytime. Any one of us. Right, Otis?"

"Yeah." He nodded, stirring sugar into his cup. "That's right."

"But we're doing some good work down here, okay? Some real good work."

When we had our coffee I followed Ada to the stairs, passing Marlon, who was wheeling the old judge away from the table, wheeling him past Shai and Otis and Maryellen, past the empty boxes of wine piling up on the counter—a tottering cardboard skyscraper threatening to fall onto the sticky tile of the floor.

"Listen. My cousin says you are to be trusted. My cousin says, this man coming down, you let him know what you can." Ada talked fast. She didn't look at me while she was talking. "So what I'm gonna do is, I tell you what I tell you. You don't ask any questions."

"All right," I said. "Who's your cousin?"

"Didn't I just say don't ask me questions?"

"Yeah."

"So? I tell you what I tell you, you listen."

Ada and I outside the house as the sun came up. The mansion at our backs was sparkling white, gabled and turreted, with polished glass doors sliding open onto the slate patio, where we sat drinking coffee. After the cramped raucousness of the night, the big quiet morning world was soft and cool. A rolling valley of a backyard, the grass true green, dew-dappled, endless.

"Now. You're wanting to know about this contract, completed a week ago now, week ago Sunday. You're wondering what went wrong."

"What do you mean, a contract?"

Ada scowled. "Are you fooling? Are you still doped up? I said *stop* asking me questions." She hissed, shook her head. But she couldn't help herself. "Goddamn right it's a contract. What do you think we're playing at down here? We're doing the good Lord's work, but we're no dummies. Cash on the barrel. Pay in advance or no one going nowhere." She sipped coffee, ran her tongue over her teeth. "But this one now, this one . . . thing is, *nothing* went wrong with this one. This one went just exactly right. Everything how it was clocked."

"*Something* went wrong," I said.

"Listen: shut up. Okay? Listen."

I loved Ada's face. It was wide, with a strong African nose and a broad forehead. She had hidden her short dreadlocks again under the orange kerchief. I wondered if that was for the benefit of the neighbors. A line of high thick hedges shielded the lawyer's property, but those neighbors would presumably be dismayed if they caught a glimpse of two black people on his patio, sitting on his tasteful outdoor furniture, talking urgently about a runaway's route.

"This boy. The one you after. He did what we told him. We got a message in to him four months ago. Told him the night, told him how to do it. Told him get sick. He did it."

I had more questions, but I held on to them for now. Ada was rolling now, talking fast. Word had come from the northern friends about a boy who needed to come out along with a package he was working to obtain. Payment was arranged.

"And we had the bay, see."

"The bay?"

A sharp glance——*No questions, dummy*——then she answered my question. "Sick bay. Two girls are assigned to western section worker care on Sundays, and that night both of them were us."

Monica Smith, age twenty-four, and Angelina Croth, age twenty-seven. Two working-class girls in starched nurse's whites, fighters in the Cause——willing to take a job in a plantation, pass whatever tests they had to, get the necessary permits from the American Medical Association to do medical care on a PB population. Work down there for however long was required to earn trust, sweeten the scheduling person in HR, get on duty on the preappointed night.

"That boy came in to worker care, puking his guts out, like we told him to, and our people had him."

This time I made my question into a statement. "Must be hard to get yourself sent to the infirmary on a plantation."

Ada nodded. "Not hard getting sick. The trick is to get sick

239

enough. They see a lot of injuries in these places. You're working with needles, band knives. You fall; you get a sleeve tangled in a drive shaft. I knew a man who had his face burned with a hot iron: they sent him down to worker care and turned him out again in an hour. Most injuries they handle in population or on the floor. They wrap you up, maybe a steroid shot, and you're back on the floor.

"The thing you want, you want to get sent down, is poison. At a garment factory, you know, you're working the floor, there's a lot of industrial strength lying around. Sealants. Chemicals and cleaners. You smart, you don't overdo it, you can get yourself real bad, get it so you almost die. Then they take you down for sure."

That sent me back down, back into the tunnel, down below Indianapolis with that boy. The pallor of Kevin's skin. Chemicals and cleaners. Oh, that boy. That beautiful broken boy.

Not to be thought of now. Work to do now.

"All right, so he comes in. He's sick as hell; he's got this package."

Ada winced, moved her head back and forth. "I don't know. Some of these details I never had, you know? But the way I understand it, the package went to the driver direct. Never came into the bay. But you'd have to ask one of them nurses, which you will never be able to do. And don't ask me, by the way, what the fuck was *in* that envelope, because I do not know, and I do not care."

So there's Jackdaw in the sick bay. The clock is ticking; the delivery is scheduled for 8:49 p.m. onto a forty-five-foot tractor-trailer. Forty-two hundred raw bolts for export, and all the rest of it crated and palleted and headed for a route along the Red Highway.

The boy is there, and somehow or other the package is, too. It goes into the jacket of the driver. Maybe the driver is playing out a crush on one of those sweet young nurses, Monica or Angelina, and maybe he stops by with flowers and it's a quick thank-you hug to slip it in his pocket.

Or maybe one of our nurses junks it out the window while the driver happens to be out for a stroll around the campus, stretching his legs before climbing in the rig.

Ada doesn't know all that. Ada says if I want to know how the package got from the girls to the driver, I'd have to ask one of them.

"Which I'll never be able to do."

"You got it."

And as for Jackdaw, Jackdaw's body, precious cargo: he went out in a barrel.

The trucks are loaded in a secure area, of course, and plantation security checks and double-checks every single item: they open every crate, shine their lights into every box on every pallet. But see, the good guys are smart, too; the good guys are always working, too. There's a workshop down in the Great Dismal Swamp, a Panthers-funded research center, with honest-to-God engineers down there, building all kinds of crazy shit, looking for those golden-ticket ideas: how to slide people past all those checks and double checks. Turns out one thing that doesn't get opened up for a final check after it's packed is medical waste. So what about a man-size rubber bladder fitted with a thin reed, like the one a scuba diver wears, so a person could survive in there, down in all that waste? What about you get a man to the infirmary, make it look like he burst loose and leaped out a window when really he's coming out in a barrel?

Ada described it, and that was a feeling you could feel. A feeling that I could feel. Wrapped up tight and clammy in some kind of rubber suit, folded over and jammed in a bucket, entombed. Rolled end over end, helpless, banging against the sides, the darkness and the heat and the stink. And then with the poison sloshing in your guts, cleaners and chemicals . . . and add to it the terror, the certainty as you were wheeled out of worker care toward the loading dock: capture was coming. This could not and would not work.

"So that's it," Ada said. "That's the hard part. Boy's in the truck, truck clears the gates, clears the Alabama border. Freedomland."

Ada clapped her hands together as if knocking dust off of them—like, *Mission accomplished*.

"That's what happened?"

Ada looked at me sideways. "That was the *plan*, I'm saying. Far as I know, yes, that's what happened. We know the truck came out. We know the nurses did their part. That's what we know."

"Okay," I said. "Okay."

But it wasn't okay. Not even close. I had learned nothing that I needed to know. Kevin leaves in a barrel, and the package is in the driver's pocket. What then?

"Where did the boy get out of the truck?"

"That's not my part of it. That's the driver."

"Where does the driver give him the package? How does he get the rest of the way north, after he's off the truck?"

"You don't listen, man. I'm telling you, I don't know."

My coffee cup was empty. I stood up. I looked out at the lawn, the sunlight. It wasn't enough. It wasn't close to enough. I looked down at Ada, still sitting on the patio chair.

"I want to talk to the nurses."

"Well, that's gonna be hard, because they don't exist." She smiled. "They never existed."

I was agitated. I was unhappy. Get to the lawyer, Barton had said, and he will point you in the right direction. So here I was, and what did I have? The sun was slowly rolling out across the lawn, brightening the green of the grass inch by inch. Closer every moment.

"All right, then, the driver. How do I get in touch with the driver?"

"I don't know."

"Ada. Please."

"I'm telling you straight, man, I don't know. The nurses came from a guy Marlon knew, a guy from Atlanta, and the nurses got to the driver once they were already working there."

"How?"

"Two pretty nurses? How you think? Listen. Okay? I got no con-

242

nect with the truck driver. I don't have a name or number. You'd have to walk into GGSI and ask."

"How do I do that?"

She barked a laugh. Looked at my face and stopped laughing.

"We help people *out* of these places, son. Not in."

Ada stood up. We were done. She yawned, spilled the dregs of her coffee onto the ground around one of Counselor Russell's flowering trees.

"And what about the girl?" I said quietly.

Ada waited before she answered; waited so long that when she said, "What girl?" I knew it was a lie.

"Luna."

This time the answer came too fast. "I don't know that name."

"You do. She's the one who got hold of the package in the first place."

I didn't know how, and Ada sure as hell didn't know how, but Luna had done the hard part. *She was the one who got your precious evidence.* Jackdaw, weeping, standing in the river. *She took all the fucking risks.*

Ada, though, was shaking her head, setting her chin. "I don't know who you're talking about."

"Sure you do."

I closed my eyes, thinking of Jackdaw, of Kevin, his life flown out of him.

"And I think you know," I said to Ada, "that she thought she was getting free."

"Yeah, well," said Ada, and it was a kind of miracle, because even though she said she didn't know who I was talking about, and even though she said she had never heard the name before, she said, "Well, it wasn't her time."

"I guess not."

"Whatever promises were made to that one, they were not made by me, you understand?" Her face now was downright defiant; the face of the woman I'd seen on the square, the one who had scowled and stared while the others were beating me into the car. "Those promises were not made by me."

She went toward the door, and I followed her, and now all I could think of was Luna—I bet Kevin had told her what they had told him; I bet she had taken some poison, too, some chemical or cleaner, gotten herself sick and gotten herself taken to worker care, and then she woke to find that Jackdaw was gone and she was still there. Left behind. The only thing worse than a lifetime of slavery: that taunting instant of hope, gone in a flash. And I knew of course what happened to her next. When the package was discovered missing and Luna was found to have helped in its disappearance, she was tortured then, Bridge had said; tortured and killed—that piece of it from Cook.

That had been the last thing for Kevin. That's what had finally done him in, hearing that, when Cook gave that sad report. *She's dead. Okay? She's dead.*

Subdued, then tortured, then killed.

But that was the aftermath. Carnage in the wake. The job itself had gone off without a hitch: Kevin had gotten himself to worker care, the nurses had packed him up in a barrel of blood and gotten him onto a truck, and then they made themselves disappear. The package to the trucker. Everything as planned. So where the hell was it?

"Hey. Hey!"

Marlon was coming out fast, crashing into Ada going in. But he was yelling at me. He took me by both my arms, sudden and fierce. "Hey! Do you know some fucking white girl?"

5.

Marlon had been washing the lawyer's three old Cadillacs, pulling them out onto the driveway, one at a time, keeping a lookout for lurkers, peepers, anything strange out on the street. And he'd found something: a pink South African hatchback, obnoxiously visible on the sedate and moneyed suburban street, with a white girl in the front seat dozing.

Down in the basement, he insisted on holding Martha at gunpoint.

I said it wasn't necessary, and Ada agreed with me, but Marlon said, "We don't know what the fuck this girl is," and Shai said, very quietly, about me, "We don't even know who *he* is," which I was glad nobody heard. So we sat in an awkward arrangement around the table, back down in the basement kitchen, a very different place in the morning: last night's dishes were a precarious pile in the sink; thin bars of sunlight found sticky patches on the concrete floor.

It was me and then Martha, her knee bouncing with nervousness, her face bleary with worry or fear. Then Shai, Marlon beside Shai, opposite Martha, aiming his .45 at her while she told her story. Ada stood by the sink, arms folded, listening.

"I saw you getting...I saw these people"—Martha caught herself—*these people*. She winced. "I saw you getting beat up. I was scared." Without her cat's-eye glasses, without any drugstore knickknack in her hair, she looked more like an adult than I was used to. "I followed the car. I tried to be careful."

"I guess that was a stupid fucking thing to do," said Marlon.

"I guess we need to be more careful about being tailed."

That was Ada, from over by the sink, and the reproach didn't much help Marlon's mood. He hissed and leaned back, sneering. Shai, very gently, laid her hand on his shoulder, and I saw it work, saw the tension ease out of his body. Love at work.

"All right," said Ada, impatient. "Look." She pointed back and forth between Martha and me.

"You know this person?"

"Yes."

Pointed to me, then back to Martha. "You trust her?"

I hesitated a half beat, and into the hesitation welled up the horror of what I was, what I was doing. It wasn't Martha I distrusted; it was myself.

"Yes." I nodded. "I trust her."

"All right." Ada shrugged. "You still want to go in there and find that truck driver?"

Ada was a maker of plans—a hatcher of plots. Like Father Barton, like Officer Cook, like me. She came and pulled a chair up to the table and explained what she was thinking. Martha could be of use now for the same reason she had been useful in getting me across the border—because of the color of her skin. While Ada laid it out, walked through the way it could work, I watched Martha from the corner of my eye and could tell how carefully she was listening. Her eyes, which I was used to seeing jump all over the place, were focused and intense. She was getting herself ready.

The plan was crazy. Risky as hell, no question about it. There were a very few things that Ada and her group could tell me about GGSI, about the layout and security arrangements of its headquarters. Most of what they knew was secondhand or thirdhand, and much of it was outdated. Rumors, whispers, gossip about the inside. Of my specific questions, they could only answer a couple: yes, we would be screened in on arrival and checked out on departure. There were cameras, yes, all over the campus, but not in the areas that were restricted to white workers only; Alabama state law forbade the surveillance of employees without cause.

It occurred to me to ask if Ada knew anything about that one building whose identity I could not figure out from the overhead map in the full file—that unlabeled structure jammed in behind the Institute for Agricultural Innovation—but of course I could not ask about it, because then I would have to explain where and how I had seen such a map.

We came to the end of the conversation. The plan was formed, as formed as it was going to get, and still Martha remained quiet. Her hands, too, were still; not fiddling with her rings, not tucking a lock of hair into the corner of her mouth. I had the odd sense of seeing her real self rise up out of the motionless form of her present body: like the person who had been inside the other person all along.

I looked at her when the talking was done. "You don't have to do any of this," I said. "You've got your money."

She turned her head slowly and looked at me.

"But what about Steubenville?" she said, and I blinked.

"What?"

"You don't think it'll work. The whole crazy business with the man in Steubenville. The guy who said he can get me into that database."

"TorchLight," I said, then, "No. No, I doubt it."

"So?"

"So?"

I knew her expression so well. I saw what she was seeing: opportunity.

"But if this plan—if her—I'm sorry, what—"

"Ada."

Martha smiled at her. "Thank you. If Ada's idea works, and we can get in there, then don't you think there will be a way to access it directly? Once we're inside? Once we're in there? Isn't that right?"

"Right."

"Right. So. So I can't miss that chance."

"But..." I started, but something in her face—in her eyes. I stopped.

"I will call my sister. She will hang on to Lionel another day."

"Yeah. I know. Martha..."

I stopped.

"It's dangerous," she said, speaking very slowly. "It is very risky. I understand. But. *But*—if there is a way to find out what has happened to that man." This was in the form of a question, but her voice had no questioning in it. "Then that is what I am going to do. I have to."

"You gotta understand, though—"

"I know."

"I can't promise anything."

My protests were halfhearted. She was firm, but I could have talked her out of it. I could have told her there was some other way. I could have opened myself all the way up, torn off the blank mask, and shown her my face. I could have told her to forget the whole damn thing.

But this was my chance, and I knew it. I told her that if this was what she wanted, I wanted her to have it. I told her that if she helped me get in, I would try to get her what she needed. I told her that because I needed her. I had to have her. My empathy was woven, as ever, with cunning.

We spent the rest of that day cosseted in the lawyer's house and with the lawyer's people, refining and fine-tuning, building our story. Shai went up and down the stairs, collecting articles of clothing from the closet of the lawyer, from the closet of the lawyer's dead wife. I ended up in a peach-colored sweater and in pants of Marlon's, black pants without pockets. "There, that's right," he said. "That's good. Trust me, man: down here they don't like niggers having places they can stick shit."

We did not see the old man himself again, but I heard him— three or four times I heard him—from an adjoining bedroom, moaning in his sleep.

6.

Thursday morning. Vivid and clear. Me and Martha, decked out and ready to go. Closing the doors of her sedan in the wide parking lot of Garments of the Greater South.

Martha, showered and shining, in a sharp red professional skirt and blazer, a piece of green jewelry pinned at her breast; timeless pieces from the collection of the lawyer's long-dead wife. Martha in good old fancy-white-lady drag, and me in the peach sweater and pocketless pants, already wearing the servant's smile, already rolling in the bashful gait. Lifting the black rolling suitcase out of the trunk, loaded with the tools of the trade.

I eased the bag down onto the asphalt while Martha waited. I pulled out the handle of the suitcase. She started, and I followed. I was in charge of the bag. This was the South. She glanced back and I looked up and we looked at each other, just for a second, one last human look to go in on.

The plantation had not been hard to find. Coming off State Route 4, we saw a big green sign, a dedicated exit, as for a university or military base or theme park. The exit sign went so far as to proclaim the company motto—AMERICAN GROWN, SOUTHERN SEWN!—along with the logo I had seen previously on Jackdaw's collarbone, the proud uppercase *G* with the other letters tucked safely inside. The logo that was supposedly waiting for me somewhere, somewhere in the endless South, emblazoned on that envelope, the needle in the haystack I was going to find.

That same logo was on each of the three buildings that together formed GGSI headquarters, three glass-walled skyscrapers standing lordly above the parking lot, blinking back the sun. The logo was on one of the flags flapping above the concrete plaza in front of the buildings. There were three altogether — one flag for the company, one for the state, and one for the United States of America. Flags and recessed concrete and a handsome fountain. There was a statue, a giant abstract bronze, rounded and swooping, which as you got closer turned out not to be abstract at all: it was a boll, a simple boll made heroic, a cotton boll like a triumphal arch.

I had seen corporate plazas. Corporate plazas in Manhattan, in Boston, in Washington, DC. This was no different. Exactly the same.

I held tightly to the grip of the rolling suitcase. I came up alongside Martha, but her sunglasses were on. Her human eyes were hidden now. She stopped just outside the door of the center building, and I rushed past her to open it. She walked past me and did not say thank you. Deep in her character, ready to go.

The lobby was vaultlike and chilly after the early-autumn warmth of the parking lot. The words GARMENTS OF THE GREATER SOUTH, INCORPORATED were six feet high on the back wall, cotton-white letters on a wall of blue-sky blue, alongside a gigantic photomontage of happy Asian children kicking soccer balls, turning cartwheels, shouldering their sturdy backpacks in their brightly colored cotton clothes.

"Yes?" The receptionist was waiting at a desk big as a spaceship between two banks of elevators. Red lipstick, blond hair, blue eyes, a tasteful gold necklace. "How can I help y'all?"

I ducked my head while Martha smiled.

"How are you this morning? My name is Ms. Jane Reynolds, from Peach Tree Management Systems. I am here to see Mr. Matthew Newell."

"O-*kay*," said the woman behind the big semicircular desk, lingering on the *kay*, teasing the word out into a question while she typed, pulling up a calendar. "And did you have an appointment?"

"Well, yes and no," said Martha, and my head was still down, eyes down, but I could hear in her voice that she winked as she said it. "We met down at the CSO, back in June? And Matty—I'm sorry: Matthew; Mr. Newell—he was sweet enough to say that if I was ever in the area I should feel free to stop by."

"Oh," said the blonde. "I see."

CSO was the Conference of Slaveholding Organizations. It was a safe bet that a plantation the size of GGSI would have sent a sizable contingent; it was an open question whether Matthew R. Newell, assistant vice president of transport operations, would have been among them. We were out on the wire here, me and Martha. Out there together.

"So would you mind just ringing up, see if he's around? Of course I should have called first—I just had an appointment right down in Blessing, and I thought . . ."

The blonde was already in motion, offering Martha an empty smile and a wait-just-a-moment forefinger. She tucked the telephone receiver under her ear and pressed a button on her console. The elevator doors opened on the far side of the lobby, but no one got out. We had gone over everything on the way, discussed every detail, various contingencies and possibilities, but Martha was in charge now—she would have to be. My job was to walk with my eyes pointed downward at about forty-five degrees. My job was to smile and keep smiling.

There was no security in the lobby. No powerfully built men with keen eyes and bulges at their hips. Probably a panic button under the woman's desk or a panic switch at her feet. Maybe a gun down there, too. And there were cameras, unhidden: one above the reception desk, angled down; one above each bank of elevators. Cameras in the public spaces, Ada had said, but not in the private areas. Not in the executive offices. That was as far as she knew; that was according to the latest reckoning. We were counting on it, but we didn't know.

The receptionist cupped one palm over the mouthpiece. "Excuse me? Hi. Where did you say you were from again?"

"Peach Tree, ma'am," I said. "Peach Tree Management Systems."

"We're consultants," said Martha, flicking an irritated look at me, servant speaking out of turn. "Workplace efficiency. But like I said, it's as much a personal call as anything. I just wanted to say hi."

I pressed my hands together while the blonde said "Hmm" a couple more times and went back to murmuring into her phone.

I stood and waited and grinned and looked at the floor, fighting back against the simple, sick, vertiginous awareness of where I was, where *exactly*. I was tottering on the rim of it. Through those doors. Up those elevators. Behind these three towers...

I was breathing very slowly. Martha stared into the expanse of the lobby, and I could not guess what she was thinking. We were deep in character, and I'd taken us into this place, and I could feel the terrible weight of it pressing my flesh, and when the receptionist looked up again and smiled, her red-lip smile was the wide, burning grin of the devil.

"You're in luck," she said to Martha. "He *is* here, and he'll be right out."

"Oh, isn't that nice," said Martha. "That's just perfect."

"Yes." She sniffed. "Your Negro will need to be cleared."

Again, as at the border. Scalp and armpits, teeth and tongue; pants down, shirt up. They had a room for it, just off the lobby, and an attendant, a tired-looking free black man who scowled and said nothing as he ran his clumsy fingers over my body. I stood absolutely still. I held my arms out. It would have been the school at Bell's, the first time, the first of such searches I had endured in my life. Lesson 1: your body is not your own.

This place, this plantation, was on a different order from Bell's. Physical size and scope of work, a different universe of slavery from the little three dozen acres where I'd been raised. Green grass, farm country, pig lots, cattle pens, silos. The world I was about to enter was a twenty-four-hour operation, ultramodern and ultraefficient, with computerized inventory tracking and comprehensive worker-control protocols. There was a camera in the upper left corner of the room, bearing cold witness to the man and me. I was here and I was there at the same time, feeling this tired guard's hands on my chest at the same time as I was feeling the rough hands of the guards at Bell's, a lifetime ago.

This is so much worse, I thought, and immediately thought, *No, no, nothing could be worse.* But it's a waste anyway, isn't it, the idea of comparison, just in general. Holding up one kind of horror against another.

"All right." The bored security man broke his silence, straightening up, pulling off his gloves and chucking them into a bin. "Bag now." Quickly he opened the rolling suitcase I was hauling, rifled through that, too—a change of clothes for Martha, change of shoes, and a laptop turned off, which he opened and closed uninterestedly.

"Okay," he said. "You're clear."

But then before I could lower my arm he wrapped something around the wrist, a thin strip of paper, bright green, which secured to itself, tight as hell, tugging at the small hairs of my arm.

"That is an identification bracelet," said the man. "That identifies you as a Person Bound to Labor and a member of our staff."

"Whoa," I said. "Whoa, whoa."

"Don't worry. You'll come back through here again on your egress from this facility. But every dark-skinned person is required to wear a band while on the grounds." He showed me his own bracelet, which was a cool red.

"But don't you have a color for folks like me? Negroes like me, just—just here for a visit?"

"No, man, we don't." His voice was dry, humorless. "We don't actually get too many of those."

Martha was waiting for me in the lobby, laughing with her hand on the arm of a short, fat white man in a sport jacket, who was laughing, too. This was Newell—instantly recognizable from his picture on the company website, where we'd found him yesterday after-noon on an old laptop belonging to the lawyer's people, making our plan.

It was Martha who pointed to him — to his weak-chinned, sappy, smiling head shot, his sad-sounding title and anemic history within the company. *There's the guy. There's the guy we want.*

And now here he was, the guy we wanted, dumpy and thin-haired and pink-cheeked, in casual slacks and polished shoes, with one of Martha's hands on his forearm, the both of them laughing like old pals.

"Well, of course I do," Matty Newell said hopefully. "You're not the kinda gal a fella's gonna go and forget."

"I do like to think so," said Martha, her laugh a tinkling false-hood. "I surely do."

"You caught me in a good mood, too, I must say. A good week for us, darn good week."

My mind jumped to Donatella Batlisch, to the footage from the motel TV: the woman flying forward suddenly with the gun blast, collapsing, limp. Good news for the southern interest, happy days at GGSI. But no, no. Newell just meant the late frost. "We're com-ing up on Halloween, and here we still got acreage coming into flower. Don't see that every year; no, ma'am."

And for a second as I approached them across the lobby, my fake smile was real, a smile of appreciation for Martha. I watched her nod admiringly. I watched her touching Newell's elbow. Jesus. She was a natural.

"Oh, Mr. Newell —"

"Please, please, Jane. Make it Matty."

"All right, then. *Matty.*" She made it sound like "Hercules." He beamed. "Matty, this is my associate."

Newell peered at me, confusion in his small eyes. He had a lan-yard around his neck, dangling an ID card in a plastic sheath. His face was soft, his hairline retreating, just as it was in the picture. Since sitting for the corporate head shot, though, he'd grown one of those little Tommy Jefferson ponytails, and it didn't particularly suit him.

"Your, uh, associate?"

"Associate, assistant." She winked at him, mouthed the word *servant*. "Whatever you want to call it. He does what he's told."

Matty sized me up, smiling weakly.

"Just seems like . . ." He shrugged. "Well. Funny work, for a nigger."

Grin grin grin. Smile smile smile. "Oh, I know, sir, I know." I glanced at Martha, at Ms. Jane Reynolds, making sure it was okay to talk. "I guess I'm a funny kind of nigger."

Matty Newell gaped for a second, then laughed, a nervous, throaty chortle, shaking his head at this strange old world of ours. The flags snapped sharply outside in the brisk wind. The Asian children in the photomontages were frozen in their happy cartwheels.

"Well, come on up to the top floor," said Newell. "Have a good look at the joint. Then we can talk about whatever it is y'all are selling."

The whole building had that same pleasing color scheme, easy white and gentle blue, and every wall was lined with more of the glossy enlarged pictures. On the way to the elevator was a housewife of some indeterminate Southeast Asian ethnicity, reaching into her closet for a stack of towels—while reaching through the closet wall from the other side was a black slave, grinning, servile and unseen, as he provided the stack of sturdy cotton towels.

I did not blanch. I did not slow. I walked past, sticking close behind Martha, noticing things.

I noticed the pattern of the light fixtures in the long hallway: a bank of two, then a bank of three, two and then three. I noticed the pants of the slaves in the photographs, black like Marlon's pants, like the ones I was wearing along with my inoffensive peach sweater. I noticed the lushness of the white carpet. I noticed everything.

The elevator raced us soundlessly upward fast enough for my ears to pop, and I stood clenching and unclenching my jaw, standing in quiet self-erasure at the rear of the car. I looked anywhere but up at the camera mounted in the high corner of the elevator. I studied the button plate on the elevator doors: MURDOCK ELEVATORS, it said. Murdock, Louisiana. Martha laughed and flirted with Mr. Newell.

"No, sir," she was saying. "Oh, no. We're up from the Birmingham office, but the company is headquartered in Georgia."

"Georgia, huh?" said Newell. "And how are things in the State of Surrender?"

"Oh, stop," she said, and slapped him on the arm.

He laughed, eyed her nervously, hoping not to have offended, and rushed to reassure her. "I'm only teasing, of course. Bygones be bygones and all that. Every state free to choose its own path. The American way."

While Newell mouthed these wooden platitudes I had another quick flash of Batlisch, flying forward, arms out, the panic of the crowd. I wondered what Martha was thinking about. The elevator dinged, and we stepped directly out into sunlight; the whole top floor was taken up by one room with windows for walls, the sun streaming in gloriously on a bright open penthouse with marble floors.

"This is my office," said Mr. Newell, and immediately snorted and waved his hands. "Just kiddin', of course. This is the observation deck, what we call the perch. I love taking folks up here. Just gives a real strong sense of the place."

He walked up to the glass and gestured for us to follow — well, for Martha to follow. My presence he had more or less forgotten: I was the rolling suitcase. I did what I was told. I was not worth thinking of.

He stood at Martha's elbow. "Really something, huh?"

"It sure is."

From inside my cloak of invisibility, I looked, too. Most of the buildings were like the one we were in, made of glass, beaming and winking at each other across wide green lawns. The buildings were gathered in clusters, divided into regions, separated by winding walkways and black-paved service roads and high chain-link fences. I was in both places at once. I was back there in the Capital City Crossroads Hotel, staring at the satellite image from the full file, and I was here for real on this plantation, in the presence of the real thing. Everything getting realer and realer, the closer you get to it, like flesh on bones.

I got busy correlating, matching up the buildings I was looking at with the blurry images I'd seen in the file: the offices, the outbuildings, the shipping and receiving center, the machine shop. The five brick towers of the population center, gathered around a tall tower with a glass cupola.

My mind saw that something was missing before I knew what it was. Where were all the people? At Bell's the yards were always full of us, hustling and hollering, singing sometimes, yelling at each other or getting yelled at by the guards and the working whites. Down there on the green lawn of GGSI, I saw not a soul. Everybody inside, I figured. Shift in progress. Slaving away. And yet . . .

"Now, okay, so those right there are the garment factories," said Matty Newell, pointing down at industrial buildings as big as football stadiums, scaffolded with exterior piping and drums, sending up streams of dark smoke. "That right there is kind of the heart of the place."

Newell was looking down at the pristine lawn and the handsome facilities with clear satisfaction, giving us his overhead tour with almost proprietary pride, as though GGSI belonged to him instead of the other way around.

"Inside there are the ginning operations," Newell added. "The cleaners and the dryers and so on. We've got the largest set of high-capacity round-base cotton gins in the state."

"Well, I'll be," said Martha. "No kidding."

My eye, meanwhile, had found it, that one abstract rectangle, shaded by the Institute for Agricultural Innovation, the small dark building that bore no number or name on the aerial picture.

I couldn't ask Newell what it was, of course. I couldn't ask Martha to ask. I was black. I wasn't there.

"Now, this is a twenty-four-hour-a-day operation, just by the way," Newell was saying, Martha still nodding, eyes big with amazement. "Twenty-four hours a day, seven days a week. We run in shifts here, morning, afternoon, night, and late night. Never a dull moment. Sabbath comes every day for one-seventh of the population, so we never have to stop the plants. We got seven Easters, too. Seven Christmases. Only thing shuts us down is a bad accident, and"—he made a fist and knocked gently, ha-ha, on his bald forehead—"none of those in twenty-nine months."

He grinned, nice and broad, and gave me a wink. "None of your cousins got a thing to complain about down here, son. And I mean it."

It seemed he wanted me to respond, so I responded. "I bet you right, Mr. Newell. I bet you right."

Newell laughed nervously, inside his throat.

"I mean it, son. This is not the slavery of fifty or even ten years ago. People think about slavery, and they still think—*still!*—about the whips and the dogs and the spiky neck chains, all of that nasty business. But this is *now*. This is the twenty-first century. You see there"—pointing again with that fat finger, a gold ring between the second and third knuckles, forcing me to look—"that there is the population center. Four thousand head in those buildings right there. We got a rec center in there, gymnasium equipment that every one of our team members is not just encouraged but also required to use. And you see that building in the center, with the turret-looking thing on the top? From up in there the guards can see into every single cell, and every single cell can see the guards, too. So everybody knows they're safe. Everybody's looking after each other. That goes back to Jefferson, by the way, that design. So you're looking at a proud tradition here."

He had fixed his hand on my arm all of a sudden, tight and congenial, like a fraternity brother.

"Forget about whips, okay? Forget about Tasers. The BLP allows it, you probably know that, but I can tell you—because I know the folks down on the sixth floor—I can tell you that we do not use Tasers here. Once in a blue moon, maybe, is it thought to be necessary. Because this here is an *incentive*-based facility, okay?" His fingers were tight as a shackle on my bicep. "And I tell you, you hear folks saying, what do they feed those poor boys? Then I go home on meat-loaf night at my house, I'm thinking, gee, I *wish* I was over in the mess hall with the peebs!" He snorted. "I only *wish*! Just don't go telling my wife!"

I laughed, good and loud. *Come on, Victor. Come on, Brother.* Get it done. Find this fool trucker, find out what happened to that envelope. Bring the damn thing home. That was all I had to do. I laughed and laughed.

Newell, encouraged by my laughter, in full booster mode, turned his attention back to Martha. "Can I tell you something crazy?" He leaned in toward her earnestly. "If Garments of the Greater South were its own country, we would have a gross domestic product bigger than that of Rhode Island!" He leaned back, goggle-eyed, red-faced. "Now, ain't that a hell of a thing?"

"It sure is," said Martha. "It sure is."

One thing that you could see from up here that *hadn't* been included in the satellite imagery from the full file were the cotton fields themselves, the unending acres of them, rolling out from the campus in all directions like the moonscape beyond a space station. And I could not see them, not from this height, but I knew they were out there, hundreds of Persons Bound to Labor too small to be seen, lost in among the long white lines of cotton. For a second or two I stared out into those distant fields, stared at the fact that when this was over, once I talked to that driver and he pointed me to the next place I had to go, I would walk out of here, and those people I could not see but knew to be suffering, they all would be here forever.

What do you do with that fact? Do you hold it like a stone in your hand? Pitch it away from this great height and watch it fall? Do you swallow it and feel it in your throat till the day you die?

The elevator dinged. "All right, now," said Newell. "Let's head on down."

Martha really was a goddamn natural.

We filed into Matty Newell's small office on the fourteenth floor, past a hallway of air-conditioner chill and the faint smell of coffee, the three of us crowded in there with the filing cabinets and his smooth black desk and computer. She and I had practiced it, going around and around, back and forth, in the lawyer's basement, and as soon as Newell closed his door behind us, away she went. Off to the races.

"Well, as long as we're here, visiting," she said, and he grinned, gave her a tsk-tsk.

"Here it comes, huh? Here comes the sales pitch."

Martha winked. "You caught me. It'll be painless, Matthew, I promise it will."

"Matty."

"*Matty*. All I want to do is ask you a simple question."

"All right." His brows were knitted. His fingers were laced together. I could read his thoughts—from back by the door with my eager smile, a good boy, an obedient boy, I could see what he was thinking: *I've got no juice anyway. I can't say yes or no to anything*. He had given us the tour. That was what he had to offer. His smile was preapologetic—soon she would find out, this pretty lady from Peach Tree Management Systems who had dropped from the sky into his little life, that he had no juice. We'd chosen him well.

My eyes flitted to the four corners of the room, one by one. Nothing. Not that a camera couldn't be small, of course. Buried in the plaster; screwed into the lights. But nothing that I could see.

"All I ask is that you answer one question," said Martha. "And it's a darn easy question, too."

"Okay . . ."

"This question is like, you know"—she palmed her forehead—"*duh*."

"Okay." Mr. Newell laughed. "Sure. I getcha."

"So here's the question. What is it that y'all are selling here?"

Newell puffed out his cheeks. Opened his hands. "Cotton? Cotton goods?" he said, tentatively, shyly, like a kid getting a trick played on him. Waited to see if that was right, then tried again. "A brand? A, uh . . ." He fumbled for the buzzword. "A lifestyle?"

"No, sir," said Martha, shaking her head slowly, exuding confidence. I could have applauded. "What you are selling is *time*."

She launched into it then, good and confident, the whole *Music Man* business, while I made my comprehensive survey of his office, moving only my eyes: two squat filing cabinets; a floor-to-ceiling tiered bookshelf, lined with binders and regulatory manuals; a sturdy industrial desk with a metal frame and a glass top, with three pictures arranged neatly (Mrs. Newell, Mr. and Mrs., Mr. and Mrs. and a handsome chocolate Lab). Hidden from view, not visible but certainly present, was the fingerprint danger button: on the underside of the desk, most likely; under the seat of the chair, second choice. Behind and to the right of where Newell sat was a single interior door. Not to any kind of executive washroom, surely. Our Mr. Newell wasn't pulling those kinds of perks. A closet, more likely. Storage.

While I crawled through his tidy junior executive's lair with my eyes, Martha was giving it to Matty with both barrels: "You got yourself four thousand, two hundred and thirty-two folks out there"—pausing, just barely, a quick sly acknowledgment that she had the figure, she'd done her homework—"and it's their *time* that you all are selling. Every hour of good work they give to the company, every darn *minute* of it, *that* is the product.

"Now, let's say we take one Person Bound to Labor," she said, "and pop him anywhere on the flowchart. Okay? He's splitting open bales. He's a loom operator. Doesn't matter. He's top-level, he's a trusty, he's punching code on a pattern maker. Okay?"

"Okay..."

"Let's say he works one hour. How many minutes are in that hour?"

Newell hesitated—he knew there was some smart answer here, but he couldn't figure it. "Sixty?"

"No, sir," said Martha, said Jane Reynolds, saleswoman of the year. "Maybe it's fifty. Maybe thirty. Maybe a hundred! It all depends on what's going on in that man's head, what's going on with that man's body. What we sell at Peach Tree, what we do is, we sell minutes. With our system of incentives and corrections, we add minutes to the hours that your PBLs are putting in, and you know what that does?"

"Uh..." He was afraid to answer. Afraid to be wrong. "It makes better clothes?"

"It makes money, Mr. Newell!" She spread her hands. "It makes more money."

Newell chortled. "Well, we sure hope so!"

For a surreal half a moment I became excited at the prospect of making a sale. Ms. Reynolds and I would return to the office in Birmingham and report on our success, log it in the system, get high fives from the other sales teams, arrange a meeting with the tech guys for follow-up. Jane Reynolds would be employee of the month. I'd get—what? What reward would a freedman associate receive? Alternate universes, other worlds.

"I tell you what," said Martha. "I'll *show* you. Can I show you?"

"Sure," said Mr. Newell. He stood up, as though maybe she was going to lead him somewhere. "Show me."

"Albert?"

I popped out of the back corner like a jack-in-the-box. "Yes, ma'am!"

"Can we get set up, please?"

She said it with mild irritation, like she couldn't believe I hadn't done it already. I saw the small look she gave to Newell, the small look he gave back: *these people.* I opened the bag, opened up the laptop, and pressed a few buttons. Newell scurried out of my way, stood awkwardly in his own office, hands behind his back, ponytail jutting out over his pink neck.

"Okay," said Martha. "Away we go. Albert, would you mind hitting the lights for us?"

"They're just there," said Newell and pointed, and I hopped over to the light switch.

"What I'm going to show you," said Martha, calling up the first slide—the logo for Peach Tree, clipped off their website—and beaming it onto the window shade of Newell's office, "if you'll bear with me, is just a taste of the proprietary technology that Peach Tree is offering. Just a sense of it. So . . ."

The slide blinked off, and no second one came.

"What . . ." said Martha in the darkness. "Albert?"

"What is it?" said Newell.

"Oh, dear," I said. "Oh, boy."

"Albert!" Her voice transformed. Sharp as broken glass. "Albert, would you be so *kind* as to turn on the lights, please?"

I did, and fast. Martha was standing, flustered, with her hands on her hips. Newell was bemused, uncertain. "Ms. Reynolds—Jane, is everything okay?"

"Yes, of course, Mr. Newell."

"Matty. Please."

"Matty, it's just, you know, they send me out here to do this, and they don't send me with equipment that actually functions. Or a . . . a . . ." It was the sole flaw in her performance; the only half a moment's hesitation. Jane Reynolds would have said "nigger," of course. "A *helper* who can do his darn job."

Newell didn't notice her skipped beat. He wasn't noticing anything but a chance to be some kind of man. He was rushing around from behind his little desk. He was handing her tissues.

"I do understand, believe me. Here, Ms. Reynolds—"

"Jane," she said.

"Jane."

Matty Newell was smiling weakly with a dim, hopeful light in his eyes. Martha took the proffered tissues and blotted tears from the corners of her eyes. Real tears. I almost laughed. I was still standing back by the light switch, just inside the door, invisible and quiet. But Jesus Christ, she was good at this.

"I have a very good presentation." She pointed to the laptop. "I mean it. That is an excellent presentation."

What she was doing was, she was letting it be his idea. She was walking him along, holding his hand tightly enough to lead him, loosely enough for him to be unaware of it. She was an absolute natural. Or maybe all women could do that to all men, if they wanted to.

"I would actually love to just do it alone, just the two of us," and she gave that quick, simple, businesslike sentence—"I would actually love to just do it alone, just the two of us"—just enough backspin. Just enough.

"I tell you what, Jane," said poor dumb Newell. "Let's head up to the cafeteria, and I'll buy you some lunch. Okay? We'll have some lunch and . . . and you can tell me what you got to tell me. Don't have to fuss around with all the tech and all that. You just lay it out for me, and we shall discuss it. Would that be all right?"

Her look of abject gratitude—Newell the savior, Newell the gentleman—was a thing of wonder.

"Oh, Matty, that would be so kind of you. And we really do have a remarkable product."

"Of course," he said. "And I'd sure like a chance to hear about it."

He stood up. She closed the laptop, which we had loaded with exactly one slide, and followed him to the door.

"Oh, wait," she said, glancing at me for just one half a second, just a quarter second to make sure that this was still our play. I nodded, a degree of head tilt well below Newell's notice, and Jane Reynolds said, "Is there somewhere my boy can wait?"

"Oh."

Newell stopped, flummoxed. I do believe the man had genuinely forgotten that I was in the room. "Well, he can wait right here, as a matter of fact. This door'll lock behind me, and it won't open until we come back. That all right with you?"

He wasn't asking me, of course. Jane Reynolds said that it would be just fine with her, and he guided her with a hand on her back out into the hallway.

I waited five minutes after the door shut. I stood perfectly still and counted. Three hundred seconds.

While I was counting I stood as Jane Reynolds would expect to find her boy standing—in the corner with my head lowered, touching nothing, like a powered-down robot.

At three hundred I sprang into motion and the beautiful new music appeared in my head, the wild rhythms from the lawyer's basement. It kicked up in me loud, so as I got to work it was with the urgency of that music. I moved through that small office like a drumroll, like an ascending scale.

I rolled Newell's chair over to the bookshelf and stood on the seat and ran my finger along the topmost row of binders: dust. Same with the second level, and so on down to the floor: dust, dust, dust, all the thick binders and regulatory volumes so much set dressing.

I rolled the chair back to the desk. I already knew where this was going—I knew I would end up having to get into Newell's computer. This was the twenty-first century: any kind of important document, anything that mattered, would be on the hard drive or on the server. But I did not want to be hacking if I could help it, so I was praying for a break here; I was hoping like crazy. I tugged open the narrow drawer of the desk, rifled past the stapler and the scissors, then I ducked over to the filing cabinet while I bent a paper clip into a twist.

Martha and I had agreed on twenty-five minutes. Fifteen minutes

in Newell's office to get the two pieces of information we were after, one for me and one for her, plus a five-minute margin on either
end.

Nine minutes had already passed, five minutes of silent counting
and four minutes of work, as I threaded the tip of the paper
clip into the chintzy lock of the filing cabinet. I felt as I had at
Saint Anselm's Catholic Promise, seven days ago now, Thursday to
Thursday and a lifetime in the past. Break into a building, crack a
desk: these were the easy assignments, the small projects outside
of thought or contemplation, beyond regret or conscience. A hard
deadline, a specific task. I twisted, caught the hook of the child's-
play mechanism, twisted again, and felt it give. The music played,
jumping, triumphant, in my head.

There were five drawers to the filing cabinet. I worked from the
top to the bottom.

Purchase orders, record keeping, maintenance logs—one thick
folder with the details of a hundred different trucks and trailers.
My forefinger ran along the spines of hanging folders. Forty-five
seconds per drawer: pull open, quick examination, push it closed.
Accident reports, insurance documents, vehicle registrations. The
bottom drawer was financials: purchase orders and invoices, sum-
maries of fuel expenditures quarter by quarter, reports on cost for
overall fleet maintenance.

Buried on the bottom of the bottommost drawer, hidden beneath the thickness of the hanging files, was a curled bundle of
papers wrapped in a rubber band.

What I was looking for would not be hidden, but I reached for
this rolled-up sheaf anyway, tugged it up from its hiding place.
It was a manuscript, typeset, dog-eared, with nervous doodles
around the edges. *I Love You, Too, Sir: A Tale of Forbidden Romance,* by
Matthew R. Newell.

"Jesus Christ, Matty," I muttered and slipped it back where it had
been. "Jesus fucking Christ."

I turned back to the desk and moved Newell's mouse to make

the computer blink out of its standby sleep. I cracked my knuckles. I did not sit. I hovered over the desk, back bent, and got to it.

Once, in Chicago, someone had slipped me the URL for the US Marshals Service open cases page. I sat in horror in a library carrel, blocking the screen with my body, blocking from the world the sight of my own five-year-old file photo. *Is that what I look like?* I remember thinking. I clicked on the thumbnail picture to make it large. *Those eyes — those eyes* — I drew back from the picture of myself on that screen as if from a picture of the devil himself. Had that really been me?

My knowledge of computers, my ability to hack a database, to punch through firewalls, all that came later. That was all Bridge's people. Four months of training in Arizona, plenty of that time in dark rooms navigating databases, penetrating secure servers, learning to follow the traces of men across the Internet.

I didn't have to breach any firewalls to get to sweet dumb Matty Newell's desktop, because he'd written his passwords in scratchy pencil on the back of the picture of himself with his wife and his dog. I trawled his hard drive. I entered search terms; I refined them; I found a spreadsheet, living on his desktop but cloned on an intranet server, called Contract Drivers Database, updated most recently ten days ago.

The truck drivers were identified here with four-character codes, and from Angie at Whole Wide World Logistics I had HR59, and now I was able to give HR59 a name: William Smith.

William Smith. I stopped, staring at the screen, my hands at rest on either side of the keyboard. The clock on the upper right corner of Newell's screen gave me nine more minutes. There was no phone number listed for William Smith. No e-mail. No evident means of communication whatsoever.

I stared at the name, feeling time slip out from under me, hearing the mad acceleration of the music in my head, wondering how many fucking William Smiths there had to be in the state of Alabama. How many Willys and Billys and Bills were we talking

about in the Birmingham metro area alone? In lieu of a phone number for Mr. Smith was a six-digit number that had to be a driver's
license number, and, after a couple of slashes, more indecipherable
coding: FWH 9, B8. Numbers and letters. William Fucking Smith.

I made a fist and pounded it down onto the desk, and the computer jumped and shivered. *Easy, Victor. Easy, Brother. Easy, now.*

If I couldn't find my man, I could find Martha's. Fulfill my other
responsibility—the other reason I was here. I memorized William
Smith's tangle of identifying numbers and closed out the spreadsheet, tunneled back into the hard drive, typing furiously, breathing
hard. I had seven and a half more minutes, and it took me just three
of them to find what Martha had been prepared to drop almost
thirty grand on—the infamous TorchLight database: every person
in bondage, all across the Four. The three million, listed by service
name, by PIN, by marks and scars, all organized and straightfor-
ward and user-friendly.

Here he was; here was Samson. Martha's love and Lionel's father. The man and his fate, in black and white on the screen before
me. I hovered there, hunched forward, eyes wide, frozen for a
minute's contemplation.

"Well, damn it," I said quietly.

I read it again, as simple a story as it was. Preparing myself to explain it to her. This is what she wanted to know, and now she would
know. Worst-case scenario.

Two beeps from the hallway. I jerked my head toward the door
as it slowly pushed open.

Three minutes early.

There was no hiding. I had no weapon. I made my hands into fists
as the door came open and saw Newell in the doorway, his loafers
on the carpet, his big belly, his thick right hand frozen on the handle. His eyes wide with confusion, trying to make sense of what he
could see: a black man upright at his desk, fingers on the keys of
the keyboard; to Mr. Newell I might as well have been an ape or a
horse, upright and clacking away. Martha was in the shadow behind

him, still in the hallway, eyes flashing, pleading apology—*I held him as long as I*—

"What..." he said. "What—what on earth are you doing?"

"Stay," I said, hard and flat. *"Stay,"* but Newell followed some ridiculous manful instinct and put his body in front of Martha's, protecting his guest from the one-man slave uprising in his office. But Martha, thinking quickly herself, had stepped into the room and closed the door behind her. She made a gun of two fingers and jammed them into his back, and Newell fell immediately for the oldest trick in the goddamn book. He stuck his hands up in the air.

"My God," he said to her. "You're..." A pink flush came into his thick neck. His eyes were wet with confusion. "Are you a part of this? What is this?"

Martha didn't answer. I kept talking to Newell as though he were in obedience school.

"Step forward slowly," I said. "Your arms raised."

He obeyed. He raised his hands higher, bending his poorly tailored sport coat out of shape, tugging the hem of his dress shirt out of his waistband.

"Just...I never—I never did anything to hurt any Negro," he said. "I never did." Sincerely he said it. Believing it.

"Get down on your knees. Lace your hands behind your head."

He lowered himself down, a series of ungainly motions, a fat, scared, graceless man trying to move unthreateningly. Down on his knees Mr. Newell risked a longing glance at his desk, at the panic button, at the telephone. He knew that he was dead. He had known for all his life in that dire, dark, late-night-fearful part of his bourgeois brain that this moment was coming, was always coming. This was the terror that was the underside of mastery. He worked in a multimillion-dollar company, economy as big as Rhode Island, built on the backs of black people kept in cages, and so there had to be a *reason* they were in cages—it couldn't just be because their suffering sowed the cottonseeds and ran the bundling machines; how could it be so? It had to be because under their skin, under the smiles GGSI had painted on their faces, they were monsters.

Now here, at last, the moment had come. I stared down at him, just me, no weapon in my hand, and he literally trembled, his moon cheeks and the thickness of his neck quivering.

"Listen, Matt," I said, calm as calm could be. "What does FWH mean?"

Newell blinked. "What?"

He was sweating; a heavy sweat on his forehead like a glaze. Martha looked from him to me, from me to him.

"FWH," I said. "It's an abbreviation. From your roster of contract drivers. Please tell me what it means."

"It's—that's . . . it's Free White Housing." His voice quivering like a ribbon. "That's—our white people. They live here . . . FWH just means—that's where they live."

He was here. The truck driver. Working white. William Fucking Smith lived *here*.

I got down closer to Mr. Newell, down on my heels. I made my eyes wide and clenched my teeth. I was not going to kill Matty Newell, but his fear was of value. I used it as a gun, as a hundred-dollar bill, as the bent end of a paper clip to spring open a lock.

"FWH nine," I said. "B eight."

"Free White Housing area nine. Unit B eight. It's . . . it's like—an apartment complex. I don't know."

"Any reason a slave would go there?"

"Go—where?"

"To Free White Housing."

"Yes. I mean, yes. Not—not usually, but yes. Niggers—I'm sorry. I'm sorry, sir. Slaves—I'm sorry . . . black persons . . . I'm sorry. Oh, Lord." He licked his lips. Snot ran from his nose. When Matty Newell told this story later, he'd say I had a shotgun, at least. Machine gun, maybe. Martha with a pistol in each hand. The both of us dripping with knives.

"Slaves go there? It's not unusual?"

"It's not."

Okay. Okay. I had what I needed, almost. The music had kicked up again, tightening my chest. There was a sickening feeling of excitement getting going in me as I realized what was going to happen. What I was going to have to do. The man was here. William Smith. He was *here*. I pulled open the top drawer of Newell's desk and started to rifle through it, thinking quickly. "Okay."

"What . . ." said Mr. Newell. "What are you doing?"

"Stay there, man. *Stay*." He stayed down on his knees, his hands behind his head.

Mr. Newell looked to Martha, but she did not even see. She was at the desk now: she had found the page I had been looking at. She was staring at the screen. Oh, Martha.

I took the scissors out of Newell's desk, and his eyes bulged. "No," he said, his voice rising. Waddling backwards on his haunches, hands behind his head, repeating his refrain, "I never did any harm to any Negro person."

"Quiet, please."

I was unbuttoning my shirt. I was stepping out of my shoes. I held the scissors in my right hand and pointed at Newell with them. "How do I get to Free White Housing area nine?"

He told me what I needed to know. While he was talking I turned the scissors to my neck and began to carve, bringing up a deep well of blood, hacking away. Right where I had my inked-in tattoo, right at the root of my neck. I needed blood. I needed a fresh wound. You had to be very sick, puking and shitting sick, to be brought to a doctor's attention around here, that I knew. A bad cut, though, was not the end of the world. Steroid shot and a bandage, you're on your way.

"Martha," I said, "there's a first-aid kit on the bottom shelf over there. Can you get me some gauze, please?"

She was still at the computer. Transfixed by the screen. Martha was not watching us anymore. Her attention was wholly on that computer screen, where Samson's face and fate were still displayed. She had taken a step forward; she had reached her hand halfway up toward the screen, a small gesture full of grief.

I got the bandage myself. Worked it slowly around and around my neck. When I was wound up, three thick layers of gauze covering my fresh, credible wound, covering where I would have borne the sheltering *G* of GGSI, when I had what I needed from Mr. Newell to get across campus, I pulled the cords from the printer and from the computer, one by one. Martha kept looking at the screen, even as it went blank.

I had a couple more questions for Mr. Newell, but when I had all of them answered I pushed him all the way to the ground.

"I never . . ." he said, sobbing. "Never . . ."

"I know," I said. "You never did any harm to any Negro person. But I'm going to tie you up now, bind your hands and feet, bind your mouth to keep you quiet, and put you in the closet."

I got to it. I did it fast. When he was in there, far from his panic button, far from his phone, I gently guided Martha away from the desk. I took her by the hands. Got her to look at my eyes.

"Here's what's happening. You take the elevator down. You walk briskly across the lobby and say thank you to that blond girl and get in your car and drive north."

"Yeah," she said. "Okay."

"Are you listening?"

Her eyes were not on the screen anymore, but that's where she was. She was with him, she was with her Samson, far away. I squeezed her hands between mine, squeezed each individual finger, trying to gather her attention, get her here with me.

"You go and get Lionel from your sister's house and get that money I gave you and drive to Canada. Or fly overseas. Go anywhere. Go somewhere good. You got it?"

"I do."

"That's enough bread to start a new life, and that's what I want you to do, okay? Get that boy out of America. Get him out."

"You . . ." She looked at me. Shirtless, shoeless. Wrapped with gauze. The simple black slacks now looking dingy, pathetic. Slave garb. "What are you doing?"

"I gotta finish this up."

"And then how are you going to get out?"

"I'll figure it out."

Her eyes at last were back in focus. She was back in the room.

"How? How are you going to figure it out?"

7.

Poor Mr. Newell, inarticulate with fear though he was, had managed to answer my questions one by one, even the one question I hadn't known to ask—what is the line around the property, the broken black line that had puzzled me when I first got a look at the full file? It was a train. A subway. Not an electric fence or a utility pipe, but an underground train. Delivering Persons Bound to Labor from the population center to their shifts.

It explained why I'd seen no actual people at work from way up there in the perch, where Newell had taken us so he could crow. The slaves were way out in the far-flung acreage of the cotton fields; the slaves were laboring in the high floors of the stitch houses; the slaves were transported belowground, where they couldn't be seen. Not past the headquarters buildings full of happy Matty Newells, meeting in conference rooms and making calls, doing no harm to any Negro person.

You'll take the service elevator, Newell had said. The door will open directly onto the platform. So down I went. Shirtless and shoeless, disguised in my five feet of bandage and bright green wristband and my own black skin, I rode the service elevator down from Newell's fourteenth-floor office with my head slightly lowered, my brain on fire.

As it descended I began to hear music, loud and martial music, and when the elevator door opened I was in a gigantic room full of men singing.

The men were shirtless and shoeless, as I was, and they were facing away from me, just backs and heads, rows and rows of backs and heads, hundreds of men standing totally still, their voices raised.

"These strong hands belong to you," they sang in chorus. "Hands and back and spirit, too." The melody was simple, a childish four-note singsong. "Every day in all I do"—I shouldered my way forward, finding a spot in the crowd—"GGSI, my heart is true."

Now I was in among them, and nobody looked at me, nobody said who the fuck are you: I was one more shirtless man with a wristband and black pants, with mummy strips of bandage covering my neck and shoulder.

"As Thou hast done in days gone by . . ." I listened to the lyrics. I got it by heart. "Oh, Lord, protect GGSI."

That was it. After that the song just started again, and now I sang it, too. "These strong hands belong to you . . ."

I found a place between two men. The first was about my age, maybe a little younger, with high cheekbones and small eyes. The other was middle-aged, with a wide forehead and bulb nose, and beside him was a man with a striking face, a square, dimpled chin and high cheekbones . . . and then there was another, and an-other—all the kinds of faces in all the colors the world calls black: brown and tan and yellow and orange, copper and bronze and gold.

"These strong hands belong to you . . ."

They sang—we sang—with no enthusiasm or joy. We used to sing at Bell's, crossing the yard or working on the pile, just like slaves used to sing in Old Slavery, spirituals and work songs, sly lyrics, silly lyrics, yearning for freedom or roasting Massa in nonsense words he couldn't understand. This, though—this was a different kind of singing. I looked from man to man, and they were singing mechanically, eyes front, mouths moving like pup-pets. Singing this dumb refrain about how much they loved their bosses and loved their work.

Nothing spiritual about this. This was something else altogether.

There were no women. The women were somewhere else. Where were the women? Things were coming loose in me, being down here with all these men. Things were coming loose. I felt like I might fall down, but I could not do that—none of these men was wavering. They stood completely still, staring straight ahead, only singing.

What I did was, I focused on the room. Focused on noticing things. I was in a subway station, a platform, a kind of place familiar to me from New York, from Washington, DC, from a hundred different hunts. A cavernous room lit dimly by over-head fixtures hanging from a high domed roof. A concrete floor ending like a cliff edge above the sunken well of the tracks. I focused on the room and the sound of my own voice, singing along. "These strong hands..."

I kept it in, I kept it all in, I had to keep it in, so I kept it in, made my face like their faces, expressionless, only the mouth moving. But I was too close, too close to their faces. For my whole career un-der Bridge I had always dreaded the page of the file that showed the photograph, the real human face of the man I was seeking, and now here I was among them—none of this peeb shit, none of this "Per-sons Bound," no slaves down here, all that abstraction torn away like skin coming off a body, and these were *people*—human fucking *beings,* each with the one life he was given, and this was the life they had.

The music stopped in the middle of a line—"and back and spir"—and we stopped singing.

"Arms out." A voice came through from on high, burred and flat-tened by the intercom. "Hands up."

Everybody did as instructed: extended their arms, raised their hands. I did it, too. This was it. My rushing emotion was subsumed in a sudden heat of panic. Newell had untied himself somehow, stum-bled, screaming, into the carpeted hallway. Or it was Martha—they'd stopped her in the lobby. They'd stopped her in the car. She was in no shape...

"Heads back."

We tilted back our heads. Stared at the ceiling. The men around me followed the instructions dully, robotically. This seemed to be an everyday occurrence. This was protocol.

On my left hand was the green wristband the guard had fitted me for. In my right hand was a piece of paper that Newell had filled out and stamped under my command. Temporary Intracampus Travel Certificate. Permission slip. Travel papers. Some of the men around me, I noticed, carried similar passes; others had none. Some wore, along with the green band, other bands of different colors in various places up and down their arms. A whole world of systems, of rules and regulations.

The intercom voice again: "Hold pose." A frozen moment. A room cramped with shirtless men, all of us with heads tilted back, arms up and out. People like trees.

"Forty-five and under, hands down."

Most of the men lowered their arms to their sides. I did, too. The older men kept their arms up.

There was a man moving through the platform. The slaves parted to let him through. He was black, as we were, but wearing a shirt and boots. He came within a few feet of me but did not look in my direction, did not see me, the infiltrator, where I stood with my eyes lowered like everybody else. The train was coming—I felt the familiar stale breeze being pushed forward along the tunnel—but nobody moved.

This guard or trusty, whatever he was, moved from man to man, all those with their hands still up, checking for something in their mouths. Push his index finger between their lips, force open their teeth, then worm his finger around, upper palate, lower palate, then out. His face was set; mean; like Harbor, the hard boy who'd haunted my childhood at Bell's. Thinking of Harbor, I thought of Castle, and I felt a dizzy sense of the world collapsing, of my lifetimes flattening together into one plane—and meanwhile this overseer type appeared to have found who he was looking for among the forty-five-plus men. He took his finger from the man's mouth, had him bend over, and began to pat down the length of his body.

The train pulled into the station, and its doors pulsed open. No-body moved.

"Up," said the overseer or trusty to the man. "Let's go."

The forty-five-plus nodded and lowered his hands and allowed himself to be led through the crowd, toward the exit at the end of the platform, and his face remained as impassive as all the other faces. But his eyes: I saw it, a flickering in his eyes—I *saw* it—a slight widening. Absolute and abject terror. I had read about the up-to-date disincentive programs that were run in plantations now; all that shit that had come online since my days at Bell's. They were permitted now to tie you to a plank, pour water in your mouth to simulate drowning. They were permitted now to employ electric shocks; the science was in place to precisely measure out the volt-age. All the uses of darkness. Of noise. Everything was carefully regulated, of course, BLP officials on hand at all times.

That man, that forty-five-plus, they took him away. At no clear signal, we all got on the train.

It was twenty-four men to a train car, twelve on either side. There were no seats. We stood, staring straight ahead. The train pulled away from the station, and we all began to sing again: endless cho-ruses of the same song, no variation. There were no windows on the train. The man across from me was barrel-chested, with a thick bull neck and deep-set eyes. The train was loud in the tunnel, rush-ing and roaring through the darkness. It was hard to think with the singing and the rattle of the train.

The train ran in a simple circle around the plantation, fourteen stops in all, but I just had to make it through four of them: head-quarters to facilities maintenance; facilities maintenance to stitch house 1; stitch house 1 to stitch house 2; stitch house 2 to Free White Housing. I looked past the big barrel-chested man. Behind him, in small letters, where one metal plate of the car's structure met the next, were the words STIPELY FABRICATING SERVICE, LOUISVILLE, KENTUCKY. Just beneath the word *Kentucky,* one tiny machine screw was coming loose—I saw its head, a flat silver insect, poking like a secret from the surface of the train wall. I watched the screw as we juddered along.

At the first stop, facilities maintenance, a middle-aged white woman got on in the bright orange jumpsuit of the Bureau of Labor Practices. The singing stopped, but the train began to roll again, and she made her way down the center aisle, counting heads, clicking a small handheld clicker, one click for each of us. She did this while whistling slightly to herself distractedly, the way you might move through a crowd of chickens in a pen. Nobody looked at her. Nobody looked at anybody else. We just kept singing. I stared at the tiny loose metal screw. "All right, folks," she said brightly. "Thanks very much," and she moved through to the next car. At stitch house 1 nine slaves got off, and nine new slaves took their places. I did not look at the new faces.

I was going to find William Smith, and I was going to ask him my questions. Find out where that package was, get the fuck out of there—*How? How are you going to figure it out?*—and go and get it.

I should have felt something. I should have been excited, I should have been reveling in a moment, an opportunity that had at long last arrived.

But there on the train car, surrounded by men who would ride this train forever, I did not feel shit. I just wanted to get this done. Get it over with and get out.

Between the third and fourth stations the train stopped again.

"Hands in," said an intercom voice, and before I could wonder what that meant, a pair of shackles dropped and dangled in front of me and in front of everybody else on the train car. One pair per passenger, they appeared and hung there like oxygen masks coming down when a plane has lost cabin pressure. I followed the others. Did what they did. Raised my hands and stuck them through the holes. The manacles tightened automatically, biting into my wrists. I still had my pass, my Temporary Intracampus Travel Certificate. It was tight between my forefinger and thumb.

The doors opened at either end, and two men came in, one at each end, black men, like the one from the platform who'd led off the forty-five-plus. Petty authorities, whatever they called them here. One of them had a dog. They wore uniforms, the same color scheme as the one worn by the guard who'd gone over me in the lobby, the same as the carpeting in Newell's office: cotton white and blue-sky blue.

"All right, y'all," said the first, from the forward end of the car. "Who's feeling good today?" The man talking was the taller of the pair, with a broad chest and dark shining eyes. His voice had a rousing, rolling cadence. "Who's feeling *good?*"

Everybody answered together. "I am."

"Good. Who's feeling strong?"

This time I was ready. I joined in. "I am!"

He nodded again, beaming. "Now, you all know this: GGSI loves you."

Every man on that car spoke it in unison: "Thank you, GGSI."

"Now, GGSI is here to *take care of* you."

"Thank you, GGSI."

The other overseer, down at the back end, was nodding heartily at everything, mouthing the answers, too. He stood there holding the dog's leash. His attentive expression matched the dog's.

"Let me ask y'all something." The overseer who was running the show here, he licked his lips. He bounced on the balls of his feet. The dog poked its nose around. I was scared of that dog. "Who is it that gives us these clothes?"

"GGSI."

"Who puts food in our bellies?"

"GGSI."

"That's right. Sing it, brothers. Sing it with me now."

And we were back into it, hands and backs and spirit, too, everybody singing with noticeably more verve now, in the presence of the law. While we sang the two overseers worked their way down the line, one on either side, checking everybody's papers.

This was not perfunctory, either—they were holding pens, checking carefully, while the singing went on around them.

"You good." Looking each man in the eye, then looking at the paperwork, nodding. "You good. You good."

My pass was incomplete. As the trusty on my side drew closer, he and his dog, I managed a good, clear look at the Temporary Intracampus Travel Certificate of the man beside me, and I could see how Newell had fucked me. At the bottom, not in any box, just jammed in where there was space for it next to the signature, this man's pass bore an inky thumbprint. By accident or by design, Newell had left mine off.

I kept singing. I considered my options. My hands were shackled. The snare was sprung, the lock in place. I had no options. I continued to sing.

I watched the overseer moving down the line, watched my madman's game sailing toward its end. I should have felt scared, I knew. I should have felt the horror of the man trapped in his fate.

Instead I was just thinking *I failed you,* a quick burst of felt thought, like a prayer—but I wasn't sure who I was praying to. Whom had I failed?

The overseer was in front of me now, running his eyes over my face. He took the piece of paper from between my fingers and looked at it closely. His expression did not harden; his round cheeks did not change. "As Thou hast done in times gone by," I sang. "Oh, Lord, protect GGSI." The man turned very slightly toward the other overseer, to check where he was, then he took my pass, and when he placed it back in my hand it had a thumbprint on the bottom.

"You good," he said and kept moving.

When the men were done the shackles loosened, just enough for us to withdraw our hands, but they stayed dangling, jostling and swinging in front of our eyes as the train lurched back into motion.

The next stop was Free White Housing, and I got off.

*　　*　　*

That is one of the moments I still think about. Lord, I do.

I've tried to enact it. The small, quick, dangerous motions: to pop his thumb quickly in and out of his mouth, drag it through Newell's signature, jam the smeary thumb pad into the corner of my paper. Furtive movements. One, two, three.

I think about that moment all the time, how nice it would have been to say thank you. To say something. This man a stranger to me. My hero. I would have kissed him. I return in my mind to Bell's, to Chicago, to the thousand small kindnesses with which we armored ourselves against the world.

Free White Housing area 9 was visible from where the train doors opened, an ugly apartment block surrounded by a high chain-link fence. I booked it over there, hustling quick, eyes front, knees up. I ran past a high guard tower, ran with my back erect and my paper held out in front of me, thinking, *One way or another, this is almost over.*

The fence was unlocked. As I was going in, a pair of whites was coming out, rumpled blue work clothes marked GGSI, and I stepped aside, angled my eyes down. They took no notice. The buildings of Free White Housing were pale sandstone apartment houses, the kind of undistinguished clustered residences you see on the outskirts of poor towns—every apartment with a tiny balcony facing squarely forward, overlooking a concrete courtyard below. Four balconies per floor, six floors up. Apartments like cages, like drawers in a rolltop desk, identical and interchangeable, like pigeonholes in a wall.

I found building B and pressed the button for apartment 8. I had to stand calmly; I had to force my body to be still. Pressed the button again and waited.

They found him out, I was thinking. William Smith. He made a run for it. He's dead.

But then when I pressed the button again there were footsteps, thumping a thousand miles an hour, coming down the steps inside.

"Stop buzzing," said a voice, muffled, through the door. "Stop buzzing!"

The door of the lobby jerked open. A rag doll of a man, with a thin neck and long greasy heavy-metal hair, jutted his head outside into the courtyard, looked around quickly.

"Get in, man. Get in. For fuck's sake get *in*."

8.

Billy Smith was in a bad, bad way.

"Oh, man, oh, man, oh, man," he kept saying, a steady mumble, all the time shaking his head, gritting his teeth, running one hand through his greasy heavy-metal hair. "Oh, man, oh, man."

"Why don't we have a seat, Mr. Smith?" I said—I kept saying—but he couldn't do it or wouldn't. He told me to call him Billy, everybody fucking called him Billy, but that was all the sense I got out of him, at least at first. I sat watching him from one of his two folding chairs while he smoked and paced the tiny apartment in caged-tiger loops, trailing ash, stepping over and around Styro-foam food cartons and empty beer bottles. Billy didn't look like any truck driver I had ever seen: lean and lank, with nervous, edgy eyes that flickered constantly into all corners of the room.

"You gotta just tell them I'm fucking sorry, man," he said over and over in our first few minutes together, no matter what I asked, no matter where I tried to start. "You gotta just tell them I'm fuck-ing *sorry*. Okay?"

"Sure," I said. "You bet. But listen. Billy."

"You'll tell them? Please?"

I couldn't make him slow down. I couldn't make him hear me. Billy was operating on some level beyond my reach. The air in the apartment was a low, thick funk, the smell of a scared little man, an addict who had run out of whatever it was that kept him bumping along life's bottoms.

"I did what I could, okay? I'm sorry; things don't always—I did my best, okay?"

He lit a new cigarette with the end of the one he was smoking and shook his head bitterly. "I don't know why I ever got involved with all this mess. I really, surely do not." Inhaling, twitching, pulsing. "It all just depends who's on the gate, you know, and it was supposed to be Murph, but it wasn't Murph, and there's nothing I could do, so I'm sorry. Will you tell them? Will you?"

"Mr. Smith?" I said, real loud, then I slapped my hand down hard on the table and for whatever reason that caught him. He stopped moving. Rubbed his forefingers into his eyes, shook his head, then took a good look at me at last: no shirt, black pants, green wristband.

"What center you sneak out of?"

"I'm not part of the population here, Billy. I'm from the outside."

"No shit?" His eyes went wide. "How'd you get in?"

"That doesn't matter."

"Jesus. Jesus fucking *Christ*." He rushed over to the window, slowly lifted one slat of the blinds, and peeked outside, clutching his chest. *"Jesus."*

And he was off, a new tense orbit around the apartment. This man had all sorts of cosmic things going on in his mind, some stew of fear and regret and, unless I missed my guess, early-stage narcotics withdrawal.

"They're coming," he said now. "They're fucking coming."

"Who, Billy?"

"Bosses, man." He gaped at me. "Bosses always coming, man. It's not my *house,* you know what I'm saying? They can come in any time they want to. They got that right, okay? It's my house, you know, but they own it. Rent comes right outta my check. Everything. Food. Water. Stove gas. Everything." He had ramped up, he was talking fast, a million nervous miles an hour. "They can come in *whenever.* My man Jackie Boy in building C, he got jacked for porn. Black-girl porn, too, which they fucking *hate.* Tossed him right the fuck out. I knew a guy—Bolo, Bowler, Bowser, something—in FW 6, he had a bunch of coke in a Baggie in the toilet tank, you know? They canned his ass in a hurry. They woulda sold him off-shore if he had a drop of nigger in him, shit you not." Billy had made his way back to the window, and he risked another glance outside. "No, man, no: they can come in any time they want to. That's why I've been so freaked out, you know?" He crossed the room in two long paces, sat down across from me, sudden and hard. "So let's *go*, okay? What do you want to know?" Banged his fist on the table. "What do you want to fucking *know?*"

"You said something about Murph. Who's Murph?"

"Fucking no one, man. Murph wasn't there. He wasn't fucking *there.*"

Murph was one of the gate men, but Murph used to be a driver, just like Billy. Murph owed Billy all kinds of favors. Billy had gotten Murph high more times than he could count—"and laid, too, man—laid and fucked up a hundred times." And it was Murph, last Sunday night, who was scheduled to be at the large-vehicle exit point doing driver clearance. The trucks and the truckers are checkpointed separately, Billy told me in his special Billy style. Trucks get searched while the cargo goes in, then they get searched again by a whole separate team before they're sealed. The loaded trailers are towed to one of the seven LVEPs, where they are connected to a tractor. That's where the truckers show up, at the LVEP; that's where they get their driver clearance before climbing in the rig.

"I'm serious," Billy said bitterly, hissing out a long contrail of smoke. "I do *not* know how I got into this fucking mess."

Maybe Billy didn't know, but I had my suspicions. Ada guessed it was sex that had roped the man in, a pair of nubile abolitionist nurses, but looking at Billy, inhaling, twitching, pulsing, I figured it had to be drugs.

"It all depends on who's doing that hand search, you know, and it was supposed to be Murph. I had the fucking envelope, though. I was holding it."

Billy had been directed to leave his jacket slung over his balcony—

unit 8, three stories up—and then when he went to put it on that Sunday night, lo and behold, a padded envelope was in the pocket. You would never approach the LVEP with anything remotely resembling contraband, except that on this night it was supposed to be Murph—the whole plan hinged on Murph's weak vigilance. Then Murph got the flu.

"You believe that?" Old cigarette out, new one lit. "The fucking *flu*."

Kevin, meanwhile, in his terrible hiding place: barrel of shit, barrel of blood, barrel strapped to the bed of a truck. The truck in lurching motion, the rattle of the wheels, the slosh of the fluid around him, the sick, close, dark air. And then after all those miles, Billy pops him out of the truck at the truck wash. He's ready for his connecting flight—and where's Luna? Where's the package?

"Billy?"

"It was just bad luck."

"Billy."

"Bad, bad fucking luck."

"Billy, where is it?"

He screwed up his eyes and stared at me. "What?"

"The package, Mr. Smith. Are you telling me it never went off this plantation? Are you telling me it's still here?"

"Yeah, it's here." He was close to the point of tears. He gaped at me. He pressed his dirty fingers into his temples. "That's what I'm telling you; it's here." He got up with a jerk, so fast he wobbled and nearly fell down. "It's in my fucking fridge."

My ticket to freedom was exactly as it had been described.

A padded envelope, five inches by seven inches. A half an inch thick. On the front, the logo of GGSI, and on the back, Kevin's initials. I traced his handwriting with the tip of my forefinger.

I felt nothing. I put my palm on it and waited for the rush of feeling I was expecting, the dream of my new life in Little America, maple trees and a frozen lake and the curl of chimney smoke from my small wooden home.

The envelope felt like nothing. If felt like a small package, five by seven, with a slight bulge in the center.

The crazy courage of this kid. Jackdaw, born as Kevin. The *balls.* Lying to those holy fools the whole fucking time. *Go and get that girl and I tell you where I put your fucking envelope.* When he never even had it. He never fucking saw it. He had never held it in his hands.

All of it a wild bluff. Tricked Barton, tricked me, tricked everyone, all to get this girl Luna out.

And now she was dead. And now he was dead.

And here I was in the inside of his world, mourning him all over again, this crazy courageous kid: he's down there dead in the water, and here I am.

Billy Smith was hovering behind me, twitching back and forth on his heels, hands in his hair, breathing heavy.

"Yeah, man, I'm just glad to get rid of that thing. I mean it. That thing's been giving me bad dreams, man. Real fucking bad dreams."

"Oh, yeah?"

"Yeah." His breath was hot and stale. "You know that lady? The lady that got shot? I *dreamed* that, man. Night before it happened. She was giving her, like, testimony, you know? In my dream. With the long table and the microphones. All those ugly men staring down at her. You know they wear those flag pins on their jackets?"

I stood facing Billy, holding the envelope, feeling its small weight in my palm.

"Everybody was just fucking freaking out, you know, calling her this and that, nigger lover and everything, and then someone just came up behind and"——he made his fingers a gun, grimaced as he fired it——"*pow,* shot her head off, you know? That was in my dream. I dreamed it, and then the next day it happened on the fucking news!"

I tucked the envelope into my waistband, at the small of my back. Still I was waiting to feel something——the rush of possibility, the thrill of victory——waiting to feel my future coming.

"So all right, so what the fuck, man?" said Billy. "Somebody coming to get you? You got something set up?"

"No."

"What? What do you—how you gonna get out of here?"

"We're going to figure it out, Billy," I said. "We'll figure out something."

"We?" he said. His eyes bulged in his narrow face. "Oh, no way, oh, no. No fucking *way*."

We were back and forth on it for a while, Billy and me. He was trying to make me understand what I already knew, what I probably knew a lot better than he did: that it was impossible. People have tried all the ways, man, he told me. Packed in crates. Sewn into seat linings. Wrapped up within a palletized load of cargo. Inside the engine block. Clinging to the chassis.

"Jackdaw got out," I told him. "You got Jackdaw out."

"Yeah, but that got *planned*. You hear what I'm saying, man? That got set up for a fucking *year*. I mean, I was part of it, I don't even *know* how long that got planned. And so what do you wanna do? Just, like, what? Fucking ride out shotgun?"

"No," I said. "Of course not."

Although that was among the options I was considering. It was on the list that was writing and rewriting itself in my mind, possibilities arranging themselves in order of plausibility. I could hold Billy hostage or appear to hold him hostage: whittle a wooden gun from one of his sofa legs; build a bomb out of refrigerator parts and strap it to his chest and let the gate men know I'd kill him.

There were so many flaws in such a plan, so many questions.

I thought through the map of the place, thought about the buildings that abutted the property's edge. What about that Institute for Agricultural Innovation? What about the black building behind it? It was marked off somehow; it was distinct. It occurred to me that a building so marked may be operated separately, may have its own separate system of entrances and exits.

Flaws and questions. Questions and flaws.

I stood. A quarter of an hour passed, then half an hour. I did my own version of Billy's dance, pacing a circuit around the small space while Billy took his turn sitting, watching me think.

Subway tunnels. Delivery trucks. Employee parking.

I looked out the window. The sun was going down on the plantation, with shadow patterns on the concrete courtyard, with the bright green lawns past the fence turning darker, when the real plan began to form itself in my head—not a good plan, not even close, but perhaps the best of all the bad.

"Billy, are you allowed to go into the town if you feel like it?"

"Course. Sure. Yeah." He eyed me warily from the table, a cigarette dangling from the corner of his mouth. "I'm not a slave, man. I just gotta sign out, say where I'm going, what time I'll be back, and then I gotta sign back in."

"All right." I nodded. This was something. I sat across from Billy. "You're gonna go into the town and find a pay phone, and then you're gonna dial the telephone number I give you. You're gonna say exactly what I tell you to say, and the man on the other end is going to say okay. Then just stay where you are. Ten minutes later the Turner Alarm will sound."

"What? What the fuck are you talking about?"

"Listen. You're going to call that number"—a Maryland number; my man in the system; deus ex machina—"and the Turner Alarm will go off. They'll go to lockdown here and send out the wagons."

The alarm was part of the Turner System. It was mutual defense. Every plantation in every county in the Hard Four was required to maintain a reinforced vehicle called a Turner Wagon, with a small armed company of guards, that could be sent out to any other plantation experiencing insurrection: a threat to one being understood as a threat to all. The system is named for Nat Turner, of course, the Virginia slave who with his confederates slaughtered fifty-odd people in 1831, although the system didn't become common until the so-called Starman Revolt, in Carolina, in 1972.

"So you got it?" I told Billy. "Sirens gonna wail, wagon is gonna roll out."

"And then what?" said Billy. "Where are you gonna be?"

"I'm going to be on the wagon."

That plan might have worked, too. There were still some pieces to figure out, obviously—one more ride on that subway, a few more choruses of "These strong hands belong to you." A couple more tricks to pull, but I was ready to try it, and I think Billy was, too, but then all the sounds started at once.

Chopper blades. A dozen automobile engines, roaring in fast. Car doors slamming, boots on the stairs. Billy's nightmare made real.

I shouted to him, looking back over my shoulder as I ran for the window, but Billy had fainted—he was flat out. The window was useless. The door was splintering inward. A dozen people were yelling *Freeze*—yelling *Get down;* yelling *Nigger, get down*. A forest of gun muzzles. Me on my knees. Following instructions: hands up, hands laced behind my head, head down . . .

I had no gun. I had no knife. I only had that envelope, five by seven and padded and marked, and it was torn from me as they dragged me down the stairs.

9.

I knew I was underground, but that was pretty much all I knew.

I had been battered. Dragged out of Free White Housing, kicked with boots and hit with batons, and thrown into an armored car. Pushed through a door and tossed onto an elevator. Same manufacturer, I noted dully, as the one in headquarters. Murdock Elevators of Murdock, Louisiana. Someone shocked me in the midsection with a Taser or stun gun, and I fell down.

Now I was lying on a steel floor. There were tender spots, budding bruises, on my arms and legs. The metal I was on was cold. I was naked. My hands were shackled to each other, my feet were shackled to each other, and a loop of chain was drawn between the two sets of shackles and then through a metal loop bolted to the floor.

I passed in and out of consciousness one or two times.

Who did I think I was? I was just gonna waltz out of there? Ride out shotgun, like the man said?

Who did I think I was?

For a while I kept thinking there was someone else in the room with me. A dark figure, huddled in the corner.

"Is that you?" I even said one time, whispering, reverential, but nobody answered, and when I managed to move my head around, there was no one. I was alone.

When I woke again, though, I could hear someone breathing. Shallow breaths, and a light tapping—tap, tap, tap.

"You up?"

I shifted my weight, and the chains rattled.

The man who spoke, whoever he was, was on the far side of the room. Still making that soft noise, tap, tap, tap.

I turned my head, fought back a rolling spasm of pain, and saw him. He was inside my cage with me, leaning against the thick steel door with his arms crossed, bored. In one hand he held my envelope, Kevin's envelope, five by seven, with a small bulge in the middle. He was holding it in his right hand and tapping it, tap, tap, tap, against his left bicep.

The man was familiar to me, but I couldn't quite place him. A wide neck, very pale skin. Dull eyes.

"Come on," he said. "Get up."

I knew where I'd seen him. The Fountain Diner, my first meal in Indianapolis. Cook's partner, thick-necked and red-faced. Officer Morris, who wouldn't know he was on fire unless a pretty girl told him so. I guess someone had told him something.

"Up," he said again. "Time to go."

Part Three

NORTH

Compromise is not the worst of sins, but it is the busiest. The only one we're all of us doing, twenty-four hours a day. Seven days a week.

—*Reverend Kevin Shortley,*
On the Urgent Necessities, *1982*

You are not alone
I am here with you
Though you're far away
I am here to stay

—*Michael Jackson, "You Are Not Alone," 1994*

1.

One more hotel room.

Motel, maybe. I don't know. Morris drove for a while, some dull collection of dark hours, with me in the back of the unmarked silver sedan he had shoved me into by the top of my head, and then I saw neon that said VACANCY. I saw a squat one-story building, and then I was at a door with a number 4 on it. One more ugly hotel room, facing one more deserted parking lot, in one more invisible town.

Morris knocked on the door marked 4, and it was Willie Cook who answered—Cook with his shark's smile, his dancing eyes. He was out of uniform, sleeves rolled up, chewing a piece of gum and holding up his hands as if to welcome an old friend.

"Well, all right," he said. "You made it."

"Oh, my God," said Martha behind him. "Oh, my God . . ." Her voice reminded me what I must look like, battered and bandaged and chained. Cook, without turning, said, "Now, you stay where you are, baby."

I watched Martha sit slowly back down on the edge of the bed. I formed my mouth into a smile. *It's fine,* I thought, just as loudly as I could. *Not as bad as it looks.* Morris had taken me out of the leg shackles, at least. At least I had my pants back on.

I let Morris push me into the room, and I stood where he placed me: in front of the rickety little motel table between the kitchen area and the bed area. Cook settled into the table's one wooden chair and put his feet up, like a working man relaxing at the end of his hard day. There was a gun on the table, too—not his service weapon; some snub-nosed thing—and a laptop showing a screen saver of the Indy 500, colorful race cars moving in patterns on the sleeping monitor.

Morris tossed Cook the envelope, and he caught it, held it a second, then set it down on the table. His big gold class ring made a hollow knock on the cheap wood.

"Well, all right," he said again. "Nicely done."

Morris fetched himself a beer before settling with a sigh into an overstuffed chair beside the window. He had the bottle in one hand and his service weapon in the other, pointed at Martha.

She looked bad. She looked half out of her mind with weariness and confusion. There were, at least, no bruises on her face, no blood at the corners of her lips. Her eyes were dark and panicky, roving back and forth between Morris and Cook, Cook and me.

God, that girl should have run. She should have run from me in Indianapolis; in Green Hollow, Alabama; at Garments of the Greater South; she should have run. She should have run from me a million different times.

"I don't understand this," I said to Cook. "What is happening? What is she doing here?"

He blew a bubble, destroyed it with his teeth. "Did you forget?"

"What?"

"Your leash, son. Father Barton's laptop, tapping into your tracker, keeping tabs." It was the same laptop on the table in front of him, next to the gun.

"I didn't forget," I said. "But it was my understanding that when I had the lost package in hand, I would return directly to Indianapolis and give it to Father Barton."

"Yep. That was indeed the plan."

Questions were struggling to the surface of my mind, one by one, then all together, like animals emerging from mud. Had they known the whole time that I was planning to double-cross them, to turn this goddamn envelope over to the marshals? Was it just Officer Cook who had been on to me, or was it Barton also? And what about Morris, who, Cook had told me, knew nothing about his Airlines service—what was he doing running these kinds of errands, not to mention how? How had Morris come by the authority to get a man sprung from the bowels of a megaplantation?

The only question I said aloud, though, was my first one again. "What is she doing here?"

"She's insurance," said Cook. "To make sure we get what we need." He pivoted in his chair, pointed at Martha. "Tell him, honey."

"They've got him," she said, her voice coming like from under water. "They've got Lionel."

I turned back to Cook, caught him poking his tongue through his gum, stretching it into a thin pink membrane. "Why?" I said. "*Why?*"

"Settle down, boy," said Morris, shifting his pistol from Martha to me. "You settle down."

Martha stood, hands clenched at her sides, and Morris brought the gun back to her. "You, too."

"Please," I said to Martha. Trying to calm her down. Calm myself, too. Whatever was going on, I didn't think these guys were kidding. "Please. Sit."

This now, for Martha, on top of everything. What she had learned only hours ago, about Samson, and now this. Martha sat on the edge of the bed and tilted her head back and stared at the ceiling, and the moonlight coming unevenly through the blinds washed the side of her face and made her look old and sad.

"I was bringing it to you," I said to Cook. There was a fresh dark feeling blooming in my stomach, filling me up like internal bleeding, and I heard that darkness come into my voice. "I was going to bring it to you all."

"Sure you were," he said. "Sure." And then, new subject—oh, just by the way: "You know, I don't think you ever told me what your man's name is. Your agent, I mean. In the marshals."

Oh, Martha, I thought. *Oh, Martha.* This on top of everything.

"Bridge," I said quietly. "Louis Bridge."

"Oh. Huh." Cook snapped his gum. "I was thinking, wouldn't it be funny if I had the same guy?"

There it was. An answer. A lot of answers, actually, all arriving together, all at once.

"Actually, my man's a lady," Cook added. "Deputy United States Marshal Shawna Lawler. I never met her, but she sounds sexy as hell on the phone. If you're into white women."

He flicked his eyes toward Martha.

"I don't . . ." she said. "I don't . . ." She stood up again, and Morris said, "Sit," and she said, "What does he mean?"

"Me and your boyfriend here, Jim, or Victor, or—what'd you call him? Brother. I like that. Me and Brother, we're just the same. Same little secret." He stood up solemnly from that wobbly motel table, pointed a finger at me, slow, and intoned: "Nigger stealer. Soul catcher. Government man." He lowered the finger, sat back down. "Just like me."

I waited for Martha to say something else, anything else, but she didn't. She might have said, *I don't believe you;* she might have said, *It can't be true;* but from that corner of the room there was nothing.

I didn't look at her again. I couldn't look at her anymore.

Cook was done smiling, at least. All the winking and smirking, all the wiseass man-of-the-world business had fallen away in an instant. Without that smile, he looked like a different human being. He sat rigid in the chair, and his face became tired, closed, with sadness behind his eyes, like the shadowy water just visible under the surface of the sea.

I wondered what *I* looked like now, when at last I wasn't trying—not pretending anything. I wondered what I was looking like in that small room, alone with Cook's revelation, with the truth of what I was at last filtering out into the world.

"Please believe me, man. I'm not happy about this," said Cook, his voice low. "About *none* of this. But you're my chance. Okay? You're my chance."

He stood up again at the table, leaned forward while he talked.

While he explained—while he tried to explain. "All I'm supposed to do is get Barton's secrets. That's the job: get the man's secrets, and they set me free. That's my deal. Two years I been at it, and two years he's been keeping me low on the pole. Errand boy, muscleman, bullshit. Two years." He put up his hand and spread apart two fingers.

He turned abruptly to Martha. "Then here comes your friend." I did not look at her. I couldn't. "Sad little mush-mouth Jim Dirkson. Talking about this wife in the mines. Here's my chance. I push you on the priest, let's do this one, let me quarterback it. Tutor me, Padre, you know? Here's my chance to learn some secrets, get into the inside. Agent Lawler keeps saying, get what we need and you're done. You're free."

Every time he said that word, *free,* I felt sick. Lord, what they had done to this man. What they had done to me. The monsters they had made us into, prowling along, sniffing for chances.

"But then you"—he pointed one finger at me, wagged it—"you go and turn out to be what you are. Turn out to be like me. And I was like, whoa, whoa. Wait. This is even *better*."

Morris belched, long and loud. Settled in the armchair, coasting through this dull guard duty with the bored confidence of a white man lording it over a black and a woman. I stared at Cook, remembering his excitement that morning on the banks of the White River. Kevin lying dead, Maris furious, Barton grieving, Cook seizing the moment. I was having my realization in that moment, and he was having his.

"I explained to Barton that he should send you to go and get this thing. I told him how we could tap your chip, how I had me a solid connect in the marshals. Then I called up Agent Lawler."

Me on the phone with Bridge, sending him to BWI airport, and Cook—or whatever this man's name was—on the phone with Lawler. Phones ringing off the hook in Gaithersburg.

"I said, listen, baby, remember this evidence Barton's been so hot on? What about I get that for you? Illegal collusion. Major federal lawbreaking. Well, she liked that a lot. She loved it."

There was no point in explaining to Cook that his agent wanted her hands on the evidence for the same reason mine did: to get rid of it.

"And better than that, I said to her, I said, what if I can get you one of me, a nigger-catcher soul-stealer motherfucker like me— except this one's gone to the dark side? He's working freelance for the Airlines. What if I get you all that? If I get you all that, you gotta let me go, right? Then you gotta set me free."

He lifted the envelope off the table, and I was surprised at the sudden pain I felt. I felt it in his hands like it was a part of my body, like it was my heart he was holding. The idea of that thing going back to Maryland, getting buried by the marshals, after all Kevin had gone through to get it, all that Luna had gone through. Even me. But that's where it was always headed anyway, wasn't it? I was never really going to bring it to Father Barton so he could announce it to the world.

But somehow in the wake of Cook's revelations, I was mourning that alternative future, longing for a victory I had never really contemplated.

"So here's what's up, man," said Cook. "We're going to take out this hard drive, hook it into the laptop here." He gestured to the computer on the table. "Just to make sure you didn't pull a fast one, like my pops used to like to say. Make sure we got what we think we got. And then I'll call Agent Lawler."

He tore the envelope open at the top. I held up my hands, the chains rattling.

"Wait, though. What if Barton's right?" I said. "What if there really is information on here that could"—what were the words, all those hopeful, lunatic words?—"shake the foundations? Change the world? Just—what if?"

"Come on, now," he said. "Barton's full of shit."

"Yeah, I know. I know." I took a step toward Cook, aware of Morris in the corner of my eye. "But we're talking about the future. The future of the country. Talking about three million slaves."

Cook said something familiar; something I had thought to myself—and not long ago, either. "I ain't thinking about the three million" is what he said. "I'm thinking about me."

"Wait . . ."

"Hey. Hey!" He had the package open. He pulled out what was inside. He looked up at me. "What the *fuck?*"

Motion from the other side of the room, Morris rising from the chair. "What is *that?*"

We were all staring at what was in Cook's palm, then suddenly Martha was moving. She was off the bed just as Morris was off the chair, quick as choreography. She grabbed Morris's beer bottle and smashed it on the edge of the table, making a weapon that caught Morris in his rush, so it was really his own running that drove the broken edges into his belly.

He screamed while Martha turned the bottle deeper, and I lurched my body forward, overturning the table into Cook, knocking him against the wall and banging his head hard into it, sending a small burst of plaster out onto the both of us.

"God*damn* it," he said and reached for his gun where it had skittered on the tabletop, but I put my hands on top of his hands on top of the weapon, and we were struggling for it when over my shoulder I heard Martha shouting, "Shit! Asshole!" I jerked up, hard, bringing all four of our hands up off the table, Cook clutching the pistol and me clutching his fingers, both of us yelling. Morris was holding his wounded guts with one hand, but the other hand held his automatic, and he was trying to get a bead on Martha, who had just rolled behind the bed.

I wrenched Cook's finger, and the shot was an explosion in the small room. Morris fell but got off one shot at me as he was falling. I did not feel the bullet—didn't feel it because it had caught not me but Cook, and a geyser of blood erupted from the center of his throat, and his eyes went wide and white, wide like Castle's eyes. His eyes in the darkness. Pleading eyes, wide in the rain. Castle wanted to go back and help Reedy, and I said no we couldn't go back, and I was scared, too, but there would be no more chances, not like this one. Reedy was dying and the rain was pounding and that fence post was loose, I had seen it come loose, and this was the only opportunity we were going to get, the only one we would ever get. I told Castle what he'd told me, so many times he'd told me, that we were different, that there was more for us, but he said not if we died! Not if we got caught running and they put us down or sold us offshore! And he was scared, I understood that, goddamn it, I was scared, too, but standing out there in the rain arguing made no sense, we had to go, we had to fucking *go*. I grabbed him by the neck and told him we were going and he said no again, fighting and pushing back at me, and I squeezed his throat and his eyes went wide and wider till he stopped fighting and then I ran, I ran away alone. Rain washed the blood from me while I was running, and everything I've gotten since I have deserved.

"He's dead," Martha was saying. Yelling. "Victor! Brother! He's dead. It's too late."

Cook was under me. We were on the ground. I had my hands on his neck, trying to hold back the blood, push it back in. I was trying to heal the man, but his eyes were open, staring, white.

Very slowly I let him go. There was blood all over me, blood on my hands and up my arms and on my naked chest. I stood up. The room was full of red.

"Okay," Martha was saying. She was trembling. I was trembling, too. "Okay. Okay. Okay."

2.

The steps of the monument were gray and slick with rain.

I stood beneath the Martyr with my hands in my pockets. I didn't smoke. I didn't tilt my head up to feel the drizzle on my cheeks. I didn't move. I stood beneath Old Abraham, quietly fiddling with the green bracelet I was still wearing on my arm. Doing nothing but waiting.

The streets were empty, more or less. Laughing voices, now and then, carried over from Georgia Street, the blocks of bars a quarter mile or so away. I saw a couple leaning into each other, climbing unsteadily into the back of a cab, way down on Market Street.

But the ring of shops and office buildings that wreathed Monument Circle were all closed this late at night. Here in the bull's-eye of the city, at this hour of night, it was just me out here, just me and the likeness of Lincoln. Both of us likenesses.

And just what was Victor feeling, anyway, as he stood there waiting? What about Old Victor—what was going on inside his mind?

I don't know. I was drained of emotion, washed out by the rain. I suppose there's a version of this story in which I'm standing there crackling with joy. Maybe I should have been crying, tears carving rivulets in my stone cheeks. Monumental. There might even have been, in some other reality, knives of regret scything away at my insides.

But none of that, not for me. Just standing, just waiting, coat shrugged close around me, my hands jammed in the pockets of my coat.

In one pocket was the gun, a loose heaviness in the pocket's depth.

In the other pocket, my right hand was clasped on one corner of the envelope, folding and unfolding one ragged corner.

Up in the sky was the dim, grubby outline of the moon. Abraham Lincoln's giant disapproving features in shadow above me, staring at the city, the country, all this unfinished business.

"Victor?"

"Yeah. Come on up."

There was Mr. Bridge, coming carefully up the steps, one step at a time, not wanting to slip, and despite myself I felt the tiniest prickle of disappointment. There must have been some part of me hoping for a surprise. What if Deputy United States Marshal Bridge had turned out to have about him the smoldering air of a secret agent? What if he'd been six foot six and thin as a rail, wearing Loyal Texan cowboy boots and a battered Stetson? What if he wore a yarmulke? What if he were *black?*

Alas. Bridge was Bridge. A bushy gray mustache and a sloping forehead below a receding hairline. Tan slacks and brown dress shoes, poorly chosen for rainy late-autumn Indiana. He stood before me, me and my Abraham, a supplicant before the prince and counselor. He was the puffy, dull-eyed middle manager of my most contemptuous imaginings. This, my tormentor.

I raised my hand as I came closer, and he raised his in return. Bridge's tie was brown and plain.

I fidgeted with the envelope's dog-eared corner while Bridge came up the steps.

Bridge was alone, per my instructions. I could see down Meridian Street the car from which he'd climbed. He'd emerged from the driver's seat, and I couldn't tell if there was someone in the back or not, but it didn't matter. Here at the steps it was just me and him, Bridge approaching, no bag or case, his hands raised as instructed. I had thought through all these details, got the setup straight: a public place, but a public place wreathed in darkness, a dead downtown in the middle of the night. It was 1:00 in the morning, Sunday morning. Two days since Martha and I returned to the North. Almost two weeks since Kevin was stuffed into the barrel, rolled onto the truck. Eleven days since I checked into the Capital City Crossroads Hotel, just down the hall from Martha and her son.

I ducked my hand into my other pocket, and Bridge stopped abruptly and raised his hands higher. I smiled. A glimmer of feeling reached me, distant but clear: it felt good to be in charge, even of one man, one small moment, one instant.

I wasn't reaching for my gun. It was the envelope I took out.

Mr. Bridge's eyes flooded with relief. He was easy to read, easier than ever, now that not even a phone line separated us. He was just here, ten feet in front of me, his features as open and plain as a child's drawing. He reached out, as though I was just going to hand it over, and I could see it all in his face, the pressure that had been applied on him from wherever it had come.

I dropped the envelope back in my pocket, and he darted out his tongue quickly, licked his lips.

"That's it?"

"Yes."

He nodded, licked his lips again. "I must hand it to you, Victor. That was well done. I don't know how you did it, but that was well done."

"I'm a professional."

"Yes." He nodded: *yes*. "Well, I hope you will not be surprised to hear that I am prepared to live up to my end of the bargain as well. If you would just . . ."

He took one more step up the stairs, and now my other hand came up, the gun hand. He stopped.

"What is it?" I said. "What's in there?"

He stopped. "Have you opened it?"

Bridge. Question with a question. I went back on him: "What do you fucking think?" His eyes above the gray mustache were growing fretful. He didn't like my tone. "Of course I opened it."

It was still open, as a matter of fact, and it was in my pocket with the open end up. I took it out and held it up in the dim rain-flecked moonlight. A small flask of sturdy plastic or polystyrene, full of clear liquid, secured with a screwed-on cap. Still floating in there, after all this time—after Luna smuggled it out, got it into William Smith's coat, after Billy panicked and stuffed it in his fridge, after I had it and Morris had it and Cook had it and I had it again—still floating inside that thin flask was something else. Something microscopically small.

"Well?"

Mr. Bridge's lips were pursed. They disappeared beneath his mustache. "I'm not a scientist."

"Yeah. Me neither."

I waited. Bridge could see what the deal was now. I wasn't turning anything over without this conversation.

"What it is . . . my understanding is . . . that what it is is cells."

"Human cells?"

"Yes and no."

I aimed my gun at him. "Bridge."

His face contorted. He didn't know how to answer. He didn't know whether he could. Of course I already knew what it was. I had been to Saint Anselm's. I had found Father Barton, as I expected to, in a wretched state, his man Cook having mysteriously disappeared along with his means of tracking me. I got the drop on Mr. Maris, whispered sweetly to him a little with my weapon in the small of his back, and then me and Father Barton had done some talking. I had done just what I was doing now—held the gun in one hand and this tiny vial in the other, held both before his pale staring eyes, and said to him, this isn't the financial records of any fucking Malaysian shell company, is it?

At gunpoint he had told me what it was, admitted what he had known all along—that he had sent me down there, run me through all that he had run me through, run Kevin through all that he had run Kevin through, all on the basis of a lie. The truth was too heavy, too serious to be trusted to the poor dumb Negroes he was working so hard to save. Another layer, another layer down.

I had held the damn thing up in front of that monster and threatened to destroy it—burn it before he could show it to anyone. I had flicked my cigarette lighter open beneath the envelope until his soft young face melted with fear. *Please,* he had said. *Please...*

And now here was Bridge, the same desperate expression, the same worried *Please.* He rubbed the corner of his mustache.

"They are hybrid cells, Victor. From eggs that are...eggs that have been harvested from human subjects."

"Slaves."

He sighed. He looked up toward the statue, as if the Martyr would provide him some relief. I just wanted it. I needed it. I needed for him to say it.

"What is it, Mr. Bridge?" Now I was walking, coming down the steps toward him, gun in one hand, envelope in the other. "You think I'll back out? You think this is the one thing I can't live with? After everything I've lived with, you think I can't live with this?"

"Okay," he said. "Okay. GGSI has a medical facility. Okay? The egg is harvested from a human subject, and—my understanding—the nucleus is removed. And then new material, not new, but taken from other subjects...look, what they're working on, on making..." He wasn't a scientist. It sounded insane, but it was true, so he said it. "On making people. It's hard to understand."

But I did understand. I understood better than he did. In that black building on the map, auxiliary to the Institute for Agricultural Innovation, they were taking girls like Luna and stealing their eggs, separating out the DNA, forming hybrids, breeding cell lines.

Barton had had his own language for it, had turned it all into biblical horror: *They are casting themselves as God. They are bringing forth the stuff of life.*

I put it more plainly still, my gun still trained on Bridge's wide midsection. "They're growing slaves."

"Well," he said, "they are trying."

It was coming up, my anger, my disgust, my wild red feeling. It was coming up fast and I knew it was going to and I struggled to keep my voice even. Keep it calm.

"What've the marshals got to do with this?"

"Elements within my service," he began, and from the way he was looking at me, weighing me, I could tell he was trying to find my breaking point. See how much I could take. "Not me, mind. But others—have been involved. In helping to make arrangements to provide some of the necessary technology."

"Arrangements."

Bridge nodded. "Again, not me. We are a large organization, Victor, with many layers. But yes. If the population held in bondage, if they were—not technically . . . people any longer. Certain constitutional issues, certain political issues . . . would be resolved."

I tilted the vial one way and then another in my hand, felt the small movement of the liquid. This is what Barton wanted to publicize, this is what the marshals were desperate to have kept secret: not some banking irregularities, not fiscal collusion. This. The next step. They'd been improving the machinery of slavery for two centuries, inventing new tortures to make people work harder and longer. Stripping slaves of their names, their families, their spirits. This is where it went next: people with no bloodline, people with no past and no future, people with no claim to freedom. *These strong hands belong to you . . . Hands and back and spirit, too . . .*

Bridge took a step up toward me. "You can appreciate, I think, why it is important, for a variety of reasons, that this experimentation, at this delicate stage, not become public. That's all." Now he was getting bold. Now some steel was coming into Bridge's voice. He saw the end; he was ready. "So you're going to hand me that package, Victor, and I'm going to take it. We are going to determine that it's the right material, then we are going to destroy it. And then we are going to do as you have asked. We are going to set you free."

"When? And who's we?"

"Right now." Just like that, his voice had taken up its old bossman confidence. "I have traveled here from Gaithersburg with a technician named Lance Cormer. Dr. Cormer works in a special division in our service, and he has come prepared."

"Prepared for what?"

"Prepared to take care of both ends of this. He can quickly do some initial testing on the materials you've provided to make sure it's what we're looking for. Make sure you're not—that you're not pulling some trick here." He rubbed his forehead. "Mind, I don't think you are. You're a straight shooter, Victor. You've always been a straight shooter."

He puffed out his cheeks a little, and tilted his head, and I felt that he had somehow shifted, started singing in a new key.

"And, Victor, further to that, I did want to say: thank you for your service to your country."

I had to laugh. I laughed. "Okay," I said. "You're welcome."

"And also, uh—good luck to you."

I didn't laugh any more. What was next? Was he going to give me a gold watch?

I tried to see behind Bridge's eyes, see how deep he went. Was he saying merely what he was saying, or was he saying he was sorry for what he had done to me, what all the world of Bridges had done to all the world of me's?

Should I have felt in that moment a matching spirit of magnanimity and grace? Should I have extended my hand for him to clasp, placed my black hand in his white one and smiled, no harm done, life goes on? I could not feel that spirit of grace, not in that moment. Not after all I had been through in the preceding two weeks and in the six years before that. I would have had to be superhuman, I think, to feel that forgiveness. I was and am possessed of all human flaws and weaknesses. I did not want to forgive him, so I did not. On the other hand, I wanted to fire the gun and watch him fly backwards on the steps, but I did not do that, either. Call that even.

"It is important we both realize, Victor, that it's merely an accident of history that created this problem. An accident of timing. Do you see what I mean? We were precipitous, and agents of my service were too eager to be helpful. That was all. But in time, this"—he gestured to the vial, and I saw the energy in his fingertips, wishing he could just grab it from me; I held it together—"will all be perfectly legal."

"I don't think so. I think in time . . ."

I couldn't finish the sentence. Because what I was thinking was, of course he's right. Of course he's right. Because this is what happens: shit gets worse. It doesn't get better. It gets worse. Incidents ripple up, then they ripple away again. Batlisch appears, troubles the surface of the world, but then is destroyed. Disappears. Time makes things worse; bad is faster than good; wickedness is a weed and does not wither on its own—it grows and spreads.

"One more time," said Bridge. "So we are clear. We walk together, four blocks, to a van, where Dr. Cormer is waiting. You continue to hold those materials. Dr. Cormer performs the minor surgery to remove the transmitter-responder from your spinal column. That will take about four and a half minutes."

Four and a half minutes, I thought. *Four and a half fucking minutes.*

"And then before Dr. Cormer and I allow you to leave the van, you will give us the materials and Dr. Cormer will conduct the verification process. When that is done, we go our separate ways. You need never see me again."

I nodded.

"Yes? Is that good?"

"Almost. What about papers?"

Bridge nodded, all eagerness now. "I have a set for you. Wilson Teller, born Albany, New York. No marks, no record. Passport and driver's license."

"Clean?"

"Clean and clear."

"How will I know?"

"You will know because . . ." He shrugged. "You will have to know because I am telling you so. Is that acceptable to you, Victor?" He smiled, very, very small. "Mr. Teller?"

I eased my head back and forth. I shifted from foot to foot.

"Victor, can you live with that?"

"Yeah," I said. "I can. I can live with that. Fine and dandy." I said those last three words with special distinctness, *fine and dandy,* to ensure they would be registered by the microphone I was wearing. Button-small, tucked inside my ear like a hearing aid. Barton had fitted me for it. He had all kinds of gadgets hidden in Saint Anselm's Catholic Promise, behind his false walls and hidey-holes. I said it loud and clear. "Fine and dandy."

Mr. Bridge drove the van, and I rode in the back with Dr. Cormer, who did not wear a white coat or any other indication that he was a doctor; just a black suit and black shoes and no tie, and—for security purposes, or so he said—a featureless plastic face mask, drawn tight across his whole face like a second skin. Eyeholes, a hole for his nose, and one for his mouth. I rode in the back in silence staring at the blank face of Dr. Cormer, forty-five minutes across from one another in the bench seats of the van, as if descending deep into some sort of meaningful dream.

We arrived, forty-five minutes outside of Indianapolis, at the only kind of place that is forty-five minutes outside of Indianapolis: a cornfield, empty and endless. I saw it out the tiny rear windows of the van. The van turned down a tiny gravel spit of a road, and we bounced along it deeper and deeper into the corn until we pulled up outside a white tent, erected in the middle of a dirt circle between two corn rows.

Bridge killed the engine, came around, and opened the back of the van. Dr. Cormer in his mask got out, and I got out behind him, and the three of us walked from the van into the tent, through that big Indiana darkness. The rain had stopped and the moon was out, a flat, tarnished coin. Stars scattered like pinprick wounds. The white tent glowed dully in the moonlight.

Inside was a table covered in white paper, surrounded by surgical lights. A generator chugged in the corner, powering the lights and a squat silver machine, no bigger than a dorm-room refrigerator.

"If you would remove your shirt and your undershirt, please."

It was the first this doctor, this ghost, had said, and by old instinct I tried to get a read on his accent, tried to find the man inside his voice. Nothing came.

"Lie down, please, on your stomach." Neutral voice. Empty. Something beautiful in that nothingness, something pure. "Yes," I said. "Okay."

I lay down and heard the machine humming to life, and I saw Bridge with my half-closed eyes, shifting from foot to foot. I heard the pin in my back, calling out, protesting.

Four and a half minutes. I counted them down. A minute of preparation, some sort of gel being spread across my back, cool and clammy, like Vaseline. A flat disk placed halfway up my back, then moved, in small circles, up and up; I heard it beeping, one beep every two seconds. Listening. Up and up the ladder of my spine, by two-second intervals. Beep, beep, beep.

Bridge watching from his corner, brow furrowed, frankly fascinated. My body trembled. Dr. Cormer moved his disk more slowly, then there was one long beep, and then a sudden sharp pinch as something was inserted into my flesh. I heard the doctor murmur, "Okay, there. There we are." I thought of Martha, sweet Martha, pulling free the bullet from my shoulder—*There! Got the little fucker*—and I smiled. Bridge saw me smiling, and he looked troubled, wondering maybe how I could be smiling, as he stepped forward, got down on his haunches.

"Dr. Cormer, are we clear?"

"We are clear," said the doctor in his voiceless voice. "We are engaged but not yet withdrawing."

"Now, Victor," Bridge whispered, "I need you to give me the package."

"What?"

"The envelope, Victor. We will need to see it right now and test its contents. You will need to wait."

"What—why?"

"We need to make sure this is real before we let you go."

"You said—"

"I know what I said, and I apologize that it was necessary to mislead you. But it's important that everyone is pleased before we complete the surgery. This is the only way."

"Mr. Bridge," I said.

"What?"

"It could have been . . ."

"What?"

"Now," I said, *"now,"* and Bridge said, "What?" but I was talking to the microphone, and the explosion was loud and immediate, a huge noise and a rush of wind from the cornfield as the tent flew away and the dirt patch was flooded with lights.

Bridge was armed, of course, a nice government handgun, and so, it turned out, was Dr. Cormer. Both of them were armed, but they weren't armed like Mr. Maris was armed. A tank of a man, black boots and camouflage pants and shirt, holding a shotgun and backlit by truck headlights, throwing forward his tall shadow while he shouted, "Drop your weapons; drop them; drop them now!"

Bridge tossed his gun so it landed in the dirt at Maris's feet. Maris fast-walked with his shotgun, paramilitary style, and stepped on Bridge's gun, pushing it into the soil. I was still down on the mat, still attached to the machine—the needle in my back, the long thin cord stretched across my back. Not yet free.

Dr. Cormer, the man with no face, wasn't ready to give up. Maris shouted "Drop it" again, but he stood defiant, surely in violation of his training, and Maris, with a burst from the shotgun, sent him spinning backwards into the dirt.

"No!" I cried from the table. "No!"

Maris said nothing. He moved swiftly around the perimeter, searching for more adversaries. Father Barton emerged from the front seat of the truck and walked calmly toward Mr. Bridge, holding in one hand the hilt of a long curved knife.

I rolled myself off the table to the place where Dr. Cormer was slumped at my feet.

I had to save him. That was all I could think of. I had to fix him so he could finish fixing me. I felt under his collar and found the edge of the mask and peeled it off. A kind-looking young black man with a pencil-thin mustache.

But he was dead. The government technician was stone dead, laid out beside me, as dead in the dirt as Cook had been on the motel carpet. Father Barton, with his left hand, held the precious envelope clutched to his chest; he held the knife in his right. Bridge was on his knees with his hands behind his back, the barrels of Maris's shotgun against the back of his head.

Barton knelt beside him, exactly like a consoling priest, though his words were a low, cruel murmur. "I do not know the extent of your crimes, sir, but I know how they are to be purged. They are to be purged in blood. They are—*no*," he said sharply and seized Bridge's face. Seized his eyelids, pulled at them. "No, you may not close your eyes. You may not."

Barton's arm, though, lacked the conviction of his voice. He raised the knife slowly, creeping toward Bridge's fat throat, uncertain of his angle. Maris held the shotgun, impatient.

"No," I said. "No; stop."

Maris looked down at me, confused. Barton, though, he was nodding. He understood—he thought he understood. "Do you want the gun?" he asked me. "Or the knife?" He didn't wait. He lowered his wicked blade, handed it to me where I was crouching on the floor, the thin wire still trailing out behind me, tethering me to the machine. "Go on, then. Go ahead."

"No," I said. I put the weapon down. "Let him go. You have what you wanted. What *we* wanted. Go on with it. Tell the world. But let this man go."

Maris looked at me coldly. "Your sympathy is misplaced."

"He was doing his job."

"No excuse," said Maris. "Absolutely not."

But Barton was not so certain. He looked like the timid young priest he had pretended to be when first I met him, at the Fountain Diner, stammering, apologetic. He lowered his knife. "I'm not . . . I don't know," he said. "How can we let him live? A man like this."

"A man like this?" I said softly. "What're you? What're *you*?"

When they were gone, when we were alone in the field of corn, Bridge stood up slowly. His pants were untucked, his hair a wild mess. Inside man, desk man. All this adventure was new to him.

"Thank you," he said. "My God, Victor. Thank you."

He held out his hand to help me up, but I crawled back up onto the table. I was still hooked up. I was ready to go.

"Mr. Bridge. Do you know how to work this goddamn thing or not?"

I could feel it as it happened. Feel it tearing free of me. Letting go the nerves, nerve by nerve, bursting stars of bright pain flying out along my spine. I screamed, but there was no turning back, there was no way to undo it now. He had grasped it, fished it out with that flat disk and conjured it up, yanked it from my flesh, and I screamed and screamed and everything went black, black as a gunshot, black as a disappearing sun.

When I woke up I was alone.

Bridge was gone. All remnants of that tent were gone, the poles and the canvas, the machines and the generator.

I was alone in the cornfield, lying on my back, aware first of the clot of bandages on my back, the blood seeping around me in a puddle. It was like I had been left behind by aliens. Like I was a fossil from an ancient evaporated sea.

I lay there until I felt I could stand, then I stood until I felt I could walk, then I started off in search of a phone.

3.

Martha's beloved wasn't dead. He had been sold offshore. He was in the Special Economic Zone. That's what I'd discovered on the TorchLight search in Newell's office.

Samson, being recaptured, after his brief, happy, free life, after falling in love with Martha and fathering Lionel and being found again, suffered the fate of many escapees who are subsequently caught: he was sold, for pennies on the dollar, to the controllers of an oil rig called the *High Water* working in the SEZ.

The SEZ was created during the Texas War, a nautical territory of the United States to be jointly administered by the Department of Defense and the Department of Energy. Because the gulf rigs and the oil they bring up are considered of vital national interest, laws have been passed to modify or suspend regulations regarding the treatment of Persons Bound to Labor inside its boundaries. No Franklins out on the waves.

At Bell's, when we were tempted to misbehave, when we got out of line, and when we cautioned each other—*Hush up, now; Don't be dumb, man*—it was always the SEZ we were thinking about. *What you trying to do?* we'd say. *Get your ass sold offshore?* In the times of Old Slavery, in Maryland or Virginia, they would trade rumors about the hot hell of the cotton lands; at Bell's we sweated over the SEZ. It floated in our imaginations then, as I saw it floating terrible now in Martha's, thinking about the man she loved. A machine island floating on dark water, shrouded in black smoke. A fortress carapaced in scaffolding and metal decks, masted with smokestacks. Gas fires burning orange in its vents, satellite dishes rotating slowly on its towers.

"Might be better," I said to her, "if he *was* dead."

"No," she said. "No."

I told her everything. I told her about you, darling. I told her the whole story. Sitting on the thin bedspread in the hotel room, told her about Bell's and about you, told her about Chicago and about Bridge, told her about Barton and Jackdaw and Dr. Cormer in the field of corn.

About what you said, about two worlds, this world and another one, us now and us later, what we are and what we are going to be.

We're in Chicago, and I still have never been to Canada. We're in Chicago, not permanently, but right now. Today. Everything I see I wish that you were seeing. I went to a hot-dog cart for lunch. I ate three hot dogs, thinking of you. I bought one for Lionel, then another one.

And here I am, on an elevator, riding the elevator up to visit a company that makes elevators. Martha and her boy are across the street at a coffee shop called Joey's. Martha is reading the *Chicago Tribune*. Lionel is reading the comics and drinking chocolate milk. Martha's hatchback is directly outside, visible from the front door of the building I'm in, parked in such a way that we can get out quickly if need be. Lionel knows only that we are on an adventure, and that is enough; that is more than enough.

In this world, in the real world, I am stepping off the elevator onto a thin green carpet. My shoes are black and highly shined, and my gait is confident and purposeful. I am a few minutes early for my appointment, here at the offices of Hugh Moorland Elevator and Escalator Company, a privately held corporation: established in 1927, annual sales of just under $1.2 billion, corporate parent to Murdock Elevators of Murdock, Louisiana.

"Good morning, sir. What can we do for you?"

"Hi. How are you? I have an appointment."

The gentleman smiles. He invites me to have a seat. I sit and leaf through a magazine.

Martha and I have learned that elevator design varies widely between companies and involves a large amount of highly technical proprietary information: the mechanical functioning of the pneumatic systems, the tensile strength of cables, the interior electrics, the design and movement of the counterweights. Even the size and shape of elevator buttons, their response times, their relative luminosity when depressed.

You never know which of these details, if any, will prove relevant to your goal, which is, in this case—as one small part of a much larger plan—to simultaneously shut down elevator service in every building on a plantation that comprises thirty-two separate structures.

"Mr. Powell?"

"Guilty as charged," I say. I hop up.

"Great to meet you," the woman tells me. "Come on back."

"You betcha," I say, finding a voice, a happy midwesterner, road warrior, traveling salesman.

This is today. More plans are in motion. More ideas are in play. Every day is two worlds; every day we split into two.

A map of the Gulf Coast with the current location of all the rigs was hard to find, but we found one. A technical diagram of an individual rig such as the *High Water* is proving much more difficult to find, but difficult does not mean impossible.

Everything can happen. Everything is possible.

ACKNOWLEDGMENTS

My first and deepest thanks go to my wife, Diana Winters, and to our children, Rosalie, Ike, and Milly. I love you.

I am so fortunate to have Joëlle Delbourgo as my literary agent—and confidante and friend—and to have Shari Smiley and now Joel Begleiter watching my back on the West Coast. It was thanks to Joëlle that this book ended up at Mulholland Books/Little, Brown and in the very good hands of editors Joshua Kendall and Wes Miller. Their sensitivity and enthusiasm were transformative.

Cheers to all my other new friends in the Hachette universe: Reagan Arthur, Pam Brown, Sabrina Callahan, Ben Allen, and their respective teams. I knew any organization that had Michelle Aielli in it was one for me.

I am very grateful to the artist Oliver Munday for creating this book's beautiful cover.

I had a lot of help in Indianapolis. Thanks to my students, colleagues, and friends in the MFA program at Butler University (named for its founder, the noted Indiana abolitionist Ovid Butler); to Officer Daniel Rosenberg and his colleagues on the Indianapolis Metropolitan Police Department; to Paul Bacon and his family; to Wilma Moore at the Indiana Historical Society; to Charles Harris and his colleagues at Peerless Pump; and to Professor Antwain Hunter, also at Butler. My respect and gratitude also go to the Indy literary community, especially the Indiana Writers Center, the Indianapolis Public Library, and the staff and supporters of Indy Reads.

I also had help from Kevin Hastie; from Brooke Pierce; from Ian "Gee" Chu and his cousin Dan; from Dr. Jason Organ; and, on issues of constitutional law, from Professor Morton Horwitz, who was extraordinarily generous with his very valuable time.

Thank you to everyone at Quirk Books in Philadelphia, especially Jason Rekulak, for putting me on the path I travel now.

I have taken liberties with its course, but there really is a little river called Pogue's Run and it really does travel for much of its length below the city. I am grateful to Stuart Hyatt for inducting me into its secrets. You can visit Monument Circle in Indianapolis, but there's no statue there of Lincoln; the Soldiers and Sailors Monument, erected in the wake of the Civil War, was the first such edifice in America built to honor the common soldier.

ABOUT THE AUTHOR

Ben H. Winters is the author of eight novels, most recently *World of Trouble,* the concluding book in the Last Policeman trilogy, a nominee for the Anthony Award and for the Edgar Award from the Mystery Writers of America. *Countdown City* was an NPR Best Book of 2013 and the winner of the Philip K. Dick Award for distinguished science fiction. *The Last Policeman* was the recipient of the 2012 Edgar Award; it was also named one of the Best Books of 2012 by Amazon.com and *Slate.*